Red Sunset Drive draws you in and holds you there. Can't wait for the next Detective O'Shea case.

— Kelly Stuhr, Senior Des Moines Police Officer

"If you're a fan of the *The Twilight Saga, The Vampire Chronicles,* or even TV reruns of *Castle,* you'll likely enjoy this ride down *Red Sunset Drive.*"

— Pacific Book Review

"A sense of slow, but unmistakable menace galvanizes the plot...A solid mystery featuring otherworldly good and bad guys, which primes its readers for future series entries."

— Kirkus Reviews

"Walters's cinematic style constructs a visual journey as the characters navigate through dangerous territory. The damp and dismal setting takes on a life of its own."

— Foreword Clarion Reviews

Red Sunset Drive

Other Books by Jan Walters

Believe

York Street—A Ghost and a Cop Series (Book 1)

Red Sunset Drive

A GHOST AND A COP SERIES

Jan Walters

iUniverse®

RED SUNSET DRIVE
A GHOST AND A COP SERIES

iUniverse books may be ordered through booksellers or by contacting:

*iUniverse
1663 Liberty Drive
Bloomington, IN 47403
www.iuniverse.com
1-800-Authors (1-800-288-4677)*

*Because of the dynamic nature of the Internet, any web addresses or
links contained in this book may have changed since publication and
may no longer be valid. The views expressed in this work are solely those
of the author and do not necessarily reflect the views of the publisher,
and the publisher hereby disclaims any responsibility for them.*

*Any people depicted in stock imagery provided by Thinkstock are models,
and such images are being used for illustrative purposes only.
Certain stock imagery © Thinkstock.*

*ISBN: 978-1-5320-1117-7 (sc)
ISBN: 978-1-5320-1116-0 (e)*

Library of Congress Control Number: 2016921427

Print information available on the last page.

iUniverse rev. date: 06/09/2017

Acknowledgments

With four generations of men in my family serving on the DMPD, going back to the 1890s, I grew up hearing all kinds of crazy police stories. Being an avid reader of paranormal novels, I created the Ghost and a Cop Series, which is based on a little fact and a lot of fiction.

I couldn't have created the characters in the series without the fab four (Bill Nye, Jerry Viers, Steve Walters Sr., and Steve Walters Jr.). We meet every weekend at the Crouse Café, and they regale me with police adventures.

I also want to thank local Des Moines photographer Cameron Fisher for the great photos I've used on the cover of this book. I wanted eerie pictures, and Cameron surpassed my expectations.

As a lifetime Des Moines resident, I have taken liberties with various locations in Des Moines and the surrounding area for the purpose of the story.

Although the Des Moines Police Department does not deal with the types of paranormal criminals portrayed in my books, they need to be commended for their hard work and dedication to protecting all area residents. I hope the law enforcement officers enjoy the adventures of Detectives Brett O'Shea and Michael O'Shea.

I'll tell you my sins and you can sharpen your knife
Offer me that deathless death
Good God, let me give you my life

—Lyrics to *"Take Me To Church"*
by Andrew Hozier Byrne

1

Detective Brett O'Shea's foot tapped on the floor as he studied the card in his hand. The card read, "John Richard Allen, President, Historical Preservation Society." He didn't know how the card had ended up in his office. As a second-year detective, he was out to prove he was damn good at his job.

He'd found the card on his office desk last week. Since he didn't have anything to do with the preservation society, he thought maybe another detective left the card in his office. At least that's what he'd thought until the phone calls and messages from Allen began.

He twirled the card through his fingers before flicking it onto the desk.

Better find out what Allen wants. He punched in the phone number on the card and waited. Just as he was ready to hang up, a squeaky voice finally answered.

"Is Mr. Allen there?" Brett replied.

"Detective O'Shea. I'm pleased that you finally found the time to return my call."

The snide comment caused him to clench his jaw. "You'll have to excuse me. I've been busy."

Allen chuckled. "Of course you have. I think we have something important to discuss."

He bit back a curse. The guy was pretentious if anything. "I'll be the judge of that. How can I help you?"

"As you can tell from the card that I left you, I am John Richard Allen. My ancestor, Captain James Allen, supervised the construction of the original Fort Des Moines back in 1843. There have been strange …"

Brett glanced at the clock. One minute on the phone and the man's high-pitched voice was already grating on his nerves. And he didn't need a history lesson. "Sorry to interrupt, but how did your card get into my office?"

Allen laughed again. "I've got connections, O'Shea—ones I'm not afraid to call on if needed."

Too bad Allen couldn't see him roll his eyes. "What the hell does that mean?" Again there came the damn laugh. "Since you're not going to answer my question, I need to go. I've got a lot of cases to work. Though I did appreciate your little history lesson."

"Tsk, tsk, Detective. There is a reason I called you. I have something to show you. Perhaps we can meet tomorrow for lunch?"

"Can't do it this week. I'm busy. Maybe next week?"

The flippant tone in the squeaky voice disappeared. "Detective, I will meet you at noon tomorrow at the ballpark. My car will take you to the site."

"What site?"

"You'll find out, Detective O'Shea." Brett winced at the sarcastic emphasis Allen placed on his title. "I'll see you at the ballpark at noon."

He stared at the receiver in disbelief. *The asshole hung up on me!*

Wind-whipped pellets of rain slammed into the glass in front of him. Ominous low-hanging clouds rolled across the sky. Another fall storm. A chill hung in the air.

A shiver rippled through him. It wasn't from the rain outside. Intuition told him that meeting Allen would be a mistake, but what choice did he have? He used to believe in absolutes, but not since he met his deceased great-grandfather, Michael, who happened to be a ghost. Cops were good; criminals were bad. Monsters and demons were supposed to be just stories—figments of someone's overly active imagination. Brett cringed. Just thinking of the possibility of dealing with more hocus-pocus crap sent shivers through his body. Without Michael's help, he wouldn't have survived the case last year—a case that involved a supernatural killer. He much preferred to be a detective who solved routine burglary cases and an occasional murder. His last big case, which made him a detective, began on a fall day just like this. It was almost the end of October.

"Call me superstitious," he muttered aloud. He'd feel better if it were December, not October.

A loud knock on his office door drew Brett's attention. Surprised, he watched Terry Anders march into his office and sit down in front of the desk. In his fifties, Chief Anders was a hulk of a man. His steel-gray hair matched the intensity of his stare. Anders hadn't changed much in the past year since they worked the serial killer case together.

Brett grinned as Anders took his seat. "I see you're still attached to a coffee cup. I figured that now you're the police chief, a secretary would be bringing you all the coffee you wanted."

Anders grunted. "Are you kidding? I still have to get my own coffee. No one has better java than this bureau. Does Jake—I mean, Captain Foster—still make you detectives bring in the premium brands?"

"Yeah, it costs me an arm and a leg. I have to admit that I

like the better coffee, but don't tell Foster. So is this a social visit, or did you come to see if my new carpet got installed?" Brett bit back a smile.

Anders slipped a quick glance at Brett's office floor. "Quit your bitchin', O'Shea. Your office is fine. You detectives are lucky to even have a view of the river." Anders straightened his arm and held up his hand. "Before we get sidetracked, I wanted to find out how things are going. Looks like you're still working out."

"Uh, yeah. I got to keep up with the new recruits. Now that I'm thirty-one, some of the guys think I'm over the hill. Plus, working for Foster is great." His smile faded. *What does Anders really want?*

Anders leaned forward and set his cup on Brett's desk. "Over the hill! Hell, they probably think I'm ready for a nursing home. It's good to hear you get along with Foster. Foster does it right." Anders paused, leaning back in the chair. "I'm only checking because when I saw you in the hall yesterday, you kind of looked frustrated."

"Frustrated?" He frowned. "Who knows what I was thinking about."

Anders smiled. "Yeah, who knows. Well, I'll let you get back to work."

Clearing his throat, Brett said, "If you have another minute, there is something I'd like to run by you."

He took a deep breath before sliding the card across the desk. Anders picked it up and turned it over.

"What's this?"

"I found the card on my desk last week. I just thought someone accidently left it here. The guy on the card left a few messages the past couple of days."

Anders's eyes narrowed. "How the hell did it get on your desk?"

He shrugged. "I asked the same question. Allen hinted

he had connections. I'll ask Foster if he knows anything about it."

"So what did he want?"

He rested his hands on the desk. "I'm not sure. Allen wants me to meet him at the ballpark tomorrow."

Anders reached for his cup and took a large swallow. "Are you worried about something?"

"I'm not sure. Something about the guy makes me edgy."

Anders's jaw tightened. "Check the security cameras. Maybe you can see who entered your office the day you found the card. After working that case last year, I trust your instinct. If you're edgy, then so am I." Grabbing his cup, Anders studied him like a bug under a microscope. "Since Allen called several times, why didn't you call him back earlier?"

Shit. Maybe I should have kept my mouth shut. "I was busy wrapping up a couple of cases going to trial. I guess I dropped the ball. Still, something is not quite right with Allen."

Lightning lit up the office. Both of them jumped as thunder rattled the windows.

"What do you mean?" Anders's mouth drew into a tight line.

"Hell, you remember last year. We almost died. I'm man enough to admit I was scared shitless."

Anders jerked to his feet and closed the door to Brett's office. Brett swallowed. A closed door wasn't a good sign.

Anders's gray eyes flashed as he leaned over the desk. "I think it's safe to say that we won't have to deal with that … that crazy shit again. But if someone is harassing one of my men, I want to know about it right away! Is that clear?"

Brett nodded. Is that what Anders thought—that fighting a demon equaled "crazy shit"? In his mind, it was more than that—much more.

"I want you to meet the guy and find out if there is any real danger. With all the frickin' loony tunes shooting cops lately,

I'm going to have Foster follow you. Send me an update when you get back. Understand?"

Brett nodded. "I'm supposed to meet him at noon tomorrow at the ballpark. He wants to take me to some site."

"Where?"

"That's exactly what I asked. I guess I'll find out tomorrow."

"I don't like this, O'Shea."

"But sir, don't you think …"

Anders gripped his coffee cup. "My orders aren't open for debate, Detective O'Shea."

Whipping around, Anders opened the door and paused, a half-smile on his face. "O'Shea, I haven't told you this for a long time, but you really are a shit magnet. Be careful tomorrow."

2

Torrents of rain poured from the clouds. Jagged bolts of lightning lit the sky. Brett winced at the continued flashes of light. He could barely see the road. Mentally, he was kicking himself for the way the meeting with Anders had played out. He hadn't shown himself in the best light. He should have returned Allen's calls earlier.

Brett's crappy mood faded as he pulled up to his house. At least one thing was going right today: Lisa Winslow, his girlfriend, was parked in her silver SUV in front of his house. He hurried to the house to unlock the door. Brett grinned as she struggled to hold on to the umbrella as she ran toward him. He held open the door as she slipped past him. He wiped a trickle of water from her nose with his finger before pressing a kiss to her cheek.

"This is a pleasant surprise. I thought you had to work at the TV station tonight."

She shrugged off her coat and tossed her shoulder-length blonde hair, now damp from the rain. "I did. But I decided to take the night off. I wanted to see you, so I took some comp time."

Brett grabbed her waist and pulled her against him. "I'm so glad you did. Come here. You need a proper hello." He leaned down, sealing a long kiss on her lips.

"Hmm. That's nice," she purred.

His hands drifted down to cup her bottom. "Yeah, real nice," he rumbled.

Her deep blue eyes narrowed as she playfully pushed at his chest. "O'Shea! You can be a caveman sometimes."

Brett leered at her, thinking of running his tongue down her neck. "Grrrr. You woman. Me man."

Lisa dissolved into laughter, slipping under his arms. She collapsed in a nearby chair. "Stop it! I'm hungry. How about I take you to dinner?"

Brett smiled. "Great. After my horrible day, I feel like going out. How about pizza?"

"Sounds good. What happened at work?" Lisa asked as she absentmindedly checked for messages on her phone.

"Police shit I can't discuss with a TV reporter who happens to be my girlfriend. I'll go change, and then we can leave." Brett winked. "Or you could come and help me change?"

"If I go with you, we'll end up staying here." She blew him a kiss. "I'll be anxiously waiting right here."

He quickly showered and went to the bedroom and grabbed jeans and a black T-shirt. The shirt slid over his large pecs and past his narrow waist. He tucked it in and picked up his razor. He stared at his image in the mirror as he shaved. Working out daily was ingrained into his DNA. Hearing Lisa's voice drift from the other room, he cleared his mind and concentrated on what he was doing. His chin dipped as he shaved the dark whiskers from his face. Tossing the razor aside, he grabbed a tube of hair gel and rubbed some into his hands before smoothing it through his thick hair. He wore it longer on top, cut short on the sides. He turned his head from side to side, looking for any gray hair. *Nope, all good.* He hurried down the hall, excited to be spending the night with Lisa. Soon he'd be ready to take the next step in their relationship.

They headed to the South Side for pizza. While driving, Brett reached for Lisa's hand. She gave him an odd look and turned to look out the window. What was up with that? Had he done something wrong? No, that wasn't it. *Probably my imagination.* He lifted her hand to his lips.

"Anything wrong?"

She shook her head, slipping away from his hold. "No, just a little tired all of a sudden. Looks like the rain will let up."

He glanced at the vacant look in her eyes. Something was bothering her. "You know we can go home. I can order in."

She turned toward him with a wan smile. "No, we're already in the car. We'll talk later if that's okay?"

As they ate, Brett noticed Lisa picked at her food, hardly eating anything. He sensed a gulf had developed between them, but he had no idea what had caused it.

After the waiter cleared the table, Brett braced his elbows on the table and leaned toward Lisa. "Okay, talk to me. What's going on? You're quiet tonight."

Lisa twirled a long blonde strand around her finger, gently nibbling on her plump lower lip.

"I wasn't going to say anything, since it's not for sure. My boss pulled me into his office today. There is a possible job opportunity in Saint Louis. He texted me right before we left your house and said a major TV syndicate is interested in hiring me."

"Saint Louis?" His fingers tightened into a ball. "What the hell, Lisa!"

Lisa's blue eyes sparkled from unshed tears. "Please calm down. I just wanted to get your thoughts."

He slumped back in the seat and stared. "Who the hell are you? You never mentioned you were looking for a new job."

Her doe eyes studied him. What did she expect him to say? He didn't want her to leave. He tore his fingers through his hair. "Why now, Lisa? I thought we had a good thing."

This whole situation sucked.

Lisa gripped his hand and squeezed. "We do. You know we do. I didn't ask for this. Frank, my boss, thought he was doing me a favor by recommending me."

He snarled. "Right."

Raising her face, she angrily swiped away a tear. "I'm not sure where we're going. Are we going to move in together ... get married? I don't know. Brett, I'm so confused. What do you want?"

His dry throat made it difficult for the words to come out. "I won't hold you back. You need to decide what you want."

"Oh, Brett," she sighed. "This is supposed to be a decision that we make together."

He leaned across the table, capturing her gaze. "Am I happy you're considering a job out of state? No, but I'm trying to understand."

Tears dotted her cheeks once again. "You know, you could probably get a job with the Saint Louis Police Department."

He closed his eyes, taking a deep breath before he met her gaze. "You know I can't do that."

"Could you try?"

"Chief Anders trusted me enough to promote me to detective. I can't just up and quit." Shaking his head, his voice cracked. "I'm the only family mom has left. I can't leave her here by herself."

Lisa bowed her head. "I know. I had to ask. I don't want to lose you. We're so good together." She yanked out a tissue from her purse and blew her nose.

His stomach clenched. Why was he feeling guilty? He wasn't the one who wanted to move away. "Don't cry. I'll always be here. I'll support whatever decision you make."

Her fingertips grazed his cheek.

"I don't know what I want or what I'll decide to do. We could see each other on the weekends ... take vacations together. We could make it work, Brett, if we both tried."

He forced a smile, not meeting her eyes. "Maybe. Maybe it would."

❦

The ride back home was painful. Brett didn't know if this was a breakup or not. It sure felt like one. A woman's tears could bring him to his knees quicker than anything. As he drove, they held hands with their fingers tightly entwined. He loved her. She was tough—a fighter. They were a good match. So why couldn't he tell her to stay? What the hell was wrong with him? Was he going to let her walk out of his life?

Standing next to her in the driveway, he tilted her chin so he could meet her gaze. "Do you want to come in and talk?"

Lisa lurched forward and wrapped her arms around his waist. "I'll take a rain check if you don't mind. I'll call you later if that's okay. They want a decision in a couple of days."

He kissed the end of her upturned nose before escorting her to the car. He watched the taillights disappear as she drove out of sight. Alone, he rubbed the moisture from his eyes before turning to go inside. Would she call him? *Maybe I should call her.*

After locking the doors, he stood in the middle of the kitchen, staring absently into space. He grabbed a book off the table and heaved it at the wall. White sheets of paper fluttered in the air, scattering about the room. With closed eyes, he gripped the back of a chair. He didn't want to lose her, but he wouldn't prevent her from leaving. Lisa was ambitious and smart. The job would be a great opportunity for her.

After setting the coffeemaker for the morning, he undressed and flopped on the bed. He tossed and turned all night. A quick glance at the clock confirmed the alarm would go off in three hours. Lisa's announcement had hit him like a truckload of bricks. Had he made a mistake? Should he have agreed to move and leave Des Moines? No, he couldn't leave his mom or his job.

Glancing at the dark ceiling, he murmured, "Okay Michael. I need some help here." Several moments later, he rolled over and punched the pillows. "Now that I want you to talk, you won't do it. Thanks, buddy."

Brett missed the crazy old coot. Although, there was nothing old-looking about Michael. He looked about Brett's age.

He punched the pillow again for good measure. The meeting with John Allen tomorrow was ever present. His brain was on overload. Pulling the pillow tightly around his head, he struggled to get comfortable. There were lots of detectives in the area; why had Allen sought him out? Tomorrow he'd start getting those answers, and—he hoped—Lisa would decide to stay.

3

The alarm's annoying buzzer vibrated on Brett's nightstand. Without opening his eyes, he slammed his fist on top of the off button. Rolling to his back, he dropped an arm over his brow. He heard the neighbor's car back out of the driveway. The loud vibrating noise made him clench his teeth. *Damn it. Can't that guy get his muffler fixed?*

A bone-jarring pop of the muffler caused his eyes to fly open. It was 6:30 a.m. already. With a groan, he pushed himself to his feet and made his way to the shower. The hot, steamy water brought him back to the living. He pulled out a new black suit with a gray tie and quickly dressed. Standing in front of a full-length mirror, he turned to the side. The suit fit like a glove, showing off his athletic build. He wanted Mr. Allen to know he wasn't some flunky detective he could order around. As he headed to the kitchen, the smell of fresh coffee greeted him. He poured a cup and tossed a frozen ham and cheese croissant into the microwave. *Home cooking— nothing better.*

Another look at the clock gave him urgency. Gulping down the last couple of bites, he tossed the dishes in the sink. Always punctual, he hurried out the door and jumped into his car.

As he walked into the Detective Bureau on the second floor, Jake Foster's towering frame filled the doorway. His gaze locked on Brett. In his midforties, Captain Foster was in peak physical condition and a fanatic about health and exercise. His buzz-cut black hair was peppered with very little gray. He swore that Foster's square jaw could break granite. He would hate to be in a fight against the captain.

"In here, O'Shea." Foster pointed to a chair. "Have a seat. I hear that I'm supposed to shadow you today." Foster's unflinching gaze flitted over him. "What's this about? Anders was kind of vague."

He shrugged. "A guy named John Allen wants me to go look at something. He hasn't been very forthcoming. I think Anders is just being careful."

Foster's gaze didn't waver. The captain didn't even crack a smile. Brett shifted his position in the chair, meeting Foster's gaze. He silently prayed there wouldn't be any additional questions.

"How long is the meeting going to take?" Foster growled.

"Not too long, I think."

Foster rose to his feet and waved toward the door. "Get out of here, O'Shea. Since I'll be the one to cover you today, I've got work to get done."

Brett jumped up from the chair, anxious to get out of Foster's office. He hurried down the hall to his office, closed the door, and leaned against the wooden barrier. *Hell! That was intense.*

The hands on the clock barely moved all morning. By midmorning, Brett had lost track of the number of cups of coffee he had downed. By the pounding of his heart, he knew it had been quite a few. He was going to turn into Anders if he wasn't careful—a coffee cup glued to his hand 24-7. With a smirk, he finished responding to his e-mails.

Finally, it was time to go. Brett grabbed his phone and keys and poked his head in Foster's office.

"Sir, I'm heading out now."

Foster nodded. "I'll be right behind you."

The ballpark was only five minutes from the station. Brett took a deep breath as he turned the ignition. After crossing the river, he turned south toward the ballpark. A black limo sat on the far east perimeter of the parking lot. He pulled up next to the car. A limo driver stood outside the vehicle, waiting for him.

The driver nodded as Brett exited his car.

The driver's formidable frame matched the uncompromising look in his eyes. Slightly over six feet, Brett had to look up to meet the man's gaze.

"Detective O'Shea?"

"Yes, I'm O'Shea." Instinctively, he glanced around the lot. There were a few cars parked in front of a nearby restaurant. A pair of joggers ran by on the adjoining trail. Foster's car was parked along the adjoining street. Nothing appeared out of the ordinary. He peered inside the limo and saw that it was empty. "Where's Mr. Allen?"

"Please step inside, Detective. My name is Terrence. I'm Mr. Allen's driver. I've been instructed to take you to him."

With his hand on the door, Brett paused. "Allen was supposed to meet me here."

"He was delayed and sends his apologies."

The chauffer's stiff mannerisms made Brett smile. The man had the look of an ex-FBI agent or military veteran, down to the short-clipped hair and unwavering gaze.

"I don't like getting the runaround. Maybe we should reschedule."

"Sir, if you'll be patient, Mr. Allen has directed me to take you to the dig site just a few seconds from here."

"Dig site for what?

The chauffer shook his head. "Sorry sir. I'm not at liberty to say anything more."

Brett settled back in the seat as the door closed. The limo maneuvered quickly through the southeast bottoms—an area that he was well familiar with from his days on patrol. The bottoms were nestled along the Raccoon River. Because of frequent flooding, the small homes built there at the turn of the twentieth century had been demolished one by one. His gaze took in the entire area, which was being revitalized a block at a time.

Unbidden thoughts of Lisa whispered through him. She had left a message saying she was visiting Saint Louis for a few days. He pulled out his phone. His fingers hovered over her name. He pressed it and waited as it rang.

Her voice mail answered. "Hey, Lisa. It's me. I wanted to call and see how things were going. Call me later when you get a chance."

He dropped the phone back into his pocket and ran his hands across his face. *Get your mind back in the game*, he warned himself. He would try to call her later.

The car stopped on a hill overlooking the junction of the Des Moines and Raccoon Rivers. Several bald eagles perched on nearby trees flapped their wings in the afternoon breeze. Standing near the limo, he turned to view the area. The need to check his surroundings was instinctive. The warm breeze did nothing to alleviate the chill that rippled through him.

A man wearing wire-rim glasses walked toward him. The slender man was dressed in sturdy hiking boots, khaki pants, and a hat that looked like the one worn by Indiana Jones. *What an odd-looking man*, he thought. The man stopped in front of him and held out his hand.

"Detective O'Shea. We meet at last. I'm John Allen."

He stared at Allen's face. One eye was blue and the other brown. A shiver of unease rippled through him. Shaking the man's smooth hand, he retorted, "Nice to meet you, Mr. Allen. Now, how can I help you?"

Stomping his feet to remove clumps of mud, Allen gave him a pointed look.

"Right to the point. Good for you, Detective. Just so you know, besides serving as president of the Historical Preservation Society, I am an archeologist and am in charge of the dig site you're about to see. Now follow me and stay close."

Brett fell in line behind him. Allen seemed to be a busy guy, which made Brett more curious. As they headed down the dirt path, Brett stepped in a pile of poop. He groaned as brown goo dotted the bottom of his trousers.

"I guess I should have told you to bring boots."

Brett muttered under his breath as he treaded carefully on the grass. The winding path twisted and turned. When they reached the end of the marked pathway, the archeological dig site lay before them. Allen's staff of individuals carefully sifted through a pile of dirt, waving to Allen as he passed by.

Allen led him to part of the site that was empty. Yellow tape blocked off this section. Allen turned toward Brett and held up his hand.

"Detective, before we go down, I want to remind you of the need for confidentiality."

Brett nodded, peering down to the actual dig site. His eyes widened as he glanced about the site. Allen smiled like a proud father. Brett had to admit that he was impressed. He remembered reading in the newspaper that they had unearthed a wealth of ancient Indian relics. Even the state archeologist was involved.

"All I see are a few old bowls and broken stuff. What does this have to do with police business?" Brett asked as he tiptoed around tools lying on the ground.

"I'm sorry to be so secretive, Detective, but once you see what I have to show you, you'll understand."

Allen might have been part of the city's founding fathers crowd and very influential, but he made Brett nervous. The man's shifty gaze never met his straight on.

Brett pointed. "Are we going down into that hole?"

"We are. Don't worry, though. There are planks to walk on. Can't have you getting that fancy suit of yours muddy, now can we?"

Grabbing the top of the ladder, Brett climbed down. At the bottom, a tunnel led away from the site.

Allen stood near the tunnel entrance, waving. "Hurry up, Detective," Allen snapped impatiently.

"I'm coming." Brett stared at pieces of pottery and wood littering the ground. "How come no one is digging down here?"

"Patience, Detective."

Allen grabbed a lantern and entered the tunnel. As Allen hurried forward, his hat bobbed up and down, giving him the appearance of a little bobblehead or a miniature Indiana Jones. Brett's smothered laughter drew Allen's attention. The man turned to Brett and glared. Brett stiffened, his smile fading.

"Is something amusing, Detective?"

He shook his head. "No. Why?" He bit the inside of his cheek to keep from laughing. Allen looked pissed.

As they again started walking, Brett asked, "I'm curious about why you do this archeological thing. Your family is pretty involved in politics."

Allen cocked his head. "You've done your homework. Even though my family is quite political and wealthy, I want to do something and be remembered in my own right."

The farther they advanced in the tunnel, the more apprehensive Brett became. He mumbled under his breath. Barely able to see his hand in front of his face, he pulled out his cell phone, using it as a light. He suddenly pitched forward as his foot dropped into a hole.

"Damn it!"

Allen kept going, ignoring Brett's grumbling. Brett swore the man increased his pace. In fact, he thought he heard Allen chuckle.

Allen appeared to have memorized the numerous twists and turns they made before coming to an arched stone-and-metal doorway. Two towering granite columns anchored it— one on each side of the door. A thick metal chain created a barrier to what was behind the opening. Brett ran his hand across the ancient-looking doorway. A look of pride blossomed on Allen's face.

After unlocking the chain, Allen tugged on the door, his chest heaving from his efforts.

Brett stepped forward, gently nudging Allen aside. With little effort, Brett pulled the door open.

"Well, come on in, Detective." Allen motioned for Brett to precede him.

Stepping past the door, Brett found himself in a small cave no bigger than twenty feet by twenty feet. Two large tombs sat in the center of the room. Large bronze-looking crucifixes were affixed to the lids. The tops of the stone tombs were chipped and weathered. Had they been exposed to the elements at some point in time?

"Whoa! What the hell?" A tremor of unease tore through him. He jarred to a sudden stop in the doorway. Between the cobwebs and the tombs, the urge to run was overpowering.

Allen set a lantern on one of the tombs. The man's eyes glittered in the dim light. "Come closer, Detective. I have a story to tell you."

"Allen, I think you need to tell me what's going on. I have several serious cases that I should be working on. You created this little drama just to show me a couple of old tombs?"

Allen's high-pitched laughter filled the room. He removed his glasses and carefully wiped his lenses with his shirt. "I think I've held you in suspense long enough. Are you aware that humans have lived in this area for thousands of years?" Without waiting for a response, Allen wiped the top of one of the tombs with his hand. "Do you remember that back in 2010 a construction company discovered a prehistoric site near the new wastewater treatment plant? The State of Iowa archaeologist and the University of Iowa found well-preserved house deposits and numerous graves."

Brett inwardly groaned. This was going to take all day at this rate. "What's the bottom line, Allen?"

Allen sighed. "As I was saying, at least three late prehistoric villages stood in or near this area during times ranging from AD 1300 to AD 1700."

Brett muttered, "Allen, I'm still not clear how any of this involves the police."

Allen cut the air with his hand. Brett jerked at the movement. An odd look filled Allen's eyes. Allen continued as if Brett hadn't spoken. Allen seemed to have a control issue.

"There were also numerous prehistoric American Indian mounds in the same area, but the early settlers destroyed most of those."

"Damn it, Allen!" Brett clenched his hands. "I don't need a history lesson. You've got ten seconds to make your point."

Allen's eyes narrowed. "And I was just getting to the good part." Spreading his arms, he slowly turned in a circle. "As you saw from our walk to the cave, the soldiers in Fort Des Moines dug these tunnels close to the original fort in order to get coal back to the fort's blacksmith. These coal tunnels were dug in the early 1840s and ended close to this enclosed cave. You'd be surprised how many of these tunnels exist." Brett frowned. "Anyway, after my team got approval to dig here, you can imagine my amazement when we discovered the existence of this cave. Of course I blocked it off, so only a few trusted people even know this secret."

Brett walked to the doorway but abruptly stopped. *Secret?*

His curiosity was piqued. "What secret? I don't see anything here but a couple of old tombs."

Allen pursed his lips. He stomped over to the corner and picked up a large crowbar. He ran the end of the tool along the top of the tomb. Strange writing was embedded in the stone.

"See this writing?" Allen jabbed his finger at the stone. "It's Romanian. You can imagine my excitement at finding these tombs here in the middle of Iowa."

Brett leaned over to examine the writing. "1359! Shit, that's old."

"Yes." Allen gripped Brett's elbow. His voice dropped to a whisper. "I'm the only one who has seen this. Now you will be part of the secret." Spittle flew from his mouth as he spoke.

Crap! Brett wasn't sure he wanted to become part of Allen's secret. Goosebumps popped up on his arms. The lantern flickered from a nonexistent breeze. Brett shivered with unease.

"Mr. Allen, the chief will want a report when I return to the office. I get that you found a couple of old tombs, but shouldn't you report this to the state archeologist or something? I can't exclude anything from my report."

Allen flapped his hands as he paced in front of Brett. "Yes, yes. I know that. Now, help me slide the crowbar under the lid to open it."

Brett swallowed hard. He didn't want to look at any skeletons. The thought gave him the creeps. Between the two of them, they managed to shove the large, flat stone sideways to reveal a gauzy shroud.

Brett threw his hands in the air and hopped away from the body. *What the hell are we doing?* "Son of a bitch! There's a body in there!"

Pushing his hat back to reveal thin blond hair, Allen chided, "What did you expect to see? An empty casket?"

"Well, kind of. This is barbaric. You don't go around

disturbing the dead. Hell!" The musty smell of the open tomb filled the cave. His stomach clenched.

Allen's laugher echoed through the small, enclosed cave. "Don't tell me you've never seen a body before?" His hands slid over the corpse.

Brett growled. "Of course I've seen bodies. New bodies—not these ancient things."

Allen's gaze locked on Brett. "I've been watching you for the past year. The serial killer case that you and Anders dealt with last year was very impressive. I'm surprised that you were able to keep it out of the papers."

"I don't know what you're getting at."

"Tsk, tsk," Allen warned. "Even though I have no proof, I think you were dealing with something that most people would dismiss entirely. Something unnatural."

Brett stared back at Allen. *The guy is bluffing.* Folding his arms across his chest, he snorted. "You have quite an imagination, Allen. The reason nothing was in the paper was because there was nothing to tell."

Waggling a finger in his direction, Allen smiled. "Whatever you say, Detective."

"Why did you ask me here? I don't see one damn thing that is police business."

Allen's eyes burned a hole through him. "Because, Officer O'Shea, I believe there is a vampire in Des Moines."

4

Brett took a deep breath and burst out laughing. His stomach muscles contracted from the deep belly laughter. "Vampire! Are you crazy?" Wiping the corners of his eyes, he smiled at Allen. "I'm out of here, Allen. Call me if you need police assistance in the future." Just as he stepped into the tunnel, a wiry hand grabbed his shoulder.

"O'Shea, wait. There's no one else I can trust."

The desperation in Allen's voice made him pause. Brett faced Allen. Gone was the cocky attitude that Allen had shown since they met.

"Listen to me! These tombs are from the fourteenth century. Ever since I discovered this cave, several incidents have occurred."

"Like what?" he grumbled.

Allen shook his head, pacing in front of him. "First it was missing animals—pets and such. Last week a homeless camp near the river suddenly disappeared. All ten people are gone—not a trace of them left."

"C'mon, Allen," Brett moaned. "Homeless people move around a lot. Since winter is coming, they probably headed south, where it's warmer."

Allen's lips narrowed. "That's possible. It is reasonable to assume that they have left for a warmer climate. I would agree with you, if I hadn't seen a man's finger lying near this cave. It was all shriveled, as if all the blood had been sucked out."

Brett's pulse increased. "A finger? Where's the rest of the body?"

Allen shuddered, a look of revulsion covering his face. "I have no idea. You should have seen it."

He felt a flash of frustration. "Do you have any idea how many people go to the emergency room every day because they chop off or saw off a finger? Where is this finger, anyway?"

Allen pointed to a bucket in the corner. After removing a rock and a jagged board on top of the bucket, Brett peered into the container of alcohol before straightening. "I'll ask again. Where's the finger?"

Allen grabbed the bucket and looked inside. "I put it right here a couple of days ago. Since the cave is sheltered and cool, I figured it would be okay here. I even put that large rock on top of the board to protect the evidence."

Brett smacked the palm of his hand against his forehead. "So you have no idea what happened to the finger."

Allen glared back at him. "Of course I don't know what happened. Why else would I tell you to look in the damn bucket?"

"Haven't you ever noticed the critters wandering around at night? With the snacks and food that your crew eat here at the site, it's going to draw raccoons, coyotes, turkey vultures—you name it. Someone probably forgot to shut the door one night, and it made an easy meal for a wild animal. I get that you tried to protect it, but you should have left that little tidbit of information in one of the messages or at least brought it to the station."

Allen kicked the bucket against the stone wall.

Brett bit back a smile. Mr. Allen had a temper. At least he could get out of this hellhole. Grabbing Allen's lantern, he marched out of the cave.

Behind him, he heard Allen swearing. "Allen, hurry up. I'm out of here."

"Detective, wait up. I can't see."

Turning back to the cave, he hollered, "No can do. I've got appointments, Mr. Allen."

He ignored the mumblings of Allen behind him and kept walking. Minutes later, he was up the ladder, walking back to the limo. As he stood by the car, he took pity on the would-be archeologist. The man's cheeks were as red as a brick, and his lips were drawn together in a tight line.

"Seriously, Allen, I'm glad you contacted me. If anything else strange shows up, give me a call. I'll be glad to take a look."

He shook Allen's chilled hand, climbing into the limo.

☙✦❧

Once at his car, he spotted Foster driving down the street. With a subtle nod, he got behind the wheel.

To quiet his growling stomach, he swung by Burger King for a quick lunch. It was almost 2:00 p.m. by the time he was back at his desk.

Captain Foster slipped into his office and sat down in front of the desk as he was returning phone calls.

He took a long sip from the Burger King cup and choked back a laugh as his superior frowned at him.

"Relax. It's diet."

Foster leaned back in the chair and kicked out his legs, but Brett wasn't fooled. The captain's brown eyes stared at him.

"So what happened out there today? You were out of sight for some time. I was about to go check it out myself."

"After I got a history lesson on Des Moines from Allen, he led me down into the dig site. His crew found a bunch of old tunnels that the military used to get coal to the original Fort Des Moines blacksmith. Anyway, one of the tunnels branched off to a cave. Only a few people know about the cave."

Brett cringed when Foster waved his hand in a circle, motioning him to get to the point. "And this impacts the police how?"

Brett bit back a smile. "Exactly what I asked Mr. Allen. He took me into a cave and showed me two old stone tombs. From the writing on the top, they are from 1359."

"1359? Does he want us to guard them?"

Brett quickly took another drink. "Not quite. He believes there could be a vampire in town."

Foster jerked to his feet. Leaning over Brett's desk, he hoarsely whispered, "Vampire!"

Brett nodded toward the doorway where a couple of the detectives stood staring at them.

Foster turned and marched over and slammed the door. Brett jerked. Was Foster pissed at him?

Foster turned and dropped back into the chair.

"O'Shea, are you bullshitting me?"

"No, sir. Personally, I think Allen has been watching too many reruns of *The Vampire Diaries*."

"What the hell are *The Vampire Diaries*?" Foster's eyes glittered with anger.

"Never mind. It was a joke."

Foster's mouth became a tight line. A muscle in his neck throbbed. "You know that Allen has a lot of pull in this town. He's in the paper every other week for donating this or that and sponsoring someone's political campaign."

"I realize that, sir."

"Why does he think there is a vampire in Des Moines, of all places? That shit isn't real."

Brett had once thought the same thing. He no longer knew what to believe. He sure as hell didn't want to think that vampires were real. But what if Allen was on to something? Had he misjudged Allen?

"I agree. He mentioned an abandoned homeless camp down by the river. He thinks it's strange that the people in the camp disappeared."

"Did you happen to tell him that most homeless people leave before winter gets here?"

"I did. He also said there have been a lot of small animals killed recently. What really convinced Allen that a vampire is on the loose is that he found a man's finger by the cave."

"Did you bring it back with you?"

"No. Mr. Allen lost it."

Foster leaned back in the chair, staring up at the ceiling. "God save me from frickin' idiots."

Brett took another long drink, accidently making a slurping noise with the straw. Foster lowered his gaze to stare at him.

"Sorry." Brett quickly tossed the empty cup in the wastebasket.

"What do you think, O'Shea?"

He cleared his throat. "I think Mr. Allen has an active imagination. But we should cover our ass. Anders will want to know what we're doing to prove or disprove Allen's allegations. It wouldn't hurt to do some checking with the Animal Rescue League to see if there is a jump in missing animals."

Foster nodded. "Good idea."

I'll check with the guys to see if anyone has gone missing the past week or so." Brett grabbed a piece of paper and jotted some notes. "If I can get a name or two on the homeless group, maybe I can track down family members and check with the shelters. I'm sure there is a logical explanation."

Foster stood and went to the door. Pausing, he turned toward him. "Get on it then. Make this your priority. Once we can rule everything out, document the hell out of it. Allen has a lot of clout. I don't want us ending up on the front page of the paper. Got it? And get a report to the chief right away."

"Yes sir. I'll get right on it."

As the door slammed, Brett blew out a deep breath. He was almost afraid to start the investigation—afraid of what he would find. Vampires didn't exist. They couldn't. Besides, this was Iowa for God's sake, not New Orleans.

5

Brett wrapped up the report for the chief. He breathed a sigh of relief once he hit Send. After clearing his desk, he logged off of the city's network. He wanted to get out of the office before Anders saw the report. Shit was going to hit the fan once Anders saw the word "vampire."

Taking the back stairs, Brett made it to his car undiscovered. He rubbed a knot in the back of his neck and turned toward the gym. With Lisa out of town, there was no reason to hurry home. Besides, he didn't want to be one of those cops with a potbelly.

With a quick smile for the receptionist, he signed in at the gym. Tension strummed through his body. He made a beeline for the treadmill. Running would take the edge off his nerves.

Ignoring the beads of sweat running down his shoulder blades, he cranked up the volume on his phone and ran until his legs shook from the exertion. The sunset was long gone by the time he hit the showers.

As he approached the gym's front desk, he spotted Detective Kevin Donnellson. The detective was built like a Viking warrior, minus the long hair. With light blonde hair and bright blue eyes, Donnellson was always a hit with women.

Donnellson leaned on the front desk, talking to the new trainer. He was obviously checking her out. Brett walked up behind Donnellson, slapping his shoulder. "Donnellson, I didn't know you worked out here."

Donnellson turned around with a big smile on his face. "O'Shea! How the hell are you? I just moved to the South Side, and this was the closest gym to home."

"You'll like it here. You ought to stop by the house sometime and have a beer."

Donnellson's phone buzzed. He glanced at it and smiled. Stepping off to the side, Donnellson whispered something into the phone. His husky laughter was a clue that he was talking to a woman.

Minutes later Donnellson pocketed his phone and faced Brett. "Hey, I've got to run, but we'll definitely get together. Catch you later."

Brett shook his head, watching Donnellson rush out the door. He couldn't figure out how Donnellson kept his girlfriends straight.

He turned to study the new trainer, Jamie. She looked as if she were in high school, but he knew that if she was a trainer, she had to be older.

"Hi, may I help you?" Jamie smiled up at him.

Her heart-shaped mouth glistened with some type of pink gloss. She was petite, yet her muscles were well defined.

He rested his elbows on the ledge and grinned down at the young trainer. "I'm Brett O'Shea. I wanted to stop by and say hi. You must be the new trainer?"

"Afraid so. I'm Jamie Brooks."

Strike one. She obviously wasn't impressed with his charming smile. "You'll like it here. It's one of the better gyms in town."

Her blonde ponytail swished over her shoulder as she turned her head. "Yeah, I know. I checked it out before I applied. Are you a regular here?"

Before he could reply, she held up her hand. She answered the phone and paged one of the guests.

Turning back to him, she muttered, "Sorry."

"No problem. I'm what you could call a regular. I'm in here almost every day."

When a couple approached the desk, Brett leaned closer. "Hey, it looks like you're busy. I'll catch you next time. See you later."

Brett's bad mood lifted as he left the building. He'd completely forgotten about the crappy day he'd had. After a quick drive home, he walked into the kitchen, grabbed a container of frozen meatloaf, and tossed it into the microwave. His mom, Sandy, was always cooking for him. He'd often come home from work and find his freezer full of home-cooked meals. He grabbed his phone and called his mom.

After a couple of rings, Sandy answered. "Brett—about time you called me. Anything exciting going on at the station?"

"No, nothing exciting. Just the same old stuff. How are you doing?"

"Fine," she sighed. "I haven't heard from Lisa for a while. How is she doing?"

He hesitated. "She's in Saint Louis for some job interview."

"Oh, Brett." Regret filled her voice. "Do you think she'll get it?"

"I don't know what she's thinking. She won't return my calls."

He could almost see the wheels in his mom's head turning.

"Why don't you come over for dinner? I'll make your favorite."

He chuckled, trying to lighten the tone of the call. "I just put some of your meatloaf in the microwave."

"Fine, but if you want to talk, give me a call night or day. I know you two will work it out. Talk to you later, sweetie."

Brett smiled. His mom was always the optimist.

He stared at the phone. Lisa hadn't returned any of his calls. Obviously she wanted some space. He wouldn't pressure her. She needed time to decide.

After eating, he stretched out on the sofa. With a bottle of beer in hand, he lazily flipped through the channels on the TV. His cell phone rattled on the coffee table in front of him.

"O'Shea here."

Anders's loud bellow nearly caused him to drizzle beer down the front of his shirt. "A vampire, O'Shea! A fucking vampire."

He bit back a smile, thankful that Anders couldn't see him. "Sir, I only repeated what Allen told me. We have no evidence that those creatures even exist."

Anders lowered his voice. "Damn it. We almost died last time. The council is supposed to formalize my appointment as chief next month. Can you imagine what they'd do if they got wind we were looking into whether there is a vampire in Des Moines?"

"No. I mean yes, I do. I sure as hell don't want a vampire in our city. We were both pretty traumatized after that last case."

"By the way, are you still seeing Lisa?"

Brett's thoughts screeched to a stop. Why the change in gears? "Not really. She's applying for a job out of state. Long-distance relationships don't work all that well."

"Oh, I'm sorry to hear that. Lisa was a great girl. She could keep our secrets out of the news." Anders growled. "If it's true, how the hell can we keep this stuff off the evening news?"

Anders was right. With Lisa gone, how were they going to avoid being a major news story? Brett rose to his feet, standing in front of the window in his front room. He stared at his reflection. His lips had thinned to a narrow line. Frown lines marred his forehead.

"Sir, maybe I should finish checking out Allen's story and

see what happens. What if Allen fed us this line of bullshit to see how we handle it?"

Anders fell silent. Brett could picture his boss pacing the floor with a cup of coffee in his hand. "Do it. I've got too much on my mind right now. If you need any help, go to Foster. I trust him with my life, and so should you. I'll talk to you later."

He muttered his agreement, continuing to stare out the window as Anders hung up the phone. It was a typical fall evening. A brisk wind shook the leaves from the trees. A full moon lit the evening sky, shining down on the quiet neighborhood. Brett ran a hand through his hair. He choked back a laugh. At least Allen hadn't said there was a werewolf loose in Des Moines.

Impulsively, he grabbed a jacket from the closet and his car keys. He was going for a ride.

John Allen skirted the edge of the ballroom. Another presidential hopeful was in town to raise funds. Since the state was the first in the national caucus race, presidential candidates were frequent visitors to Des Moines. He shook hands with several acquaintances as he shouldered his way through the crowd.

He hurried to the car. Terrence, his driver, was waiting in the circle drive.

"Where to, sir?"

"I need to go back to the dig site. Did you bring the clothes I requested?"

"Yes, sir. They're in the backseat."

He smiled. "Good. Let's get going."

Once parked at the site, Terrence opened the door. Allen jumped out, turning on his flashlight.

Terrence closed the car door and looked out into the dark. "Sir, shall I go with you? It could be dangerous."

He patted the driver's shoulder. "No, that's fine. I shouldn't be long."

Terrence nodded before getting back in the car. Using the light to guide his way, Allen made it down the ladder. He wanted to check the tomb. He didn't remember locking the chains earlier. A light mist rolled across the ground. Droplets of moisture coated Allen's face. The beam flickered. Shaking the flashlight, he continued to make his way through the dark tunnels.

Coming to the cave entrance, he saw the chains lying on the ground. *Damn it.* He must have forgotten to secure the door. He would have to enter to make sure nothing was missing.

The dampness made it difficult for him to grip the door. He tried several times before it began to open. A snapping sound made him whirl toward the noise. He pointed the flashlight into the darkness behind him. The pounding of his heart blocked all other sounds. He swore it sounded as if someone had stepped on a twig, causing it to snap. He breathed a sigh of relief on finding the tunnel empty. He reached into his jacket and felt the wood stake in his pocket. No vampire was going to get John Allen. He'd convince O'Shea that something evil was in their city. His harsh breathing echoed in the tunnels. Allen stood quietly, watching and waiting. As time passed, he relaxed. He considered that perhaps he should have brought Terrence with him.

Pushing the cave door open enough for him to squeeze through, he stood with his back against the wall, making a circle with the flashlight in his hand. Nothing appeared to be missing. However, one of the lids on the tombs was ajar. Picking up the crowbar, he tucked the light under his chin as he adjusted the lid to seal the tomb. He quickly closed the door and secured the lock and chain.

Taking a deep breath, he rushed out of the tunnel, wondering what had possessed him to do this late at night. He skidded to a stop when he saw a pair of glittering gold eyes watching him. With shaking hands, he pointed the light at the strange eyes. He nearly laughed aloud. A fat raccoon turned and waddled toward him.

He scurried up the ladder. Once back on solid ground, he glanced down into the dark hole. His body trembled, chilled from the fall wind and wet conditions.

The sound of husky laughter drifted through the mist. Not sure where it came from, he quickly turned around. Terrence walked toward him. He took a deep breath.

"Sir, are you okay?" Terrence's voice boomed through the night.

"I'm fine. Let's head home."

Before walking back to the car, he took one last look down into the pit. Using the light, he surveyed the site. Was he paranoid, or was he being watched? As he walked toward the car, the faint sound of laughter whispered in the wind.

6

Darkness settled within the reaches of the damp cave. The locusts in nearby trees created a symphony of sounds that echoed within the enclosure. As the stone cover on the casket began to inch open, the creatures of the night stilled, waiting.

Dragos's eyelids flew open. Darkness surrounded him. He jerked to a sitting position and slammed his head on something hard. Instinctively he reached out to feel the container in which he was enclosed. Panic rose up in his throat. He moved his legs only to kick a solid mass. Where was he? He heart hammered in his chest as he struggled to catch his breath. Focusing his energy, he pushed upward, opening his dark prison. He shakily crawled out of whatever he'd been stuck in and stood on the floor. His breathing was labored. He turned and gasped, staring at an ornate burial casket. His vision blurred when he realized he had been lying inside it. Where was he? Nothing made any sense. More importantly, why was he sleeping in such a morbid place? Another casket was nearby. Whose was it? Nothing looked familiar.

His senses alert, he slowly turned in a circle. A shiver ran up his spine. His head dipped, causing thick black hair to fall across his brow. He was in a cave, but it was not like the caves at home in England. Even the smell in the air was different. He was used to controlling every minute detail in his life. Nothing was left to chance. Whatever was happening to him was beyond his imagination and comprehension.

He crept toward the other casket and peered inside. It was empty. Had there been someone else in the cave? More importantly, how the devil had he gotten here?

The last thing he remembered was sharing a carriage with his close friend Marcus and a new acquaintance in Bucharest. A sharp pain flashed across his brow. Why couldn't he remember more details?

A musty smell filled the air. His brow furrowed as he walked the perimeter of the enclosed space until he found a doorway.

He turned as a familiar sound drew his attention. A river flowed nearby. He stumbled. How could he know that? He was shut in a cave, surrounded by walls of stone. How was it possible to hear the sound of water?

A sharp pain brought him to his knees. When the pain subsided enough, Dragos shakily stood, bracing one arm against the wall. He rubbed his mouth. His teeth ached. Tentatively, he poked a shaking finger inside his mouth. *What the hell!* The canine teeth jutted downward. They felt razor sharp. He clamped his jaw closed, and he winced when his teeth cut his lower lip. Blood trickled down his chin.

Dragos staggered to the side. The room felt as if it were spinning. Groaning, he closed his eyes and concentrated on what he remembered.

He and Lord Marcus Needingham had been traveling across Europe, making their grand tour. They had arrived in Bucharest, the home of his mother, and a few days later a letter had arrived. His mother had written that his father,

William Eldridge, the Earl of Albemarle, was ill and that he should return with the utmost haste.

Instinctively, his hands smoothed the wrinkles from his dress coat. A glance down at his boots brought a frown to his face. He was filthy. Impatience flashed through him. What had happened that night with Marcus? He vividly recalled they were to meet up with a man—an aristocrat with polished manners, who dressed liked a king. His thoughts were vague. He couldn't remember the man's name. He recalled only that his smile never reached his eyes. Dragos knew he didn't particularly care for the man, but he couldn't remember why. On their last night there, he and Marcus were to attend a royal ball. Marcus had eagerly accepted the offer, agreeing to ride with the man. Dragos's attempt to decline the invitation was hastily brushed aside by Marcus. His friend was impressed by the man's riches and manners. Dragos gave in and agreed to go to the ball. After all, one more night in Bucharest would make little difference. Or so he had thought.

He roared with anguish. He pounded his fists against the stone walls, heedless of the pain that rippled up his arm.

He recalled feeling uneasy as they entered a seedy tavern. Supposedly the man's carriage would deliver them to the ball—a ball at which the crème de la crème of society would be on display, trying to arrange strategic marriages or simple midnight rendezvous. Yet why would a wealthy man with royal connections want to meet in a place such as a run-down tavern? It'd made little sense to him at the time. Why hadn't he turned around and left? Was it fate?

Like an idiot, he had chosen to enter that run-down tavern. When he and Marcus walked in, other occupants had slowly backed into the shadows. It was as though they had the plague. This was, he felt, another reason he should have left.

They both jerked as a barmaid slammed two large cups of

ale in front of them and quickly scampered away. The fearful look on her face did nothing to calm the uneasiness he felt.

"I don't like this, Eldridge. Let's leave," Marcus hissed.

Rising to his feet, Dragos dropped some coins on the table. The tavern door blew open, slamming into the wall. A dark stranger filled the doorway. At closer look, he saw that it was the man who had invited them to the ball. Dragos remembered his thin, gloved hands resting on a tall, black cane adorned with an ivory skull. This unknown man flashed a look of distain about the room. One by one, the occupants of the bar fell silent. No one moved. The man whipped his cloak over one shoulder. The richness of his garments glistened in the golden glow of the nearby candles. The man's dark gaze locked on Dragos and his friend.

Dragos shook his head as pain cut through his ruminations. He couldn't remember what happened to Marcus. Had they left the tavern and returned to the hotel? His last memory was that of meeting the man's empty gaze.

Filled with the sudden need for fresh air, Dragos stormed to the doorway. With barely a push, the thick stone door flew open. He stood quietly, taking several deep breaths to force the tension from his body. His thirst building, he slowly made his way to the rushing water. Dead leaves crunched beneath his boots. Stars twinkled between passing clouds as a stiff breeze caressed his face. The satisfaction of freedom coursed through his body. He almost felt giddy. He nearly growled at the childish thought.

The roar of something in the sky drew his attention. White and red lights flew across the sky at a speed that he thought not possible. The roaring sound seemed to be connected to the lights in the sky. His gaze followed the lights until they dipped so low that they were lost from sight. *What the devil?* What was this place? Some type of witchery was evident. He reached for his knife in his boot, but it was missing. With his senses on alert, he knew he must find shelter and food.

A nearby bush rustled, causing him to stiffen with awareness. *A scrawny wolf?* His head tilted, studying the animal. No, it was smaller—a dog, perhaps. It crouched in the shadows, watching him. Dragos felt his canine teeth lengthen. Fear nearly blinded him. He clutched his stomach. Hunger pains nearly brought him to his knees. *No need to hunt when an unlucky animal is so readily available.*

He straightened, frightened by his bloodthirsty thoughts. He was a gentleman—a member of the ton. His thoughts were likely due to delirium. After all, he couldn't remember when he last ate or drank. He needed water. He turned and lunged toward the creek, where he furiously gulped from the stream.

In the blink of an eye, he found his hands wrapped around the animal's neck. He bit into a major artery. Warm blood filled his mouth. Before he could spit it out in revulsion, he greedily drank until there was no more forthcoming. Minutes later, he thrust the dead animal to the ground. He jerked a yellowed handkerchief from his pocket. He rubbed the blood from his mouth. Disgusted by his behavior, he stuffed the dirty piece of linen into his pocket. He felt life coursing through his body. The blood warmed him. A sense of satisfaction enveloped his chaotic mind.

He thrust back his head and roared with anger. What had he just done? He was no better than the poor animal he had attacked. Bending over, he spat the remaining taste of blood from his mouth. He felt he must be seriously ill. This was not normal behavior. *Perhaps I have been poisoned.* He needed to find help and go home.

He stared down into the pit that he had climbed out of earlier. Evidence of human presence was scattered about the ground: shovels, hammers, and ladders. It appeared to be some type of dig site. People would be returning. Were they friend or foe? He felt trapped. The urge to flee this place consumed him. He ran blindly through the forest, stopping only when he discovered a large tree with a rotten center. He could hide there if needed.

He spotted a leather strap lying on the ground and used it to tie back his hair. Straightening, he stood with his shoulders back. He would get through this. He had to.

He was young and wealthy and had his entire life before him. Or did he?

7

The next morning, Brett called the local animal shelters. With no results, he checked with the other detectives and realized he'd hit a dead end. There had been no unusual spikes in the reported number of missing animals or the deaths of small animals.

He stared at the to-do list before him. With a black marker, he crossed off the first item. *On to the next.* He picked up the phone and called two shelters near the river. He set up appointments for later that afternoon.

Suddenly he had an idea. With his calendar clear for the rest of the morning, he pushed back from the desk and walked next door to Foster's office. He knocked on the doorframe and paused.

"Get in here, O'Shea." Foster stood, sorting through stacks of paper on the desk. "I'm going to kill Anders. The paperwork that goes with this job is insane."

"I can come back later."

"No, sit down." Foster plopped back into his chair, his lip half-curled upward. "What's up?"

Foster rarely smiled. *What is up with that?* "Well, I checked on missing animals, but nothing turned up. I have a couple of appointments this afternoon at the shelters. Maybe I'll get a lead on the homeless group that left or disappeared."

"Good. So what do you need from me?"

Brett shifted in his seat. "I thought I'd go back to the dig site and look around."

"Sure. Why?" Foster's phone rang, interrupting their discussion. Leaning past Brett, Foster called to the secretary sitting outside his office. "Marge! Can you get my phone?"

Brett smiled as the white-haired woman mimed Foster's order and then slammed a desk drawer before answering the phone. Brett knew that Marge could have retired ten years ago, but with no family nearby, she had made the police department her family. She could be quite a harridan at times. Most of the brass chose to look the other way when she went on a rampage. After all, she had taken many of them under her motherly wings once or twice in their careers. All the sergeants brought the rookies upstairs to meet Marge. Years ago when he was a rookie, she had stopped Brett in the hall.

Pointing to his shirt, she barked, "What the hell happened to your uniform? Did you sleep in it?" She lowered her chin, looking over her glasses with a look of distain.

She reminded him of his deceased grandmother—a spitfire. This was the one day he had forgotten to take the clothes out of the dryer, and he had to run into her. "No, ma'am. I guess I forgot to iron it."

Her wrinkled cheeks puckered as her finger jabbed him in the chest. "Don't you be forgetting again. Next time I'll take you to the chief's office. You rookies are all the same. Now don't disappoint me again, young man." And off she went, leaving him trembling and relieved at the same time.

Foster winced as Marge banged around at her desk. "I'm going to regret asking her to get the phone, aren't I?"

Brett held up his hands. "I'm staying out of it. I've had my share of run-ins with her. You can't win."

Foster grumbled. "I know. I can't even ask her to

make coffee. She threatens to charge me with sexual discrimination."

Brett stood. "I'm not sure I'll be back before you leave. I'll send you a report in the morning."

When Foster's phone rang again, Marge hollered from her desk. "I'm busy. You're going to have to answer your own phone or use that damn voice mail that we're supposed to use."

Foster groaned before picking up the phone.

Brett stopped by Marge's desk, which was immaculate. A fresh bouquet of flowers sat in front of her. He leaned down and took a whiff.

"Got a boyfriend, Marge? I bet you're holding out on me."

Marge flashed one of her uncommon smiles and swatted his arm. "Don't you be trying to get in my good graces. I heard you and Foster in there talking about me."

Brett held a hand to his chest. "Who, me? You know that I'm your favorite cop."

"You think so?" she snapped. Her blue eyes glittered with what appeared to be amusement. She adjusted the purple glasses on her nose and peered up at Brett.

Brett pulled out a flower from the vase on her desk and held the stem between his teeth. Leaning closer, he growled. Her white-powdered cheeks turned a rosy hue. Marge's deep laughter caused several detectives to stop and look at the pair.

"O'Shea, if I were thirty years younger, I'd be knocking on your door."

He placed the flower back in the vase. "You just made my day, Marge. I'm flattered. Don't let Foster work you too hard."

Marge tittered, making him smile. "You don't have to worry about that, O'Shea."

As he passed Foster's office, the captain mouthed, "Kiss ass."

After grabbing his file from his office, Brett hurried down

to the dig site. The site was swarming with young wannabe archeologists. A young man in a white shirt and tie bent over a makeshift desk as Brett approached.

When the man looked up, Brett held out his badge. "Hi there. I'm Detective O'Shea. Is Mr. Allen around?"

The man grunted and returned to looking at the papers on the desk. "Matt Beyer. And no, Mr. Allen just left for lunch. He didn't mention anyone coming today."

Brett smiled. "I was with him yesterday. He gave me a tour of your site. I want to check things out again if you don't mind."

Matt finally looked up. He must have passed the assessment, because Matt nodded. "Sure. Go ahead. But don't disturb anything on the ground or dig anywhere."

Seeing that Matt's attention was diverted back to the paper, Brett turned. Several young women stopped digging and smiled as he walked past them. It made him feel good, especially since Lisa had left.

He smiled back. "Good morning, ladies." Their interest was blatant. Laughter followed his progress through the area.

On reaching the edge of the hole, he pulled out his cell and took several photos of the site.

"Brett? Is that you?"

Slipping the phone into a pocket, he turned. Jamie, from the gym, stood next to him. She removed her sunglasses, wiping the lenses.

"What are you doing here?" she bubbled. "You don't look like you're dressed to help us dig."

He laughed. "Afraid not. I'm here on business."

Looking puzzled, she tilted her head. "Let me guess. You're with the insurance company?"

"Not even close. I'm with the police department."

Her smile faded. "Police? What happened?"

"Mr. Allen called me. He wanted my professional opinion on some things. I wanted to look around on my own."

Absently brushing the dust off her jeans, Jamie rose and stretched. Brett's brow rose. He wondered if she realized how attractive she was.

"Well, I'd better let you get to work. It was nice to see you again."

"Same here. See you at the gym."

He turned, hurried toward the tunnel, and quickly climbed down the ladder. Several groups of people were scattered throughout the area, sifting through mounds of dirt. Careful not to step on anything, he spotted the tunnel. Pulling a flashlight out of the bag, he advanced toward the enclosed cave.

Luckily the chain was unlocked and the door ajar. There was a lantern in the room. Clearly Allen had been here earlier. He dropped the flashlight in the bag before setting it on the floor, and then he walked to the tombs. One lid was slid open.

With hands on the edge, he peered in to look at the body. It was empty! Gone! *There was a body here yesterday. What the hell happened to it? Did Allen move it?* The light flickered several times before the cave went black. Reaching down to find his bag, he cracked his head on the stone tomb.

"Shit! Where's the stupid flashlight?" Holding his head with one hand, he used his free hand to locate the light.

"Finally!" He grabbed the flashlight and shone it about the cave.

He glanced around the room, expecting to see Allen standing nearby. He picked up his bag and turned to leave, having seen what he wanted. He stopped in front of the door, which was now closed. He was sure he'd left it open. The heavy stone slab was closed tight, shutting him into the cave. Fear coiled in his stomach.

He lunged against the door, pressing until his shoulder ached. His chest heaved from deep breaths. He stepped back and wiped the beads of sweat from his forehead.

"What the fuck?"

Brett tried again, using his other shoulder. Unable to move the rock, he pulled out his phone. No coverage. *Great, just what I need.* No one at the office would even miss him today. Vampire or not, he didn't want to spend the night in this cave.

He turned and ran into a large cobweb. He frantically clawed it away from his face. If possible, his heart beat even faster. He glanced at the tombs. *Maybe I should go close the lid.* He didn't want to see any spirits flying about the cave. After dragging the cover into place, he slid down the wall. With his head back against the wall, he groaned. "Why does stuff like this happen?"

A loud voice boomed in his ear. "Because you're a shit magnet, like Anders keeps telling you."

"Argh!" Scrambling away from the voice, he rolled to his feet in a single movement. Familiar laughter ricocheted against the stone walls.

"Damn it, Michael! Why did you lock me in here?"

The brawny ghost leaned against the wall with folded arms. His green eyes glittered with what looked like mischief.

"How the hell did you get shut in a cave anyway?"

Brett wagged his finger at the ghost of his great-grandfather, Michael. "Oh no, I get to ask the questions. After the last case, your spirit was supposed to go to heaven so you could be with grandma."

Michael's laughter faded as he removed his fedora and ran his fingers through his sandy-brown hair. "Don't worry. We talked about things. You're my great-grandson, and I can't abandon you in your time of need. Besides, I didn't lock you in here."

Brett grunted. "Yeah right. You forget that I'm well aware of your jokes. Like sticking drunks on freight trains and sending them to Chicago. Or the night you went target practicing and shot out a window in the squad car."

"Listen here, sonny. I'll say it one more time. I did *not*

lock you in here." Michael yanked out an unlit pipe from this tweed jacket. "Just because I've been dead since 1933 doesn't mean I don't know what's going on."

Brett stalked toward his ghostly great-grandfather. His lips thinned. "Yeah? Then tell me what is going on, 'cause I sure as hell don't know."

Michael glanced around the cave and shrugged. "As an experienced detective, I'd say someone wants you out of the picture. The question is, what are you investigating?"

Brett rolled his eyes, ignoring the question. "You can't just come back and stir things up again. I work for Foster now, not Anders. So I don't need your antics or trouble."

A swirl of dust filled the cave. He closed his eyes and coughed. When he reopened his eyes, Michael was gone.

Fear dissipated as the cave door began to inch open. A whoosh of air filled the cave. When the opening was wide enough to squeeze through, he wiggled his way out. He took a deep breath and fell against the tunnel wall. Michael stood there watching.

"Thanks! I was getting a little claustrophobic in there."

Michael grinned. "I could tell. I accept your apology. Now tell me, what were you doing down in the tunnels? And what about the empty coffins down here?"

Brett walked toward the ladder. "You're not going to believe it, but John Allen called me. He discovered these tunnels are connected to Fort Des Moines. Yesterday one of the tombs had a body in it. Allen believes there is a vampire in Des Moines."

Michael's jaw dropped open. "You don't say! A vampire?"

"Before you get too excited, I've done some research and come up with zero. No increase in missing animals. No uptick in missing people. I'm wondering if Allen is a few bricks short of a load."

Michael tapped his index finger against his chin. "Allen?

That name is familiar. Is he related to the Allens who founded the city?"

Brett nodded. "He's related to Captain James Allen. The Allen family has a lot of political clout. Needless to say, Anders wants this kept out of the papers. The good news is that I haven't been able to find any proof a vampire even exists."

"I hope you're right. After our run-in last year with a demon, I sure don't want to deal with more hocus-pocus. I don't know anything about vampires. Do you?"

Brett paused after climbing the ladder. "Only what I've seen on TV and in movies. Wooden stakes can kill vampires. Garlic may or may not keep them away. Let's just hope that Allen is wrong. I'm not prepared to deal with vampires."

8

Dragos knew the sun had set the minute it did so. His eyes flew open, and he quickly exited the cave. There had been too many people going in and out of it. Although several days had passed, he had spent the nights hunting in the woods. This was his last day to sleep in the cave.

His priority was to assuage his hunger. He knew something was seriously wrong. Some type of illness had taken hold of his body. It made him hunger for blood. Try as he might, he could not overcome that horrific need on his own. He needed to seek out assistance. He thought perhaps there was a physician in the area who could rid him of this disease.

Over the past few nights, he had expanded the area in which he hunted, hoping to find someone to help him. He had come across a camp of people. Curious, he glided from tree to tree, watching the group from the shadows. Being alone, he was hesitant to walk into their camp and announce himself. His sword and gun were missing, so he was cautious, thinking it better to be prudent than lose his life. Besides, based on their appearances and the strange clothing they wore, they seemed to be down on their luck. He doubted that there was anyone in their midst who could heal him.

Up to this point, he had been able to catch several small animals each night—enough to satisfy this unending thirst he was forced to endure. Each night, the search for food became more difficult.

Now, he stood alone, confused and most of all hungry. He hadn't eaten last night. Spasms tore through his body. With no animals nearby, he had to broaden the area he hunted. Nearby lights drew his gaze. They cast a golden glow to the sky. His canines lengthened. He winced from the constant need pushing from within. Blood was all he could think of.

He stumbled over a downed tree, falling to his knees. Head hung low; he dug his fists into the wet, black soil, his harsh breathing breaking the silence of the forest. Clutching his stomach with one arm, he staggered to his feet, absently brushing the shoulder-length hair from his eyes. His body was racked with pain. His humanity was slipping, and yet he had no idea how to break the evil spell that consumed his soul.

Unbidden, he walked toward the lights—toward the people. The fallen leaves littering the ground crunched as he walked through the forest. Hiding in the overgrown brush and scraggly trees the strange world beckoned Dragos.

Odd carriages with wheels traveled down the roads, drawn by an unseen power. *How do they move without horses?* Their speed was unimaginable. Groups of people walked nearby. He shook his head at their manner of dress.

"Good lord! A foul witch!"

He gasped and ducked behind a tree.

Sure enough, a witch walked down the street as happy as you please. Her pointed black hat waved in the evening breeze. She cackled gleefully and tucked her broom between her legs. Rather than flying away, she hopped around, enjoying the laughter of people passing by. It was then that he looked at her face. She was young and quite pretty. Her figure was attractive. She had nice, full breasts and slender hips, yet her scraggly black hair was a sure sign she was a witch. He became convinced that a spell had been placed on him.

No one tried to subdue her. Was no one going to capture her and lock her away? What was this place that allowed witches and strange people to wander the streets?

Before he could ponder what to do about the witch, he spotted a fairy following the witch. The fairy danced down the street, her supple movements enchanting everyone who looked at her. Men either smiled at the beauty or shouted coarse remarks. *For God's sake! The woman needs protection.*

"Hell, would I have five minutes with that beauty," he hissed between his teeth. The blonde seductress wore a green dress that barely reached her knees. And what nice knees she had. Fragile wings came out of her back. Blonde ringlets hung down the middle of her back, bouncing over her derriere. Dragos growled and stepped toward her. He wanted to grab her tiny waist and sink himself into her depths. His cock thickened, imagining the heat wrapped around him.

His eyes narrowed as he shook his head. He was bewitched indeed! It was the witch that he needed to watch. Reluctantly he gave the fairy one last look. If luck were with him, he would find the beauty again.

Careful to keep his lips drawn tightly to hide his protruding canines, he fell into the crowd of laughing, raucous people. A couple of men glanced at him, looking him up and down. They held up their thumbs, and one of them muttered, "Nice costume, dude."

He nodded. "Thank you." *Costume?* Why would they think he wore a costume? He cursed as the witch entered a building. Where was she headed now? He wanted to grab her and take her back to the cave. Witches were known to have special powers. He would make her lift the spell of his cursed affliction.

He stopped at the door, glancing at the sign: "High Life Lounge." *High life indeed.* He boldly entered the tavern. A sea of heads stood just inside the entrance. Wall-to-wall people filled the tavern. Where was the witch? He had to find her. A bearded man weighing at least twenty stone bumped into his shoulder.

Dragos glared at the man. "Watch yourself."

The man stopped and stared at him. With a sneer, the man asked, "Who are you supposed to be?"

Dragos straightened his shoulders. "Pardon. I am Mr. Dragos Eldridge. My father is the Earle of Albermarle."

The stranger burst out laughing. Even his friends joined in. "Well, whoop-de-do. And I'm the president of the United States."

The men surrounding him laughed louder.

He had to find the witch. "Leave me," Dragos brusquely demanded.

Not wanting to waste another minute on the idiot before him, he turned, looking for the witch. He couldn't let her escape. The top of her hat bobbed above the heads at the opposite end of the bar.

Before he moved, a tap on his shoulder drew his attention. His head whipped around, and a beefy fist slammed into his nose. Bright lights flashed in his eyes. The metallic taste of blood filled his mouth. *Damn it!* He bent over as his teeth sharpened. He quickly covered his nose with his hand, trying to hide his canines. Once in control, he drew himself up and towered over his attacker, who shuddered.

"You blackguard. A man with principles does not attack a man when his back is turned." Dragos's lip curled upward, daring the man to attack again.

The man clenched his fists, looking as if he wanted to punch Dragos.

"Fuck you! Blackguard? Who the hell talks like that?" The man's mouth opened and snapped closed. The blood drained from his face as he stepped back. "Your eyes are red. How the hell did you do that?"

Dragos froze. *Red? Curse the witch!* What other maladies

were going to befall him? The bearded man looked increasingly afraid by the moment.

"It is part of my costume." He ran his fingers through his hair, which fell about his face, and straightened his jacket. He would have the witch before the night was done. Then he could return to normal.

"Uh huh. Right. I knew that." A brittle smile on his face, the man drifted away, glancing over his shoulder at Dragos.

Dragos's nose began to swell. At least the bleeding had stopped. With a deep sigh, he renewed his search. The witch remained in the corner of the tavern. He wove through the crowd, ignoring the sexual-laden glances from scantily clothed women. After reaching the bar, he turned and leaned back. Dragos gazed out at the crowd of people. He tried to relax and look like he fit in. The witch stood next to him. How easy it would be to snatch her up and carry her outside. Yet he waited, listening intently to her conversation with the man next to her. The man easily laughed, hinting at his good nature. His green eyes glittered with amusement at the witch. Dragos watched as he reached up and brushed dark brown hair—hair much shorter than his own—from his brow. Was he the witch's lover?

Dragos's brow rose as she wrapped her arm around the man's neck and pressed a kiss to his cheek. He winced, waiting for the man to repel her actions. Instead the man laughed at her antics. Becoming impatient, Dragos stretched his leg, knocking her broom to the floor. A windfall! He would take her broom. She'd be forced her to come with him. He reached down toward the broom. Suddenly she leaned down and slapped his hand.

"Hey! That's my broom."

Her light green eyes glared at him. Her full pink lips were pursed together, seemingly waiting to be kissed. His gaze searched her face. Freckles dotted her cheeks. She looked like a sweet young maid, not a violent witch who had cursed his existence. His pleasant ruminations ceased as he stared at her coarse black hair.

She continued to stare at him, her frown fading.

"Well hello there. I'm Candy."

"I am sure you are." He blushed on realizing he had verbalized his thoughts. "I apologize. I meant to say that Candy is a beautiful name. Very unique."

Her tinkling laughter confused him. How could a witch be so young and beautiful?

The muscular man on the other side of her stared at him. "Actually her name is Candice. She never tells anyone her real name." The witch slammed her fist into the man's arm. "Ouch! Careful. Just because you're my friend doesn't mean I won't arrest you."

Arrest? Is the man a constable or sheriff? The man was obviously very fit. He seemed to carry himself as a man of authority. His green eyes didn't miss a thing. Dragos felt the intensity of the fellow's gaze.

"Then mind your own business, Brett. Besides, you're off duty."

Brett waved at the bartender. "Three Bud Lights." He slid a bottle down the bar to Dragos.

Dragos had never heard of Bud Light. He tipped the bottle, swallowing the cold beverage. A smile lit his face. It was like ale. At least some things hadn't changed.

9

Brett was suspicious of the man next to Candy. He had no reason why. It was just one of those instinct things— something Michael had drilled into him. A good cop knew when to listen to his gut.

The man's costume didn't seem right. The clothes were dirty and tattered. They almost looked real, which could mean the guy was homeless. Why else would any sane man wear clothes or a costume like that?

The man appeared to be in his twenties, younger than him. Although the guy might have been homeless, there was something in his stance that gave Brett pause. The man was confident, especially in wearing shoulder-length hair. His granite features would make anyone think twice about starting trouble with him. With the man's imposing height and whipcord frame, he would be able to take on any guy in the bar—except him, of course.

Even with all these red flags, he could tell that Candy was interested. *How is she not picking up on the warning signs?* Brett had known Candy since high school. They went out on one date and realized they were better friends than lovers. Halloween was her favorite time of year. She always took the opportunity to dress up as some zany character. Even he'd barely recognized her tonight. The black wig and face makeup were deceiving, but her bubbling laughter gave her away.

Nodding at the towering stranger, Brett remarked, "I don't think I've seen you in here before."

"No, this is my first time."

"Do you live in Des Moines, or are you traveling through?"

The man's eyes darkened. *Why?* Brett thought. His brain flipped into detective mode.

"Just traveling through."

Brett frowned. *That was kind of vague.* More red flags waved in his head. According to Candy, he was always suspicious, but this guy was beyond suspect.

"Jeez, Brett. Quit playing detective. The poor guy looks exhausted." Candy rested her hand on the man's arm.

If she thought he was going to let her wander off with this guy, she was crazy. It was so not happening!

Brett finished his beer. "Sorry, I'm not trying to overstep myself, but Candy is my friend."

The man frowned and leaned past Candy. "I would be protective of her also. Excuse my manners; my name is Dragos Eldridge."

Brett held out his hand. "Brett O'Shea. Dragos? I don't think I've heard that name before. Is it Russian?"

Dragos shook his head. "Not Russian. English. My mother is from Romania. My father is the Earl of Albemarle. You must be Irish."

He laughed. "My great-great-great-grandparents came from Ireland back in the 1840s. We're American."

Dragos's body sagged against the bar. He held the bottle of beer in his hands, staring into the swirling contents. "America. That's right. You Americans fought us a couple of times to win your independence."

"Yeah, over two hundred years ago. Are you here for business? I bet you're in IT. Des Moines is a hub for startup companies."

Dragos didn't acknowledge his comment but calmly drank his beer. Candy glanced at Dragos and back to him.

Brushing his black hair out of his eyes, Dragos asked, "Mr. O'Shea, may I ask you a question?"

He nodded. "Sure, but call me O'Shea."

"I sustained an injury recently. I'm afraid that I occasionally forget things. Could you tell me what year it is?"

Brett's gaze jerked to Candy. He barely stifled a groan. He knew that look. Candy looked at Dragos as if he were a lost puppy and she needed to save him. *Crap!*

"Sure. It's 2017. What year do you think it is?"

Dragos's head dropped to his chest, his long hair hiding his face from view. His deep voice rumbled from his chest. "Candy, are you perhaps a real witch?"

Candy shook her head. "No, silly. I'm dressed up for Halloween. You know what Halloween is, right?"

When Dragos turned toward her, frown lines marred his brow as he reached out to touch her hair.

She tittered, "Oh, you think … my black hair. No, this is just a wig—a crappy one at that." She yanked off the wig and dropped it on the bar. Thick auburn hair fell about her shoulders.

Dragos straightened and stared at Candy. He reached out, wrapping a thick strand of her hair around his finger. Slowly lifting it to his face, Dragos ran his finger across his lips. Candy sighed.

What the hell! Brett stiffened. *What is Dragos doing?*

"Dude, I hate to ask, but are you smelling her hair?" Brett took a step toward Dragos, ready to separate the pair if needed.

Dragos's heated gaze locked on Candy. "Just getting my bearings, O'Shea. A beautiful woman is always a sight to behold."

Candy's face turned bright red. "Oh. Thank you. I don't know what to say. You're so different from the other men

I know. No offense, Brett." Candy patted Brett's hand as if trying to comfort him.

Brett swore under his breath. His gut was churning. She was going to take the guy home. He knew that look of hers. Infatuation was written all over her face. They didn't even know if Dragos had a job or where he lived. Nothing. The guy could be a serial killer for all they knew.

10

Brett waved the bartender away and slapped a couple of twenties on the bar. Only a few people were left in the bar. He'd lost track of the number of beers that Candy and Dragos had drunk in the past few hours. It was closing time.

"Hey, Candy. The bar's closing. Why don't I drive you home? You're looped."

She gripped Dragos's arm, falling against his body. Her body seemed to melt against the stranger. Brett cringed. He felt the heat coming off the pair.

In a shrill voice, she waved Brett away. "I'm fine. You go ahead. Dragos can drive my car and make sure I get home. Won't you, baby?"

Dragos's eyes widened. The Englishman stared down at Candy, who staggered; she would have fallen if Dragos hadn't wrapped his arms about her waist.

"Yes, I will ensure that you arrive home safely."

Couldn't the guy take the hint? Brett was ready to carry Candy out of here. Normally she was very reserved around people she didn't know.

Tired and ready to go to bed, Brett snapped, "Okay, guys. We're all going home now. It's late, and they want us to leave." He grabbed Candy's hand and pulled her out of Dragos's arms. She fell against him, nearly knocking him off his feet.

"Sorry," she chortled. "Oh my God. The room is spinning."

When Dragos reached for Candy, Brett muttered, "I got this."

The trio exited the bar and walked toward Brett's car. Candy began singing at the top of her lungs. Brett glanced back at Dragos, who trailed behind them. Dragos's grin faded as Brett glared at him. *Good! About time the guy took the hint.*

"Your friend's singing appears to be slightly off-key," Dragos snickered.

"No shit!" Her off-kilter voice was giving Brett a headache. "If you hadn't encouraged her to keep drinking, she might not be in this condition."

"I apologize. I had no idea of her condition until she fell into my arms at the tavern." Dragos jammed his hands into his pockets.

Brett grunted. *Yeah, right. He had no idea? Probably though he'd get an easy lay.* On reaching his car, he propped Candy against the fender until he could get the door open.

"Here we go. Let me help you get buckled up."

Candy fell into the front seat, laughing so hard that her costume fell off one shoulder. Her legs stuck out the door. Her head leaned against the center console. As Brett lifted her legs to stuff them into the car, Candy jerked and wiggled.

"Stop. You're tickling me."

Brett heard Dragos smother a laugh as he struggled with Candy. After several minutes, Dragos tapped him on the shoulder.

"Please, allow me."

Brett stepped back. "Be my guest."

Dragos ran his hands down onto her legs. Brett took a step toward Dragos, ready to rip his hands off of Candy. Suddenly her movements and laugher immediately stopped.

"M'lady, may I assist you?"

Candy sat up, brushing her riotous curls out of her face. "Why yes, you may." Leaning past Dragos, she stared up at

Brett. "Did you hear that, Brett? He called me *m'lady*. Isn't that cool?"

Brett rolled his eyes. Candy was like a limp noodle in Dragos's hands. Within minutes, she was sitting upright in the front seat. Dragos grinned and turned to him.

"Your friend is quite lively. I like her." Dragos smiled from ear to ear.

Brett leaned down and fastened her seat belt and shut the car door. "Yes, she is. She is a good friend of mine. A really close friend." With a nod, he walked around the car. "Well, it's been interesting. Take care."

He hopped in behind the wheel. As they pulled away from the curb, Dragos remained standing on the sidewalk. *Why is he just standing there?* Candy pressed her face against the window and moaned.

"Hey, don't get sick in my car." Brett glanced at Candy. "Why did you drink so much?"

"Oh come on, Brett. It's been a tough week. I let loose a little. It's no big deal."

Brett grumbled. *No big deal?* She would have gone off with Dragos if he hadn't been there. Then where would she be?

A light mist drifted through the air, leaving droplets of moisture on the windows. The sound of the windshield wipers broke the silence. Just before he turned the corner, a glimpse in the rearview mirror showed Dragos staring after them.

Brett jumped when Candy slapped his shoulder.

"Ouch! What was that for?"

"We can't leave him there. Turn around."

Candy grabbed the steering wheel, nearly sending them into a pole.

"Stop it. Are you trying to get us killed?" Brett pulled her hand off the wheel. "Damn it! What's wrong with you tonight?"

"Brett," Candy whined, "go back. At least ask the guy if he

has any money. What if something bad happens to him? It will be our fault."

He gritted his teeth. "Candy, be reasonable. Dragos is weird. He didn't know what year it was. He's probably a mental case who went off his meds. You don't need that kind of trouble."

"Let me out of this car right this second. I'll go back and get a cab for him, but I'm not leaving him alone in a strange city on a rainy night," she ordered.

"Damn it!" He whipped the car around, heading back to the parking lot. "Maybe he'll be gone."

She flung out her fist, hitting his shoulder again.

"Will you quit hitting me?"

He slowed the car as they approached the empty lot. Dragos was gone. He bit back a smile. "Well, it looks like he's gone. Can I take you home now?"

Candy lowered the car window, peering out to the low-level fog rolling in from the river. "I can hardly see anything. Where is he?" she muttered.

Brett ignored her mumbling about poor Dragos. *The hell with Dragos.* He was tired and wanted to go home to bed. Relieved the guy was gone, he turned the car.

Suddenly Candy screamed. "Stop! Stop! There he is."

Before the car came to a complete stop, Candy opened the car door, nearly falling to the ground. She ran to the riverbank at the edge of the parking lot. Brett slammed the car into park and took off running after her.

By the time Brett caught up with her, she was on the ground, cradling Dragos's head in her hands. Dragos held his stomach. On his knees, his black hair swung free, shielding his face from view. The man's low moans echoed in the still night. The sound gave Brett the heebie-jeebies.

Brett jerked as Candy pulled his hand. "Brett, help me get him up. We need to take him to the ER."

When Brett leaned down to grab Dragos, a deep growl

rumbled from the man's chest. Brett dropped his arm, stepping back.

"Hey, man, we're just trying to help."

Without looking up, Dragos shook his head. "Just leave me be. I will be fine tomorrow."

Brett shrugged. "Are you sure?" He pulled his keys from his pocket.

Candy patted Dragos's back. "No, he's not sure. For God's sake, we're not leaving him here on the ground. C'mon Brett; let's get him to the car."

He slipped the keys back into his pocket. Leaning down, he reached around Dragos's waist, pulling him to his feet. "Sorry, but if I'm going to get home before dawn, we need to get you to the hospital."

His head bowed, Dragos nodded. "I am beholden to you."

Brett bore Dragos's weight on his right side. By the time they reached the car, Brett was breathless. Dragos was as heavy as a ton of bricks. After two tries, Candy opened the car door, and helped get Dragos situated in the backseat. At one point, Brett was sure Candy was going to fall across Dragos' lap.

When they reached the hospital, Brett jumped out and grabbed a wheelchair nearby. He gasped as he caught a glimpse of Dragos's face. His skin was a grayish-white: the color of dirty snow—the color of dead people. He'd seen countless bodies, and he had never gotten used to the sight.

He squeezed Dragos's shoulder. "Hang in there, man. They'll get you fixed up in no time."

Dragos nodded. "I pray so. I can't continue like this."

Brett glanced at Candy, whose eyes welled with tears. At the check-in desk, a nurse took one look at Dragos and motioned for an orderly to take him back to a room. When Candy started to follow him, Brett grabbed her arm.

"Let's wait here. He might not appreciate our hovering over him."

Candy gave him a lopsided grin. "Fine. Not that I agree with you, but you may have a point. I need to go find a bathroom."

The nurse cleared her throat. "I need to get some information on your friend. Let's start with a name and address."

Brett gave the name that he knew. The nurse frowned. "What about insurance?"

"I just met the guy a few hours ago at a bar. You'll have to ask him."

After Brett was dismissed, he turned to see Candy teetering down the hallway toward him. They found a corner with two empty chairs. *Halloween in an ER room. Just where I want to be. Not!*

A guy dressed up as a mummy sat nearby. Blood oozed from his head. *A fight or a fall*, Brett idly thought. A young woman with heavy makeup sat across from Brett. Her red vinyl boots clashed with an orange miniskirt. *A costume or hooker?* He blushed as she caught him checking her out. She gave him a piercing stare and slowly eased her legs apart. That answered that question. He studied her face, trying to figure out how old she was. One half of her head was shaved. Bright blue hair hung down over the eye on the opposite side.

"Hey, honey, what are you doing?" she coyly asked.

He opened his mouth to respond, but Candy glared back at the woman. "Good lord. We're at a hospital."

Blue Hair rose to her feet, tugging on the short skirt. "Hey, bitch! I ain't talking to you."

Brett grinned and watched as Candy's eyes widened. *Oh shit! Girl fight!*

The woman approached standing directly in front of him. Wiggling her butt, she smiled. "Like what you see, honey? How about stepping outside for a few minutes? You look like you like to ride."

He choked back a laugh. "Sorry. I'm waiting for a friend." As if he would consider hooking up with her.

Blue Hair smiled, running her fingers through Brett's hair. He jerked away and grabbed her wrist. "Not interested. Understand?"

Her lip curled downward. "I understand that you can't handle a real woman," she muttered in a snarky voice.

Candy's laughter surprised him. "I suggest you take a hike, sweetie. He isn't interested. If you're really stupid, just keep talking. He can get you a one-way ride to jail if you're not careful."

Blue Hair stared at him as if to ask if that were true. He nodded. She whipped around and stomped back to her seat, turning so she now faced the other people in the waiting room, ignoring Brett and Candy.

A chuckle escaped him. "Thanks."

Candy rolled her eyes. "God, I thought she was going to stick her twat in your face."

He grinned at his friend. "Maybe I should have reconsidered."

"You're so bad." Checking her cell phone, she asked, "Should we go check on Dragos? It's been almost an hour."

Brett stood and stretched. "I'm going to go find you some coffee—get you sobered up. If we haven't heard anything by the time I return, I'll go check."

"Just flash your badge," she snorted before bursting into giggles. "The nurses will tell you cops anything."

"Yeah, right," he grunted. "You've been watching too many CSI reruns. See you in a few."

He sighed to himself and zeroed in on the coffee vending machine. Three o'clock in the morning, and here he was hanging out in the ER for some guy he didn't even know. At least it was the weekend. He could sleep in tomorrow. Dragos was a mystery. His mannerisms, the way he talked, and the way he dressed were all red flags that screamed "Run!" at his subconscious.

He was pretty sure Dragos's clothes weren't part of a costume. Something was wrong. He needed to find out what it was before Candy ended up falling for the guy. He didn't want her to get hurt.

Jostling the hot drink from hand to hand, he walked back to the waiting room. He rubbed his throbbing head. *How do I get into these predicaments?*

Candy jumped up as he approached. He handed her the coffee and then turned toward the nurses' desk. Turning on what charm he had left at this time of night, he leaned on the counter, doing his best to flatter the middle-aged nurse.

"Hi, I wanted to check on the man we brought in here. It's been over an hour, and we haven't heard anything."

The nurse at the desk peered over her glasses. "Name," she growled.

"I'm Brett O—"

"Not your name. The patient's name."

He cleared his throat. "Sorry, it's late and I'm missing my beauty sleep." The woman gave him a deadpan look. "Uh, his name is Dragos. I can't remember his last name. He is dressed in a costume that looks like something from the eighteenth or nineteenth century."

The nurse turned to her computer screen and began typing away. "I hate Halloween."

His hand covered a smile. Nurse Ratched wouldn't have been amused. Minutes later, she looked up. "The doctor has just finished the paperwork. Your friend left about fifteen minutes ago."

Where did he go? The guy doesn't have a car, so did he just walk away without telling us? Now he had a throbbing headache.

Candy tapped his shoulder. "Well, how is he?"

"Hell if I know. He was released fifteen minutes ago."

With a toss of her long auburn curls, she glanced down the hallway toward the ER rooms. "Well, what are we waiting for? Let's go find him."

Before he could disagree or convince her otherwise, his friend slipped through the double doors. He had no choice but to follow. *There had better be a good reason that Dragos disappeared.*

11

Dragos sat on the edge of a bed. Scores of tubes, blinking lights, and strange sounds overwhelmed his senses. The nurse wheeled him into this room with curtains as walls. He heard the moans of the sick and smelled the fresh scent of blood. His teeth lengthened. He lowered his head as his stomach twisted into knots. *Damnation! Where is the physician?*

He fought the urge to seek out the source of blood. If he harmed anyone, he would not be able to forgive himself. His nostrils flared as the scent of blood consumed him. He couldn't stay in this room another minute. The bloodlust was too strong to remain.

Suddenly the curtain jerked apart. In walked a man wearing a long white jacket. He glanced at Dragos and looked at a square object he was holding. Words filled the object.

The man held out his hand. "Hi, I'm Dr. Hirsch. I see you've been enjoying a night out on the town."

Dragos stood, shaking the doctor's hand. "Good evening. I am Dragos Eldridge."

The doctor laughed and patted Dragos's shoulder. "Glad to meet you Dragos. I understand that you've been experiencing stomach pains tonight. Why don't you sit up on the table and let me examine you?"

Dragos let the doctor push him back on the cold table. His muscles tensed as the doctor's fingers pressed into his skin. Occasionally the physician would grunt or mumble something to himself.

"Any vomiting?"

"No," he muttered. "Something is very wrong, Doctor. Can you heal me?"

The doctor straightened and looked at Dragos. "Are there other symptoms you are experiencing?"

A thrill of excitement coursed through him. Finally, they were getting somewhere. Brushing the hair from his eyes, he nodded. "Yes, I have strange urges. I may have been bewitched."

"Really, I can assure you that I've heard everything. Why don't you tell me exactly what is going on with you?"

The pain gripped his body once again. He jerked upward, grabbing his stomach.

"Here, let me give you something for the pain. I'll get X-rays ordered and we'll find out what is going on."

As the doctor turned to leave, Dragos snagged the man's arm. In a thick, hoarse voice, Dragos pleaded, "Blood. I need blood."

The doctor's face turned white. His eyes widened as he stared at Dragos. The doctor pulled from Dragos's grip, looking as if he were going to run from the room. Instead the doctor drew a deep breath before breaking out in hysterical laughter. Tears ran down the doctor's cheeks. He shook his head.

"Okay, you got me. Who put you up to this? Was it Dr. Campbell? No, I bet it was Dr. Davis. She loves Halloween. It has to be her."

Dragos stared at the strange physician. Why was he laughing? Who were Campbell and Davis? His pain intensified. He gripped the edge of the table rather than shake the doctor like he wanted to. He had to convince the doctor of the seriousness of the situation.

"Doctor, I know not what you are accusing me of. I can assure you that my condition is real. One day I was fine, and the next day I was crushed by this need for blood."

Dr. Hirsch grinned, patting Dragos's knee. "I'll bet you are. It's that time of year, you know."

Dragos blinked, gawking at the physician. *How is my condition connected to the season?*

Eyes narrowing, Dragos said, "I do not wish to be this way. Am I cursed? If so, give me medicine to heal me."

His fingers tightened around the edge of the table, diverting his attention from the pulse pounding in the good doctor's neck—a pulse that created temptation and a desire for blood.

The doctor wagged a finger at Dragos. "Oh, you're good. I don't know what she paid you, but it wasn't enough." The doctor appeared to write something on a flat surface and turned to leave. "It was nice to meet you Mr. Eldridge. You take it easy. No more drinking blood tonight."

Then the doctor was gone. Was that it? No medicine. No help for this cursed condition that was destroying his life. He slammed his fist into the padded table, which blunted the sound of his agony.

He had to get out of here. *Should I tell Brett or Candy about my condition? Perhaps they would know what to do.* Somehow he had to figure out how to get back to where they waited. He slipped into the hallway. Dr. Hirsch stood at the end of the hall with several people clustered around him. They were laughing and sneaking glances in his direction. A man even bowed. *Hospitals are worthless. Where is the compassion?* He growled and turned in the opposite direction. He would learn to control this illness. He would survive in any way that he could.

As he stormed down one corridor after another, he came

to the realization that he was going in circles. As he turned another empty corner, a man pushed a cart past him. He nodded as the man smiled. Dragos abruptly stopped and slowly turned. What was that smell? He gazed at the cart as it continued down the hallway. The aroma of blood flooded his senses. He gaped after the cart. It was loaded with bags of blood. Dragos could almost taste it.

He crept after the man, pausing to duck into a doorway to avoid being spotted. After several turns, the man and the cart went through a door. Just before the door completely closed, Dragos slipped into the room. Crouched near the floor, Dragos hid between two metal storage containers. The man stood at another door, waving a badge in front of a red light. He continued to wave the badge as he let loose a volley of curses. Apparently the badge was supposed to make the door open. The grumbling man left his cart and exited the room.

Quickly! This was his chance. Dragos jumped upward and hurried to the cart. The blood was stored in some type of clear substance. It seemed durable enough to prevent the leakage of the liquid. But how would he extract the blood? He picked up a bag, turning it all different ways, looking for an opening. Frustrated, he bit into the bag. Cool liquid flooded his mouth. He groaned as the chilled blood ran down his throat, coating his stomach. Immediately his stomach pain eased. Yet he frowned. Was this to be his future—relying on blood to feel normal?

He tossed the empty bag to the floor and ripped into another bag, draining it in only a few gulps. His gaze returned to the cart. There must have been at least fifty bags of blood sitting in front of him. He knew he must act immediately, as the man would return any minute. The major sticking point was how to get the blood out of the hospital.

Dragos tore into the numerous drawers and cupboards lining the room. Nothing. Shoulders sagging, he stared at the cart loaded with blood. He could not leave here empty-handed.

Suddenly his foot bumped into something. A container filled with crumpled paper sat on the floor. More importantly, a black bag lined the container. Hastily, he dumped the paper on the floor and shoved the bags of blood into the black bag. He tied the top of the black bag together and hurried from the room. Every sound heightened his fear of discovery. He forced himself to walk slowly down the hall. As he turned a corner, a young woman with a badge approached him.

"Are you looking for something?" she asked.

He smiled into her eyes. "Yes, I am looking for my friends in the waiting room."

Her eyes widened as she studied his clothes. Her smile growing, she pointed in the opposite direction. "Take a left and then a right. Look for the signs, and they will take you back to the ER. I like your costume. You look quite dashing."

It was irritating that people seemed to think his clothes were some kind of costume. "Thank you," he reluctantly murmured.

Once the woman was out of sight, he hurried down the hallway. Fear filled him. He'd never stolen anything before. He felt ashamed, but what choice did he have? The physician would not take him seriously, and it appeared he needed blood to survive.

He skidded to a halt as he rounded another corner. Candy jumped up when she spotted him and ran to his side.

"Are you okay? Brett went looking for you."

He slid the lumpy bag behind his back. "I am much better. Shall we leave now?"

Candy pulled out her cell phone and dialed. "Hey, Brett. He's here. Okay, we'll wait here." Candy put the phone in her pocket and glanced up at him. "Well, you do look better than you did when you went back there. Was it a stomach virus?"

He had no idea what a virus was, but it sounded good. "Yes, they told me it was indeed a virus."

Candy took his arm, patting it affectionately. "I'm so glad it wasn't anything worse. In a day or so, you'll be back to normal. Trust me; I've had the bug more times than I can remember."

If Candy is correct, then perhaps I do have this thing called a virus. Maybe I will be better in a few days. Hope took seed. He felt optimistic for the first time in days.

The sound of a door opening drew Dragos's attention. Brett strode through the door and headed toward them. He stiffened when Brett's eyes narrowed, for he knew he was the focus of the intense stare.

Forcing a smile, Dragos nodded. "I have a virus. It will pass soon."

Brett stared at him for several seconds. "Great. I hope you're ready to go home now. It's 5:00 a.m., and I'm beat." Brett's gaze lowered as he nodded. "What's in the bag?"

"Medicine." Dragos met Brett's unflinching gaze.

Shrugging, Brett started walking toward the outside door. "It looks like they gave you enough for an army. I'll go get the car and pick you guys up."

Dragos smiled. "Yes, the doctor ordered me to take the medicine for the next several weeks. I have a very serious virus."

As Brett walked away, Candy grabbed Dragos's forearm. "Are you okay?"

He nodded. If only circumstances were different. He could see himself courting Candy. She was very attractive and had a beautiful spirit.

Dragos's heart thudded as Brett's vehicle pulled up to the entrance. He tried to calm his pounding heart. Although he barely remembered the ride to the hospital, he knew it was faster than any carriage or horse he had ridden. He climbed into the rear seat and glanced at Brett and Candy. They did not appear concerned. Gripping his blood supply, he studied this thing his friends called a car. As Brett turned a key, loud music blasted from inside. Dragos covered his ears, nervously glancing over his shoulder. *Where is that music coming from?*

Brett's gaze met his in a mirror. "What's wrong?"

Dragos felt his bones vibrate from the loud music. He forced a laugh. "Nothing. The sound ... it ... Never mind." He couldn't even think clearly.

As Brett drove away from the hospital, Dragos struggled to keep his wits about him. The lights and buildings were astonishing. In his wildest imagination, he could have never thought this world was possible. There were so many inventions and things that he could not name.

What kind of world had he entered? More importantly, how had he gotten here?

12

Brett pulled up next to Candy's car in the lot near the bar. The horizon was streaked with rays of pinkish light.

"Okay, here we are. Are you able to drive?" Brett studied Candy.

"I'm fine," she muttered.

"Great. Call me tomorrow afternoon. I should be up by then."

With the engine running, Brett turned to the backseat. "Dragos, it was nice meeting you. I'm glad you're feeling better. Now, where are you parked?" Dragos shook his head. He had that deer-in-the-headlights look again. "Dragos, did you drive to the bar or take a taxi? I can drop you off at your hotel." Dragos ducked his head again. *What is it with this guy that he can't answer simple questions?*

In a low voice, Dragos remarked, "You have been most accommodating Mr. O'Shea. I appreciate your assistance tonight. I will return to my lodgings near the river. I will be fine, I assure you."

Brett scratched his chin, looking out toward the river. "I'm sorry, but I missed where you said you were staying. What's the name of the hotel?"

"It is not a hotel," Dragos haltingly replied, "I'm staying outside by the river."

Candy's mouth formed an O as she gasped, startling Brett. "Absolutely not. You just got out of the hospital. You can't sleep outside, for heaven's sake. You can sleep in my extra bedroom."

Both Brett and Dragos responded at the same time with a resounding "No."

Candy jumped out of the car and tore open the back door, motioning for Dragos to get out.

"Guys, it's nearly dawn, and we're all tired. Dragos needs a place to sleep tonight, so he is coming home with me," Candy demanded. "End of story."

Brett stared at Candy. What was she thinking, offering to take in a complete stranger? *Shit!* "No, he's not. He's coming home with me, and that's final," Brett snapped.

Dragos hopped out of the car, holding his bag. With a forlorn look on his face, Dragos stared down at Brett. "I appreciate your kind offer, but I will not impose on your generosity any longer. Good night, and best wishes."

He felt his blood pressure rocket upward. "Dragos, get in my car before I throw your ass in jail. Candy, get your ass in your car now and go home."

Seeing the forlorn look on Dragos's face made him impulsively do something stupid. He was such a sucker for a sob story. *God, I'm as bad as Candy.*

Candy winked and slammed the back car door shut. She blew Brett a kiss. "Thanks, buddy. Talk to you later today."

Dragos slipped into the front seat of the car. Brett sighed. "Seat belt."

Dragos's blank look faded as he fastened his own seat belt. Neither man spoke as Brett drove home. He quickly parked the car and stomped toward the house with Dragos following. Brett switched on a light and headed to his bedroom, where he grabbed some clean sweats and a T-shirt. Dragos stood in the kitchen, looking awestruck. Why? Brett was too tired to even guess.

"Here are some clean clothes. Come on and I'll show you the bedroom. I hate to be antisocial, but I'm dead. If you get up before me, help yourself to the food in the kitchen. We'll talk more when I get up."

Dragos nodded, brushing his hair behind his ear, and followed him to the extra bedroom.

Brett switched on the light. "Here you go. There's a bathroom through the other door, and the remote for the TV is on the nightstand. Do you need anything?"

Dragos cleared his throat, still gazing about the room with a perplexed look on his face. "Thank you. I will be fine. Good night."

Brett flashed a smile and closed the door behind him. Once in his bedroom, he quickly undressed. Tossing his dirty clothes on the floor, he stared at his closed bedroom door. How was he going to get any sleep tonight with a stranger sleeping down the hall? The guy could be packing heat for all he knew. *Damn!* He realized he should have searched Dragos. He engaged the lock on his door.

After showering, he slid between the cool sheets. With his arms folded behind his head, he stretched out. His Glock was within easy reach. He listened intently for sounds coming from the other bedroom. Water was running. Minutes later it was off. *Quick shower? Hell, why am I worrying about if the guy gets clean or not?* He yanked the pillow over his head.

Several hours later, Brett nearly fell off the bed. The sound of a TV in the other bedroom ricocheted throughout the house. Suddenly the house was silent once again. Brett fell back on the bed. His head was pounding, his mouth as dry as a camel's ass. But he was too lazy to get up and get a drink. His eyes drifted closed once again.

A few hours later, sounds from the kitchen woke Brett. *Now what?* Instead of investigating, he turned over and slapped the pillow over his head.

His rumbling stomach woke him. He popped open one

eye to look at the clock. It was nearly two. No wonder he was hungry. Stretching, he tossed the covers off. He grabbed his sweats and made his way to the kitchen. He stopped in the doorway, shock frozen on his face.

All the cupboard doors were open. A carton of milk sat out on the counter. Half-eaten apple cores littered the table. Cracker crumbs created a trail from the cupboard to the table.

He swore before picking up the mess his houseguest had left. He opened the lid on the milk and sniffed. Gagging, he dumped it down the drain. He rinsed the sink and turned. He jerked and instinctively took a step backward. Michael was seated at the kitchen table.

"Damn! How about a warning next time you decide to pop in?"

Michael pushed back his hat with the back of his hand and flashed a crooked smile. "Jeez, Sonny. I thought you understood by now that I come and I go."

Brett growled. "And I thought you quit calling me Sonny."

Michael guffawed, slapping his hand on the table. "You think you're so clever. Not to criticize, but you look like hell. Long night partying?"

Brett shrugged as he slid a frozen sausage biscuit into the microwave. "I wish it were that simple."

"Just spit out what you're trying to say. You're worse than an old woman."

He narrowed his eyes at ghostly great-grandfather. "Candy and I met some guy at the bar last night. He got sick, so we took him to the emergency room."

"That was nice of you. The guy still in the hospital?"

Brett shook his head. "No, he's staying here."

Michael rose to his feet. "What!"

"I didn't have a choice. Candy was going to let him stay at her house."

"What's wrong with him staying at his own place?"

Brett hung his head. "The guy was staying down by the river."

"River, smiver!" Michael slapped his hat on the table. "You need to get him out of here."

Brett swore he heard his grandfather mutter "idiot" before vanishing.

He sat down at the table with his breakfast in front of him. He'd give Michael five minutes. Sure enough, a couple minutes later, Michael popped back into the room.

Pushing his fedora back off his forehead, Michael let out a puff of air. "Who is the guy?"

"Dragos Eldridge. He's from England."

"There's something wrong with your guest. He's as white as a sheet. He's lying there sleeping, not moving. It's like he's barely breathing."

Brett shook away his imaginations. "Did I mention that he was at the ER earlier today? He has some virus."

"Hmmph! There's something weird about the guy."

Leaning across the table toward Michael, Brett grumbled, "Maybe. I can't put my finger on it, but he's kind of odd. Can you help me figure out what's going on with him?"

Michael's brows arched upward. Excitement lit his face. "Of course."

He grabbed his now lukewarm breakfast and started to eat. Unfolding the morning paper, he stared at the front-page headlines. *A murder!* A woman's body had been found north of downtown, near the freeway. He picked up his cell phone and called Jake Foster.

Foster quickly answered. "Foster."

"Sir, it's O'Shea. Hey, I just saw the paper. Do you need me to come in?"

A pause ensued. "I've got one of the new guys here with me, but I could use someone with experience. Come on in."

With the phone pinned to his ear, Brett was already walking down the hall toward his room. "I'll be there in thirty." After hanging up the phone, he quickly dressed. On his way out, he peeked in on his houseguest. Dragos slept like a baby. *The guy must be very sick.* He wanted to wake him and get him to leave, but there wasn't time. With a sigh, he closed the door.

As Brett got into his car, Michael sat in the front seat. "Great. Glad you're still here. I need you to keep an eye on Dragos. I have to go to work. I don't feel comfortable leaving him here, but he still looks sick."

Michael rubbed his hands together, letting loose a mischievous-sounding cackle. "Sure. This is a prime example of why I love hanging around you. A stranger and now a murder—how exciting."

"Go watch Dragos. I'll catch up with you later."

❧

Brett hurried into the station. Entering the multistory building, he took the stairs two at a time. Foster was at his desk, which was covered with crime scene pictures. Brett nodded to the man standing near Foster's desk.

"Tim Randall, meet Brett O'Shea," Foster absently muttered. Foster's eyes focused only on the pictures in front of him.

"Hi, Randall. I was out last week when you started with the bureau. How do you like working with everyone?"

Randall looked to be several years younger than him. His light brown hair was buzzed; it looked like a military cut.

Randall grinned. "So far so good. I've got my first murder to work on. Can't beat that."

Foster glanced up at Randall. "O'Shea will be the lead. You're working for him."

Randall's grin faded. "Yes, sir. That's not—"

Foster jabbed a finger at one specific picture. "O'Shea, look at this. What do you see?"

Brett steeled his emotions. He'd never get used to looking at dead people. Pictures of dead people were just as bad.

The woman's throat was ripped apart. Every stitch of clothing was gone. Garish eye shadow and bloodred painted nails drew his gaze.

Without glancing at Foster, he sifted through the pictures. "Do we know the woman's name?"

"Her name is Ramona Smith—a known prostitute. She usually works the loop area."

Brett traced the fatal throat wound with his finger. "What do you think? A knife?"

Foster picked up the picture, staring at the woman's neck wound. "Don't know. I'm hoping the coroner will have some answers for us. We should be getting the report in a few hours."

Brett laid the picture back on Foster's desk. "Who saw her last?"

"That's your job to figure out. I know it's the weekend, but Anders wanted you on the case. Have a report ready by Monday morning. If anything comes up, just let me know. Randall, do whatever O'Shea tells you."

Brett went into his office and turned on his computer and pulled up Ms. Smith's record. She had an extensive arrest history. Prostitution and robbery were the most recent charges. For being only thirty-eight years of age, she looked older. The deep wrinkles on her face indicated that she smoked. She was one hard-looking woman. Still, he felt sorry for her. Hers hadn't been an easy death.

The neck wound puzzled him. *What could have caused that type of injury?* He finished his notes, jotting down her most recent known address, place of employment, and family members.

Afterward, he and Randall headed down to the parking lot and got into a car.

"Where are we headed?" asked Randall?

"I want to see where they found the body."

"Foster and I were the first detectives on the scene. There are plenty of pictures. If you tell me what you're specifically looking for, I could do it later. It would save you some time."

Brett gripped the wheel and took a breath. He needed to remember that Randall was inexperienced. He'd need some patience.

"That's okay. We'll do it my way."

Randall pulled out his cell phone to check messages. "I'm not trying to be disrespectful, but she was just a prostitute." He jerked forward when Brett slammed on the brakes.

"Knock it off. You need to show some respect." *Son of a bitch.*

Randall rolled his eyes. "Quit sounding so sanctimonious. I've heard rumors about you. There are several of us who can't figure out why Anders and Foster think so highly of you. You do know that my uncle is the mayor of Des Moines, don't you?"

Brett hated kiss-asses. "I don't give a rat's ass who you are. Either you do your job right or I'll make sure it will be your last job."

Once at the murder scene, Brett got out and surveyed the area. Older two-story homes that somehow escaped being demolished when the freeway was built in the early sixties dotted the street. Several buildings had boarded-up windows. Others looked like they should be razed. Brett knew that the area north of downtown had its share of drug dealers, prostitutes, and drunks, as well as immigrant families trying to get established. Ramona had lived on the south side of town and usually worked that area. So what led her here last night?

He ignored Randall, who stood nearby. Turning, he caught

a glimpse of a shade dropping back into place. Someone was watching them.

He walked toward the dilapidated Victorian home. The flagstone sidewalk was cracked and missing several stones. He knocked on the weathered door, noting the name on the mailbox. Tattered lace curtains covered the glass in the door. Footsteps approached the entrance.

The door inched open, revealing a stout older woman. Her gray hair, streaked with shades of black, was pulled back into a ponytail. Baggy blue jeans and a paint-splattered gray T-shirt completed the look. She glared at him with a cigarette clenched between her lips.

"Hello, Ms. Moore? I hope I'm not interrupting you. My name is Detective Brett O'Shea." He held up his ID. "Are you aware that a woman's body was found outside your house last night?"

The door eased open a little further. The woman leaned against the doorframe, puffing away on her cigarette. "Hell yes. I couldn't go back to sleep with all the flashing lights and noise. Why are you here? I was already interviewed by an older detective and some young cop." She grinned. "Actually, the older one was good looking. Like you."

He felt himself blush. "That was Detective Foster, my supervisor. His notes did indicate that he visited briefly with you. I just wanted to stop by and introduce myself, as I'll be working the case."

She ground out the cigarette on the front porch. "Great. I told Foster that I didn't see or hear anything. With all the cars racing up and down the street, a person can't hear anything." She paused and scratched her head. "Now that I think about it, I did hear a couple of gunshots. The woman wasn't shot, was she?"

"I'm afraid I can't say. Do you want to add anything else? I thought that since you live on the corner, you probably keep an eye on activities in the neighborhood."

She nodded vigorously. "Damn right. The damn dealers aren't going to hang out in front of my house and sell their shit. Between them and the whores, this neighborhood has gone downhill. It's gotten to the point where decent folks can't take a walk at night anymore." She held out her hand. "By the way, I'm Charlene."

Brett smiled. "Nice to meet you, Charlene. We need more people like you who take an interest." Handing her a business card, he turned. "If you see anything, please give me a call."

The woman waved. "Thank you, Detective O'Shea."

As he walked back to the car, Randall approached him.

"What was that all about? We talked to her early this morning. She doesn't know anything."

"Good ol' Charlene is a watcher. She was watching us. She may or may not know anything about the case. The point is that I want to get on her good side so she'll feel comfortable about calling us with leads."

As soon as he returned to the car, his phone rang.

"O'Shea here."

"O'Shea, it's John Allen. We haven't spoken in a while. Have you followed up on the leads I gave you?"

"Allen, I'm working a case right now. This isn't a good time."

"Oh, come now. You've had several weeks to check on things."

He frowned. Randall intently watched him. "Just a minute." He slipped out of the car.

"I'll give you two minutes. First of all, there are no leads on missing people from the homeless camp. I also checked with all the animal shelters in town. No one is reporting missing animals. I just can't buy your theory."

"Listen, O'Shea. I've got a missing body"

"A body is missing?" He'd thought Allen had moved the body the last time he was in the cave.

"Yes. Both tombs are empty."

Brett's patience ended. "Why didn't you report this sooner?"

"Detective," Allen snapped, "I've been out of town and just discovered the loss. You need to keep checking and find out what is going on. Do I make myself clear?"

"Perfectly." Brett fumed with anger.

"I saw the morning paper. I know there was a murder last night. Could it be connected to my theory, Detective?"

"Allen, quit grasping at straws. I'll be in touch."

The bastard hung up. It was just as well, because he would have screamed if he'd had to talk to Allen again. Right now his priority was Ramona's murder. He didn't need Allen calling Anders to complain.

He slid behind the wheel as the cell rang again. This time it was Foster. He ordered them to the coroner's office.

13

Brett and Randall met Captain Foster outside the coroner's office.

Foster's squared jaw was clenched. The muscle on the side of his neck throbbed. Brett had seen that look before.

"Did you learn anything?" Foster asked before turning to enter the building.

"Ms. Moore was watching us survey the area where the body was found. I think she knows something. I left her my card. Maybe we'll hear from her."

Randall snorted before glancing down at his feet.

Foster stepped within inches of Randall's face. "What's your problem?"

"Uh, I don't think Ms. Moore knows anything. She's just an ol' busybody."

Foster stepped forward, forcing Randall to step backward. "Are you telling me that you, a new detective only on the job for a short time, know more than my experienced detective— the same detective who cracked the serial killer case last year with Chief Anders?"

Randall had enough sense to blush. "No sir. My mistake."

"Mistake? For a new guy, you're becoming a serious pain in my ass. Do you know what that means?"

Randall shook his head.

Foster's lips tightened. "If you want to find out, keep mouthing off about something you know nothing about."

Brett bit his lips to keep from smiling. *Bam!*

"Let's go. Doc Burns wants to go home and enjoy his weekend—something you gentlemen will not be doing."

Brett's smile faded. Foster knew how to take the joy out of life.

As the door opened, the men could see Ramona's body laid out on the cold steel table in the center of the room, split open. Randall made a gagging sound and rushed from the room.

Dr. Burns smiled at him and Foster. "A newbie?"

Foster grinned. "Gotta break them in. What do you have for us?"

"Well, we have an interesting situation. A majority of the blood was drained from her body. The way the throat was cut open is concerning; it's not a type of wound I've seen before."

"Wouldn't she have bled out on the ground?" Brett asked.

"The blood by the body didn't account for the amount of missing blood. I did take a skin sample around the wound to see if animal saliva could be found. We also dusted the body for fingerprints. Everything came back negative."

"What does that mean?" Foster demanded.

Sighing, the doctor washed his hands in a nearby sink. "We know she died from major blood loss, but we don't know what or who made the injury. Whatever ripped her throat, it was sharp, and the attack was quick."

"Hell," Foster swore. "Send us your formal report. I know Anders is anxious to review it."

Foster shook the coroner's hand and motioned for Brett to follow.

His mind was reeling. *What kind of killer would do this? Did she know her killer?*

"O'Shea, I want you and Randall to visit the known

whorehouses in the county. See what you can find out. Someone had to see her last night."

"Will do. You wouldn't consider reassigning Randall, would you?"

Foster growled. "No. Are you having trouble with him?"

He shook his head. "Nothing I can't handle. He just needs an attitude adjustment."

As he and Foster exited the building, Randall waited in the car. After nodding to Foster, Brett and Randall drove across town to check out the whorehouses. Brett's thoughts kept drifting back to Allen's concern about a vampire being in the area. There was no proof that vampires existed, but in the dark recesses of Brett's mind, the question lingered: *If they don't exist, why am I still worried?*

14

Michael sat in the corner of Brett's spare bedroom, watching Dragos sleep the day away. The guy barely breathed. Michael shifted in the chair. He had been here for hours. Boredom was beginning to set in.

It wasn't long before Michael's eyes closed. His thoughts reluctantly drifted to the past—a simpler time when he thought he had it all: wife, kids, and a job. Back in the depression, he was one of the lucky ones to be working. Then, in the blink of an eye, it was all gone.

Suddenly the man on the bed gasped and jerked upward. Dragos sat on the bed, his feet on the floor, running a hand through the shoulder-length black hair swirling about his face.

Dragos stood and glanced out the window. Michael was surprised to see it was nearly dusk. Dragos walked toward the bedroom door and glanced down the hall to Brett's room.

"Hello. Mr. O'Shea, are you here?" he called.

Shrugging, Dragos walked into the kitchen. The man looked completely bewildered. He opened the fridge several times, each time staring at the food before he closed it. He then opened a cupboard and took out a box of crackers.

Michael wrinkled his nose. *Crackers?* Dragos then walked into the family room and sat on the sofa and stared at the blank TV screen. *Why doesn't the guy pick up the remote and turn it on?* Bored to tears, Michael decided to go check on Brett for a few minutes. Obviously nothing was going on here.

◦❦◦

Dragos was at a loss as to what to do. Brett was gone, and he was left to wander about this home with nothing to occupy himself. It was nothing like what he was used to in England or his travels in Europe. He casually flipped a switch on the wall, jerking as the ceiling light brightened the room. He quickly shut it off, shaking his head in amazement. *I truly did jump forward in time two centuries. There is no other explanation. Hot water comes out of a pipe. Lights ignite at the flick of a switch. But where are the servants? How am I supposed to get clean clothes or meals prepared?*

Dragos glanced down at the baggy, untailored clothes that Brett gave him to wear. He looked at the pile of his own clothes and frowned. Even though Brett's clothes were somewhat distasteful, they were clean. He wisely decided against wearing the clothes he had arrived in. He would ask Brett later who could clean them.

His stomach clenched, reminding him of his illness. He wrapped his arms around his middle, hoping the pain would quickly go away. He wondered when this virus would pass. It was becoming worrisome, this need for blood. In fact, it frightened him. What would he do if his blood supply ran out?

He hurried to his room and pulled out a bag of blood. A quick puncture and the bag was emptied. Power and energy surged through him. He hid the empty bag and shoved the black bag under the bed.

Tearing his hands through his hair, he roared. No, he

would never take blood from a live person. He would not let that happen—ever.

He jumped to his feet, needing something to take his mind off the fearful thoughts. He tore off his clothes and stepped into the warm shower. The palms of his hands slammed against the walls. With his head lowered, a choked sob escaped him. Rivers of warm water flowed over his body. He let the water course down his face. He stood under the water until it began to cool. Sighing, he turned off the water and grabbed a towel. He then reluctantly picked up the clothes that Brett had provided and put them back on. He stood in front of the mirror, surprised at what he saw.

His brown eyes looked dark—almost black. His face was leaner and more chiseled than he recalled. His once dark brown hair was now black with bluish tints. Just a hint of whiskers graced his jaw. His eyes widened as he traced his face with his hand. He looked different and felt different. His hearing was keener. His eyesight had improved. His body felt as if it were coiled, ready to explode with power and speed. Had this virus somehow improved his senses? Would his body return to normal when he got better?

He glanced in the mirror and untangled his thick hair with his fingers. It was thicker and longer than he remembered. Realizing no answers were forthcoming, he returned to the kitchen and began to explore the house, room by room.

After his search, he returned to the large chair by the window and stared outside. Modern-looking homes lined the street. Odd vehicles roared by. What was to become of him? It was 2017. His family was dead and gone. His best friend, Marcus—also dead. He had no money, no connections, and no family. With a fist pressed against his thigh, a single tear ran silently down his cheek.

Michael buzzed back to Brett's. Dragos was in the shower, so he returned to the living room and waited. When Dragos came out of the bathroom, he wandered around the house. Michael closely followed to make sure he didn't steal any of Brett's stuff. Finally, Dragos sat down. Invisible, Michael leaned against the wall and watched Dragos. The guy looked devastated. Michael's feelings of distrust dimmed somewhat. He was filled with an urge to sit down and comfort Dragos. He would talk to Brett later and discuss what they should do about Dragos. Even though he had these sentimental feelings for Dragos, something bugged him about the guy.

15

It was late as Brett and Randall pulled up to the towering three-story Victorian house near Drake University. The house had been kept up enough that it didn't draw attention. With an alley behind the house, customers could come and go with relative anonymity. Known as Eden House, this brothel catered to a rougher clientele based on the frequent police trips to this address. Brett was relieved it was the last stop on their list. He hated going to these whorehouses. He always felt dirty when he left. Brett and Randall had interviewed prostitutes all afternoon and evening. No one had seen Ramona on the day she died. One of the whores did confirm that Ramona occasionally worked the area north of the loop, which might explain the reason she was in that area the night she was killed. They still didn't have much to go on.

Brett got out of the car and started toward the back door. Turning, he noticed that Randall still sat in the car. "Are you coming?" he hollered.

Randall held up his cell. "I've got to make a quick call. I'll be right behind you."

Brett groaned. He wanted to get this last interview over so he could go home. "Fine. Just hurry up."

Brett followed a customer into the house. An attractive brunette woman in her twenties met him at the doorway.

Long tendrils of hair brushed against his hand. Her pink heart-shaped lips parted as she checked him out.

"Hi there. I'm Heather. What would you like tonight?"

She would have looked like any young professional except for the clothes she wore. Her lacy black V-neck shirt showcased her breasts. He tried not to stare, but every movement caused her nipples to pop out. Her short leather skirt barely covered her bottom.

Smiling up at him, she grabbed his hand and led him down a dim hallway. A cloud of smoke from cigarettes hovered in the room, burning his eyes.

Unhooking her hand, he asked, "I'd like to speak to the person in charge." He flashed his badge to emphasize his statement.

Uncertainty flitted across her face. "Oh, you mean you want to know the special rate for cops?"

His attention sharpened. "What do you mean by that?"

Disappointment filled Heather's eyes. "Nothing. I just thought you might be interested."

"Heather, you can leave us now."

A woman approached him. She looked to be in her fifties. Heavy wrinkles lined her face. Her brassy blonde hair hung limply around her puffy face. She took a drag from a cigarette. Her pale blue eyes narrowed.

"I'm Detective O'Shea. Are you in charge?"

"I am. What do you want?"

"I'm investigating a murder. There was a body found east of here early this morning. The woman might have worked here at one time. Her name was Ramona."

The woman ground out her cigarette in an ashtray. "Never heard of her. I mind my own business, if you get my meaning."

Brett walked around the woman and glanced down the hall.

"Hey, where are you going?" she demanded.

Brett looked back over his shoulder. "I didn't get your name."

She stepped in front of him. "It's Darlene."

He smiled. "Darlene. That's a nice name. Now, Darlene, I was just going to take a look around. You wouldn't happen to have a Coke that I could buy, would you?"

A man entered the back door and stopped. Brett smiled at him. The man took a look at Darlene and then Brett before turning and hurrying out the door.

"Oh darn. There goes a customer. I'm sorry. I must be blocking the hall."

Darlene's eyes flashed at him. Brett bit back a laugh and said, "Well darn. He left. Should I go and convince him to come back?"

In a crusty voice, Darlene snapped, "What do you want, Detective?"

His smile faded. "I'm just trying to do my job. I need information about some poor girl who was viciously murdered."

"Okay, I knew Ramona. She worked here a year ago. She was particular in what she would do. Some of the customers can be a little rough. She decided she could do better on her own."

"Do you know how she was doing? Did she have regular customers?"

"How the hell would I know?" Darlene's lips pursed together.

"What about one of your regulars? Did someone get a little too rough? Maybe one of them wanted to hurt her?"

Darlene glanced behind her, appearing to hesitate. Maybe he was hitting a nerve. "Follow me," she ordered.

She led him into an office and shut the door before moving behind a large desk. He remained near the door, loosening his jacket.

"Too many nosy people out there. I can't give you any

names, Detective. I'd be out of business tomorrow if that happened."

He shrugged. "Of course."

"Let's just say I will keep my ears open. Leave me your card, and I will let you know."

"Darlene, I'm not sure that I can trust you to let me know. Maybe I should come by on a regular basis."

Darlene's eyes narrowed. He could barely keep a straight face. She looked as though she had just eaten a lemon. He could play these mind games all night if needed.

"Shit! What are you trying to do to me? I've got bills to pay." She slammed a fist on her desk.

"I need information. Do you want to see other women murdered?"

"Of course not." She took a deep breath before adding, "I might know of one guy who was capable of doing something like that."

"What's his name?"

"I don't know." She jerked open a drawer and pulled out a bottle of whiskey, pouring herself a large shot. "I'd offer you one, but I know you're on duty." Darlene smirked at him. He smiled. "Anyway, he's a new guy who came in last night. Never saw him before. I don't know if he'll even be back."

"What did he look like?"

Darlene shrugged. "Honestly, I didn't pay much attention. Tall. Dark hair." She tapped her chin with her index finger. "Now that I think about it, the collar of his coat was pulled up around his face. It was like he was covered by a shadow. Strange, now that I think of it."

Brett tossed a card on her desk. "If he comes back, you call me immediately. Day or night. Understand?"

Darlene nodded. He opened the door and saw Randall standing in the hallway with Heather draped over him. As soon as Randall saw Brett, he moved away from the woman.

Darlene muttered a curse.

Brett drew up beside Darlene. "Randall, what are you doing?"

"Uh, looking for you."

Brett wanted to smack the smart-ass in the head. "Yeah, you looked real worried."

He made a point to brush against the new detective as he made his way outside. Randall followed and hopped into the car.

Once at the station, Brett pulled up alongside his car and got out.

"I'm going home. Get the car checked in, and be back here tomorrow morning."

Randall nodded. "Sure thing. See you in the morning. What time?"

He didn't even bother looking at Randall. "Eight." The guy was a moron. He didn't even realize his job was on the line.

Once home, Brett tossed the keys on the table. There were no lights on in the house. Maybe his houseguest had left. He could only hope. Grabbing a beer out of the fridge, he headed toward his recliner in the family room. He sat down and took a long drink. His eyes drifted shut as he thought of the events of the past twenty-four hours.

Without warning, a voice echoed in his ear.

"Sonny. We've got problems."

He jumped up, dropping the beer. He quickly flipped on the light. Stiffening, he glanced around the room. Michael was sprawled on the sofa. Amusement lit his face.

"What the hell are you doing?"

"Didn't mean to scare you. I wanted to talk about your guest, Dragos."

Brett whispered, "Is he still here?"

Michael leaned forward. "Of course he is. He's in the guest room now."

"Hmm. I thought he'd be gone. What did he do all day?"

"He slept until dusk. Then he just sat and stared out the window. He didn't even turn the TV on."

Brett rubbed his throbbing brow. He didn't want to think about Dragos. He had a murder investigation to get done.

"What do you want me to do? The guy is sick. I will talk to him in the morning and try to find out what his story is."

"Fine. I'm just saying there is something weird about the guy."

He sighed. "Don't worry. I'll take care of it tomorrow. I'm going to clean up the mess you caused and go to bed. Catch you later."

Michael waved and disappeared. As Brett walked past the guest room, he paused and pressed his ear against the door. *Should I knock and try to talk to the guy? No. Not now. Maybe tomorrow. Besides, what could happen at this time of night?*

16

Brett hurried into roll call and spotted Detective Donnellson.

"What did you do this weekend?" asked Donnellson.

"Worked the prostitute case with Randall." He watched as Randall joked with the other officers as he made his way to the back of the room, where several detectives sat.

Donnellson leaned toward him and whispered, "Lucky you. What do you think of our new guy?"

"He's a prick."

Kevin laughed. "You hit the nail on the head. Did he give you a spiel about being related to the mayor?"

Brett cringed as Randall's laugher rumbled behind him. "Yeah, as if that was going to impress anyone. He seems to have an issue with whores. Do you know why?"

"No, haven't heard anything. I'll keep my ears open and let you know."

Once roll call wrapped up, he went upstairs to meet with Foster. The captain was on the phone, so he sat down on the edge of Marge's desk. The older woman peered over her glasses, giving him a mock glare.

"Don't you have anything better to do?" she snapped.

"C'mon, Marge. I wanted to see if you had a hot date this past weekend."

Her throaty laughter made him smile.

"I waited for you to call. Your loss."

He slapped his thigh. "Darn it. I knew I forgot something."

"Are you waiting for Foster or just bothering me?"

"I need to give him an update." Leaning forward, he glanced at Foster to make sure he was still on the phone. "What do you know about Randall?"

"Hmmph," muttered Marge. "Did Foster pawn him off on you this weekend?"

He glanced over his shoulder and nodded. Too many ears in this place.

Marge shook her head. "Several of the guys have worked with him. So far he's not winning any popularity contests. Why?"

He smiled. "Just doing some homework. Hey, when are you bringing in cinnamon rolls again?"

Marge playfully shoved him off her desk. "Maybe Friday, if I feel like making them. Now leave me alone so I can get some work done."

He stared at her clean desk and laughed. The woman was always caught up on her work. Foster slammed down the phone and rose, motioning for Brett.

Foster's mouth was stretched in a thin line. Stress lined his face.

"I read your report. It doesn't sound like we have much to go on. Do you have anything else to add?"

"As I mentioned, Charlene Moore may be able to assist. I think she knows something."

Foster rubbed his temples. "So how did you and Randall get along?"

"Different. He's a little … I don't know … insensitive."

Foster glared back. "Insensitive?"

"He acts like it's not a big deal that a whore is dead. It was clear he thought I was wasting my time talking to Charlene Moore."

"Seems he's rubbing several of the guys the wrong way."

Foster rubbed his brow. "Just try to teach him something. His transfer request came from the mayor's office. Anders wants us to make it work."

"Great, but if he doesn't show up for work one day, don't blame me."

Foster smiled. "Get out of here, O'Shea. I think you're on the right track."

Brett headed to his office and went through e-mails and voice mail messages. John Allen had called, wanting a progress report. He determined to call him back later. More importantly, he had a phone message from Charlene Moore. She had remembered something and needed to talk to him right away. Maybe this was the lead he was looking for. As he came out of his office, He saw that Randall was visiting with Marge. On second look, he noticed that Randall was actually talking to the secretary, who was ignoring him.

"Randall, let's go." Brett tore down the stairs.

Once they were in the car, Randall immediately took out his cell and began texting. He glanced at Brett before asking, "What's up with the harridan of a secretary? Why does Foster keep the bitch around?"

His fingers tightened about the steering wheel. "Her name is Marge. She's part of the history around here. You'd better be careful what you say about her, or you'll get your ass in a wringer."

"Well, the old hag better stay out of my way."

Randall went back to texting. Brett cast an angry glance at the detective. Randall's nose looked like it had been broken—more than once if his guess was right. In fact, he'd like to break Randall's nose again just for the hell of it. Smiling to himself, he jerked the wheel hard to the right as he turned a corner. Randall dropped his phone on the floor.

"Watch it, O'Shea!"

God, that felt good, Brett thought.

Minutes later they pulled up in front of Charlene's house. Randall groaned.

"Shit, what are we doing here?"

"Listen and learn, Grasshopper."

Randall shoved his phone into a pocket and followed Brett up the sidewalk. "What the hell do you mean 'Grasshopper'?"

Brett chuckled, ignoring Randall's question.

Charlene waited in the open doorway. "Detective O'Shea. Thanks for coming."

He placed a hand on her shoulder. "Let's go inside and you can explain what happened."

Randall followed him into the house. After they were seating in the living room, Charlene's hand shook as she pulled out a cigarette. "Hope you don't mind."

"Not at all. It's your house." Brett gave her a reassuring smile. "Just take your time and relax."

After several long drags of the cigarette, she leaned back on the sofa. "Around 1:00 a.m. last night, I heard a noise. So I got up and looked out my bedroom window. At first I thought it was my imagination. Then I saw him."

Shit! Who did she see? The killer? Brett's pulse quickened, and he pulled out a recorder. "Do you mind if I record this?"

Charlene shook her head.

"I may need you to come to the station for an official interview, but for now I'll use the recorder. Can you tell me what you saw?" He softened his tone to encourage her.

"At first there was nothing there. Suddenly he just flowed out of the shadows. He was tall with long, dark hair. Then—"

Randall interrupted. "Flowed? What does that mean?"

Brett swore under his breath. *Damn it, Randall.*

Charlene shrugged. "One second there was nothing. Then he was there. He stood there for several minutes, looking around where the body was found. He glanced toward my house. He almost saw me. I jumped away from the window. I have to tell you that my knees were knocking together."

Brett leaned forward. "What scared you, Charlene?"

She cast a nervous glance to the door and windows, which were shuttered.

"When he turned to my house, I saw his face. I'll never forget his eyes."

"His eyes? How could you see his eyes? It was dark," Brett stated.

Charlene ran her hands up her arms as if she felt a chill. "I could feel his eyes on me. His red eyes." She snuffed out the cigarette and lit another.

"Red eyes? What do you mean?"

"Red," she shrieked. "Like, fire-red eyes."

Brett took a deep breath. Charlene looked as if she were ready to collapse. "Could it have been red sunglasses?"

Charlene rolled her eyes. "Really. I know what I saw, and I'll never forget."

What could he say to that? Nothing.

"Can you think of anything else?"

When Charlene shook her head, he clicked off the recorder. The three of them sat in silence for several minutes. Brett cleared his throat. "I've got to be honest, Charlene. I don't know anyone who has red eyes."

"Me neither," she gruffly muttered.

He rose to his feet to leave but turned back to Charlene. "Do you need a place to stay for a few days?"

"Nah, I've got a friend who will come over. Besides, I've got a .45 I keep by my bed."

He patted her shoulder. "Promise you will call me right away if you see him again. I may need to bring you down for a formal interview. I'll let you know."

Charlene stood and shook Brett's hand. "No problem. Thanks for listening. I was afraid you'd think I was crazy."

Brett grinned. "Trust me. I've seen and heard all kinds of crazy shit. I just want to make sure you're okay."

Surprising him, she jerked forward and hugged him.

"Thanks, Detective. Don't worry. I'll be fine."

Brett glanced at Charlene standing on the porch as he drove away. Again his thoughts returned to Allen's warning about a vampire. Was he letting his imagination run wild or what? Had he watched too many Dracula movies?

"What do you make of that?" Randall chuckled.

He couldn't talk to Randall about vampires. He shrugged. "Who knows? She believes it."

"In my opinion, that interview was worthless. So where to now?"

Let it go, he thought to himself. "We're going to visit Darlene again."

Randall straightened. His look of amusement faded. "What for?"

"I don't have to justify myself to you. It can't hurt to go check things out again."

Randall turned and stared out the window of the car.

Good. He'd pissed off Randall. He had bigger problems to think about.

He pulled up to Darlene's house and got out. He noticed that Randall remained in the car. "Randall, let's go," he yelled.

Randall slowly got out of the car. "I'm coming. Go ahead, and I'll be right in."

Brett's pissed-off look failed to get a response from Randall. It was just one more strike against the guy in his book.

Once inside the house, he knocked on the door to Darlene's office.

The hard-looking woman opened the door.

"Well, if it isn't Detective O'Shea."

"Thought I'd stop by and say hello."

Darlene threw back her head and laughed. She shoved aside the papers scattered across her desk. "You've got balls, O'Shea. I'll give you that." A cloud of cigarette smoke filled the room. The ashtray was piled high with butts. "Sit yourself down."

He made a fist and covered his mouth as he coughed. His eyes burned. He could barely breathe.

"Are you okay?"

He waved his hand, hoping to clear a hole in fog. "Fine," he croaked.

With a smirk on her face, she got up and inched open a nearby window. "There." Darlene glanced at a clock on the wall. "Sorry, Detective, but I've only got a few minutes. I saw something weird last night." She picked up an unlit cigarette but paused before putting it in her mouth.

Brett took a deep breath, relieved that she didn't light it.

Darlene pointed to the open window. "As I was saying, I looked out the window early this morning. There was a tall guy hanging around the alley. I sent Bobby, my security guy, out to see what he was doing. I didn't want him vandalizing clients' cars. About ten minutes later, Bobby came running back in the house. His face was whiter than a sheet."

He tensed and pulled out his recorder. "What happened?"

She cast him a pained look. "Why don't I get Bobby in here."

Darlene picked up the phone. "Bobby, I need to speak to you."

Minutes later, a knock on the door preceded Bobby's entrance.

Bobby's bulky figure filled the doorway. He had deep-set eyes and a bald head. The towering man gruffly asked, "What did you want, Dar?"

Darlene nodded at Brett. "Tell the detective what happened with the guy out back this morning."

The pair exchanged an odd look before Bobby nodded in agreement. He licked his lips before speaking. "I tapped the guy on the shoulder. When the guy turned around, he just stared at me. Didn't say a word. Didn't move. Nothing."

Brett studied Darlene and Bobby. Bobby looked anxious if the tightness to his face was any indication.

"Do you have a description of the guy?"

Bobby grunted. "Taller than me by several inches, so at least six foot four. And he had long, dark hair. It looked black."

Brett tugged at his ear as he felt a chill enter the room. He glanced about, expecting to see Michael. Bobby stared at him, waiting.

"Do you know what the guy was doing?"

Darlene lit up another cigarette. "No. He was watching my house. It was just creepy."

As if on cue, Michael sat on the edge of Darlene's desk.

A loud crash from down the hall drew everyone's attention.

Darlene rose. "I need to check on the staff. C'mon Bobby. You're welcome to join us, Detective."

Brett rose and trailed after the woman. He jammed an elbow into Michael's stomach as he passed. "What are you doing now?"

Michael adjusted his hat. "Calm down. I wanted to see if you needed my help."

"Stay out of sight. I don't need any distractions," he tossed over his shoulder. He glanced down the hall looking for Randall. *Where did he go?*

When Brett entered the kitchen, several young women were clustered about a large table, enjoying lunch. The smell of coffee filled the air. One woman flashed a suspicious gaze at him. A brunette let her robe fall open, attempting to spike his interest. He winked at her.

"Damn it, Keri. He ain't here for a social visit." Darlene pointed to a pile of pots littering the floor. "Cover the girls up and clean up the pots you knocked over. Where's Suzi?"

Keri shrugged and chomped on the wad of gum that filled her mouth.

Darlene rolled her eyes. "Can't hire good help anymore."

Brett smiled and bit back his laughter.

"Sorry to rush off Detective, but I need to call in more girls for tonight."

"No problem." Brett glanced at Bobby. "Can you continue with what you saw?"

"Well, I usually walk the back parking lot to make sure no one gets rolled on our property. Darlene wanted to me to go check out the lot. By then it's usually pretty dead around here. I went out for about ten minutes and didn't see anyone." Bobby's voice faded. He looked shaken. "Then I turned and saw someone step from the shadows. The man came toward me. He was dressed in black." Fear filled Bobby's eyes. "The way the guy moved wasn't natural. In a blink, he moved at least twenty feet."

Brett's gaze narrowed on Bobby. "What did he look like?"

"He had long, dark hair that blew around his face." Bobby paused, swallowing hard. In a whisper, he added, "I don't know why, but I didn't want to see his face."

Brett pressed closer. "Why? Did he threaten you?"

Bobby shook his head. "The closer he got, the harder my head pounded. It was like a vibration. I'm man enough to admit that I was scared. When I went to get my gun, he left."

The kitchen had cleared by the time Bobby finished speaking. Brett gratefully took the cup of coffee that Bobby offered. Holding the steaming brew, he mentally rehashed what Bobby had said. *Tall man with dark hair. Dragos fits that description.* Had he made a fateful mistake taking in the man?

A woman's scream erupted from down the hall.

Brett jumped up, hurrying after Bobby. Bobby flung open a door to reveal Randall struggling with one of the girls who worked in the house.

"What the hell is going on?" Brett roared.

Randall's hands dropped to his side. Straightening his jacket, the detective wiped his face with the back of his hand. A deep scratch marred his face. Beads of blood were welling on his skin. Red hand-shaped marks stained the woman's cheeks.

Randall raised his arm, pointing to the woman. "The bitch attacked me. I was defending myself."

"Liar!" she screamed as she lunged forward. Bobby grabbed the woman and hauled her to his chest.

Darlene joined the fray and swiped her hand in the air. "Enough! Bobby, take her upstairs. Randall, I want you out of here. Don't come back."

Randall's lip curled. "You don't have to worry about that. You couldn't pay me to come back here." Randall glared at Darlene as he stormed from the room.

Brett stared after the detective and turned to Darlene. "What am I missing?"

Darlene took a deep breath. "He's a regular customer. Unfortunately, he likes to play rough. Several months ago, he broke the arm of one of the girls. I told him that if things got out of hand again, he wouldn't be coming back."

"I don't suppose anyone pressed charges?" Brett asked, bristling with anger.

With a slight smile, Darlene shook her head. "C'mon, Detective. You know how the game is played. He's a detective and could make my life difficult. I had to give him a chance to play nice."

"Is your girl okay?"

"She'll be fine. But I don't want any more trouble from him."

His jaw tightened. "Oh, you don't have to worry about that. I'll take care of Detective Randall." Shaking her hand, he thanked her for the tip.

His job was complicated enough without Randall adding more problems. Foster would be furious with the detective. Randall was a sadistic son of a bitch—one Brett wasn't going to work with.

17

Silence filled the car as Brett and Randall drove back to the station. Brett was furious. A quick glance at Randall confirmed that he was pissed as well. Heat flared from Randall's gaze. Brett hated this kind of tension. There was a murder to investigate.

As soon as they pulled in the city lot, Randall jumped out, slammed the car door, and walked away. Brett stared at Randall's back, wishing things had turned out better with his partner. With a sigh, he headed to his office. With Randall's uncle being the mayor, shit was going to hit the fan.

Marge glanced up as he paused near her desk. "What did you do?"

Brett placed his hand over his heart. "Marge, you wound me. Why would you say that?"

With a glint in her eye, the secretary smiled. "O'Shea, I know you. You've got that look on your face."

Reluctantly, he chuckled. "Thanks, Marge. I needed a laugh. Is Foster in?"

After a quick glance at the phone, she nodded toward Foster's office. "Go in. He just got off the phone."

Brett closed the door behind him. Foster glanced up and frowned.

"Now what, O'Shea?"

"It's Randall. We stopped at Darlene's place earlier. She might have a lead on the murder case."

"Great. I need some good news today. Get your report to Anders." Foster glanced down at his desk, dismissing him.

Brett cleared his throat. "While at Darlene's, Randall roughed up one of the girls."

Foster's jaw clenched tightly. "What! Where is he?"

Brett looked toward the closed door. "Sir, I assume he's in his office."

Foster stormed to the door and threw it open. "Marge, call Detective Randall and tell him to get his ass in my office now."

Foster turned back to O'Shea. "File a report on what you saw with Randall."

"Yes, sir," Brett quickly responded.

Raking his hand through his hair, Foster took a deep breath. "Now, what did you get on the prostitute's murder case?"

Brett pushed Randall from his thoughts and explained what Darlene and Bobby had seen.

Foster nodded. "Send a sketch artist over to Darlene's."

"I'll get right on it," Brett said, happy to get out of here before Foster exploded.

Foster glanced at his phone as it rang. "Once we get that sketch, get it circulated. Maybe we'll get lucky and someone will recognize the guy."

Brett hurried out of Foster's office. The elevator doors opened, and Randall stepped out and gave him a seething glare. *What the hell?* It wasn't his fault that Randall screwed up.

Brett jumped when Randall jammed his shoulder into his own. He stopped and stared at Randall's shuttered gaze.

"Watch it, O'Shea."

Brett cocked his head to the side. "I think you should heed your own advice." He turned and walked down the hall before he said something he'd regret.

Once in his office, he e-mailed the guy who did the drawings for the department and then wrote up his reports for the day. He had never been so glad to see 5:00 p.m. His head throbbed.

Thinking about his houseguest, he called Candy. Until they knew more about Dragos, she needed to stay away from him. When her voice mail answered, he hung up.

A workout would alleviate his stress. It would also give him a chance to see Jamie again. He had texted Lisa a couple of times but didn't get a response. He kept telling himself to let it go and forget her. He had to start dating sometime.

The gym was packed. Jamie was at the front desk. Donnellson towered over her. *Damn!* His friend was close enough to kiss her.

The pair jerked apart as he approached the desk. Donnellson smiled at him.

"O'Shea. Someone kill your dog? You look like shit."

"Very funny. Looks like you're done working out already."

Donnellson slung his bag over his shoulder. "Yeah, I was off-duty tonight, so I came in here early."

Brett winked at Jamie. "Well, I'll keep Jamie company while you're gone."

Donnellson smiled back at him. "You do that."

Jamie's throaty laughter drew their attention. "C'mon, guys. Quit teasing."

Donnellson waved and left the gym.

Brett turned back to Jamie. "So are you still working for Allen at the dig site?"

She nodded. "Just for a few more days. The ground is starting to freeze. They'll be shutting everything down soon."

"Do you enjoy working for him? He seems pretty intense."

Jamie's smile faded. "There were some odd things going on at the site. There was a tunnel blocked off. Whenever someone asks about it, Mr. Allen threatens to fire them. The tunnel is off limits."

"Hmm. I wonder what is so special about the tunnel?"

Jamie leaned closer to him. "I don't know, but a couple of employees told me that there was a lot of weird stuff going on at night."

He thought back to the time he got locked in the cave. What else was going on down at the site?

Several people entered the gym and walked toward them. "Hey, Jamie, I'll catch you later."

He definitely wanted to find out more about the tunnel. She knew something.

By the time Brett finished his set, Jamie was gone. Disappointed, he drove home. He immediately headed to the kitchen and grabbed a beer. A yellow piece of paper on the table caught his attention.

> Brett, I stopped by to see how Dragos was doing. He hadn't been out of your house in two days, so I took him out. I'll bring him back later tonight. Don't worry.
>
> —Candy
>
> PS: I've got my gun. ☺

He crumpled up the note, tossing it in the garbage. Rubbing a hand across his face, he groaned out loud. *Shit!* Now Candy was alone with Dragos. He didn't even know where they were. He yanked out his cell and dialed Candy's number. Voice mail picked up. *Again!*

"Candy. It's Brett. Call me as soon as you get this message so I know you're okay. Damn it! You know better than this."

He finished off the beer and grabbed another. He went to the family room and stared out the front window. From here he could watch the street and know the minute Candy pulled in. With a cell phone next to him, he sat in the dark and waited.

18

Candy pulled into Brett's driveway. She knew Brett was still at work, but she had worried about Dragos all day. She had called several times with no success. Dragos had been so sick the night they took him to the hospital that she wanted to see how he was doing.

Candy knocked on the door. It eased open. Dragos peered out at her. A bright smile lit his face.

"Candy! How are you? Please come in." Dragos stepped aside so she could enter.

She was struck again by his arresting looks. His alluring gaze caressed her as she moved past him.

"Thanks. I'm not intruding, am I? I wanted to see how you're doing. I hope you're feeling better." A flush heated her cheeks. She was rambling. His intense stare sent pulses of electricity through her body. God, he was so hot!

She bit her lower lip, tossing her purse on the kitchen table. He continued to stare at her without saying a word. Her pulse quickened.

"So what have you and Brett been up to over the past couple of days?"

"I believe Brett has been working. I haven't seen him since the night we met. The good news is I am much better."

"You look great." Her face infused with heat. She shook

her head, feeling like a sixteen-year-old girl meeting a boy for the first time. "You haven't left the house?"

He shook his head, causing his thick hair to swirl about his face. "No, I haven't."

She blew out a puff of air. "Well, we need to remedy that. How about I give you a tour of our city and take you out for dinner?"

A look of bemusement crossed his face. "I have not had a woman make me such an enticing offer before. I am honored to accept."

Candy glanced at the floor to hide the thrill of excitement that coursed through her. He had such an odd way of speaking. It was quaint, but she liked it. When she looked up, she gasped.

Dragos stood only inches away. If possible, the look in his eyes had intensified. An unnamed emotion held her in place. Was it fear or something else? She nervously twisted the edge of the beige cashmere sweater that clung to her curves. She pushed her auburn curls over her shoulders.

He closed the distance between them. His stare never wavered. There was something in his heated look that burned to her core. Moisture collected between her legs. Her breasts ached. No one had ever looked at her like that before. She tilted her head back to watch myriad emotions flash across his face. Thick midnight hair draped forward as he bowed his head toward her.

His hair caressed her face as he leaned in for a kiss. The chiseled planes of his face created a map of shadows and light, while the darkness of his gaze was fathomless. Her lips parted ever so slightly. She inhaled when he grabbed a fistful of her hair, pulling her toward his mouth. His hot breath traced a path up her neck toward her lips. She couldn't breathe. Never had she felt her heart pound this hard. Without warning, her knees buckled. His arm whipped out and grabbed her waist. With one arm, he pulled her up against his iron-hard body.

At the moment of contact, she felt his body tremble. So he wasn't immune to this growing attraction between the two of them. They were barely touching one another, and she was ready to strip off his clothes and bang the hell out of him.

"You drive me crazy, woman," he hoarsely muttered. He reached down and drew her legs apart. His hand inched upward, reaching her heat.

She threw her arms around his neck and clung to his lips. Their moans filled the room. Continuing to hold her with one arm, he struggled to loosen her trousers.

"Wait." She struggled to pull their lips apart. Her brain wasn't cooperating. She could barely utter a coherent sentence. Brett could come home at any minute. He'd be furious to find the two of them together like this. Dragos was hot, gorgeous, and oh, so tempting, but did she want to have sex with him? She glanced at his face. Though his eyes were heavily lidded, he watched her. She struggled to catch her breath.

"Why?" His lips continued to nuzzle her neck.

He ran his tongue down the side of her neck. His teeth nipped at her skin.

She gently pushed his chest, creating some distance between the two of them. "Quit doing that. I can't think"

He raised his head, meeting her gaze. The corner of his mouth turned upward. "If you insist." With a slight bow, he turned away.

She grabbed her purse and scribbled a note for Brett before she changed her mind. She picked up the car keys and turned toward the door. "As much as I want to stay and finish what we started, let's slow it down. If you're ready, let's go eat. Then I'll give you the tour that I promised."

Dragos flashed a crooked smile and smoothed back his hair. He looked as rattled as she felt. "Lead the way, my auburn goddess. My life is in your hands."

She grinned back at him. *"Auburn goddess?"* She liked

that. Suddenly realizing she was gaping at him, she turned and walked outside. "Well, let's go then."

As she pulled out in the street with Dragos sitting next to her, she mentally kicked herself. Maybe driving off with a strange man wasn't a wise move. Her impulsiveness had won again. She hoped it wouldn't bite her in the ass.

19

Brett woke with a start. Headlights lit up the room. Jumping up from the recliner, he peered outside. Candy's car was in the driveway.

"About time," he muttered. A glance at his phone indicated it was nearly midnight. He marched into the kitchen and leaned against the counter with his arms folded against his chest. His foot tapped impatiently on the tile floor as he waited for the door to open.

He heard the lock click as Candy used her key. The door opened, with Candy leading the way. Dragos's arm was draped over her shoulder. The pair giggled, which caused him even more irritation.

As Candy flicked on the kitchen light, she screamed. "Damn it, Brett! You could have said something when we came through the door."

He glared over Candy's head at Dragos. "This is my house. It could have been someone breaking in."

Candy swore. "Yeah, and there could be gold at the end of the rainbow. Don't be an asshole."

He shoved off the counter and sauntered over to the pair. Dragos stepped in front of Candy.

"Is there a problem, Brett? Candy left you a note that indicated where we went."

Well, one point for Dragos. He was defending Candy.

"Actually, there *is* a problem. It's midnight, and my friend was out with you. With you being a stranger, I was worried about her."

Dragos stiffened. "I understand your worry, but it is unjustified. I will protect her at all costs."

Brett ran both hands through his hair. He turned and yanked open the fridge. "Anyone want a beer?"

Dragos and Candy flashed a look to each other.

Brett rolled his eyes. She was obviously falling for the guy.

Dragos shook his head. "Not for me. Candy took me out for Italian food and wine."

Candy stood on her toes and pressed a kiss on Dragos's mouth. "I'm going home. Too much testosterone in this place. Talk to you tomorrow, Dragos. Bye, Brett."

Once she left, Dragos sat at the kitchen table and watched Brett.

"So what's going with you and Candy?" Brett asked.

Dragos smiled and shook his head. "We just had dinner together."

"Sure looks like more than that."

"Gentlemen do not gossip about conquests or affairs of the heart."

"Where do you come up with language like that?" he grumbled.

Dragos's smile faded. "It is something I picked up over my travels."

He took a sip of his beer and cradled the bottle in the palms of his hands. "So I'm not trying to be nosy, but what are your plans? It looks like you're back to normal."

Dragos lowered his head. His eyes closed. "I do not know. One minute I had a normal life, with a home, family, and money. Then, in an instant, it was gone. I have taken advantage of your generosity, and for that I apologize."

Pushing away from the table, Dragos stood. "I will be gone tonight."

"Sit down." Brett cringed. "You're not leaving in the middle of the night. Besides, where would you go without any money or anything?"

Dragos's fists tightened until they turned white. "I pledge to find the man who did this to me and kill him."

"Slow down. You can't kill anyone. You do know that I'm a cop and would have to arrest you if I thought you were really going to kill someone, don't you?"

He studied Dragos. Brett knew he should kick Dragos out, but something held him back. Did he feel sorry for the guy? Maybe. One minute Dragos seemed to be down and out, and the next he was filled with arrogance.

Brett's gaze shot up as Dragos snapped, "I do not want your pity or charity, O'Shea. I will leave immediately."

"Calm down. No one is asking you to leave. I will help you find the guy you're looking for. Then we can arrest him—do it legally. Got it?"

Dragos held out his hand. "I truly appreciate your help in this matter. I am beholden to you."

"You don't owe me a thing. Just don't hurt Candy." He patted Dragos on the shoulder. "Get me a description of the guy you're looking for and any other information that will help us find him."

His phone vibrated. It was Foster. He answered. "O'Shea … I'll meet you there … Got it."

Grabbing his coat and gun, Brett met Dragos's gaze. "Foster wants to see me. I'm not sure when I'll be back." Brett clapped Dragos's shoulder. "Don't worry; I want you to stay and make yourself at home."

20

Brett jumped out of the car and slipped under the yellow tape that surrounded the scene. A sheet covered the body lying on the ground. As he looked at the address of a nearby house, he realized that the previous murder had occurred less than a block away. *Coincidence?*

He approached Foster, who grimaced as he surveyed the area. They had a second body. "Foster, what do we have?"

Foster glanced up. "I'm not sure. Check the body and see if it's anyone you're familiar with."

Brett walked over to the body and slowly lifted the sheet. Dread coursed through him. He'd never get used to viewing bodies. He studied the woman's face. Open yet unseeing eyes stared up at him. Her face was distorted in the throes of agony. A large wound on the side of her neck drew his attention. He leaned down to take a closer look. An unbidden chill ran up his spine. Bite marks and torn skin on the neck obviously contributed to the cause of death. He choked back stomach acid in his throat as he dropped the cover over her face.

"Well, anyone you know?" Foster queried.

He forced out a breath. Foster tilted his head to study him.

"Yeah. It's the woman that Randall harassed at Darlene's."

Foster rubbed his brow. "Anders suspended him for three days. We'd better bring him in for questioning."

"Crap. That will go over like a lead balloon in the mayor's office," Brett absently remarked.

"We can't show favoritism just because he's a cop."

Brett nodded.

"Did you notice the injury to her neck? It's similar to Ramona Smith."

Brett stared at the covered body. He blinked hard, forcing himself to think of something other than the cold body on the ground.

"Yeah, I did. I wanted to hear what you thought."

Foster paused and glanced at a vehicle pulling up to the scene. "I see the coroner has arrived. Hopefully we will have specific details on the cause of death soon. You might as well go home and get a few hours of sleep. It's going to be a long day."

Brett waved and turned toward his car. He then jerked to a stop as Michael appeared before him. "What are you doing here?"

"I was bored. Your houseguest and Candy are busy talking on the phone. It's like watching paint dry. I sensed you were upset, so I came to see what was going on."

He tightened his fists as Michael peered down at the body.

Minutes later, Michael returned to his side. "Did you see her neck?"

"Yes, I'm not blind,"

"Don't you think it's a little odd that we have two prostitutes with their necks ripped apart?" Michael prompted.

He glanced up and spotted Foster watching him with an odd look on his face. *Shit!* He spun around so his back was facing the crime scene. At least now the other detectives wouldn't see him.

"Yeah, I do."

"I think Des Moines has another problem."

"I'm one step ahead of you," Brett groaned. "I plan on talking to Foster in the morning. Call me crazy, but I keep going back to Allen's concern that there is a vampire."

"Hmm," Michael muttered as he rubbed his chin. "I read Bram Stoker's *Dracula* years ago, but I'm not sure what they look like. I wonder if it would be worth our time to watch *The Vampire Diaries*?"

He was ready to slap Michael when he noticed the grin on the ghost's face. "Be serious, would you."

Michael's grin faded. "I'm not a believer in coincidences. Have you considered that the murders didn't begin until your houseguest, Dragos, showed up?"

Brett opened his mouth to argue but quickly clamped it shut. His eyes narrowed in speculation. "No, I haven't, but Dragos isn't a vampire."

Michael's brow arched. "And we know that he isn't a vampire because ...?"

"Shit!" He suddenly remembered Darlene's description of the strange man outside her house: "tall with long, dark hair." Dragos fit that description, but he didn't have red eyes. Now that the seed of doubt was planted, he rushed to his car, where he grabbed his cell phone as he inserted the key.

After four rings, Candy's husky voice answered. "Hello."

"Candy, are you okay?"

"Brett? What the hell are you doing calling me this time of night?"

His heart slowed to a normal pace. "Did Dragos do anything strange or odd when he was with you?"

She yawned. "No. What's this all about?"

He drove the empty streets toward home. "I want you to stay away from Dragos. Will you do that?"

"Damn it. You'd better tell me what's going on."

"Candy, just trust me on this one," he pleaded.

"I'm working a case myself, so we weren't planning on

seeing each other for a couple of days. You have two days to tell me what's going on with Dragos."

"Fine! I'll get back to you." He ended the call and tossed the phone on the seat beside him. Was he housing a vampire, or was his imagination in overdrive? Had he been completely blind this whole time?

He parked down the street from his house and watched. He eased the car door closed. He ran through the neighbors' yards, staying away from the streetlights. He didn't want Dragos to see him coming. Damp, moist grass cushioned his footsteps. Low-lying fog rolled through air. Droplets of moisture coated his heated face.

He slipped the key into the lock, quietly easing into his home while drawing his Glock .45. The house appeared dark except for a lone light underneath the door to the guest room. Murmuring voices resounded from the television. Dragos must have figured out how to operate the remote. He was probably on the bed, watching TV.

Brett inched down the hall, his back pressed tight against the wall. Shadows shimmered in the air from the glow of streetlights filtering through the windows. An eerie quiet filled the house. He paused and took a deep breath just before kicking in the bedroom door.

He twisted from side to side, looking for Dragos. It took a minute for his brain to register that the room was empty. Momentarily relieved, Brett moved from room to room, only to find the house empty. Dragos was gone. Where was he? He didn't have a car, and he wasn't with Candy.

Pumped full of adrenaline, Brett set the gun on the kitchen table. He tore a hand through his hair. What was going on? He pulled a Coke from the fridge and then locked the back door and pressed against it to make sure it was closed. He then yanked out a chair, sat down, and took a long drink. It was nearly dawn. Was Dragos coming back? Should he try to get a couple of hours of sleep and miss Dragos's return—or, worse yet, risk getting murdered himself? The house was locked tight. There was no way for Dragos to get in without him hearing the door open. He paced about the room. He needed to call Foster and fill him in on his suspicions.

As he held the phone to his ear, the back door vibrated. The knob slowly turned back and forth. The hairs on the back of his neck rose in alarm. He dropped the phone and lunged for the gun as the door burst open.

21

Dragos filled the doorway. The breeze from the open door swirled the dark hair about his face, hiding his eyes from view.

Brett's fingers squeezed the grip of the gun. The barrel was aimed toward Dragos's chest.

"Hold it right there!" He ordered while switching on the kitchen light.

Dragos swept the hair off his face. His eyes narrowed when he spotted the gun pointed in his direction.

"How did you get in? The door was locked." Brett's gaze didn't waver as Dragos glared back at him.

"The door was stuck. When I pushed against it, it opened. Why are you pointing a gun toward me?" Dragos's fists clenched.

Brett couldn't shake the doubts from his mind. He didn't want to shoot Dragos, but he was prepared to pull the trigger.

"There was another murder several hours ago. Two women have been attacked and murdered since you showed up at the bar on Halloween. Since you have a tendency to disappear, I thought you might know something about it."

Dragos swiped his arm before him. The corner of his lip curled. "You know I was with Candy last night. When you got called out, I stayed here. Where would I go?"

When Dragos turned his head, Brett saw something beneath Dragos's lower lip. He stepped forward and wiped Dragos's face with his finger.

Dragos jerked backward. "What are you doing?"

He studied the reddish-black substance on his finger. Alarm bells rang in his head. *Blood!* Trepidation filled Dragos's eyes. *Shit!* The man looked as guilty as hell. Yet something made Brett hesitate. He couldn't believe that both he and Candy had totally misjudged Dragos. He felt he should arrest Dragos. He could always come up with a charge and hold him.

"What are you waiting for? Call the station," Michael ordered.

Brett's gaze didn't shift from Dragos. Michael's timing was always something to be desired.

Without thinking, he muttered, "Not now. I'm kind of in the middle of something."

Dragos's brow rose. "What did you say? Can you put that gun down? You're making me nervous."

"Ha! As if you're dumb enough to put the gun down." Michael stood next to Brett with his hands on his hips.

Brett held up his finger in front of Dragos. "See this? It's blood. You'd better have a good reason for having blood on your face."

Dragos quickly wiped his mouth. "I don't know what you're talking about. Why would I have blood on my face?"

"That, buddy, is the million-dollar question," Michael cracked.

Ignoring Michael, Brett stated, "That's my question. Start talking or I'll be forced to arrest you."

Dragos's shoulders drooped forward. His head bowed.

Dragos's mind raced. Fearful of discovery, he'd moved his supply of blood to the garage. He'd just finished a bag before returning to the house. Damn his luck! He had no money, no friends, and no transportation. Basically he had no options. A slight glimmer of hope remained. Would Brett understand his situation? If he wanted to survive in this time, he was going to have to trust someone. Now might be the time to do so.

"Please, may I sit down?"

Brett nodded. Dragos collapsed in a chair. "I'm afraid that I have not been quite honest with you."

"Go on."

Dragos shook his head. "This is extremely difficult. I have traveled here from England, as I mentioned. But I neglected to inform you that I have no idea how I found myself in your country."

Brett frowned at him. "What do you mean? You flew on a plane, right?"

He laughed shakily. "I have seen a plane on your television, but I have never flown. In my time, such things do not exist."

Dragos saw Brett glance to the side once again. What was he looking at?

"In your time?"

"Yes. I was born in 1812. I find myself in this tenuous situation with no logical explanation."

"Are you saying that you time-traveled?" Brett scoffed, slightly lowering his gun. "There is no such thing as time travel."

"Be that as it may, I somehow ended up in your time with no money, no family, no friends—nothing. I am at your mercy."

"Ha ha. If the situation weren't so serious, I'd go along with the joke."

Dragos sighed, squeezing his eyes shut. It was not going as well as he hoped. Gritting his teeth, he confessed, "I have a serious illness. When we met, I was stricken with terrible pains—pains so bad I thought I was going to die."

"Yeah, I know. You had a virus."

Dragos held up the palm of his hand. "Please allow me to continue. Although I am much improved from the night we met, my illness persists. The virus that has attacked my body still eats away at my soul. If you have a cure, I beg you to tell me now so I may go live a normal life rather than hiding in shadows."

Brett looked again at the blood smeared on his finger. "What are you trying to tell me?"

"I need blood to survive."

Brett shook his head as if he hadn't heard correctly. "What did you say?"

He met Brett's gaze. "I drink blood."

Brett raised the gun so it was pointing at Dragos's chest. His finger was back on the trigger. "And you killed those two women for their blood."

Anger filled him as he jumped to his feet. "I killed no one! I would not sink to that level."

"You just confessed to drinking blood. By the wounds on the women's necks, I'm guessing that you bit their necks and drank their blood."

Dragos vigorously shook his head. "You are out of your mind. I have killed no one."

"Then where did you get the blood on your face?"

"When I was at the hospital, I took quite a bit of blood. I have survived by rationing it out. I hid the blood in the garage so you wouldn't discover my secret. I would never stoop so low as to take blood from a human."

"Took? As in stole it?"

Dragos filled with shame. "I had no choice."

Brett waved the gun at him. "Let's go. You're going to show me this bag of blood—if it really exists."

Fury coursed through Dragos. His hands clenched. The man had insinuated that he was a liar. Duels were fought over lessor accusations. He stepped forward.

"Don't do it. I will shoot you," Brett softly whispered.

Dragos hesitated.

Brett motioned outside. "Let's go."

With a gun pointing at his back, Dragos walked to the garage. Once inside, he flipped on the light. Beneath the tool bench, he pulled out the box from the bottom of the pile. He tore off the lid and tossed it on the floor.

"There."

Brett peered into the box. "I don't see any blood."

With a growl, he yanked out the black bag and tossed it at Brett's feet. Brett picked up the bag and dumped the contents onto the floor. Forty or more small bags of blood fell at his feet.

Brett picked up a bag and glanced at him.

"You've been drinking this blood."

Without a word, Dragos nodded. His lips clenched tightly.

"Where are the empty bags?"

Dragos pulled out a second bag and gave it to Brett. After a few minutes, Brett motioned him back to the house. In the kitchen, Dragos sat and watched Brett. Brett scraped the dried blood from his finger onto a sheet of paper and carefully folded the edges.

"I'm going to have the lab analyze the blood from your face. You'd better pray that it doesn't match either of the murdered women."

Brett set the gun down on the table and grabbed a beer. "Do you want one?"

Dragos shook his head. He wasn't feeling very thirsty, having just been threatened with a gun pointed at his chest.

They sat in silence while Brett sipped his beer. He hoped Brett believed his story; otherwise, he'd be lost.

"Tell me about your life in England growing up."

Dragos sighed, feeling relief. Brett was giving him a chance to prove that he wasn't a killer. He apparently didn't have any answers about his illness, but it was a start.

22

Brett stoically listened to the unbelievable tale that Dragos spun. He continued to ignore Michael, who leaned against the counter with his arms folded across his chest. He had to admit that the level of detail was quite specific. His life as an English gentleman sounded like something from a movie. Brett wasn't a history buff by any means, but it sounded legit.

By the time Dragos finished his story, Michael paced the floor.

Brett tilted back in the chair and rubbed both hands through his hair. "Okay, I admit that some of your story is plausible. I still don't understand how you got to this century or how you're still alive. You were attacked by Victor. The next thing you remember, you woke up in this century as a vampire."

Dragos erupted from his seat. The chair crashed to the floor before Dragos kicked it across the room. "Vampire!"

Michael jumped as the chair slammed into the cupboards. "What the hell?"

"Every … you calm down!" Brett yelled.

"You called me a vampire." Dragos marched across the room and jabbed a finger into Brett's chest. "I am an English gentleman, not a damn vampire. I'm sick. Even you said I had a virus."

Michael moved closer to Dragos. He sneered at Brett's houseguest. "He's a bloodsucker. You'd better kill him now."

"For God's sake, not ..." Brett's voice trailed off as Dragos eyed him suspiciously. "Viruses don't cause people to drink blood, Dragos."

Dragos's hands gripped the edge of the kitchen table. "But how ... how did this happen to me?"

Brett studied Dragos. He seemed truly upset, even angry, about being a vampire. It appeared the guy had no idea what he was. A thread of sympathy took root. "If what you say is true, I bet the guy you and Marcus were with that last night did something to you."

Brett watched confusion fill Dragos's gaze as he began to put the pieces together.

"I never knew. Yet it all ties together. How could I have ever trusted the man?"

Michael threw his hands up in the air. "Well, hell. Now we have two vampires to worry about."

With Michael being distracting as usual, Brett focused on Dragos. "You had no way of knowing the truth." Brett cleared his throat. "I know this is traumatic for you, but you're asking me to believe you. Well, you're going to have to trust me. I'm going to run your prints and have the lab check the blood sample. If everything comes back clean, then we will go forward."

"Go forward?"

"I won't arrest you," Brett clarified. "One more thing. If you're in this century, then we need to be prepared to believe that the man may also be here."

With a heaving chest, the anger faded from Dragos's face. He slumped against the wall, his long legs bracing him upright.

"My God. His name is Victor! Candy showed me how to use the TV at her house. I just watched *Dracula Untold* on TV. Am I evil?"

Brett picked up the chair and shook his head. "Evil? I don't think so. The blood thing will likely scare most people. I don't think Des Moines is ready for a vampire. For now, let's keep that a secret between us."

Brett knew he'd have to bring Anders and Foster up to speed. But how?

Straightening, Dragos growled. "Why did Victor turn me into a vampire? Why not kill me? Could Victor be the one killing the young women?"

"Perhaps. First let's get you cleared; then we can search for him."

Streams of light peaked over the horizon. Brett rolled his shoulders, alleviating some of the tension that strummed through him.

"I'm going to get cleaned up, and then we'll go to the station. I assume since you sleep most of the day that you are affected by the light."

Dragos nodded. "Somewhat. Drinking blood seems to help diminish the pain."

As Brett turned toward the bedroom, he saw Michael standing behind Dragos, pantomiming the act of stabbing him with a stake. Brett rolled his eyes.

Michael jumped forward, trying to tackle Dragos. "Don't trust him! He's a vampire for God's sake."

He saw Dragos shudder and glance around the room.

Brett froze. "What's wrong?"

"I don't know. It's chilly all of a sudden."

"I'll get my coat and we can leave." Brett nudged Michael as he left the room. He had enough on his mind without putting up with Michael's antics.

By the time Brett and Dragos left the house, dark thunderclouds had rolled in. Torrents of rain slashed against the windshield. Brett swore, as he could barely see the road. Looking in the rearview mirror, he saw Michael. Michael leaned over the front seat and glared at Dragos.

"I don't know how you can trust this guy. He's going to suck you dry," Michael warned

Brett grabbed an empty soda bottle off the floor and tossed it into the backseat, aiming at Michael's head.

Dragos flashed a quizzical look.

"Hey! What was that for? Michael whined. "I'm trying to help you."

Brett bit back a smile when Michael disappeared.

On arriving at the station, Brett and Dragos darted into the building in between raindrops. Brett studied Dragos's figure. The vampire was dressed in black from head to toe, and the storm blew his hair about his shoulders. Raindrops glistened on his high cheekbones. The steely look in his eyes caught Brett off guard. For a moment, it was as if he were watching a character from a Marvel movie running toward him. He shook off the unusual case of the nerves. Michael's warning still rang in his mind.

Even though the station was fairly quiet at this time of day, he took the back stairs. The fewer people that saw Dragos, the fewer questions he'd have to answer. Once inside his office, Brett called for an ID technician. Dragos paced the floor, looking out the window.

The technician knocked on door as he entered.

"O'Shea, what's going on?"

"Hey, Sanders. Can you run the prints on my friend here and analyze this blood sample?" Brett handed the technician a plastic bag containing the blood from Dragos's face. If Sanders was surprised at Brett's request, he didn't show it. "I'd like the results ASAP."

"All you detectives are the same. ASAP! Hurry up! Yada yada."

He felt the tug of a smile. "If you can keep this under your hat, I'd appreciate it."

Sanders cast a quick glance at him while taking Dragos's prints. "As long as you don't box me in a corner."

"Don't worry. I'll be reporting to Foster and Anders."

"Fine. I have a couple of things to do for the chief, so I'll get back to you by lunch."

After Sanders packed his gear and left, Dragos stood. He returned to the window and stared at the river. Dragos's wide shoulders bunched together. Brett felt the tension rolling off of him.

"Now what?"

"I take you home so I can get back to work."

Dragos whipped around and faced him.

"If we discover Victor is here, I want to help you catch him."

Suddenly the door to his office burst open. Chief Anders stormed in, coffee cup in hand. The eyes of the burly chief narrowed as he studied Brett and Dragos.

"O'Shea! When are we going to have some answers for the mayor?" Anders paused, nodding at Dragos across the room. "Who's this?"

23

Brett blinked in disbelief. The chief was never in the office this early. "Uh … uh …" He struggled to form a coherent sentence.

Dragos stepped forward, his hand outstretched. "Hello, sir. I'm Dragos Eldridge, son of the Earl of Albermarle."

Anders shook Dragos's hand. "Good morning. I'm Chief Anders."

Dragos's unique accent was very pronounced. Brett glanced at Anders's face. Sure enough, the chief's head tilted as he studied Dragos.

"Dragos is staying with me for a few days."

"Hmm. I didn't think England used titles nowadays." Anders took a sip of his coffee as he watched Dragos.

The chief's nonchalant action didn't fool him. The chief always nursed his liquid caffeine when he was thinking.

Brett jiggled the car keys. "Was there something you needed, sir? I was getting ready to take Dragos home." He glanced at Dragos and nodded toward the doorway. Unfortunately Dragos didn't take the hint. He and the chief were staring each other down. *Shit!*

"I read your report about Detective Randall. After I suspended him, the mayor called and wanted me to retract my decision."

That was news. "What did you tell him?"

Anders set his coffee cup on Brett's desk before settling in the side chair. He stretched out his legs. "Why don't you guys have a seat?"

"Dragos, why don't you wait outside my office," said Brett. "I'll come and get you when the chief is through."

Anders's brow wrinkled. "Dragos, have a seat."

Fuck! What is Anders up to?

Dragos frowned. Obviously he wasn't the only one confused. Brett walked behind his desk and sat.

"Anyway, I informed the mayor that I would talk to you. You've always been by the book, O'Shea. Do you think Randall had anything to do with the murder of the two prostitutes?"

"I don't know. He obviously has issues, but the coroner's report has indicated that the women bled to death as a result of the bites on their necks."

Anders scratched his cheek. "I assume you have some thoughts on what made those bites."

Brett forced his gaze to remain impassive. He wasn't going to discuss vampires at this point. "We've ruled out animal bites. They could be puncture wounds of some sort."

Anders turned and stared at Dragos. "I'm sorry, but I think I missed Brett's explanation as to why you're here at the station?"

Suddenly the collar of Brett's shirt felt too tight. Before Dragos could say anything that would get them in trouble, Brett leapt to his feet.

"I'm giving him a tour. You know, he wanted to see where I worked."

Anders's gaze locked on Brett. "Sit your ass down. I'm getting a crick in my neck." Anders reached for his coffee and took a drink. "Nothing better than a hot cup in the morning to get the pistons churning."

Anders rose and walked to the doorway, where he paused.

"I know something is going on. Just tell me one thing. Does this case involve any hocus-pocus shit?"

Brett's throat went dry. The words would not come. He nodded.

Anders winced. "Damn it, O'Shea. A fucking shit magnet— that's what you are! What are we dealing with?" The chief suddenly jerked up his hand. "Stop! I don't want to know. I've got the mayor breathing down my ass and now this."

Brett's mouth opened and closed. What could he say at this point? They weren't even sure what they were looking for.

"A report on my desk in forty-eight hours. Got it?"

"Yes sir. Once I know what we've got, I'll let you know right away."

The chief nodded. "Better include Foster. We'll need to get him up to speed. Is your 'friend' Dragos helping you on this investigation?"

Dragos stepped forward. "Yes, sir, I am."

Anders shook his head. "Do what you need to do, O'Shea. Keep us out of the papers and off the evening news."

Anders's footsteps faded away.

Dragos tilted his head. "Hocus-pocus?"

Brett motioned for Dragos to follow. He entered the stairwell and took the stairs two at a time. He gasped for breath as he swung the door open and a blast of sleety rain hit his face.

"Last year Anders and I caught a serial killer—a killer who was possessed by a demon."

"A demon!"

"Yeah, a frickin' demon who almost ripped me to shreds."

Dragos visibly shivered. "My God. I never knew such a creature existed."

A reluctant grin graced Brett's face. "Well, now we know that demons, ghosts, and vampires exist."

"A ghost? When did you see a ghost?"

His grin faded. "When we worked the demon case. Come on. If you're okay with the daylight thing, I want you to show me where you were before we met."

24

Dragos flinched as lightning lit up the early morning sky. His skin tingled where the dull light reached. He pulled the hood of his jacket over his head, shielding most of his face. Was this his fate—to never enjoy a sunny day again?

Rumbles of thunder vibrated around them. They picked their way to the cave. The threatening skies thrust sleet and razor-sharp raindrops at their heads.

The only thing they had going for them was that the storm kept workers away from the site. He and Brett ran through the dig site until they reached the tunnels. Brett reached the cave door first.

"It's locked. Allen probably wanted to keep curious eyes out."

Dragos stepped forward and yanked on the thick chain, causing it to break in two.

"Whoa! How'd you do that?" asked Brett.

Dragos stared at the broken chain in his hand and shrugged. "One of the several changes I've noticed since I came down with this ... this whatever I have."

With Brett close on his heels, he stepped into the cave, slowly turning to survey the place where his nightmare began.

"So tell me what you remember from when you first woke up."

Dragos ran his hand over the top of the tomb that he had been encased in. The absence of answers plagued him.

"I couldn't breathe. The darkness was overpowering. I couldn't escape fast enough."

"You were inside that thing?" Brett asked.

"Yes. I have no idea how I got there." Dragos sighed, staring at the tomb.

Brett nodded to the other tomb. "What about the other one. Who was in that one?"

"At first I feared my friend Marcus was inside. I was afraid to look—afraid of what I would see."

"Wasn't Marcus the guy you were with when you met Victor?"

Dragos swallowed hard. "It kills me that I don't know what happened to him. Now it's too late. He'd be dead by now."

Brett stared at him. Was that pity he saw in the detective's eyes?

"Maybe we could do a genealogy search. Who knows; you might find some relative of his."

"No! We can't change the past. Let it lie."

After a few moments of silence, Brett asked, "Do you recognize the writing on the tombs?"

"No. I know it's Romanian. My father wanted me to focus on English. Family traditions and all that."

Footsteps echoed from the tunnel. The men glanced at one another. Brett motioned Dragos to move behind the tombs. Brett dodged behind the door and drew his gun.

Dragos pressed his back against the damp stone wall. He tensed, ready to assist his friend if needed. With his newly found strength and speed, he had no doubt that he could reach Brett in time.

Moments later, a male voice hissed, "Damn it."

When a thin, short man wearing a hat stepped inside the cave, Brett groaned and lowered the gun.

"Allen," Brett murmured. "It's Detective O'Shea." He stepped from behind the tombs.

Allen's eyes widened as Dragos approached him. Allen turned, looking as if he were going to run from the cave. Brett flung out his arm, blocking Allen from leaving.

"Shit! O'Shea, you scared me to death. What are you doing at my dig site?"

Brett holstered his gun, taking a deep breath.

Allen turned to stare at Dragos. "Who's that?"

Dragos stepped forward. "Hello, I am Dragos Eldridge, from England. I'm …"

"He's working a case with me," interrupted Brett

Allen's bony chin jutted upward. "From Scotland Yard?"

Dragos bit the inside of his cheek. *Who is this fellow?*

Brett cleared his throat. "Not exactly. I've been working the recent murder cases."

"Then why are you here, on my property?" A glint shone in Allen's eyes. "Unless you think my vampire idea has merit."

Brett snorted. "You know I can't say anything about the investigation, Allen."

"Did you guys break into the cave? I noticed that the chain was cut."

Both Dragos and Brett shook their heads. "No, the door was open when we got here a few minutes ago."

"Damn vandals. It's been hard to keep unwanted people out of here. I'm going to have to hire a few guards for the night shift."

"Sorry if I overstepped my authority in coming here today. I don't want to create any ill feelings between us," Brett said.

"No problem, Detective. I'm always glad to help. Though I'm not sure how my property has anything to do with the murder of the prostitutes."

"Just checking all avenues." Brett nodded at Dragos.

"We'll get out of your hair. Let me know if you see anything unusual."

Dragos followed Brett back through the tunnel. As they neared the opening, screams ripped through the air. He and Brett glanced at one another and ran outside.

A crowd of people grouped together stared at something on the ground. Brett shouldered through the crowd, flashing his badge. People were crying.

Dragos gasped. A body lay on the ground. It looked as if she had dropped dead where she stood. One leg was bent at an unnatural angle. He felt sick. He'd never seen a body before.

"Get back! Get back." Brett whipped out his cell phone. After a clipped request for backup, he crouched down next to the body and felt for a pulse. Long blonde hair covered the woman's face.

"Dragos, get everyone out of here until we can take their statements."

As one young man pulled out his phone to take a picture, Dragos grabbed it and flung it into the nearby river.

"Hey! Dude, you can't do that," the man complained.

Dragos snarled, "Have some respect for the dead."

The man pointed to Dragos's face. "Your eyes. They're glowing."

Dragos felt a surge of fear lash through him. He strode toward the man. His lip curled in disgust. The young man hurried off, looking over his shoulder to see if Dragos followed. Times did not change. People were always drawn to death.

The rain had almost stopped. A fine mist lingered in the air. Thunder continued to rumble in the distance. A sheen of moisture dampened his face. He reached up and wiped his eyes. The people grumbled but slowly made their way to the parking lot to wait to be interviewed.

He laid a hand on Brett's shoulder. Brett leaned protectively over the woman, his head bowed.

"She's dead, isn't she?"

Brett nodded. He slowly brushed long hair to the side, revealing a puncture wound in her neck.

Dragos hissed, staring at her neck. "Did the other murdered women have the same type of wound?"

Brett rose and dusted off his pants. "Unfortunately, yes."

The muscles in Brett's face were taut. His eyes smoldered. An invisible wall of despair seemed to surround the detective. Brett looked shaken.

"Do you know her?"

"I do. I did." Brett's voice cracked.

Sounds of sirens drew closer. Brett's gaze didn't waver from the pale body on the ground. A single tear fell from the detective's eyes. The professional veneer around the detective threatened to snap. Surprisingly, Dragos felt protective of the detective.

"Detective! What is going on?" Allen marched toward them. His steps faltered upon spotting the woman on the ground. Allen's mouth gaped as he pointed. "What happened?"

Dragos reached out to block Allen from touching the body. The archeologist was as white as a sheet.

"I'd better get some answers real quick, Detective. What the hell happened?" Allen demanded.

Brett leaned down and brushed the hair off the woman's face.

Allen gasped and clutched his chest.

Brett glared up at Allen. Dragos feared that the detective was going to pounce on the little man.

Brett wiped his cheek with the back of his hand. He snapped, "It's one of your staff. Jamie Brooks."

25

"I don't even know how old she was," Brett muttered.

Allen's throat convulsed. Brett grabbed Allen's arm and jerked him away from the body. All at once, Allen leaned over and vomited, splattering the ground around them.

Dragos wrinkled his nose as the acid smell blossomed around the trio.

Bent at the waist, Allen pointed to the body. "Look at her neck," he moaned. He struggled to stand, holding his stomach. "I knew there was a vampire."

Brett grabbed Allen's shoulder. "Shut your mouth."

"But you saw the ..."

"I said shut the fuck up." Brett rubbed an open hand over his face. "Are you trying to create mass hysteria?"

"No, but ..."

"There are no buts. Let the police work the case. We will catch the guy who did this."

Allen's body trembled. His bony hand reached out and gripped Brett's arm. "Don't you see? I warned you. You thought I was crazy."

Brett struggled to remain calm, not wanting to invoke any hysteria.

"Listen, Allen. I know what you think, but there are a lot of sick bastards out there. We see them all the time. If you knew the crap that went on in this city, you'd be shocked. Until we gather all the evidence, no one knows what happened. Trust me; if we're dealing with something supernatural, I'll let you know."

Allen took a deep breath and nodded. The color slowly returned to the man's face.

"Well, I suppose you're right."

The ambulance pulled up nearby. He leaned near Allen, urgency in his voice.

"Let us do our job without talking to the media. Okay?"

Allen wiped his brow with the back of his hand. "For now. I expect to be updated on a regular basis."

He bit back a curse. Allen was delusional if he thought the police were going to invite him to sit at the table. "I'll see what I can do. Now, can you get Jamie's family information? We will need to contact her family before they see this on the morning news."

Brett waited as Allen left to call his office.

Dragos nudged him. "Here comes your boss."

The body remained on the ground until the coroner pronounced her dead and evidence had been collected. Foster knelt and glanced at the body before approaching the men.

"How did you get here before anyone else, O'Shea."

"I wanted to check out dig site and ran into Allen. When we came outside, the body had just been discovered."

Foster glanced at Dragos. "Who's the guy with you?"

Brett had to update Foster on the case, but this wasn't the place. "Sir, I spoke to the chief earlier today. He is aware that Dragos is helping us."

"Dragos? Who the hell is he?"

Dragos stepped forward. "My name is Dragos Eldridge. I'm from England. I have information that may help solve the case."

"England—like Scotland Yard," Foster said.

Brett hesitated. *Not the Scotland Yard thing again.* "Well, it's complicated." The lies were accumulating.

"Do we need to talk?" Foster's mouth tightened into a thin line.

Brett watched the tech unit pull up to the site.

"I've got to go. My office at noon." Foster turned to leave. He stopped to speak with the other officers who had arrived. A camera crew trekked across the grounds but was stopped by Foster.

The day was going to hell quickly. Jamie was gone. Dead. He couldn't believe it.

As they walked toward the car, his phone rang. He saw Candy's number flash on the screen

"Candy, what's up? Yeah, he's here."

Dragos took the phone. A bright smile lit his face. Brett rolled his eyes. Dragos's deep, husky laughter surprised him. He'd accepted the fact that Dragos and Candy liked one another, but a serious conversation was needed. He had no idea how Candy would react to the idea of dating a vampire.

Dragos nudged him, drawing his from his musing.

"Here's your phone."

"So what's going on with Candy?"

Dragos had an odd look in his eyes. "Well, she was surprised to learn that we are working together. She is going to come by your house later today."

He opened his car door. "Great." Another call came through. It was the ID tech who had taken the blood sample earlier.

"O'Shea ... Okay ... Really, that's good news. Thanks for doing it so quick."

Dragos hopped in the car. "Did I hear 'good news'?"

"Yeah. The blood on your face doesn't match the murdered woman. You're not a wanted fugitive either." Brett's smile faded, and his eyes narrowed. "Wait a minute. Did you hear what was said?"

The vampire nodded. "I didn't mean to. It's just that I can hear so much better now."

"Well," he growled, "what other special abilities do you have?" Brett threw up his hands. "Never mind. Tell me later."

Dragos laid his head on the seat and closed his eyes. "Damn. I was afraid that I would not be proven innocent."

Brett winced as a splinter of guilt rose up. "Sorry, but I had to know for sure."

Steam rose off the pavement—a result of the morning sun drying the wet streets. Dragos cringed as sun lit up the car.

"Damn it!" Dragos growled. "My skin burns." He turned from the car window and scrunched down, tugging the hoodie over his face.

"We need to get you home." His eyes widened. Dragos's cheeks were red.

"I'm sorry about your friend. It must be difficult for you."

"Thanks." Brett didn't want to think about Jamie right now. The image of her body on the ground was ingrained in his memory. He had to catch her killer. Then he would sort out his feelings.

He tore down the streets, noticing tiny blisters on Dragos's face. He didn't know how much more Dragos could take. The blisters looked painful.

"I think we need one of those daylight rings they wear on *The Vampire Diaries*," Brett teased.

Dragos scowled. "Does such a thing exist?"

Brett shook his head. "No, it's just a TV thing."

Dragos actually growled.

Brett pulled the car as close to the back door as he could get. Dragos ducked his head and ran into the house. Worried about his roommate, Brett turned off the ignition and followed Dragos inside.

Brett drew to a stop, taking in the situation in front of him. Dragos stood sighing in the kitchen as he held a cool rag on his face. Michael held up a cross and glared at Dragos.

Ignoring Michael, Brett muttered, "Hey, the blisters are already gone."

Tentatively, Dragos reached up and ran his hand over his face. He gasped. "Do vampires always heal this fast?"

Brett shrugged. "Since you're the first vampire I've met, I'm not sure."

Dragos pointed past Brett. "Who's that, and why is he holding up a cross?"

Dragos was glaring at Michael. Michael smirked before setting the cross on the table.

"Shit! You can see Michael?"

"Is he making fun of me because I am a vampire?"

Brett shook his head. "No, he's … he's just being Michael."

"Well, he's a fool if he thinks that the cross will stop me." Dragos drew back his upper lip, revealing his teeth.

Brett involuntarily took a step back. Those things looked real. And sharp. "Ignore him. Michael is my great-grandfather. He's the ghost that I told you about earlier."

Dragos's fangs receded as he walked toward Michael, who rose to his feet. Dragos smiled and held out a hand. Michael studied Dragos.

"So, you're a bloodsucker."

Dragos's hand dropped to his side. His head tilted as he leaned in and drew a deep breath.

"And you're an old ghost. Where does that leave us?"

Michael puffed out his chest. "Brett is special. If you even try to take any of his blood, I'll stake you in the sun myself."

Brett took a step, coming between the men. "Hey guys, let's take it down a notch." He put a hand on Michael's shoulder. "I'm a big boy and can take care of myself, as you well know." Taking a deep breath, he glanced at Dragos, who had backed away.

"I'm not worried about Dragos. He didn't ask to become a vampire, you know. Has he done anything to make you think he would hurt me?"

Michael shook his head.

"Good. Then I need you two to get along if we're going to solve this case."

"But how can you trust him?" Michael grumbled.

Dragos threw up his hands and stormed from the room.

"Damn it!" Brett turned to leave. "I thought you were sent here to help me. Apparently I'm wrong." With that, he slammed the door behind him.

26

Michael swore. He stomped down the hall. Instead of knocking on the bedroom door, Michael shimmered into Dragos's room.

Dragos lay on the bed. An arm covered his face.

"What do you want?" Dragos muttered without looking. "Aren't you afraid I will sneak up and bite your neck?"

"I'm a ghost. You can't suck my blood." He rubbed his neck.

"A pity. I would have liked to try."

"How did you know I was in the room?"

Dragos removed his arm and peered up at him. "Really? That is what you want to know?"

Michael opened his mouth to argue, but in the blink of an eye, Dragos stood before him.

"Shit. You're almost as fast as I am."

Dragos stared down his patrician nose to glare at him.

"Must you wear that hat indoors? Your manners are sorely lacking."

Michael wanted to punch the vampire, yet he hesitated. "Well, Mr. High and Mighty, this is the twenty-first century. Things like etiquette have changed." Walking to the nearby mirror, Michael adjusted the fedora. "Besides, this was a gift from my wife before I died."

"My apologies," Dragos mumbled.

Silence reigned for several minutes. Michael grunted. "Okay, now what?"

Dragos plopped back on the bed. "Excuse me for asking, but how can you, a ghost, help solve the case? After all, we're after a vampire."

Michael let a chuckle rip from his chest. "Boy, can I tell you a few stories. If you had been around last year when Brett and I had to get rid of a demon, you would have seen our skills in action."

Dragos nodded. "Brett has told me about the case."

Michael's gaze narrowed on the vampire. "I will do anything to keep my boy, Brett, safe."

Dragos's mouth turned downward. "I would not hurt Brett. He's the only one who has helped me in this time."

Ignoring Dragos's comment, Michael added, "You should have seen me go after the son of a bitch with a flamethrower."

Dragos's brows came together. "What the hell is a flamethrower?"

He sat down next to Dragos. "A type of hose that big flames come out of. I forgot that you've been in the ground for the past couple of centuries."

Dragos cast a sideward glance at him. "I am unclear. Are we going to work together or not?"

Michael rose to his feet. "I want to apologize. If Brett says you're okay, then I'm okay. Catch you later."

Ha! I don't trust this Dragos any further than I could throw him. But I'll play nice. I'll watch Dragos like a hawk. No damn vampire is taking any of my grandson's blood.

With those thoughts swirling about his brain, his figure shimmered into droplets and immediately evaporated.

27

Victor stood beneath the towering old oak tree. He watched and waited. His eyes narrowed as he followed the detective's movements. A calculating gleam lit his eyes. Hunger gnawed at his bones. He had to feed soon.

The detective went into Darlene's place. Victor had been here before and knew that the man liked to frequent this particular house. The blond detective liked to brag about being a cop. He seemed to believe it entitled him to special privileges.

In a way, Victor felt a camaraderie of sorts with the human. They both enjoyed torturing women—something that Victor excelled at. The man was a mere amateur compared to him.

He shifted position, blending into the dark shadows. Traffic at the house was slow tonight. His options for feeding would be limited. A flash of disappointment surged through him. He so preferred young women to taste. Nothing was quite as satisfying as a beautiful woman suddenly realizing that the moment of death was upon her. Oh, he wasn't a fool. He always sampled their physical attributes prior to draining them. He reveled in the thought of their upcoming struggle and surrender. His body hardened as he visualized his last conquest.

A breeze tossed his shoulder-length hair about his face.

His woolen black turtleneck sweater kept the night chill from his body. He had quickly adapted to the casual style of clothing worn in this time. Clothing in this time was much less restrictive than it had been in the nineteenth century. He had always opted for dark clothing. A long trench coat clung to his body. The upright collar framed his jaw. His lips narrowed as the rear door to Darlene's opened, letting light flood the grounds.

With heightened senses, he ran his tongue over his sharp fangs. He could almost taste warm blood coursing down his throat. Anticipation built.

Two burly looking men shoved the detective out the door. He tumbled down the stairs, landing face-first in the dirt. The man jumped to his feet, holding a large rock in his hand.

"Darlene! You bitch. Paybacks are hell," he yelled while throwing the rock through a window. Cursing under his breath, the man turned toward his car.

Victor shifted next to the man. He reached out and put a hand on the man's shoulder. The man jerked and turned to see who had touched him.

"Hey, get your hands off me." The man whipped out a badge and flashed it at him.

Victor paused, pretending to be surprised. He flashed a smile at the detective.

"Excuse me. I thought you might need some help."

Victor watched the detective's hand inch toward his gun. He wanted to laugh. *As if a gun could hurt me.*

"It appears that you do not to need my assistance after all." Victor shrugged and turned away.

"Wait," the man called out. "I'm so pissed off right now that I can't think straight."

"No problem. I can relate. How about the two of us getting a drink?" Victor asked, veiling the smugness he felt.

"Deal. There's a bar just two blocks east of here."

"I have quite an elaborate bar at my home if you're up for a short drive."

The officer appeared to hesitate before patting the gun hidden under his jacket. "Sounds good to me. What's the address?"

"Thirteen thirteen Red Sunset Drive—one of the new housing developments west of here."

"I'll put the address into my GPS. By the way, my name is Tim Randall, detective with the DMPD."

"Nice to meet you. I'm Victor Sinclair."

Randall glanced around. "Where's your car?"

"A friend was to meet me here an hour ago but never showed." He shrugged, sighing loudly. "I was getting ready to call a taxi."

Randall pointed to his car. "Get in. I'll take you home."

As they drove to his place, Victor learned all about the young detective and his lofty ambition to become chief one day. Randall seemed to think he knew more than other officers. Purportedly, because he was related to the mayor of the city, his boss and other detectives discriminated against him—left him out of the big cases.

Victor bit back his laughter. Poor Randall. The world was against him. He was the perfect person to manipulate and control.

Resting his arm on the seat behind Randall, Victor nodded. "I don't know how you stand working for those people."

Randall squeezed the steering wheel. "Yeah, me neither. They're all assholes. Especially O'Shea. What a prick. For some reason, Chief Anders has taken him under his wing. Whatever O'Shea wants, he gets."

"Well," Victor murmured, "that sucks." Victor pointed to the left. "Take the dead-end road." Within minutes, they pulled up to the large sprawling house that he owned in Des Moines—one of several throughout the country. "Here we are."

Randall pulled into the driveway and got out. He whistled. "Nice place. I don't know how people can pay the taxes on places like this." He shot Victor a sly look. "But it doesn't appear that you have to worry about that."

Victor smiled as he opened the front double doors. "You are correct. Welcome to my home."

A large foyer with a winding staircase greeted them. The marble tile on the floor reflected light from the chandelier. Hand-scraped bamboo floors flowed from the foyer. The house had a modern feel, which Victor liked. Damp, dreary castles were a thing of his past. This house, with its conveniences, was a nice diversion.

"The family room is this way."

Victor sauntered down the hallway, hearing Randall's steps behind him. Upon entering the room, he kicked off his Italian leather loafers and walked to the bar.

Holding up a glass, Victor asked, "Okay?"

Randall nodded as his mouth gaped. Randall's attention was focused on the painting above the bar. The detective appeared to be transfixed on the artwork. Victor ducked his head, hiding his amusement.

He handed a drink to the detective. "Do you like the painting?"

The subject in the massive painting was that of a woman dressed in a long white shift. Her pale blonde hair cascaded forward, hiding her face. Her bound hands were outstretched. Only Victor knew what the painting represented.

Randall continued to stare at it as if he appreciated real artwork. "That's some serious piece of work. Where did you get it?"

Victor smiled, running a long, tapered finger down his chin. "I had it commissioned many years ago."

"Damn! The blood trailing down the dress makes it looks so real. The clash of the red and white is very startling."

Victor closed his eyes, savoring the thoughts from the

past—memories of a night many centuries ago. "Yes, it was … is."

Quiet descended in the room. Randall shifted. Victor inhaled, capturing the essence of sexual excitement in the air. The painting aroused the young detective. He bit back a smile. His plans for his guest had just changed. With Randall in law enforcement, he might prove valuable. At the least, Victor would be able to easily manipulate the detective.

"Let's sit down and talk. I'd like to know more about you."

Randall threw back his drink, quickly draining the contents. "Not much else to say." Randall sat down across from him.

"Haven't I seen you at Darlene's before tonight?"

A smug look settled across Randall's face. "The girls there are hot. They don't mind it if you smack them around a bit."

"You like to play it rough, then?"

"Yeah, but Darlene has those damn rules. She thought I was *too* rough, so she kicked me out. Fucking bitch. I'd like to make her life miserable, but I have to be careful. According to my uncle, if I do something stupid and end up in the paper, I'm on my own."

"Really? Well I might have a proposition for you. That is, if you're interested."

Randall sat on the edge of the chair. "I'm all ears."

Victor set his glass on the table. Coolly, he leaned back on the sofa, resting his arm across the back. "I also have specific needs, like you."

"What kind of needs?" Randall asked. "Nothing illegal, I hope." Randall's laughter trailed away as Victor glared at his guest.

He rose, standing over Randall, who scooted back in his seat. Trepidation filled Randall's eyes. "Nothing you should concern yourself with. I can supply you with women who like your form of foreplay. I like to watch. When you are finished, I will take care of them."

Randall's gaze turned calculating. "You can do that?"

"Yes. I would be honored to help a friend."

Randall stood and slapped him on the arm. "Man, I appreciate it. I will owe you big-time."

Mortals were so simpleminded. He needed only offer them their heart's desire, and they became putty in his hands. It was almost too easy. Victor turned to hide his disgust.

"Well, there is one thing you could help me with."

"Sure. What do you need?"

"I'm looking for a friend. He was to join me here in Des Moines, but he failed to contact me. I fear he may be in danger."

"All I need is a name and I can find him."

"Dragos Eldridge. He is from England. With him having no friends or family here, I am worried."

Randall typed the name into his phone. Covering a yawn, he muttered, "I'll look it up first thing tomorrow. I need to head home. It was nice to meet you, Victor."

"I'm glad you joined me tonight. I look forward to our next meeting," Victor smoothly added.

Randall flipped open his wallet. "Here's my card. Let me know when you have one of your get-togethers. It sounds fun."

Victor escorted his guest to the door. After bidding Randall farewell, he locked the door and headed to the basement. He needed a diversion.

Soft moans echoed from the locked room. Excitement filled him. He unlocked the door and glanced down. A woman was huddled in a corner, her knees drawn up with her arms wrapped around them. Tears silently trailed down her sunken cheeks. The puncture wounds on her neck were inflamed.

"Please, please. Let me go. I won't tell anyone about you." Her voice trailed to a whisper. "I just want to go home."

He reached down, tilting her face upward. "My poor little

bird. So sad looking. Come, let's get you cleaned up. I have some clean clothes for you."

Hope blossomed in her wide eyes. She scrambled to her feet. "Are you letting me go?"

"Yes, we are leaving, but first let's get dressed. Let me help you."

He took her arm and led her down the hall to the bathroom. Opening the door, he nudged her forward. "Everything you need is here. Take your time. I will be waiting."

Minutes later, he heard the sound of running water. He had taken Madeline a week ago. In her weakened state, she wouldn't last much longer. He enjoyed watching hope blossom in her eyes, but it was time for a new toy. He leaned against the wall, trying to decide which type of woman he would take next. Madeline was a redhead. He'd had a blonde. Or two.

With a quick glance at the clock, he growled. Impatient, he tapped on the bathroom door. "My dear, it's been fifteen minutes. Are you ready?"

The bathroom door eased open. Wide green eyes stared back at him. Her body was half hidden by the door.

"Come out. I want to see how the clothes look."

Madeline shook her head. "I can't. You can see through the gown. Isn't there something else I can wear?"

He laughed and grabbed her hand, pulling her into the hallway. The black lace nightgown hugged her curves. The V-neck dipped nearly to her navel. Her full breasts bounced with any movement. The dusky pink of her nipples peeked through the lace.

He reached out, weighing her breast in his hand. He tweaked the nipple until she squeaked with fear and pulled away.

"Now, now. You are perfection."

He tugged on her wrist, pulling her up the stairs. She tripped over the edge of the gown and nearly fell.

"Madeline, you are being clumsy tonight. Where are your manners?"

Ignoring her whimpers, he yanked her against him. He wrapped her hair around his hand, jerking her even closer.

"You smell so good. I don't think I can resist. Do you mind if I take a bite?"

Madeline pushed against his chest. Raising a fist, she beat against his face. His fangs descended. Terror filled her eyes.

He paused, enjoying the way she trembled in his arms and her pathetic attempts to escape.

"Do not provoke me. I can make your death easy or difficult. It's your choice."

Her legs gave way. "But I don't want to die," she wailed.

He gripped her waist to keep her neck in reach. Her feeble tears and pleading increased his arousal.

"Why? Why can't you let me go?" she whispered.

He lifted his head and met her gaze. "Because I am who I am. I am a predator, and you are a victim."

His eyes closed in anticipation of the ecstasy about to consume him. He clamped down until blood flowed into his mouth. The thrill of taking coursed through him. Blind lust filled his body. By the time he was finished, she was still, her eyes vacant. He released her body, allowing it to fall to the floor.

He straightened, flexing his muscles. *Another body to get rid of.* Perhaps he would leave the body near Darlene's house as a warning. Randall would appreciate his effort even if he wouldn't know who did it.

It was time to find a new victim for his playroom.

28

Brett woke with a start. Shadows danced on the bedroom walls. He rubbed his eyes, casting a quick glance at the clock. His imagination was in overdrive. He tossed the sheet to the side and slowly shuffled to the bathroom. It was nearly 5:00 a.m.—time to get up anyway.

This week had been a fiasco. The death-look on Jamie's face haunted him. He hadn't known her that well, but she'd seemed like a nice girl. He couldn't accept the fact that someone that young was gone in the blink of an eye.

He hadn't seen Michael or Dragos when he got home last night, much to his relief. Their feuding grated on his nerves.

Wandering to the front room, he stared out at the empty street. He liked this time of day. It was quiet and allowed him to collect his thoughts. A click of a switch in the kitchen indicated the coffeemaker had kicked on. Soon the smell of freshly brewed coffee filled the house.

He turned and walked back to his bedroom. As he passed the spare bedroom, Dragos stepped into the hallway. Brett's arm shot out to keep himself from slamming into him.

"Sorry, I didn't know you were up yet," Dragos yawned.

Brett wondered why Dragos was still up. It was nearly time for him to go to sleep.

"Couldn't sleep." Brett wondered why Dragos looked so cheery.

Dragos smiled. The satisfied look gave Brett pause.

"Candy picked me up, and we hung out at her place."

"How's she doing?"

"Great. She caught some guy cheating on his wife. He threatened her. I don't know why she chooses to work as a private investigator. Would it be safer to be a police officer?"

"Not really. I'll call her."

Dragos flashed a wicked smile. "Do not bother. I offered to meet the man and make him reconsider."

"On that note, I need a cup of coffee." Brett headed to the kitchen and grabbed a cup. He then sat at the table, reluctant to get ready for work.

Dragos sat across the table. "Anything new on Jamie's murder?"

Brett shook his head. "I wish we knew for sure that Victor was in town. With three bodies, it won't be long before the media starts using the label of 'serial killer.'"

"What does your instinct tell you?"

Brett bit his lip, mulling over the question. "I think Victor is behind the killing."

Suddenly Michael appeared in the middle of the kitchen. Dragos jerked to the side, nearly falling out of the chair.

"Damnation!" Dragos yelled.

Brett chuckled. "Welcome to my world. What's up, Michael?"

Michael tossed his fedora on the table. A bleak look was plastered on his face. Brett rose.

"Another body was just found."

Dragos jumped up, staring at Brett "What can I do to assist you?"

Brett slammed his fist on the table. "Shit! We've got to stop this guy." He stormed down the hall and threw on work clothes. When he returned to the kitchen, Dragos and Michael were silently waiting.

"Brett, I think the three of us need to go after this guy. If you believe Victor is behind the murders, then Dragos needs to go with us."

Brett glanced at the two of them. While jerking on his sports coat, he snapped, "So you two are talking now?"

Michael shrugged. "Yep. We're fine. What do you say?"

Brett grabbed his keys. "Let me talk to Foster and see what he says. Good idea, though."

He turned to Dragos. "Better get some rest. We'll need you later today."

Brett tore through the streets, relieved at the lack of traffic. His throat tightened with emotion. There were so many dead women. *Why now? Why in Des Moines?* He had more questions than answers.

After parking the car, he rushed into the station. As he entered the detective bureau, Randall came out of Foster's office and glared at him. *Asshole!* Randall acted as if it were Brett's fault that he had been suspended. Randall brushed against his shoulder as they passed one another.

Brett pasted on a smile. "Still under suspension?"

"Fuck you," Randall hissed. "Better watch your back, O'Shea."

He smirked back at the detective. "I'm not a woman that you can smack around, Randall. I'll hit you back. And trust me, you won't get up."

The door on Foster's office flew open. Foster stood, eyeing both of them.

"O'Shea, get in here. Randall, get out of here."

Brett opened his mouth but quickly closed it. Foster's eyes glared like wildfire. Everyone was cranked up, and it wasn't even 7:00 a.m.

Foster slammed his door and marched behind his desk.

Brett cleared his throat. "I heard there was another murder last night. Want me to work it?"

"I've assigned Donnellson."

Surprise filled Brett. Why would Foster bring in Donnellson?

"Any reason you didn't show up for the noon meeting yesterday?" The muscles in Foster's cheek twitched.

Brett suddenly wished a hole in the floor would swallow him up. "Crap. I forgot. Sorry, sir. I don't know how it happened."

Foster held up his hand, indicating that Brett had better shut up. "Nothing annoys me more than staff who can't follow orders."

He struggled to find the right words to pacify Foster. All he had was blanks.

"So tell me what this Dra … Dragos guy is doing working with my detective?"

"Well, Dragos Eldridge is from England. I think I mentioned that." Seeing a snarl settle across Foster's face, he rushed on. "So, he's staying at my place. Visiting me, I mean. I came down to the station when we had the last murder, and Dragos tagged along. He wanted to see how we do things here in the States." He gulped. His thoughts were jumbled together. He was lucky to get a coherent sentence out.

He rushed on. "The chief thought Dragos might be able to help our investigation. I was supposed to bring you into the loop. I apologize for not getting around to it sooner."

His voice trailed off. Foster's lips were pinched together.

"Do I have the word 'stupid' stamped on my forehead?" Foster glared back at him.

Foster yanked open a desk drawer and stuffed a piece of

gum into his mouth. The captain's gaze never wavered. What could he say to that? Brett felt a flush spread across his face. He'd loosen his tie, but he didn't want Foster to think he was nervous.

"What's so special about this guy?"

Brett inwardly groaned. *More lies.* "Dragos has some special abilities and may be able to help us catch the murderer."

"Special abilities? What the hell does that mean?"

He'd never seen a man's face pulled so tightly. Foster looked as though he were ready to explode.

"Dragos has an idea on who may be committing the murders."

Foster rose to his feet. "Damn it, O'Shea. I'm about ready to suspend your ass. Why didn't I know this sooner?"

He ran a hand through his hair. "It's not that simple, sir."

"I suggest that you make it simple then, 'cause I really need to understand what the hell is happening in my department."

Foster's face looked as tortured as he felt. "Sir, you remember when Allen told me that he thought there might be a vampire in Des Moines? Well, I am beginning to think that's the case."

Foster plopped back down in his chair. In a whisper-soft voice, he pointed toward the door. "I don't like smart-asses, O'Shea. Jokes and stupid comments like that have no place in our offices. Now get the fuck out of my office."

Brett stood, walked to the door, and opened it. There was Chief Anders, with his arm outstretched as if he were entering the office.

"O'Shea! I'm glad you're here. I want to talk to you and Foster."

Brett glanced back at Foster. By the looks of things, if Foster had a gun in his hand this minute, he'd be dead by now.

"Uh … Foster wants me to go, sir."

Anders's bushy brows drew together as he looked at both

men before entering the office. Anders waved toward an empty chair. "O'Shea, sit down. You too, Foster."

Anders folded his arms across his broad chest. "What's going on?"

Foster leaned forward, placing his elbows on the desk. "O'Shea believes that a vampire is committing the murders. I told him to get the hell out of here. That kind of bullshit is not something I want to hear from one of my detectives."

Anders slapped his hand palm-down on the desk. "Everyone needs to calm down."

After a couple minutes of simmering silence, Anders got up and opened the office door. "Marge! Would you bring me a cup of coffee please?" he hollered.

Anders returned to his seat. "Now, where were we? Jake, I need to tell you something confidential. No one other than O'Shea and I know what really happened last year when we worked the serial killer case."

Brett shifted in the chair. Foster's narrowed eyes zeroed in on him. *Crap.* This wasn't his fault.

Marge peeked her head in the door. "Here's your coffee, Chief. Anyone want anything else? Maybe some pie, egg rolls, cookies? After all, I'm not doing much."

Brett bit back a laugh as Foster's angry face turned in his direction. Marge was in rare form today. Anders waved her out of the office.

Anders took a sip of the steaming drink. "O'Shea and I solved the case all right, but it wasn't a normal case."

"Nothing about a murder is normal," Foster muttered.

Anders smiled. "True. It is also not normal for cops to deal with a serial killer possessed by a demon."

Foster's mouth dropped open. His snarl slowly dissolved as laughter escaped. Foster's chuckles faded when he realized he was the only one laughing.

Foster gulped before asking, "A demon? Like from the movie *Poltergeist*?"

"Actually, those were ghosts, not demons," Brett corrected.

Foster's eyes widened even further. "Fuck, O'Shea. Ghosts or demons; what difference does it make. Neither exist. Do they?"

Anders nodded. Foster then glanced at him.

"C'mon guys. Quit pulling my leg."

Anders rose and walked to the window overlooking the window. "I was like you, Foster. I didn't believe things like that even existed—not until I saw it for myself. O'Shea and Al—I mean Michael—saved my ass a couple of times. I saw things that I can't even describe."

"Who's Michael?"

"O'Shea, why don't you tell him about your ghost?"

Foster's face turned ashen. Brett feared that the stern, unbendable chief of detectives was about to pass out.

"Sir, are you okay?"

Brett took a deep breath when Foster nodded. "Michael is my great-grandfather, Detective Michael O'Shea, who was murdered back in 1933."

Foster pushed back his chair and bent over at the waist.

"Sir, are you all right? Chief, should I go get medical help?"

"No, I'm fine," Foster croaked. He grabbed a nearby water bottle and chugged half the liquid. "A ghost and a demon?"

Anders returned to his chair. "That's right. Now it appears we've got a vampire to catch."

"But how do we do that? This is crazy! I mean, how can human cops go after a vampire?"

Anders burst out laughing. "That's the thing, Foster. We're not normal. O'Shea is a shit magnet who talks to ghosts and dodges flying pitchforks. And I've seen more hocus-pocus than I care to admit. If my guess is right, Dragos knows how to catch a vampire."

Brett reluctantly added, "He believes that the man who made him a vampire is the guy we're after."

Foster weaved back and forth in his chair. "Dragos is a vampire? He isn't with Scotland Yard?"

"No. He's a vampire. Don't worry, though; I ran his prints and got a blood sample. Nothing matched the crime scenes."

"Don't worry? He's a frickin' vampire!" Foster jabbed a finger into Brett's chest. I don't know about you, but I'm going to worry." Foster grabbed the wastepaper basket and held it on his lap.

Brett's stomach twisted into knots. "We also have a problem with Allen. He also believes there is a vampire. Now with the murdered women—one of them his employee—he going to go batshit crazy."

Anders's mouth tightened. "You need to keep him quiet, O'Shea, but be careful. His family has a lot of influence."

"Chief, if you approve, I have an idea. Since the murders are occurring at night, I'd like to start working nights."

"That's fine. You know the drill. Daily reports to me and Foster."

Brett nodded. "I'll be taking Michael and Dragos out with me."

"So," Foster choked out, "we're going to have a detective, a ghost, and a vampire working a murder investigation?" Foster squeezed his mouth closed, causing tension lines to form on his face.

Anders nodded. Although his face was grim, his eyes twinkled. "Don't sound so glum, Foster. O'Shea is the best one to work the case. We just need to give him whatever he needs and provide a cover when strange things start occurring. Our job is to catch the killer and get rid of him without letting the public know the truth. Are you in?"

Shakily, Foster set the basket on the floor and rose to his feet. "I'm in."

"Good. O'Shea, keep us in the loop. Get this son of a bitch off my streets." Anders patted Brett's shoulder before he left the office.

Foster continued to glare at him. He jiggled the keys in his pocket, shifting from foot to foot. "I'm heading home, sir, to prepare for tonight. I'll talk to you tomorrow." He hurried to the car and flung himself inside. He gripped the steering wheel and rested his head against the frame. It was déjà vu all over again—cops versus evil. If only he knew they could win.

29

Brett tossed his keys on the kitchen table and threw open the refrigerator. He grabbed a beer, tossing the cap in the sink. Taking a large drink, he leaned against the counter with closed eyes.

"That bad, was it?"

When he opened his eyes, Michael was standing nearby. Dragos sat in a chair, watching him.

Brett nodded. "Foster knows the truth now. I think that having Anders in the room kept him from killing me."

Michael slapped his shoulder. "So did Anders approve of our plan to work nights?"

"We've got the green light. We need to finalize a plan. Let me change, and we can work on it."

Michael nudged Dragos with his hip. Dragos quickly shook his head.

Suspicion reared its head. "What's going on?"

"Tell him, Dragos."

Michael's innocent look didn't fool Brett. "Tell me what?"

Dragos shrugged. "It's not a secret. Candy called, and I told her that you and I were working a case. She wants to help and is going to stop by."

Brett drained his beer and set the bottle on the table. "Guys, this is a secret. No one but us is supposed to know what's going on. You can't be telling anyone what we're doing. You're going to call her back and tell her not to come over."

Confusion filled Dragos's eyes. "But what am I going to tell her?"

"Not my problem. She's a good PI, but we can't tell her what is really going on. I'm not putting her life at risk."

He sighed, noting Dragos's crestfallen face. He'd have to be the hardass.

"Just make something up. Tell her I put the kibosh on the idea. She can be mad at me. Anders and Foster would fire me if I allowed her to work with us."

Dragos and Michael sat in silence after Brett went to his room.

"Are you always so irritating?" Dragos muttered.

"Well, what did you expect? He needed to know before she got here."

"I was going to tell him." Dragos rose and flashed his teeth at Michael.

Michael stepped back, making his fingers into the sign of a cross. "Can't scare me."

Dragos smiled and leaned down, his face inches away from Michael's. "Believe me, if I were trying to scare you, you would be scared."

"Hmmph. You seem to be getting the hang of the vampire thing with those nasty-looking fangs."

"Speaking of which, I believe I need some nourishment. Care to join me?"

Michael shuddered. "Nope. I don't eat or drink, but what I wouldn't give for a cold brew."

Just as Dragos turned to leave, the doorbell rang.

Michael rubbed his hands together. "This is going to be fun." In a flash, Michael disappeared.

Dragos heard the water running in Brett's room. *Damn!* He'd have to answer the door.

He slowly opened the door, bracing himself to tell Candy that she had to go home.

His trepidation faded when he saw the tall blonde woman standing in the doorway. Wearing a fitted jacket and a short skirt, she had an air of confidence.

"Hello. May I help you?" Dragos's gaze took in her tall, slender frame.

The woman smiled at him. "Hello. Is Brett home?"

He opened the door and motioned her inside.

"I hope I'm not interrupting anything."

"No, he is in the shower. May I get you something to drink?"

She shook her head. Waves of blonde curls clung to her shoulders. She was quite stunning, with a lithe body, tiny waist, and full, sumptuous lips. If he hadn't already met Candy, he would definitely be interested.

She sat in the chair near the window and absently played with a bracelet on her arm, twisting it back and forth. Her gaze darted around the room, taking everything in. Dragos bit back a smile as he caught her look.

"I'm so sorry. I should have introduced myself. I'm Lisa Winslow. Brett and I are friends."

Dragos held out his hand. "I'm Dragos Eldridge. Also a friend of Brett's."

"Lisa! It is so good to see you again." Michael threw his arms around Lisa, nearly sweeping her off her feet.

She pressed a kiss on Michael's cheek. "Michael. How are you? I missed you."

Dragos was dumbfounded. How could Lisa see Michael? Or kiss him? It seemed that Lisa perceived Michael to be as solid as he or Brett. *Interesting.*

Michael took her hand and led her to the sofa. "Here, sit next to me. Tell me how you like the new job."

"It's going okay. It's hard adjusting to a new place. I really miss you and Brett."

As if on cue, Brett walked into the room. His thick, wet hair was combed back off his face. A dark green T-shirt was molded to his chest. Brett came to a sudden stop upon spotting Lisa in the room.

Lisa jerked to her feet. "Brett!" Her voice contained a breathless quality.

Brett took a step forward before abruptly stopping. "Lisa, what are you doing here?"

"For heaven's sake, give her a kiss," Michael ordered.

Lisa's face turned a deep shade of red. Brett stuttered like a schoolboy.

Dragos pitied Brett. His friend obviously didn't need an audience for his reunion with the young woman. "Excuse me. I believe I will take my leave," he stated. He stiffened when the doorbell rang a second time.

Michael's eyes twinkled. "I wonder who *that* is?"

Dragos growled, casting Michael an irritated look. He flung open the door. Candy pressed a quick kiss on his cheek as she breezed by him.

"Hi guys. I'm ready to work. What are we doing?" Candy tossed her coat and purse onto the sofa. Hands on her hips, she whipped around and gasped.

"Lisa, are you back for good?" She grabbed Lisa and hugged her.

Lisa grinned and returned the hug. "I'm not sure. Are you still doing the PI stuff?"

"Yes, I love it. Now that I get to actually work a case with Brett, I'm really excited."

All eyes in the room riveted on Brett.

"Uh, well, that might have changed," Brett mumbled.

Candy turned to look at Dragos. "But I thought I was going to help you guys?"

Dragos felt his frustration melt under Candy's confused gaze. "Brett and I were just discussing things before you arrived."

Lisa cast a strange look at Brett. Something was going on that Dragos didn't understand. It seemed odd that Candy wasn't looking at or acknowledging Michael. Michael remained perched on the edge of the sofa, a gleeful grin splayed across his face.

Lisa turned to Brett. "Well, that's kind of why I am here. I heard about the murders. I was worried about you. I wanted to make sure you're okay."

"Well, I'm fine," grumbled Brett, avoiding eye contact with Lisa. "Don't worry about us when you go back to Saint Louis."

Lisa stiffened as if Brett had slapped her.

Brett's lips tightened into a thin line. He abruptly turned on his heel and left the rest of them standing in the front room.

Lisa stormed after him. Michael zapped out of the room. Dragos glanced at Candy and shrugged.

"I don't know about you, but I'd like to know what is going on. Shall we join them?"

30

Brett leaned over the kitchen sink with his arms braced on the counter. What was Lisa doing here? They hadn't spoken in weeks. She hadn't even taken the time to return his calls. She'd left him for a damn job.

Every memory of them together came rushing back. How could he forget how beautiful she was? Eyes squeezed shut, he tried to block out the image of her standing before him.

A hand touched his shoulder. His body shuddered. *Lisa!* He had memorized her touch—her smell. He hadn't forgotten anything about her, although he'd tried. If he turned, he would take her in his arms and kiss her as he longed to do, never letting go again.

His throat tightened. "Why are you here, Lisa?" His voice was barely a whisper.

"I had to make sure you were okay. When I heard about the murders, I couldn't help but think about what happened last year."

Slowly, he turned. He fixed a hard gaze on her face. "Why didn't you call me back? Your mother told me that you took the job in Saint Louis. You didn't have the common courtesy to tell me or even send me a text message."

Lisa flinched.

"You know why. I couldn't. I had to see if I could start over … without you." Unshed tears filled her eyes.

He willed himself to ignore his emotions. He had erected a wall around his heart when she left. He wasn't ready to tear that wall down until he knew what she wanted.

Someone cleared his throat. Brett blinked to clear his burning eyes. Everyone stood in the doorway, staring at the two of them. No one seemed to know what to do. He gripped Lisa's arm.

"Damn, guys, give us some privacy."

After the room cleared, he sat down across the room. "So what did you discover? Was it easy to start over?"

Her head lowered. "No, I want …" Her voice faded away.

Silence filled the air. Brett slid from the chair to stand in front of Lisa. With a finger under her chin, he gently tilted her head upward. He studied her crestfallen face.

"What do you want, Lisa?" he whispered.

She wet her lips, watching him. "I want you. I want us back the way we were."

Shaken, he stepped back. His hands fell to his side. "It may be too late for that. You crushed me when you chose your job over me."

She grabbed his hand. "I thought I knew what I wanted, but I was wrong. Can't you give us a chance?"

He slipped out of her grip and turned his back. *What does she expect?* He'd gotten over the pain of her leaving. Could he trust her not to leave for another job? He'd be opening up his heart again. Was he willing to do that?

He couldn't make a decision now. It was too sudden. "I don't know what I want, Lisa. I don't want to go through a breakup again."

Lisa wiped the tears from her cheeks. "What does that mean?"

He sighed. "We'll take it a day at a time and see what happens."

She flashed a timid smile

"When do you have to go back to Missouri?"

"I don't. I quit my job yesterday."

His mind raced. *What does that mean? Is she serious about fixing the relationship?*

He nodded. "Okay then."

With a deep breath, Brett hollered to the people in the other room. "Hey, guys. C'mon; let's go." He turned to Lisa. "You might as well join us."

After everyone returned and was seated, Brett studied each of them. He hesitated when he got to Candy.

"Candy, you are one of my best friends and a great investigator, but I need to ask you to leave. You do not want to be involved in what we're doing."

Her blue eyes narrowed before she snapped, "Brett, you know me better than that. I'm here to help no matter what."

Brett shook his head. "Trust me; you need to stay out of this. It will be too dangerous."

Dragos draped an arm about her shoulder. "I can protect her."

"Can you? She doesn't even know who you are." Brett stared at Dragos, hoping he'd take the hint.

"Of course I know him. I can take orders and get things done. I'm the best investigator in Des Moines, and you know it." Candy rose with her hands on her hips.

Dragos pulled her back down in the chair and gripped her hand.

"I'm serious. I think you'd better leave. Your involvement will get you hurt—or worse, killed. I'll call you tomorrow."

Candy's face crumpled. Dragos leapt to his feet, looking as though he wanted to punch Brett. Michael jumped up and stood next to Brett.

"Everybody calm down. Lisa was able to help us with the case last year, so why can't Candy help?" Michael argued.

Candy stared at Michael. "Wait! How … who are you? How did he get in the house? Brett?"

No one spoke. It was as if they were afraid to speak.

Candy's head turned to each of them. "What's wrong?" Her body trembled.

"You can see Michael?" Brett asked.

"Of course I can," she snapped. "I'm not blind."

Michael flashed him a smug look and sat down. *Leave it to Michael to add fuel to the fire.* Brett wanted to throttle the ghost—not that it would do any good.

"Candy, meet my great-grandfather, Michael O'Shea."

Her laughter echoed around room but quickly faded.

"Quit teasing. Now, who is he?" An uncertain look flashed across her face.

Everyone nodded when she glanced at them.

Michael tipped his fedora and smiled. "Pleased to meet you, young lady. I've seen you before, but unfortunately, I couldn't talk to you."

Candy's body went limp. Dragos grabbed her before she hit the floor.

Dragos fanned Candy's pale face. "But you died years ago. Brett told me you died."

When her eyes rolled back in her head, Dragos pulled her onto his lap. He gently smoothed the red curls from her face.

Lisa jumped up and pulled a washcloth from a drawer. She wet it with cold water and placed it on her brow. "Brett, can you get Candy something to drink?"

Glad to have something to keep his mind off killing Michael, he nodded.

Dragos held the glass to her lips. He murmured something in her ear that brought some color back to her cheeks.

Michael tapped his fingers on the table. "So are we ready to discuss business?"

Brett punched Michael's shoulder, glad his ancestor had a corporeal body at that second.

"Ow! What was that for?"

"Shut up," Brett snapped. "You've caused enough trouble tonight."

"It's better to air all of our dirty laundry tonight if we're all going to work together," Michael argued.

Brett lowered his head to his chest. *Shit! Can it get any more confusing?* Lisa grabbed his hand beneath the table and squeezed. She knew him too well. Tension drained from him as he squeezed back.

Candy straightened on Dragos's lap. In a low voice, she attempted a smile. "It's okay. He's right. I want to understand."

Michael rubbed his hands together. "Now we're getting somewhere. Candy, I'm not trying to upset or scare you. We're up against a paranormal killer. Can you handle that?"

Candy trembled. "Paranormal? Like what? Ghosts? Vampires?"

Dragos jerked, nearly tossing Candy off his lap. Michael bit back a smile.

"Not ghosts. Although I'm probably the first ghost you've talked to."

Candy stared at him, as if wanting confirmation. He nodded.

"A ghost?"

Michael smiled. "Watch this."

Michael disappeared and then reappeared behind Dragos. He leaned over and tapped Candy on the shoulder.

"Damn it! How did you do that?"

Dragos growled. "Quit scaring her, or you will deal with me."

Michael flashed two fingers in the sign of a cross at Dragos. "I never asked why I can appear or disappear or turn into a solid mass. All I know is that it is very handy. It's one of the mysteries of life. Now, I think Dragos has something to tell you."

All heads swiveled to look at Dragos.

"You're a dead man," Dragos hissed.

"Michael! Stop causing trouble," Brett muttered.

Lisa and Candy continued to stare at Dragos.

Brett wanted to protect Candy. He wasn't sure if she could take another shock—especially one regarding a man she seemed to care for.

"For Candy's sake, I need to explain what we dealt with last year. If you remember, there were several murders last year."

Candy nodded. "People were afraid to go out at night. Everyone was petrified."

"That's right. Like you, I didn't believe ghosts were real. When Michael showed up, I was freaked out. Bottom line: with Michael's help, we were able to catch the killer."

"I remember seeing something on the news one night, but didn't the killer escape from jail?" Candy met Brett's gaze.

Brett rose from his chair and walked over to lean his back against the counter. "Yeah, he escaped, but we got him. He's never coming back."

"Really? I never did hear what happened on that case." Candy looked at the group

"It's because those of us working the case decided to keep it from the public."

Candy stiffened. "Why would you do that?"

"Because if the public knew the truth, there would be mass panic."

Candy jerked from Dragos's lap. Her hand clutched her throat. "What are you trying to tell me, Brett?"

"The killer was a man possessed by a demon—a demon that morphed into the scariest creature I've ever seen."

Michael shook his head. "Damn ugly thing. Almost killed Brett and Anders.

"Yeah, and Michael almost killed all of us by burning down the house."

Michael waved his hand. "Quit complaining. I saved your life, Lisa's, and Anders's."

Candy threw the wet rag at Michael's head. "Please quit interrupting Brett. So Chief Anders knows what happened?"

"He does. Very few people can see Michael. For whatever reason, you can see and talk to him now. Candy, no one wanted to believe the killer was really a demon. But when he morphed into a creature right in front of me, I had to believe it. It scared the hell out of me."

Lisa took hold of Candy's hand. "Brett is telling you the truth. I was there the night it almost killed all of us. Michael and his backup saved our asses."

Candy was as pale as Michael. Her lower lip trembled. "You guys are serious, aren't you?"

"Deadly serious," Brett added. "That is why I don't want you involved. Your life would be in danger."

Candy studied each of them. "And so would yours. I won't change my mind."

"My darling, why don't we talk about it later?" Dragos draped an arm around Candy.

Candy laid her palm against Dragos's cheek. "Sweetie, you're not going to change my mind. I'm doing it."

Dragos leaned against her shoulder. In a muffled voice, he rasped, "I need to tell you one more thing. If you never want to see me again, I understand."

Dragos raised a finger and gently turned Candy's head. His dark eyes searched her face. "I'm a vampire," he whispered.

Lisa screamed and ran to Brett's side. Candy scrambled off Dragos's lap, nearly falling to the floor. She straightened and gaped at him. Her mouth opened and closed, but no words came out.

"With that settled, let's start planning." Michael pulled out a chair, ignoring the terrified women.

Brett pulled Lisa's arms from around his neck. "Stop! Dragos is not going to hurt you."

Dragos rose and placed his hand over his heart. "I did not choose to become this … this creature of the night. I am appalled that I have to drink blood to survive. I would give anything to go back to the night that changed my life."

His eyes shimmered with moisture. He looked as if he'd lost his last friend. When Dragos turned to leave the room, Candy grabbed his hand.

"Wait. I'm sorry. But a vampire? It will take some time to soak in."

Hope flared in Dragos's eyes. He brought Candy's hand to his lips and pressed a kiss to it. "You don't hate me?"

Candy pulled his head down and kissed him deeply. "Are you kidding? But I won't lie to you; it's hard to believe that ghosts and now vampires exist." She turned to face Brett.

"So Anders knows that Dragos is a vampire?"

He nodded. "Yeah. Foster too."

Candy glanced at Dragos. "What about food? Do you need … need blood?"

"Yes."

She met Dragos's heated gaze. "Human blood?"

He shook his head. "Not directly from people."

On seeing Candy's puzzled look, Dragos added, "I have bags of blood that I took—"

"Whoa there!" Brett interrupted. "No one needs to know. It's sufficient to know that Dragos has a supply."

"Yes," Dragos solemnly swore. "I would never drink blood from a human person."

Brett placed his hands on the table. "Well, now that that's settled, let's get—"

Candy cleared her throat and looked at Lisa. "Sorry to bring this up, but Lisa's a reporter. Is that going to be a problem?"

Lisa smiled. "I kept the last case out of the papers and off the TV. I can keep my mouth shut. After all, what happens in Des Moines stays in Des Moines."

Everyone started laughing except Dragos and Michael, who looked at each other and shrugged.

Brett opened the fridge and handed out beers and sodas to everyone. "Okay, now that the drama is over, let's finalize a plan. We start tonight."

31

Randall spotted O'Shea leaving the station with a man he didn't recognize. The man with O'Shea looked like ex-military. The black T-shirt clung to his abs. His long, dark hair swung as he walked. With hair like that, the guy couldn't be law enforcement.

By the scowls on their faces, Randall could tell the two men were having a serious discussion—probably about the whores. With a body count of three, everyone was edgy. He didn't feel sorry for the murdered women. He believed the old adage "You reap what you sow." It wasn't his fault that they were dying.

He got behind the wheel, staring at O'Shea's back. *O'Shea thinks he's so damn smart.* Someone someday would give him a reality check, and he wanted to be there to see it. With his uncle being the mayor, he knew Anders was in the hot seat. As far as he was concerned, he'd like to see both Anders and O'Shea get the boot.

He spit a toothpick out the open window as the two men got into a car and drove away. He was tempted to follow them, but his shift was over. Anders had him assigned to traffic, which he hated. Hauling out the damn radar equipment was a pain in the ass, and lucky him—he got to do it each day.

The only good thing was that he worked days. His nights were open.

He and Victor had visited a couple of whorehouses the previous weekend. He had thought he liked rough sex, but Victor was *really* rough—enough to give him pause. Randall shook his head on remembering the kinky shit the man did to one of the whores. Victor carried a bag filled with all kinds of whips, nipple clamps, and other torture devices.

In a way, he was in awe of Victor. The man was relentless when it came to rough sex and getting pleasure. He was an amateur compared to Victor.

Almost by coincidence, his phone rang.

"Hey Victor, what's up?"

"Good evening, Detective. I'm going to have a little soiree this evening. I have something I think you will like."

Randall gripped the phone tighter. "Soiree? Count me in. What time?"

"Oh, after nine will work."

"Do you need me to bring anything? Liquor?"

Victor laughed. "Thank you, but no. Just bring your usual appetite."

He rubbed himself. "A blonde?"

"Detective, you will just have to see for yourself."

"Victor, I owe you. See you later."

As he sped out of the parking lot, excitement coursed through him.

Right on time, Randall pulled onto Red Sunset Drive. The winding road led up to Victor's house. Rolling black clouds obscured the half moon. Tree branches waved back and forth as if whipped by an angry wind.

He shivered as he walked toward the front door. Out the corner of his eye, he spotted several cars lining the driveway.

Before he could ring the bell, the door eased open. Victor framed the door, tuxedo and all.

"Detective Randall. Prompt as usual. Come in and I will introduce you."

Randall winced, taking in his own faded blue jeans and worn leather shoes. *Why didn't Victor tell me it was a formal event?* "Maybe I should go home and change into something more formal?"

Victor clapped an arm over his shoulder, drawing him close. "You're fine. Who needs clothes for the type of entertainment we enjoy, right?

He nodded. *Yeah, I don't plan on staying dressed long.*

Victor led him to a large entertainment area. A low fire in the fireplace cast a golden hue across the room. Numerous candles lit the area. It seemed odd to him that they didn't just turn on the lamps about the room.

Five men rose in tandem from the sofa. Randall inwardly groaned on seeing they were also dressed in tuxes. The first thing he noticed was that the men were similar in appearance. They were all at least six foot three, with dark hair, stormy eyes, and chiseled facial features. Each one of them looked like a fashion model. He wouldn't have a chance of getting a decent-looking woman tonight with them here.

He sucked in his stomach and straightened his back.

"This is Detective Randall, my honored guest. Anything he wants is to be his."

One by one, the men nodded in strangely robotic fashion.

Motioning to a chair, Victor handed Randall a drink. "Sit. Our entertainment shall arrive shortly."

Randall took the glass before sitting.

"Excuse me for a moment. There is a matter I need to take care of. If you need anything, one of my men will help you."

Slowly sipping his drink, he tried to ignore the five pair of eyes watching him. He felt like a mouse surrounded by five hungry cats. After taking a breath, he forced himself to lean back and pretend to enjoy the drink.

Logs crackled and popped in the fireplace. Eerie shadows danced on the walls. He jerked, feeling the hairs on the back of his neck stand on end.

The man nearest to him snorted. "Nervous, Detective?"

"No. I thought I saw something." He forced a smile. "Who are you guys, anyway? Models? Security?"

The man's gaze hardened. "Our names and what we do are unimportant."

Jeez! Talk about being sensitive. The guy looked agitated, so Randall wisely decided against any small talk.

Everyone's attention jerked toward the front door when the doorbell rang. Randall saw Victor walk toward the door.

Laughter and high-pitched giggles echoed down the hallway. Randall set his drink aside as Victor reentered the room with several women. The scantily clothed ladies wore tall, spiked heels and heavy doses of makeup. Randall counted seven women—one for each of them. He smiled.

One of Victor's men pulled a tall, busty brunette toward him.

Victor's eyes narrowed. "No! Our guest has first choice."

The man dropped the woman's arm and stepped back into the shadows.

"He can have her," Randall said. "I actually prefer the blonde."

All eyes turned toward a young blonde hiding behind one of the women. She looked very young. Her blue eyes rose to meet Randall's. She bit her trembling lip. It looked as if it were her first time.

Victor looked questioningly at him. "She doesn't appear to be much of a challenge. Would you prefer another?"

Randall swung toward Victor. *Can he read my mind?* A tremor shook his body. He thought about leaving but quickly quashed that idea when he looked at the blonde girl. For some reason, Randall felt a twinge of sympathy for her. "No, I'll break her in."

Each man wrapped an arm about a woman and led her down the hallway.

"First door on the right is open," Victor offered.

"That will work for me," said Randall. "C'mon, honey; let's go make some magic."

Randall opened the door and shoved the young woman ahead of him. A large bed monopolized the room. Ropes were attached to the headboard. A strap and whip lay on the bed. He smiled. Victor knew his preferences.

The woman stood woodenly in the corner. Her wide eyes focused on the bed.

Randall knew he'd come to regret picking her. He must be getting soft in his old age.

"Hey, what's your name?"

"Abby," she whispered.

"Have you done this before?"

She nodded. *Good.* At least he didn't have to break in a virgin.

"Abby, take off your clothes and get in bed."

Her eyes widened. A surge of excitement coursed through him. She was frightened—just how he liked it.

"Hurry up," he ordered as he whipped off his belt. He rubbed himself as he hardened.

She stood watching him.

"If you're good, I'll let you have some of this."

She turned her back to him and slipped out of her dress before hopping into the bed and pulling up the sheet. Her lean athletic build wasn't his preference. Her breasts were small and perky. Her long hair was pulled back in a ponytail. She looked like a cheerleader instead of a whore.

He walked to the edge of the bed and ripped the hair tie

from her hair. *That's better.* He picked up a strap, smacking it against his palm.

"Lie on your stomach and spread your arms and legs."

She looked up at him. Tears filled her eyes. When she was in position, he struck her bare bottom with the strap. Her body jerked upward. A red welt marred her skin. She muffled a scream into the mattress.

Randall swung the strap three additional times. By the time her bottom was red and swollen, moisture dotted his face. His breath came in short pants. Suddenly he dropped his arm to the side. Her boyish body had negatively impacted his desire. Even his dick lost interest.

He cursed under his breath as he shook her shoulder. "Hey, get dressed."

She rolled over, wiping the tears from her face. "What? Don't you want to do it?"

"How old are you?"

"Eighteen."

"I bet. Get dressed before I change my mind."

He turned as she dressed. He was turning maudlin in his old age.

She gasped as a scream echoed from down the hall. *Someone is having fun,* he thought. It was just his luck that the only blonde was a dud.

"Abby, I suggest you get out of here. Don't come back. Got it?"

She nodded. "Thank you for not … you know."

He grunted. "I suggest you get some new friends. Next time you might not be so lucky."

He walked her to the door and watched as she took off running down the street. After closing the door, he walked back to the room where he had left his drink. He quickly drained it, grabbed a bottle from the bar, and poured a liberal shot of vodka.

More screams and moans came from down the hallway. A

loud thump drew his attention. *Maybe I should go check? No, it's none of my business.* He sunk down into the sofa, nursing his drink. He needed to go home. He already regretted his decision to let Abby leave. It was late, and he wasn't getting lucky. Besides, he was tired. How Victor kept these late hours he didn't know. Maybe he was getting old. Decision made, he rose and set the glass on the bar. He didn't want to go wandering down the hall, peeking in rooms, looking for Victor. He'd call him tomorrow.

He was walking past the hall toward the foyer when a sound startled him. He turned and staggered backward.

A brunette was leaning against the wall, naked and holding her neck. Blood trickled down the valley between her breasts. She spotted him and tried walking toward him but stumbled to the floor.

What the hell is going on? He ran forward, reaching down to help her to her feet. Her head lolled to the side.

"Hey, wake up." The hand on her neck fell forward when he shook her body. The puncture wound oozed blood.

Something about the wound looked familiar. He slipped to his knees to closer examine her body. His heart pounded. *No, it can't be.* His body was numb. It looked similar to the wounds on the murdered women. He staggered to his feet and fell against the wall. His chest heaved as he gasped for air.

He turned to the door. He had to leave now. The car keys slipped from his hand and fell to the floor. His hands trembled. He glanced down the hall. He expected Victor or one of his goons to come out any second. He had to get out of here. Somewhere to think.

Gasping for breath, he ran toward the front door and pulled it open. His feet slid on the frozen ground, and he nearly fell on the sidewalk. Once inside his car, he struggled to take a breath.

"C'mon, c'mon," he muttered, attempting to put the key in the ignition. He fumbled with the keys, and they dropped to the car floor. Nothing was going right. His gaze darted toward the house. No one had noticed he was gone yet; he still had a chance. He bent over, frantically searching for the keys. He knew he couldn't turn on the dome light, as it would draw attention to him. Just as he was about to give up, his hand curled around the keys.

He jerked upright and stuck in the key. One last gaze toward the house was a mistake. His heart stopped. Victor and all five of the men stood directly in front of the car. Six pairs of glaring red eyes zeroed in on him.

Victor calmly walked to the car door and opened it. He held out an arm, motioning for him to exit the vehicle.

"Going somewhere, Detective Randall?"

32

It was nearly dark. This late in the season, it was completely dark by 6:30 p.m. Brett strapped on an ankle holster, thinking, *One can never have enough guns.* This was their first night working as a team. The women weren't too happy about being excluded, but no way was he dragging them along. Chief Anders would suspend him in a flash if he did so.

A crisp November wind tore through his jacket as he unlocked the car. He honked the horn.

Where is everyone? We need to get going.

The front door opened. Dragos stood in the doorway, Candy's arms wrapped around his neck. The two were locked in a kiss that went on forever.

He leaned out the car window. "Do you want to get a room or go to work?"

Dragos flipped him off.

Whoa! Where did he pick that up from?

Brett jerked as Michael's laughter sounded in his ear.

Brett frowned at Michael. "Grow up, will ya?"

Arms folded across his chest, Michael snorted. "Tried it. Didn't like it. Besides, it's much more fun to scare you."

Brett stared at Dragos when he hopped into the front seat. "What's wrong with you? I was just kissing Candy good-bye." Dragos swung around toward the backseat. "Michael. I didn't know that you had arrived."

"He arrived, all right. If you two are finally ready, can we leave now?" Brett complained.

Brett pulled onto the street and drove toward the downtown area. They would check out the places north of the loop first. As they drove west on Grand Avenue, they found themselves surrounded by vehicles full of teenagers. Windows were rolled down, and kids hollered back and forth at each other. Friday night was always a good party night. When he was a teenager, he scooped the loop just like these kids.

Brett slowed to a stop at a light that changed from green to yellow. Moments later, a green Mustang roared through the now red light.

"Shit!" Brett exclaimed.

Michael leaned forward, sticking his head between him and Dragos. "Hey! I recognize that car." He punched Brett's shoulder. "Well, what are we waiting for?"

Brett sighed. He didn't want to deal with that idiot again. Since it was still early, there wouldn't be much going on at the whorehouses.

"I'm on it," he growled.

Sticking the lights on the dash, he tore down the street and came up behind the Mustang. He'd had several run-ins with this guy the year before. The young man had crashed the car the last time they met. Daddy must have fixed it up or gotten him a new one.

After he tailed the car for two blocks, it finally pulled off in an empty parking lot.

Brett walked up to the parked car. He tapped on the window, indicating for the driver to open it.

The young driver's smile faded as he looked up and saw Brett smiling.

"Officer O'Shea?"

"In the flesh, though it's now Detective O'Shea."

The driver glanced back at Brett's car. "I didn't think detectives could pull people over."

He chuckled, enjoying the obvious discomfort of the young driver. "Well, you learned something new today. You whizzed through the red light, so I decided that you and I needed to catch up and visit."

The young man groaned. "Sir, it was yellow."

Brett shook his head. "No. I stopped on the yellow light. You decided to run a red light."

Someone tapped his shoulder. Brett looked up and saw Michael standing next to him.

"Give him a ticket."

Brett caught himself before he began arguing with Michael. Instead he leaned down and looked in the car.

"Where are you going? Party?"

The driver's long blonde hair fell into his face. He hurriedly pushed it back with one hand. "No … no, I'm not."

Brett bit back a smile. *I shouldn't enjoy tormenting the poor kid.*

"Well then, where you headed?"

"Why? I didn't know you could ask that."

"License and proof of insurance, please." He held out his hand.

The driver fumbled in the glove compartment and finally handed him the insurance paper and his license.

Brett took the license back to the car to run the plates.

Dragos yawned, covering his mouth. "Excuse me. Is this part of your official duties? I'm not sure why you pulled him to a stop. Surely he realizes his mistake. Let the poor man go."

Michael popped into the backseat. "No, don't let him go! The kid needs a ticket. He ran a red light—could have killed someone."

"Would you two quit your bickering? I'm trying to concentrate."

The driver was clean. No outstanding warrants. No recent tickets.

He walked back to the young man.

"Consider this your lucky day. I see that you've avoided trouble for the past year, so you can go."

The driver collapsed back in his seat. "Whew! Thank you. My dad said that if I get one more ticket, he's taking the car."

Brett rested his hand on the top of the car and bent over. "I don't want to see you in the loop again. Got it?"

"Ever?" Looking at Brett's face, the young man suddenly nodded. "No problem, sir."

"Keep your head out of your ass and pay attention to your driving. Now get out of here."

The driver gave a half wave and inched out of the lot.

"You were too easy on the lad," Michael growled.

Brett got back in the car and flipped on the heater, ignoring Michael.

"Hey, sonny! Are you listening?"

"Yeah, what choice do I have?" he bit out.

Dragos turned to face him, a big smile on his face. "You two are an odd pair. I do admit enjoying your repertoire of insults to one another."

"Careful, bloodsucker. I've seen several Dracula movies on TV. I know how to stake you." Michael snorted and leaned back, glaring at both men in the front seat.

"Enough! We don't have time for this shit." Brett jerked the car into gear and continued their westward drive.

They pulled up in front of a large two-story house, where Brett shut off the car and got out. As he knocked on the front door, Dragos rushed to join him and leaned in close. "Who lives here?"

"Charlene Moore. She reported the first body."

The porch light popped on just before door opened. Charlene's eyes widened when she saw the two men on her porch.

"Detective O'Shea, what's going on?" She ran short, stubby fingers through her tousled hair. The smell of cigarette smoke drifted from the house.

"May we come in for a minute? I won't keep you long."

She waved them in. "Honey, you can keep me as long as you like," she murmured.

Brett felt his cheeks heat up. Dragos's husky laughter filled the hallway.

Once they were seated on the tired-looking sofa, Brett whipped out a pen and small pad of paper.

"You probably heard that there have been two more murdered women found. Both were found not far from here."

She grabbed another smoke and lit it up. "Yeah, I heard the news. You cops have anyone you're investigating?"

Brett nodded. "We think we have a good lead. I wanted to see if you remembered anything new since we last talked. Maybe you've seen someone hanging around the neighborhood that doesn't live here?"

She shook her head. "Nope. It's been quiet as far as I can tell. I lock up after dark—too scared to go outside anymore. My social worker wants me to go to counseling. Said I'm paranoid—whatever that means."

Brett rose and dusted cigarette ashes off his pants. "Well, I'm sorry if we bothered you, Charlene. Be careful. Call me if you see or hear anything."

With a coy smile, she winked at Dragos. "Can I call him too?"

"Sure. In fact, I'll make sure Dragos stops by to see you from time to time."

Her raspy laughter made them smile.

"Seriously, you boys come back anytime. It does my heart good to see such good-looking men. Makes me remember my younger days"

Brett hurried out the door, turning to wave at their new admirer. "Bye, Charlene."

What would Charlene have done if we had taken her up on her offer? Chuckling to himself, he joined Michael and Dragos in the car.

"That was interesting," Dragos growled. "Do not volunteer me to visit that woman. She makes me uneasy."

"Jeez, chill out. I was just joking."

"Hmm. The killer would most likely be attacked if he dared enter her home. That woman is on the prowl."

Michael's head lifted as he shoved the fedora to the crown of his head. "Is she what people call a cougar?"

Brett shuddered. "Yeah, that's Charlene."

Michael snorted. "What's wrong with you two? You've seen ghosts and vampires; Brett even fought a demon. You're not really scared of an older woman, are you?"

Dragos winked. "I thought she was going to cop a feel. That's why I got out of there before Brett."

"Where did you hear that?" Brett asked. "Never mind; I don't want to know. Let's grab a bite before we visit Darlene's place."

Since the other two men didn't eat food, he went through a drive-thru. As he finished his dinner, Dragos pulled out a bag of blood and sank his teeth into it, quickly emptying the contents.

Michael watched Dragos with avid curiosity. "Whoa! That is really disturbing."

Dragos's tongue licked away a drop of blood on his lower lip. He glowered back at Michael. "Perhaps I should sample some blood from your neck."

Michael shrugged. "Can't. I'm already dead."

Dragos turned toward Brett and groaned. "I want

to strangle him. How do you put up with having such a cantankerous ghost around?"

"I'm cursed with his existence."

"Hey! I've got feelings." Crossing his arms across his chest, Michael glared at them.

Brett choked back a chuckle. The guy didn't need to know that they loved harassing him.

After several hours of driving in areas frequented by prostitutes, Brett was getting tired. They were on the western edge of the city and traffic was still heavy.

Dragos stretched and glanced at the clock on the dash. It was nearly three in the morning. "How long are we going to be out here tonight?"

Brett began to question whether it was a good idea to have Dragos and Michael ride along with him. "I don't know. Why?"

Dragos stretched. "Just wondered. This driving around is growing tedious."

Michael suddenly grabbed his shoulder, pointing ahead. "Look!"

A young woman limped down the sidewalk. She clutched her side, constantly looking over her shoulder. Who was she looking for? Or was she being chased? Long hair streamed down her back as she stumbled toward them.

Brett leaned against the steering wheel, trying to see clearly. His hands gripped the wheel as he studied the woman. Where were her shoes—her coat? She had to be freezing in that skimpy little dress. Without stopping at the crosswalk, she nearly fell when she stepped off the curb. Passing cars honked and flashed their lights. A truck skidded to a halt a few feet from the woman. She was going to get herself killed.

Brett jumped out of the car and ran toward the woman. He reached her side as she tumbled to the ground. Her eyes filled with fear when he touched her arm.

"Leave me alone."

Tears ran down her flushed cheeks. *What the hell happened to her?* Her body shook from either cold or fear—he couldn't tell which.

"Miss, it's okay. I'm a police officer Let me help you."

She gave a slight nod of her head, and he scooped her up into his arms. He gently leaned her against the car so he could open the back car door. Her body stiffened when she glanced into the car. Without warning, she reached up and shoved his chest. He struggled to keep his balance.

"No. Let me go!"

He tightened his grip, careful not to bruise her thin arm. "What was that for?"

"I want to go home. Let me go," she whimpered.

Her gaze darted to Dragos and then back to him.

"Are you scared of the man in the car?"

Her lips thinned as she shook her head.

He wasn't fooled. Clearly she was terrified.

"That's Dragos. He is working with the police"

She struggled to escape.

"I want to go home. I can walk from here. Just let me go."

Michael shifted from the car to Brett's side. "She's scared."

"I know."

She peered up at him. "Know what?"

"Nothing. Please, miss, get in the car. You're freezing. I'll take you home or wherever you want."

Minutes later, she slid into the backseat. Brett whipped off his jacket and wrapped it around her slim shoulders. Crouched down next to the car, he gently patted her shoulder. "Better?"

She nodded. He needed to get her to the emergency

room to have her checked out. The bottoms of her feet were bloodied. Who knew how far she had walked.

He took out his badge and held it up for her to see.

"Can you tell me your name?"

A small whimper escaped her.

"Do you need to go to the hospital?"

She violently shook her head. *Hell!* This wasn't going well.

Dragos turned back toward them. He draped his arm over the seat, nearly touching her leg. With fear in her eyes, she slid to the opposite corner of the backseat. Dragos looked at Brett and shrugged.

"Don't be afraid of Dragos. He won't hurt you."

Dragos smiled at the woman. With a hand placed over his heart, he pledged, "You have my word as a gentleman that no harm will befall you while you're with us."

Her brows drew together. "What?"

Brett chuckled. "See what I mean? He's a big teddy bear."

She took a deep breath and pulled the edges of his jacket tighter around her body.

"I'm sorry. I'm Abby Hay … Hayes. I want to go home."

Brett rose to his feet and closed the car door. Michael had reappeared in the backseat.

"Abby, are you sure you don't want me to take you to the hospital? They can clean up those cuts on your feet and make sure you're okay."

"No, I need to get home. My parents will be worried sick. I should have never gone to that stupid party."

He quickly got in the car and started toward the police station. He studied the distraught woman in the rearview mirror.

"I didn't do anything wrong," she mumbled. "I just want to go home."

"Hey, don't worry about it," Brett encouraged. "No one thinks you did anything. You can trust us. We're here to help you."

"I trust you. I'm not sure about him." She pointed at Dragos.

Brett glanced at Dragos, who rolled his eyes.

Dragos turned slightly in the seat. "No worries, young lady. You are obviously distraught."

"It's just that ..."

Brett shut off the car, parking along the curb. He slid in his seat so he could see her. "Just what?"

Her eyes had a haunted look.

"It's just that he looks like the men at the party."

Dragos hissed. Brett reached over and nudged Dragos's shoulder. He didn't want to frighten the girl.

A heavy sigh escaped from her downturned mouth.

"The party?"

Silence.

He tried again. "Did they hurt you?"

They sat in silence for several minutes. He was tempted to repeat his question but instinctively knew to be patient.

She whispered, "I went to a party tonight with some friends. They're older than me." She stared at Dragos. "When we arrived at the party, there were six men that looked a lot like you. Tall with long, dark hair. Foreign. You know."

"Did they hurt you?" Dragos asked. "Bite you?"

"Bite? No, but I think I would have been hurt if I had stayed. The guy that was with me was different than the other men. He looked different than the rest of them. He let me leave. I don't know why."

Brett glanced at Dragos. *Who was the other guy?* He suspected that the men she described were vampires. But six of them? It was worse than he thought. *Was Victor one of them?*

"Can you describe the guy that let you go?"

She shrugged. "Uh, I don't know. He was average. Short hair like yours but a little lighter color. He was heavier and wore jeans with some kind of sweater."

Her description could fit thousands of guys.

"Why did he tell you to leave? Was there something wrong?"

"I'm not sure why he let me go. We heard several of the other women scream. Horrible screams. Then it was like he got spooked or something."

"Do you know where you were at?"

"Not really. A driver took us to the house. It was on a dead-end road, but the house was huge, like a mansion."

Michael grumbled, "Well that narrows it down. Not!"

He tried again. "Do you know what street you were on? Is it far from here?"

"I'm not sure. I've been walking for a long time." She straightened, her face brightening. "The street has some long name like … like Summerset Road … Summerset Lane?"

"There's a Summerset south of town. A winery also. Does that sound like the place they took you to?

Tears welled up in her eyes. Her body trembled. He didn't want to push her, yet he wanted to make sure the other women weren't injured. She was giving him nothing—not one solid lead.

"Could you identify the guy you were with if you saw him again?"

"I think so. He seemed really mean at first. He beat me. I don't know what made him stop."

Brett cringed, wondering how men could hit women. He understood that some liked it rough like that, but he could never hit a woman for any reason.

"Do you want to press charges?"

Her cheeks flushed. "No, I want to forget tonight ever happened. I shouldn't have gone with the girls. I'll never, ever do that again. It was horrible."

"Sounds like you got lucky. We'll be at the station in about ten minutes. One of the officers will take you home. I want to keep your contact information. I'll give you my card. Please call me if you think of anything else."

"Thanks. I just want to go home."

The remainder of the drive to the station was quiet. Brett was caught up in his own thoughts. They were never going to solve the murders at the rate they were going.

They pulled into the police parking lot, where a squad car was waiting for them. Brett got out and opened the door for the young woman. He slipped a card into her hand.

"Call me if you change your mind. I'd like to find that guy you were with."

She flashed a timid smile and slid out of his jacket. The waiting officer opened the back squad car door for her. Before the officer could shut the door, she reached out and pushed the door back open.

"Detective! When we walked into the house, I heard someone say the name Victor. I didn't hear any other names mentioned. I hope that helps."

33

Brett glanced back at Dragos. Dragos's eyes narrowed, turning a dangerous shade of red at the mention of Victor's name.

Brett turned back to Abby. "Victor's a very dangerous man. Stay away from him for your own safety."

She nodded and waved as the other squad car drove away.

Brett hurried back to the car and hopped behind the wheel.

"I suspected that Victor was involved," Dragos raged. "No wonder the girl was terrified when she first saw me."

"Calm down," Michael urged. "We'll find him."

"We need to put our heads together and figure out where the party was held. Summerset Road isn't much of a lead."

Michael scratched the side of his head. "Didn't she say it was some fancy house? Where are there a bunch of fancy houses?"

"South of Grand, I suppose. We're not too far from there." Brett leaned over and rested his forehead against the steering wheel. Nothing was ever easy. "It's late. We can't do this by ourselves. I need to call Foster and give him an update. Patrol can start checking the surrounding area until we can re- group. If they don't turn up anything by morning, we'll start a search for Victor's house." He stared at Dragos. "And what will you be doing?"

"Plotting how I will kill Victor. My physical abilities are limited in the daytime."

Michael laughed. "Didn't I tell you that you need one of those daylight rings like they use on *The Vampire Diaries*."

Sensing the deterioration of the evening, Brett straightened and started the car. "That's it. We're done. Dragos, are you coming home with me or going to Candy's?"

"Why would I go home with you? No offense."

Brett sighed. "None taken. I'll drop you off at her place. Have her bring you over as soon as it's dusk tomorrow. Hopefully we can have a better plan."

Brett tugged the pillow tighter around his head. A noise of dishes rattling in the kitchen made him wish he could go back to sleep. *Who the hell is in my house?* He was too tired to find out. He considered that maybe if he ignored them, they'd leave.

When he woke later, the smell of coffee filled the house. His stomach rumbled. Bright sunlight filtered through the curtains. *Midafternoon already?* He'd slept the day away. He forced himself to sit up. Shuffling into the bathroom, he did his thing and grabbed a toothbrush. He splashed some water in his eyes. *Nope, that didn't help.* He was still tired.

Brett pulled a gray T-shirt over his head as he walked toward the kitchen. He paused in the doorway and called Foster.

"It's O'Shea. Any word on the search for Victor?"

"No. I just reviewed the report. We re-assigned most of the shift to cover all the streets in the area where the woman was found. They didn't find anything. It seems even the normal criminals took the night off." Foster swore aloud. "Got to go. Anders is calling a meeting. I'll check in with you later."

Brett clenched his phone. His eyes closed. He hadn't expected them to find Victor. It would have been too much to expect. He took a deep breath and entered the kitchen.

With an apron wrapped around her waist, Lisa flipped a pancake. Bacon simmered on the stove. Michael sat at the kitchen table, laughing and joking with Lisa.

Crap. He wasn't ready to for this level of a relationship with Lisa—not yet anyway.

"Hi. Cooking dinner?"

Lisa dropped the spatula on the stove with a small screech. "You scared me to death. Next time make a little more noise, will you? Sit down. It's about ready."

Brett poured himself a cup of coffee and joined Michael at the table. Inhaling the steaming brew, he leaned back and sighed. Minutes later, Lisa set a plate in front of him. He dug into the hot food, ignoring the baleful gaze that Michael cast toward it.

"Sure looks good," Michael moaned.

Biting into a strip of bacon, he grinned. "Yep."

Michael glared back at him. "You could at least feel sorry for me. I don't get to eat like you."

"Sorry," he muttered as he stuffed more bacon into his mouth.

"Well, while you were sawing logs, Lisa and I searched on the Internet. You know, it's amazing what you can find on a computer. We used something called GPC."

Brett covered his mouth to muffle his laughter. "Was it GPS?"

Casting a heated glance in his direction, Michael went on. "Anyway, we looked at pictures of houses in some of the ritzy neighborhoods we talked about last night. Nothing seemed to fit Abby's description of the house."

"Thanks for doing that. I wish Dragos would hurry up and get here so we can hit the streets. My first thought is to check out the Grand area. It's only a few miles away from where we picked up Abby. There are a lot of winding dead-end roads there. Who knows; maybe we'll find the house."

Lisa cleared the table, listening to their conversation. Suddenly the dishwasher door slammed closed.

"What?" Brett glanced over his shoulder.

Lisa's chin jerked upward. "Nothing. You just go ahead and plan how you're going to solve the case."

He stared at her backside as she stormed from the room. "What the hell is wrong with her?"

Michael winked. "Don't ask me. She's your girlfriend, isn't she?"

Was she? He wasn't sure.

Voices and laughter came from the front room. Dragos and Candy had arrived. *About time.*

Brett rose to his feet and cleared his throat. "Hey guys. Are we about ready?"

Dragos's dark hair gleamed in the dim light. Once again, he was dressed all in black. Candy was nestled within his arms; his chin rested on the top of her head.

Lisa sat in his recliner, her arms folded across her chest, glaring at him. Obviously she was pissed off at him, but now wasn't the time to deal with it.

"If you guys are ready to go, I'll go change."

Michael appeared at Lisa's side and patted her shoulder.

Dragos dropped his arms, pressing a kiss to Candy's forehead. "Fine, hurry up," Dragos grumbled.

Candy grabbed Dragos's hand. "Be careful. I want you back in one piece."

"Don't worry. Everything will be fine," Dragos murmured, meeting Brett's gaze from across the room. Dragos's eyes darkened.

Brett turned down the hall and quickly dressed, grabbing

his Glock along with extra ammunition and weapons. As he loaded his bag, he heard his cell phone ring. He'd left it in the kitchen.

Brett called out, "Hey, someone check my phone and see who it is."

When he returned to the front room, Dragos was holding his phone with a strange look on his face. Everyone turned toward him.

"Who was on the phone?"

Dragos shook his head. His eyes burned like molten lava.

A shiver coursed through Brett.

"Chief Anders called. It's bad, Brett."

What could have happened? His pulse hammered in his head. "What's wrong?"

Dragos trembled. His fingers curled into fists. "I'm going to destroy him! I swear to God!"

Brett strode over and grabbed the front of Dragos's sweater. "You have one second to tell me what the fuck is going on!"

"I'll tell you what's going on," Dragos roared. "Someone found the bodies of six women."

34

Dragos's chest ached from pent-up fury. Anders hadn't known the cause of death when he called. The bodies were being sent to the coroner. In his heart, Dragos knew the cause. They had been drained of blood—by vampires.

Candy cupped his cheek. He leaned into her, breathing her fresh scent. A calmness soothed him.

"Are you okay?" she whispered.

He was unable to speak. His throat choked with emotion. He nodded, angrily wiping his eyes. Victor had ruined his life. Now the bastard continued to ruin lives of people in this century. This madness had to stop. He had an obligation to stop Victor. He wasn't sure how he would do so, but he would not relent until the vampire was no more.

"Anders said we're supposed to report as soon as possible."

"Let's get going then," Brett tersely announced. Lisa rose to embrace him in a hug.

"What can I do to help?" she asked.

With a grim look on Brett's face, he ordered, "Stay here. Lock the doors and don't open them for anyone."

Dragos watched Brett storm out the door. Lisa glared after Brett with her hands on her hips. Dragos felt thankful she was not his woman. Candy was warmhearted and soothing to his soul—not argumentative like Lisa.

"Go. You look after Brett. I'll look after Lisa," Candy whispered.

Dragos pulled her forward until she pressed against his body. He angled his mouth and deepened the kiss. Her fingers tangled his hair, pulling him closer. His breathing hitched higher. He was lost.

Someone cleared their throat. Reluctantly, Dragos broke away. A few seconds more and he would have been unable to leave.

"Do as Brett says. Stay here. I'll be back as soon as I can. Farewell, my sweet."

Without looking back, he marched out the door to where Brett waited.

A grin spread across Lisa's face. "My sweet?" Lisa teased.

A blush graced Candy's face.

"Yeah, you know—Candy. Sweet. It's my special nickname."

"Aw. That's so cute. Brett doesn't have a nickname for me." Her smile faded. "Right now he probably thinks I'm being a bitch, which I am. Grrr! Men are so frustrating."

"What did he do wrong?"

"Nothing, really. He's ignoring me and won't let me go out on the investigation."

Candy chuckled. "What's wrong with that? He cares about you."

"I hope he still cares. I feel like I'm being shut out. If I was good enough to help with the last big case, why can't I help with this one?"

Candy held up several fingers. "Gee, let me see. One, you

were kidnapped. Or wait, did that happen twice? I forgot. You were lucky that you didn't die."

Lisa dipped her head to her chest. "I know. But I think I—we—could help."

Eyes wide, Candy shook her head. "Oh, no. You're not dragging me into this. Dragos wants me to stay here. I don't want to piss off a vampire. He might bite me." She wiggled her eyebrows.

"That is so bad!" She tossed a pillow at Candy's face.

Sighing, Lisa flopped back on the sofa. "You know, we could just follow them. We won't get involved—just make sure they're safe."

Candy shook her head. "No."

"But you're a PI. You have experience spying on people without getting noticed."

"No."

"Don't you carry a gun? You know how to use it. With your skills, and if we stay in the car, we will be safe."

"No."

"Aren't you worried about Dragos? You can help keep him safe."

"Well …"

Lisa felt Candy's resolve begin to crumble. "We will stay in the car. No one will ever know."

Candy bit her lower lip, clearly distraught.

"Do you think we will really help?"

She took Candy's hand. "I do. My experience with supernatural beings is that the more people that can fight them, the better chance we all have. Believe me; I do not want to put Brett's life or ours in jeopardy. All we will do is follow them. We won't even get out of the car to go to the bathroom. I'll take a jar."

Candy laughed as she rose. "We're not taking any damn jars. If we're doing this, then you will do what I tell you. I've tracked husbands, abusive boyfriends, and all kinds of creeps with outstanding warrants. We are not going to risk our lives or the guys'."

She jumped up and hugged her friend. "Okay. Hurry up; we need to get to the station so we can follow them."

Candy grabbed Lisa's shoulders and looked into her eyes. "Don't make me regret this, Lisa."

"Don't be a worrywart. Nothing will happen."

35

Brett waited outside Anders's office. Dragos paced the marble floors in front of him. The guy was wearing a path in the marble tile. Brett's head pounded. *Six more murders.* The women's bodies were being examined by the coroner as they waited. He needed to get his hands on the report as soon as it was ready.

The door to the chief's office flew open. Anders filled the doorway. Tufts of grayish hair stood on end. Frown lines marred his flushed face.

"O'Shea, get in here."

Brett jerked to his feet and motioned for Dragos to follow him. They stood before Anders's desk, waiting for orders.

"Sit down. I'm getting a crook in my neck looking up at you two." Anders reached for the bottle of Tums on the desk. "Damn heartburn." Popping the lid, he shook out two of the pastel tablets and shoved them into his mouth. *Crunch.* "Hmm. Better." He slid several photos across the desk. "Do you know any of them?"

Brett tentatively picked up the pictures. One by one, he stared at the faces of six women. They were all young, in their twenties. Lots of makeup and red lipstick—or was it blood?—smeared their faces. He handed the photos to Dragos.

"Well, do you know them?" Anders snapped.

"No," Brett shook his head. "What do you think?"

Anders shrugged. "Don't know. Could be a bunch of college girls out on the town. You need to figure it out, quick, before all hell breaks loose. Do you want Randall to help you?"

"No. Dragos and I will handle it," he grumbled.

"We've got less than twenty-four hours before this hits the paper. Maybe less if someone comes looking for their daughter."

Brett stood, picking up the photos. "All right to take these?"

"Take them. I'm counting on you, O'Shea."

He nodded. "Sir, I'll do my best."

Neither he nor Dragos said a word as they walked to the car. Once he was in the car, Brett gripped the wheel. How were they going to find Victor? Suddenly Dragos slammed his fist onto the dash of the car. Brett jerked, staring at him.

"Hey! You'll break my car."

Dragos glared at him.

"Don't be pissed at me. We need to direct that anger toward Victor."

"So, Detective O'Shea, do you have any idea where to start?"

"Maybe. Something has been bugging me. Abby said she was at a party with six girls."

"Yes, and your point is …?"

"Now we have the bodies of six women lying in the morgue? I don't think it's a coincidence."

Dragos blanched. "I was thinking the same thing."

Brett squeezed Dragos's shoulder. "Stay positive. We'll get him"

"I'm glad you think so." Dragos flashed a wry grin. "Do you still have that girl's address?"

Brett whipped out a piece of paper. "Got it. Let's make a house call."

They walked up onto the porch of a two-story white house. There wasn't a car on the quiet street. A mix of older and modern houses lined the street.

Brett rang the doorbell. Minutes later, an older woman opened the door.

"Can I help you?"

He handed her a card. "Good evening, ma'am. I'm Detective O'Shea from the Des Moines Police Department. I have a couple of questions to ask Abby. Is she at home?"

The woman's hand flew to her chest. "Is she in trouble?"

"Absolutely not. I just have a couple of questions about people she may know."

"Well, in that case, I'll go get her. Please come in."

They stood in the living room, glancing at a wall of pictures of Abby. Obviously she was quite a track star; a number of trophies and ribbons adorned the wall.

Footsteps thundered down the stairs. Abby skidded to a halt once she spotted them. The color drained from her face.

"Detective? What are you doing here?"

"Abby, let's sit down."

Abby grabbed her mother's hand, and they sat on the sofa.

Once seated, he pulled out the photos. "I have some photos I'd like you to look at."

Brett saw her glance at Dragos before zeroing in on him. Her brows drew together. Was she worried? Nervous?

Brett took a deep breath. *Better to get it over with.* "Do you know any of these women?" He had given Abby photos that weren't too shocking or graphic. He didn't want to traumatize the young woman for the rest of her life.

"Dear, you don't have to do this," her mother murmured.

Abby picked up the top picture. It vibrated in her shaking hand. Her lower lip trembled as if she were going to cry.

Her mother wrapped an arm about Abby, offering reassurance.

Brett reached out to take the photo from her. She jerked back, holding it to her chest. Dragos's brow rose in surprise.

"What happened to her? Is she dead?"

"Do you know her, Abby?"

She slowly nodded. "I'm pretty sure it's Christy Wilson." Staring down at the photo in her lap, she whispered, "Is she dead?"

This time he was able to slide the picture from her grip.

"She's dead, isn't she?" Abby jerked to her feet. Tears trickled down her cheeks.

Abby's mother stared at Brett before tightening her arm around her daughter.

"I'm afraid so."

"Did those guys kill her?"

Brett shrugged. "We don't know. Now that we have a name and know that you were with her at the party, it will help the investigation."

Wiping the tears away with an angry swipe of her hand, she pointed to the other photos. "What about the other girls? Are they all dead?"

His gut rolled. He hated doing this—showing a nice girl photos of dead bodies: girls she knew. The poor kid would probably have nightmares for many nights to come.

"I'm sorry, but if you could give us any names, it would help. I know this is difficult, but you can make a difference."

He pulled out the photos and one by one, and Abby was able to provide a name for each of the pictures. Her mother quietly stood near Abby; her hand anxiously rubbing Abby's arm.

After identifying the women, Abby began to sob uncontrollably. Her mom wrapped her in a tight embrace.

"I'm sorry to ask, but I have a couple of additional questions." Brett struggled to keep emotions steady. "Did you notice whether the house was a ranch style, two story? Were there a lot of trees? Anything unusual in the area? A park or school?"

Abby's tears slowed. Her mom handed her a tissue to blow her nose. With a blotchy face, the young girl drew in a deep breath. "A ranch. There were empty lots around the house."

Brett smiled in encouragement. "Sounds like a new house?"

Abby nodded. "On the way to the house, we passed a lot of big fancy houses."

"That will help us find the people who did this. Thanks, Abby." Brett reached over and patted the young girl's hand. "If you think of anything else, anything at all, give me a call. Day or night."

The older woman glanced at Brett, fear filling her eyes.

"Abby told me everything that happened. Is she safe? I didn't know if we should go stay with relatives out of state. What do you think?"

Dragos nodded at the woman.

Brett nodded in agreement. "It may be for the best. Just let me know how to get a hold of you and Abby."

"Promise me that you will catch whoever did this. I don't want my baby hurt."

Brett took the woman's hand. "Ma'am, trust me; we will do our best to get these guys. I'm sorry that I had to put you and Abby through all of this, but she's been very helpful."

He slid a business card from his pocket and left it on the table. After quickly collecting the photos, he and Dragos hurried from the house. They had identified the victims. Maybe they could find out the location of the party.

36

After writing up Abby's statement back at the office, Brett e-mailed it to Foster and Anders. Minutes later, the chief stormed into Brett's office. The sound of the door hitting the wall reverberated in the office. Dragos jumped to his feet.

Anders stomped past his desk and glared out the window. The chief's teeth gritted together, creating a sound that was worse than fingernails scraping a chalkboard.

"What do you see out here, O'Shea?"

Brett went to the window to look outside. *Shit!* "Is that a news crew setting up outside?"

Anders took a swig from his coffee cup. "It's worse than you can imagine. Shit! I'll be lucky to have a job by the end of the week."

"Do you think they know?"

Anders turned on his heel and poked his head out the door. "Marge! Can you get me a refill?"

Anders motioned for him to move and sat behind Brett's desk. Hands on either side of his head, Anders massaged his temples.

Marge knocked on the open door and set a steaming cup in front of the chief. She opened her mouth as if to say something, but Brett shook his head. With a hand on her hip, she nodded and quietly left his office. That was a shocker in itself.

Brett glanced at Dragos, who stood stiffly against the wall. He sighed and took a seat in front of Anders. "Any ideas on who called them?"

With eyes closed, Anders murmured, "Allen is holding a press conference in an hour. He called me to warn me. Damn asshole."

"But how did he find out about the six women?"

Anders shook his head. "I don't think he knows yet. The family of the murdered woman who worked for him at the dig site has been pressuring him for answers. He is going to tell the world that he believes there are vampires in Des Moines."

Brett's stomach churned as he mentally connected the dots. "Oh shit! After word gets out about the six women, people will panic."

"Exactly! The governor will involve the national guard. The FBI will want to take over the case."

Anders opened one of his desk drawers, glancing at Brett. "Where are your Tums?"

"Top drawer. Left side. Do you want me to talk to Allen—try to get him to call it off?"

Anders rolled his eyes. "Of course I want you to call him. Do whatever it takes to keep him quiet—as long as it's legal."

Dragos grinned. "I can handle Mr. Allen. He will not be a problem for much longer."

"As much as I would like you to handle it, O'Shea is in charge. I want it done right. No more bodies. Got it?"

Brett and Dragos both nodded. Anders rose and marched out of the office, slamming the door behind him.

Brett whipped out his cell and punched in Allen's number. After three rings, Allen's squeaky voice answered. He quickly hit the speaker so Dragos could hear.

"O'Shea. I wondered when you would get around to

calling," Allen quipped. "I take it you heard about the press conference."

Allen's voice hit a nerve. Brett needed to play nice when all he wanted to do was kick Allen's ass.

"What do you hope to gain from all of this? You're creating a fuckin' circus."

"Tsk, tsk, Detective. I warned you weeks ago. I know that you and the department are covering up something. It's time for the public to know so they can protect themselves."

Dragos growled, his teeth lengthening. "I will show the little man what vampires can really do."

Brett frowned at Dragos. He'd not seen this type of aggression from Dragos before.

"What did you say, O'Shea?" Allen muttered.

"Nothing. I want you to reconsider. People will be frightened, and who knows what kind of crap this will trigger. We're working hard to get to the bottom of what's going on. But be real. You know that there are no such things as vampires or the like."

Allen's laugh spiked Brett's blood pressure. Brett silently counted to three. The guy was loony tunes.

"Sorry, Detective. My public awaits."

Brett stared at his phone in disbelief. *The asshole hung up again.* Rushing to the window, he peered down to the street. Sure enough, Allen's limo pulled up in front of the police station.

"C'mon," he yelled at Dragos.

He and Dragos took the stairs two at a time, nearly slamming into one another when they reached the landing at the same time. Brett thrust the door open on the first floor, not caring that it banged into the wall. He ran through the lobby of the station. He skidded on the marble floors. His arm flailed to prevent him from hitting the wall. Dragos grabbed Brett's shoulder, shoving him toward the outside doors.

As he tore through the bronze-and-glass doors, he slammed into Foster, who was entering the building.

"O'Shea! Where the hell are you two going in such a hurry?"

"Allen is … Anders told me …" Brett tried to form the words as he gasped for air. They were going to be too late! He pointed toward the gathering crowd in front of the station.

Foster turned and studied the growing crowd gathering across the street. He saw the comprehension flash across Foster's gaze.

"Son of a bitch," Foster hissed. "Let's go."

Allen stood in the center of the crowd. His personal bodyguard stood behind Allen, surveying the reporters. When they approached, the guard whispered something in Allen's ear.

Brett, along with Dragos and Foster, worked his way through the crowd, trying to get close to Allen. There had to be a way to get the man to walk away.

Allen cleared his throat and stood a little straighter. Voices in the crowd drifted away as reporters jockeyed for position with their cameramen.

"Thank you for coming today. I—"

Brett grabbed Allen's shoulder, causing the smaller man to pitch forward. The crowd gasped. A second later, Allen's guard grabbed Brett's hand and twisted. Pain tore through his wrist.

"Let go!" Before he could identify himself, he saw Dragos grab the guard's hand and effortlessly lift it off of him. With the guard distracted, Brett pulled Allen away from the crowd.

"We need to talk," Brett hissed.

His face red, Allen shook off his grasp. He raised a finger, pointing in Brett's face.

"I warned you, Detective. You're too late."

Allen straightened his suit jacket and tie and walked back to the crowd. With a wave of his hand, he addressed the crowd. "Sorry for the disruption. I want to thank you all for coming today."

Brett and Foster edged closer to Allen. The idiot reveled in the attention he was getting. Brett wanted to wipe the shit-eating grin off of the man's face.

"As I mentioned in my earlier statement, we are facing trying times here in Des Moines. You are all aware of the recent murders of several young women. Well, I am here to tell you that these women died needlessly."

Brett saw Foster clench his fists. Dragos stepped forward, looking as though he was going to attack Allen.

"Wait!" Brett growled. "It's too late. We need to use our heads. Follow my lead."

Foster and Dragos nodded, their attention fixated on Allen.

Once the mumbling of the crowd quieted, Allen held up his hands. "Yes, you heard me correctly. They didn't need to die. The police have ignored my warnings. Now, we need to work together and catch this killer. With your help, you can warn the public so no more people get hurt."

With a smirk on his face, Brett tilted his head toward Allen.

Brett watched as a reporter stepped forward. "Mr. Allen. Can you be more specific? Who is the killer? Why won't the police cooperate with you?"

Several other reporters shouted out questions before Allen could respond.

"Quiet. I can only answer one question at a time. As I stated, I warned the police several weeks ago about a possible danger. They chose to ignore me. Now look what happened; people are dying."

Several reporters glanced toward him and Foster, whom they knew from previous cases. Brett plastered a smile on his face and shrugged, as if he didn't have a care in the world.

He elbowed Foster in the side and muttered, "Smile, sir."

Allen placed his hands on his hips and turned to gaze at the crowd. *Shit. All the guy needs is a soapbox.*

"You sound like you know who the killer is. Who is it, Mr. Allen?" a reporter shouted.

Brett's grin grew. *Here it comes!*

"I know that many of you don't believe in the paranormal, but I am here today to tell you that unworldly creatures exist."

Muffled laughter rippled across the crowd. A couple of cameramen lowered the cameras. Confusion flashed in Allen's gaze. He tried to regain control of the crowd.

"Yes, the paranormal exists. You all should take precautions," Allen warned.

"Hey Allen," a reporter called out, "have you seen these things yourself?"

Laughter blossomed across the parking lot. Allen's face turned beet red.

"I'm talking about vampires. There is a vampire in Des Moines killing innocent people."

Silence prevailed as people looked at one another, some in disbelief. Some chuckled.

Brett began to laugh loud, gut-busting laughter. Foster and Dragos joined in. Soon others in the crowd joined them.

"I'm scared," a man jeered. "Dracula's in Des Moines."

"Better buy some garlic or get holy water," someone else hollered.

Allen tore his hand through his hair. His eyes narrowed. "Listen to me! I'm not joking. People are dying. You could be next."

Foster nodded at the reporters. "O'Shea, look."

Reporters and the camera crews were putting away their equipment. People started drifting down the street.

One reporter walked up to Brett. "Detective, I saw you standing here. So how are you guys going to catch a vampire?" Before Brett could think of an answer, the reporter chuckled.

"God. You guys really have to deal with screwed-up people, don't you?"

Brett nodded. "All the time. It seems Mr. Allen might benefit from some psychiatric help."

As the reporter turned to leave, he paused. "Maybe you should wear a cross or some garlic around your neck just to be sure."

He smiled back at the reporter and gave him a half salute. "You never know. Thanks for the suggestion."

With arms folded across his chest, Brett waited until everyone left before approaching Allen.

"That went well," Brett sniggered.

Allen took a deep breath and turned toward him. "You may think you have outwitted me, but there will be another time—another place."

"Allen, I've told you before that there is no such thing as vampires. Besides, why would any of them want to come to Des Moines?"

Allen spotted Dragos watching them in his dark glasses and overcoat. "Who's that?"

"A friend."

Allen tilted his head, studying Dragos from head to toe. "Where is he from? He looks foreign."

Brett smiled. "I suppose you think he's a vampire because he has long, dark hair and wears a long coat?"

"Of course not," Allen scoffed. "There's just something about him. Does he talk?"

Dragos grinned as he walked toward Allen.

"Yes, he talks," Dragos responded in his clipped English accent. "Are you always such an annoying little man?"

Allen's bodyguard grabbed Dragos's coat. Dragos's grin grew wider.

"Do not touch me." Dragos eyes glittered dangerously. "You will regret it."

Foster rolled his eyes as Brett fought to contain his laughter.

"C'mon, Dragos. Leave the guy alone before I have to throw you in jail."

"Dragos? What kind of name is that? He looks like a vampire," Allen bellowed. "I'm going to call in experts who will support my claim."

Brett folded his arms and smirked at Allen. "Good luck with that.

Foster snapped at the bodyguard, "Get your boss out of here!"

The bodyguard did just that.

The three men let out a sigh of relief as Allen's car disappeared from view.

"We narrowly escaped that bullet," Foster muttered.

Brett shook his head. "I'm not sure. Even though Allen looked and sounded crazy, someone out there will believe it. And with this airing on the evening news, Victor and his goons will be warned."

Dragos nodded. "We must find Victor soon."

37

Randall peeked through the blinds from his bedroom. A black Lexus sat outside his house. He suspected that inside was either Victor or one of his men.

Since the night of the party, he had tried distancing himself from Victor. He could have sworn he saw puncture wounds on the dead woman, but when he returned to the house, the woman's neck was fine. She even smiled at him. Something was going on. Something that made him want to avoid Victor. The women's screams still reverberated in his mind. Truth be known, he was afraid of Victor. Victor's gaze was like staring into a deep well with no bottom. It gave him the creeps.

Victor had invited him over a couple of times during the past few days, but he had scrambled to come up with excuses. He suspected that Victor believed he was lying. The stress had him jumping at shadows and strange noises. He carried a loaded Glock from room to room in his own house. Something had to change.

As he got into his car to report to work, he glanced in the rearview mirror. The Lexus was behind him. There was no subtlety, and this wasn't a hint. Someone wanted him to know he was being watched. Who else could it be but Victor?

After parking the car at the station, he glanced at the

street. The car slowly eased down the street. Even though the windows were heavily tinted, he knew the driver was staring at him. With a shiver, he hurried into the building and clocked in. He was tired of traffic detail. Maybe Anders would reconsider and let him go back to the Detective Bureau.

Absorbed in his thoughts, he turned the corner and collided with O'Shea.

"Whoa! Sorry about that," O'Shea apologized as he reached out to steady himself.

"No problem." He knew that if he wanted to go back to being a detective, he'd better get on O'Shea's good side. He didn't understand what there was between O'Shea and Anders, but they were close. In a way, he was envious.

Randall then noticed the man with O'Shea. The man seemed stiff and withdrawn. Those dark eyes bore into Randall, causing a shiver to run up his spine. Pasting a smile on his face, he asked, "Hey, who's your partner?"

O'Shea seemed to hesitate. Randall became instantly suspicious.

"A friend. He's from England and helping the department."

"Really? That's great. You still working the whore murders?"

"Yep. And they're not all whores, as you put it."

Randall smirked. "Yeah, whatever. Got any good leads?"

"We think so. With the latest murders, we need to catch the killer soon."

"Latest murders? The last murder I heard about was that young girl—Jamie, I think—found down by river. That was a week or two ago."

O'Shea shrugged, looking impatient to leave. "We believe that the killing is escalating."

"Really? I haven't seen anything in the paper about other murders."

"You will soon. Anders is holding a press conference later today. Six bodies will put the heat on us. All of us."

Randall swallowed hard, forcing the stomach acid back down his throat. *Six bodies! Shit! No, it couldn't be. Could it? No way would Victor have killed all those women. Only a frickin' maniac would do something like that.*

"Are you okay, Randall? You look a little pale." O'Shea's eyes narrowed as he stared at him.

The buzz in Randall's head grew louder. He shook his head. "Nope. Just thinking about something. Hey, I've gotta get to roll call. Catch you guys later."

Randall heard nothing that the sergeant said during roll call. *Six more women murdered? Could it be a coincidence?* Six women were at Victor's party. He could try to find one of those women, and then he'd know for sure. But how? He didn't know any of their names, and he wasn't going to ask Victor.

After absently loading the radar equipment, he headed for the selected intersection. He was kept busy for the next several hours by writing tickets. As traffic slowed to a crawl, he glanced down the street. The Lexus was back. Mixed emotions warred inside him. As much as he wanted to stay away from Victor, he needed to talk to the guy in an attempt to get information.

Slowly walking toward the car, Randall casually adjusted the visor on his hat.

The driver's window eased open. Sure enough, Victor sat inside. Instinctively, Randall's hand moved to rest near his gun.

"Detective Randall. What a surprise to see you."

Victor's thin lips stretched into a resemblance of a

smile. He wished he could see Victor's expression, but dark sunglasses masked Victor's eyes.

"Are you following me, Victor? If you have a problem or something you want to discuss with me, then let's talk. I don't like being followed."

"Detective," Victor drawled, "why would I follow you?"

Randall leaned down and rested his arm on the side of the car. "Let's not play games."

Victor sighed, his head momentarily dipping to his chest. Before he responded, his cell phone rang. Holding up a finger, he turned. "Detective, could you give me a minute?"

"Sure, I don't have anything better to do," he snapped. *Damn! Who does Victor think he's talking to?*

Although Randall stepped away, he could still hear Victor talking. Whoever was on the other end was getting an ass chewing. After popping a piece of gum into his mouth, he pulled out his cell phone and pretended to check for messages as he continued to eavesdrop.

"It is beyond me how you can't find him. I am surrounded by incompetence. Do whatever it takes. I want him found," Victor snarled.

Randall bit back a smile. Victor was seething. He'd never seen the man unruffled before.

After Victor ended the call, Randall murmured, "That didn't sound good."

Victor's lip curled. "Do not provoke me, Detective. You do not want to be on my bad side. Trust me."

"Uh huh. Maybe I can help. I couldn't help but overhear, but you seem to be looking for someone."

Victor's long fingers tapped on the steering wheel. Minutes ticked by. *Hell. I'm over this.*

"I need to go. You'd better get those windows fixed. You can't have car windows tinted that dark. You're lucky I'm not writing you a ticket." He turned and walked back to the squad car.

"Wait," Victor called out.

Randall stopped, expecting Victor to get out of the car. Instead, Victor waved him back to the car. He forced himself to walk back toward Victor.

"Yeah?"

"Perhaps you can help me find a relative. I believe I mentioned this before. I want to help him."

"Help him? How?"

Victor shrugged. "I owe him some funds. I can help him get home to England."

England? The guy with O'Shea tonight was from England. "What does this guy look like?"

Victor rubbed his chin as if in thought. "Tall. Over six feet. Dark eyes and hair."

Crap! It sounded as if Victor was describing the guy he'd met tonight.

Randall's eyes narrowed. "Kind of sounds like you're describing the guys who work for you."

"They're all my cousins. I promised my sisters to watch over them. I must admit it has become quite tedious."

Randall nodded. It sounded reasonable to him, though he still had his suspicions. He decided to pretend to help Victor, hoping it might keep the man off his back.

"I'll keep my eyes open," he said. Slapping the side of the car, he smiled. "Well, I need to write up some tickets or I'll be stuck on traffic duty forever. Catch you later."

Watching the Lexus disappear around the corner, Randall returned to the squad car with a renewed sense of survival. He had to get more information on the man with O'Shea. He could play nice if it meant that Victor left him alone and alive.

38

Brett dropped Dragos at Candy's house and hurried home after lunch. Anders was holding the press conference at 5:00 p.m.—just in time for the evening news. After working all night, he needed to catch a few hours of sleep before going out again.

He tossed the keys on the table and automatically opened the fridge and grabbed a bottle of water. He headed toward the family room, kicking off his shoes and dropping his holster on the floor before parking himself in the recliner. *Just the place for a nap.* Quickly emptying the bottle, he leaned back in the chair. His eyes drifted shut.

"Shouldn't you be out on the street looking for, Victor?" Michael bellowed in his ear.

The deep voice jarred him to his senses. Brett jerked to his feet, instinctively drawing back a fist and swinging in the direction of the voice. His body relaxed as his fist sailed through the shadowy apparition.

"Damn it, Michael! Don't you have something better to do than scaring me to death?" Brett sat back down, ignoring his pounding heart.

Michael tossed his hat on the sofa and sat in a nearby chair. "Are you going to the press conference?"

"How do you know about that?"

"I made the rounds at the station today. I saw you talking to Randall. What did he have to say?"

"He asked about Dragos, but other than that, he didn't say much. Why?"

Michael's brow furrowed.

"I don't trust Randall. Be careful."

"Yes, Grandpa," Brett muttered. "I'm a big boy and can take care of myself."

Michael glowered at him. "Yeah, just like you handled the demon last year."

"That was different," Brett muttered.

"Hmm. I seem to remember that I saved your ass a couple of times, sonny."

He pointed his finger at Michael. "Don't call me sonny. You know I don't like it."

"Then pay attention. I've got a feeling about Randall."

He paused. He had learned that when Michael got one of his "feelings," it was usually wise to pay attention. "Okay, so what about Randall?"

"I don't know. Something is going to happen."

"That's kind of vague."

Michael grabbed his hat, plopped it on his head, and disappeared.

Brett turned around to find an empty room. His head throbbed. *Forget the nap. There isn't enough time. Maybe caffeine will help. Or a hot shower.*

Opting for a shower, he tossed his clothes into a basket and quickly headed to the bathroom. As soon as he stepped out of the shower, the phone rang.

"Hello."

"Hey, Brett. Are you busy?" Lisa asked.

"Give me a minute. I just got out of the shower." He grabbed his gym shorts and pulled them on. "Okay, what's up?"

"Not much. I stopped by the news station today. There might be a job opening here in Des Moines."

What was he supposed to say? He didn't know what he wanted. Frankly he'd been avoiding that issue altogether.

"You still there?"

He heard the tension in Lisa's voice. "Is that what you want to do? Work here in Des Moines?"

Without hesitating, she answered, "I do. I'd like for us to have the opportunity to start over again."

He dropped onto the edge of the bed and squeezed his eyes closed. "Lisa, I don't … I … Are you sure you want to be here? I can't make any promises."

"I'm sure. In fact, I accepted the job."

He smiled. *Lisa always could make quick decisions.*

"Well now, we'll just have to see what happens." He paused before adding, "I did miss you, you know."

She sighed. "By the way, I missed you too.

They sat there in comfortable silence for a few moments.

"Before I forget, the station manager told me that the chief is doing a press conference later this afternoon. Are you going to be there?"

He stretched out on the bed, cradling the phone between his neck and shoulder.

"I'll be there. Hey, I hate to rush off, but I have a couple of things to do before the conference."

Okay. Catch you later, O'Shea."

He tossed the phone across the bed. Physically the attraction was still there. But having been burned once, did he want to take a chance with her again?

"Argh," he growled. It was time to get his mind back on work. He rolled out a map of the city on the kitchen table. *Hell, maybe if I throw a dart at the map, it will land where the party was held.* Dropping his head into his hands, he studied the map, looking for street names that fit Abby's description.

A car honked outside. He glanced out the window. Candy was dropping off Dragos, which meant it was only thirty minutes until the press conference.

Brett quickly pulled on his trousers and slipped into a starched white shirt.

"Where are you? It's getting late," Dragos called.

"I'm hurrying. Cool it."

Brett rushed to the kitchen and tossed a jacket on the table while he secured a shoulder holster.

"You seem stressed. Anything wrong?" Dragos lounged against the counter with his arms folded across his broad chest.

"Michael popped in to warn me about Randall. Then Lisa called. She took a job here at a TV station. Plus I'm fucking exhausted."

Dragos's brow arched. "I think she still cares for you."

He slipped on the jacket and punched the vampire in the arm.

"Not going there. I'm worried about what Michael told me. Michael gets these 'feelings,' and he's usually right. Let's watch Randall. Are you ready?"

Dragos nodded.

"Hurry up. Anders will be pissed if we're late."

They arrived at the police station as Anders, the assistant chief, and the press secretary entered the lobby. Anders glanced at his watch.

"Glad you could make it, O'Shea."

Great! Sarcasm was all he needed today.

Anders turned and walked out to the front steps where a crowd of reporters had gathered. Brett hoped the lightning flashing on the horizon wasn't an omen of how the announcement would go.

Anders stepped up to the microphone and cast his formidable stare over the crowd. Conversations died away.

"I want to thank everyone for coming on such short notice. I wish I had better news to announce. Our officers were called to a scene where the bodies of six women were recovered."

An audible gasp came from the audience. Reporters glanced at one another in disbelief.

Anders held up his hand to forestall questions. "As you know, several women have been murdered in recent weeks. First I want to emphasize that the public is not at risk. Our best detectives are working the case and have legitimate leads. At this time, I would advise that young women avoid situations where they are out alone after dark. Travel in groups. I ..."

The crowd parted to let Allen walk to the bottom of the station's steps.

Brett stiffened. *Oh shit.*

"Quit lying, Chief Anders. Tell the truth and let the public know who you're really looking for," Allen yelled.

Cameras whipped toward Allen. The man's eyes glittered, as if he were crazed or had been crying. Somehow Brett knew it was the former.

"Our police department has been lying to all of us. We have a serial killer in Des Moines. We're all in danger."

Several people looked about in fear. Panic filled their faces.

Damn Allen! What is he trying to do?

Anders's cheeks became mottled as he descended the steps. Brett watched Anders stop in front of Allen. Brett quickly closed the distance between Allen and the chief.

"One more word and I will have you arrested for inciting a riot," Anders hissed.

Allen's mouth opened and closed several times. Allen then glanced up at the top of the stairs. He lifted his arm, pointing toward Dragos. "Ask that man who they're looking for. He's one of them."

When the crowd turned their gaze upward, Dragos had thankfully disappeared. People in the crowd shrugged, trying to figure out who Allen was pointing at. Luckily no one besides Allen had noticed Dragos.

Appearing to grow even more agitated, Allen sputtered, "See? They're hiding the truth. They don't want us to know what's going on. The guy was just standing there a second ago. Then poof, he's gone."

A reporter, standing nearby, asked aloud, "What's he talking about?"

Brett moved closer to the chief. With a relaxed smile, he stared into the camera lens. "Mr. Allen believes that vampires are killing people. He believes the police are sheltering vampires. I don't know about you, but the only vampires I've seen are the ones in movies and on television."

Snickers and jeers broke out across the crowd. Yet there were several people who stared suspiciously at the police.

Anders squared his shoulders and glanced at the crowd. "As Detective O'Shea said, we are not searching for vampires, because they're not real. We do have substantiated leads that we are following, and we hope to catch the killer or killers any day. If you have any knowledge or leads relating to the murders, we have set up a special toll-free number for the public to contact our team working the case. My press secretary will answer any other questions you have."

Brett felt a jab in his stomach and followed Anders back inside the building. Anders threw open the heavy bronze-and-glass doors of the station. He winced as the doors shuddered. Dragos darted into the elevator and joined them as the doors started to close. Once inside, Anders's cell rang.

"Anders here."

Brett turned away, trying not to eavesdrop. The voice on the other end of the phone screamed at the chief.

"Yes sir. We will." Anders slipped the phone in his pocket.

Marching off the elevator, Anders stopped at his secretary's desk. "Would you please call Foster and have him meet me in my office ASAP?"

The secretary nodded and picked up the phone. Brett

and Drago followed the chief into his office. As the door to the office closed, Anders snapped, "Take a seat. Both of you."

Dragos pushed off from the wall he was leaning against. Brett didn't know who looked more pissed off—Dragos or Anders. He knew why Anders was upset but wasn't sure what Dragos's problem was.

Maybe I should have kept my mouth shut at the press conference. Damn it! It's not like there is a procedural manual on how to handle situations like this.

A knock on the door preceded Foster's entry. Foster nodded and slid into the chair next to him. Anders's face twisted with worry. Anders looked as if he had aged several years in the past hour.

"Well, we have a hell of a mess. The mayor just called and ripped me a new one. He said that I lost control of the interview—as if I could stop Allen from running his mouth. To top it off, he is questioning the validity of whether there are vampires. I was given an ultimatum to catch the killer by the end of the month; otherwise, the council may be looking for a new chief."

Brett and Foster looked at one another.

A second later, Foster slammed his fist on the chief's desk. "That's bullshit! You can't put a deadline on when to catch a killer. They're frickin' idiots if they let you go," Foster ranted.

Anders attempted a wry smile. "Calm down. My wife would love to have me home full time. My getting shot last year scared the crap out of her. Don't worry; they're going to have to drag my ass out of here." He leaned forward, resting his elbows on the desk. "Let's focus on how to catch this guy. O'Shea, how's the surveillance going?"

Suddenly Brett's throat tightened. "Nothing solid yet. We're making the rounds and covering places where we suspect Victor has been. We'll find him soon."

"Dragos, do you have anything to add?"

Dragos straightened in the chair, squaring his shoulders. "No, but I pledge here and now that we will find him."

Anders popped the top of the Tums container sitting on his desk and shoved two of the tablets in his mouth, angrily crunching his teeth together. "Don't give me that fancy bullshit. Just find the guy. Now!"

Brett pulled Dragos from his chair. "Yes, sir. We're on it."

The pair hurried out of the office. Neither talked as they made their way outside to the car.

"Now what?" Dragos grumbled.

"We go catch a vampire."

39

Victor's razor-sharp nails beat against the marble-topped table. His men stood in a half circle in front of him, their bodies stiff and unmoving. Only an ancient, like him, was able to see the fear lingering in the shadows of their eyes.

Impatience coursed through him. How could one single vampire hide from him? Him—an ancient with skills and abilities that the others did not possess. *Damn it all! Idiots. I should kill them all and start over, creating new followers.*

"Sir, we have searched everywhere you requested. No one has seen him," Alto bravely stated. A twinge of regret hung in the air.

Victor's eyes narrowed, causing the young vampire to wince and take a step backward.

"Quiet!" Victor gave a wave of his hand, and Alto slammed against the nearby wall. Chunks of drywall fell on his sprawled-out body. "You all have failed me. No more excuses. Get me Randall. Bring him here tonight."

Alto scrambled to his feet. He met Victor's stare and briefly nodded.

"Do not fail me again."

The vampires backed out of the room, fading away into the darkened corners of the house.

Brett drove home. It was nearly midnight, and he could no longer see straight. He needed sleep, but that wasn't an option.

"We've got to find Victor," Dragos grumbled. "Things are out of control."

"No shit, Sherlock!" he muttered as he peeled off his suit jacket and tossed it on the bed.

"So where are we going tonight?"

Brett tugged a shirt over his head. "Why not go back to where we found the first body?"

Dragos shrugged. "Fine. I don't have a better idea."

His phone vibrated. It was Lisa.

"Hi there. What's going on?"

"Are you working tonight? If not, I thought Candy and I could bring pizza over."

"Unfortunately we're working. Anders is on a rampage. I take it you saw the interview?"

"What the hell is wrong with Allen? Was he trying to scare the shit out of everyone?"

Brett braced the phone with his shoulder as he tossed additional ammo into his pocket. "I don't know what he was doing. Obviously the guy has lost it. Dragos and I need to get going. Maybe we can all get together for dinner tomorrow, if that works for you."

A slight sigh whispered in his ear. "Sure. That should work. Be careful, okay?"

For a second, he stared at the dark screen of his phone. He then snapped, "Let's go!"

Lisa tossed the phone into her bag and smiled. "You're right. They're at Brett's, but they're going back out."

Candy rattled her car keys. "Well, let's go follow those boys and make sure they stay out of trouble."

The women jumped into Candy's car and quickly drove to Brett's house. Candy slammed on the brakes as they came to a four-way stop down the street from Brett's house.

Lisa's head jerked forward. "Hey! What the hell?"

"Duck! They're headed this way." Slumping down in the seat, Candy grabbed a ball cap and thrust it on her head. With her head bent, she pretended to play with the radio as the guys went by.

"Did they see us?" Lisa straightened and watched the taillights of Brett's car.

Candy glanced behind them. "I don't think so. That was close. I'm going to wait a few seconds before following them. Brett's too observant for his own good sometimes."

Lisa smiled. "You think so? Sometimes he can't see the forest for the trees. Can't he see that I care for him?"

Candy reached over and gripped her hand. "Don't worry. Things will work out. Besides, I have it tougher. How do you think it will go when I introduce Dragos to my dad? 'Dad, I want you to meet Dragos, a vampire. Don't worry; he won't bite.' Man, I dread that meeting."

She laughed. "Okay, you've got it worse."

The women did a high-five, congratulating themselves on their narrow escape.

Dragos kept his gaze locked on the outside mirror. There was something familiar about the car behind them. It reminded him somewhat of Candy's car, but he wasn't sure.

Brett's brow wrinkled as he cast a quick glance at Dragos. "What's so interesting?"

Dragos straightened and shrugged. "For a moment, I thought Candy was following us."

He saw Brett's gaze swing toward the rearview mirror. "I don't see her car. You do know that there is more than one blue Chevrolet Malibu on the road, don't you?"

"I don't know or care about your American cars. I just told you what I saw."

Brett's gaze returned to the mirror. Dragos jerked when Brett suddenly changed lanes and hooked a quick left. They narrowly missed a parked car on the side of the street. Several cars honked at them. One man stuck his hand out the window and held up his middle finger.

His head swung toward Brett. The smug look on Brett's face fueled his annoyance. "Was that necessary? You could have killed someone."

"Look behind us. Whoever you saw is long gone. No one is behind us now."

Dragos turned and looked out the rear window. The street was empty. Slowly turning forward, he frowned.

"Now what's wrong," Brett sighed.

"Why do you think anything is wrong?"

Brett rolled his eyes. "Well, for starters, you're frowning again. A moment ago, you hissed at me."

Dragos growled.

"See, you're pissed about something." Brett tossed his cell phone in Dragos's lap. "Call Candy at home and see if she answers. She probably has her laptop out and is researching her next case."

Dragos hesitated. Did he want to know the answer to his question? What would he do if Candy was following them? Women in this century were very independent—nothing like women in the nineteenth century. He'd give her credit, though; Candy was a sought-after investigator. She went into situations that many men avoided. The fact that she was proficient with a gun made him think twice about ordering her to do anything.

Brett chuckled, drawing his attention. "Are you going to make love to the phone or use it?"

Annoyed, he turned and flashed his teeth at Brett. He knew his eyes had turned red.

Brett recoiled and held up his right hand. "Dude! Chill. I'm joking."

Dragos was amazed that he had learned how to use a cell phone. It was Candy who had insisted that he learn. Without thinking, he pulled up the list of contacts and pressed Candy's number. His grip on the phone tightened as it rang. Would she answer? He turned in the seat to look behind them once again. There was nothing but emptiness—not a car in sight.

Finally, on the third ring, her cheery voice answered. "Hey, Brett!"

"No, it's me." Dragos's voice deepened. The sound of her voice filled him with heat.

"Dragos?"

Just the sound of his name on her lips made his blood simmer.

"Candy, are you busy?"

His acute hearing picked up Lisa's voice nearby.

"No, not really. Just working. You know. What are you doing?"

"I'm working with Brett tonight. I just wanted to hear your voice."

Brett pressed loud kisses against the back of his hand. Dragos reached over and punched him in the shoulder.

"Aw. That is so sweet. I can't wait to see you again. When do you think you'll be home?"

She'd never asked that question before. "I'm not sure. You can call Brett later; we may know more then. Is Lisa with you?"

Candy's nervous titter increased his wariness.

"Yeah, she came over tonight so we can work on a project."

"So you two are at your house?" Anxiety filled him as he waited for her response.

She quickly answered, "Yeah, just sitting around working. Hey, I need to run. We ordered pizza delivery and they're here."

"Sure. I will speak to you later. Good-bye."

He pondered her words. *Why did she seem so anxious to hang up?*

Brett rubbed his shoulder. "See, you called her home phone and she answered. Nothing to worry about. We're almost to Darlene's. Better get your game face on; it's time to go to work."

40

Randall pulled into his driveway. It was Friday evening, and he had no plans at all, and it sucked. Since his last encounter with Victor, he had gone to work and returned directly home. He didn't want to see Victor and his goons again. He didn't know what they were exactly involved in, nor did he want to know.

He entered the small, cluttered apartment. Standing in the middle of the room, he saw the pile of dirty dishes from the day before. A faint odor filled his nose. *Shit!* There was no way he was staying home tonight. He couldn't stand this place, but after his wife had filed for divorce, this was all he could afford. It still rankled him that she got to keep the house. Besides, two weeks without any pussy was too damn long.

He decided to go to Darlene's place. It had been over a month since she kicked him out of the place. By now she'd probably forgotten that he wasn't supposed to be there. As long as he had money, the old hag would let him in.

❦

Randall saw Bobby standing at the back door, assessing every man that entered the house. The man's six-foot-plus frame and thick body were intimidating to most, but not to him. He was a cop, and cops got special privileges—well, most of the time. Sometimes he wished that he worked before the advent of cell phones. Nowadays he couldn't even punch a suspect without worrying about being recorded.

Randall took a deep breath and walked toward the door. "Hey, Bobby. Busy tonight?"

Bobby's brow rose as he stood in front of the bouncer.

"No, but I can't let you in without Darlene's okay."

He bit back a curse. "Well, ask her then."

Bobby's head dipped to the clipped mic on his shirt. Silence. Finally Darlene's voice came on.

"Let him in."

Bobby opened the door, glaring as Randall passed through. *Jeez, I feel like a bug under a microscope. I just want a quick fuck. What's the big deal?*

Randall's smile faded when he saw Darlene waiting in the hall outside of her office. She crooked her finger at him, indicating that he should follow.

By the time he entered her office, she was sitting behind an imposing black lacquered desk. Some kind of scented candle stunk up the room.

"What the hell is that smell?" he muttered

Darlene lit a cigarette and leaned back in the leather chair. "Damn, Randall. Don't you have any class? Sit your ass down."

"Nice to see you too, Darlene. Did you do something with your hair? You look younger."

With her head tilted, her eyes narrowed. A smirk blossomed

across her face. "Don't give me your bullshit. You're lucky to be in my house after the last stunt you pulled."

He was smart enough to plaster a sorrowful look on his face. "Sorry. Things just got out of hand."

"If I let you go up to see one of the girls, how do I know that things aren't going to get 'out of hand' again?" She flicked the ashes into the empty wastebasket.

He shrugged. "I'll tone down my enthusiasm if that helps."

Snuffing out the cigarette, she rose. "I'll hook you up with Ivana—a Russian girl. If you get out of line, she has my permission to break your arm or whatever else she wants. Room three upstairs."

Randall's head sagged to his chest. "C'mon Darlene. How old is she? Sounds like she's at least fifty. Probably looks like a man. You know that I like them young and pretty."

She walked from behind her desk and stood near the doorway. "Well, we don't always get want we want, now do we? Besides, you're on probation as far as I'm concerned. If you don't like it, you can always leave."

He stood and faced her. "Ha ha. If that's how you want to play it, fine. She'd better give a good blow job or I want a refund."

Darlene's cackle echoed down the hall as he stomped up the stairs. He rapped on the door, and a deep, husky voice ordered him to enter.

"Hmm," he muttered. Maybe tonight wasn't going to be as bad as he thought.

His smile widened as opened the door. Ivana, a platinum blonde—not natural if the dark roots were any indication—lay invitingly on the bed. Her voluptuous yet muscular body was curved in all the right places. She had rounded hips and a narrow waist. Dark nipples were visible through the thin red silk negligée. She was a little beefier than he normally liked, but she definitely had some good points. She lay on her side, allowing him to see most of her body. The plunging neckline revealed big tits. He licked his lips, thinking about what he was going to do to her and those honking jugs.

"Come here, beeby," she whispered. "I know you like it rough. Ivana is going to give it to you rough. I make you happy. Yes?"

His dick immediately hardened and lengthened. Tossing his coat onto a chair, he groaned as she rose to her knees. The material covering her body slipped lower with every breath she took.

He stared, fixated on the sight before him. He blurted, "How big are those girls?"

Her catlike green eyes narrowed. She reached up and plumped up her breasts as if she were putting them on a platter—a platter he wanted to lick clean.

"Forty-four D. Are they big enough for you?"

"Yeah, baby. They're just right. Why don't you take off that thing you're wearing before I tear it off of you, and lie back on the bed."

With a slight wiggle of her hips, the red silk slid down past her knees. Laughing, she rolled onto her back and tossed the garment at him.

He caught the silk in one hand and brought it to his face. He watched while her hand dipped between her legs. He inhaled, and her scent filled him. He was near bursting when she pulled out a finger glistening with moisture and put it in her mouth. She slowly slid the finger in and out of her mouth, her pouty red lips tightening and tugging. *Damn.* He swore he could feel her mouth tugging on his dick. At this rate, there was no way he was going to last.

He yanked off his clothes, letting them drop to the floor. He then stood beside the bed, his throbbing member standing at attention.

She reached up and grabbed his arm, pulling him beside her. His mouth latched onto a hardened nipple, his teeth raking across her tender flesh.

With a gasp, she clasped his head to her chest. "You feel so good. You bite harder."

Darlene's cautionary words still rang in his ears. *Screw this!* He needed to fuck now. He was ready to explode and didn't care about her getting off. He was the customer. He snapped his teeth together one last time, rolling the tight nub over his teeth. She moaned as her body tightened. He pulled back and positioned himself between her legs. He glanced down at her face. He wanted to watch as he thrust inside her. It was going to be hard—really hard. The bitch was going to feel it up in her throat.

Her body stiffened. Her moaning ceased. Narrowed eyes watched him. Her red lips pursed together. Now what?

"What are you doing?" she hissed.

Reaching down between her legs, Randall thrust a finger inside. "Fuckin'."

Her body bucked upward, tossing him to the side of the bed.

"Hey, what the hell are you doing?" His arm swung out to hold her to the bed.

"No fuck now." She wiggled to a sitting position in the bed, her nipple nearly poking him in the eye.

He froze. Who was she to give him orders? Hadn't she heard the old adage "The customer is always right"?

"Listen, bitch. We're doing this my way. Understand?"

Without warning, she pounced on his chest. His face was locked between her muscular thighs.

She leaned forward, her bony finger poking his chest. "Pudgy man. You listen."

Before he could respond or toss her off of him, she whipped out a pair of handcuffs. She snapped one cuff on his wrist and attached it to the metal bed frame.

"Get those off me. Now!" he roared.

Smiling, she reached over and grabbed his free hand and

locked it in a cuff already attached to the bed. How had he not seen that?

He jerked his arms. He didn't care if the bed frame fell to pieces. *Shit!* It didn't budge.

Ivana jumped off the bed, her husky laughter irritating him more.

"We do things my way now."

"Argh! You'd better let me go, bitch, or I'll have you arrested for kidnapping.

Her hand tightened around his flaccid penis and squeezed.

"Ow. That hurts."

"Tsk, tsk. You like pain. Darlene told me, so I give you pain. Shall we begin?"

She leaned down and licked his nipple.

He thrashed on the bed. The handcuffs clanged against the headboard. His face grew hotter by the moment. Darlene had just made an enemy. He was determined to shut her down, one way or another. He swung his leg to the side, trying to kick Ivana as she walked around the bed.

She then unexpectedly grabbed his foot and slammed her fist into his thigh.

"Darlene! Get your ass up here now! Son of a bitch! She's killing me!"

Darlene glanced up at the ceiling. A loud crash above her office brought a smile to her face.

Bobby, sitting in her office, grinned up at the ceiling.

"Should I go cut him loose? He sounds pissed off."

She laughed. "Not yet. Let's see how our detective likes a little pain."

The screams upstairs became muffled. Darlene assumed

Ivana had duct-taped his mouth by now. They were the perfect pair but just didn't know it.

One of the other girls hurried into her office. She wrapped the loose robe about her slim frame upon seeing Bobby in her office.

"Dar, my customer is complaining about all the noise. Can't Bobby go quiet them down?"

"Tell your guy that I will give him a discount tonight. How—"

A loud thump shook the room.

"Crap," muttered Bobby. "Sounds like someone just got body slammed."

They all looked at each other and burst out laughing.

"My bet is on Ivana. He didn't know she was a professional wrestler."

Bobby shook his head. "Remind me not to get on your bad side, Darlene."

She turned and lit another cigarette, blowing the smoke toward the ceiling. "Damn straight. Randall needed a wake-up call before he killed someone."

A knock on the office door drew her attention, and Detective O'Shea filled the doorway. She glanced up. *Oh shit! This is bad—so bad.* A loud thump rattled the ceiling light, drawing everyone's attention, including that of her guests.

"Detective O'Shea. What a surprise. How can I help you?"

41

The rattling walls from above drew Brett's glance. Dragos's gaze swept upward before he bit back a smile. Whatever was going on was causing quite a bit of amusement for the people in Darlene's office.

"Sorry to interrupt the entertainment." Brett's gaze darted upward. "Do you have a few minutes to talk?"

Bobby jumped up from a chair and nodded to the detectives as he left the office. The woman in the robe quickly followed.

"Sure. Have a seat. Do you want any coffee, water?"

"No thanks. I wanted to see if that strange guy Bobby saw out back a few weeks ago had been back here lately."

Darlene seemed distracted tonight. She kept glancing to the room above them. *What is going on up there?* He sure as hell didn't want to know—not his business. He was here to focus on Victor.

She leaned forward and put out a cigarette. "No one has said anything to me lately. But let me check." She rose and poked her head out of the doorway. "Bobby!" she yelled.

Moments later, Bobby reappeared in the office.

"These officers want to know if you or anyone has seen that weird guy hanging around back lately. Seen anything out of the ordinary?"

Bobby muttered, "No. Just the usual customers."

Brett sighed. "Well, thanks. It was worth a try."

"I've seen the news today." Bobby looked questioningly at Brett. "What was up with the guy ranting about vampires?"

"I think Mr. Allen experienced a psychotic breakdown." Brett smiled.

Laughing, Darlene nodded toward Dragos. "From what I've seen in the movies, you could pass for one of those vampires."

Dragos stiffened, a deer-in-the-headlights look on his face.

Brett broke out laughing. "Now that you mention it, he could pass as a vampire."

Darlene flapped her hand toward his companion. "Naw. He's too good looking to be a vampire."

Dragos flashed a look of relief. "Thank you, dear woman."

"See? His manners are better than most men today. People are just plain crazy anymore."

"I couldn't have said it any better, Darlene." Brett shook her hand. "Thanks again. You've got my number."

As the men walked toward the back door, a loud scream from a man filled the air.

Brett bit the inside of his cheek to keep from laughing. "What's going up upstairs?

Dragos grinned. "You do not want to know. Detective Randall is up there."

Brett drew to a stop and looked back toward the door. Darlene gave a little wave, laughter lighting up her eyes.

"Damn your superior hearing," Brett chuckled. "Let's get out of here before I have to do something I don't want to do."

Dragos trailed behind. "I'm curious. What don't you want to do?"

"Help Randall, of course."

Their laughter quickly faded once they were inside the car. "Now what?" Dragos asked.

Brett rubbed his head. "I have no idea. I don't want Anders to be fired, and we sure as hell don't want any more people to die."

Dragos turned and looked out the rear window.

Brett smiled. "You don't think the girls are still following us, do you?"

Dragos shook his head. His dark hair swung about his face and shoulders. "I guess not, but I am uneasy. Something feels off."

"Don't worry. We'll get Victor."

Suddenly, someone in the backseat coughed. Both Brett and Dragos turned. Michael sat looking at them with his familiar cocky smile on his face.

"Where have you been?" snapped Brett. "All kinds of shit is going on. The mayor is threatening to fire Anders."

Michael tipped back his hat. "Well, it's a good thing that I'm here, then, isn't it?"

Dragos turned back to the front. "Is he always so arrogant?"

Brett smiled and raised both arms in the air like goalposts. "Finally someone else sees what I have to put up with."

Michael reached forward and smacked the back of Brett's head.

Dragos growled, "Do not even think of doing that to me, ghost. It will be the last thing you ever do."

Michael yanked down his fedora until it nearly covered his eyes. "Hmmph! I know when I'm not wanted."

The next second, he disappeared.

"Is the bothersome man gone?"

Brett whipped around for a look. "Yep, he's gone."

Full of mixed emotions, Brett was silent as they drove. Michael had been so helpful in the past. They had been partners on the last big case. But anymore he barely saw Michael. He wondered whether Michael was upset because he and Dragos were partnering on this case. Surely Michael understood why it was important to have Dragos help them. They were chasing vampires, after all.

Candy eased the car out of the alley. Careful to stay far behind Brett and Dragos, she and Lisa made their way past Darlene's house. Being a PI, Candy had investigated more than one husband who frequented this place.

Lisa gasped and grabbed Candy's arm.

"Is that Dragos by the tree?"

Candy stopped the car and peered into the darkness. Squinting, she whispered, "It looks like him. Why didn't he leave with Brett?"

"Darn it. Candy, we need to get out of here. If he sees us, they'll be furious."

Her hands shook as she gripped the wheel. "Dragos is staring at the house, so maybe he won't notice us."

At that moment, the man by the tree turned and stared at the women. Even though they were at least fifty feet away, Candy shivered at the intense stare and the flash of bright white teeth. The man drew back in with the shadows, barely visible. His dark clothes and long hair were very similar, but yet something was different.

"That's not Dragos," Candy cried. "He has night vision like a cat. He'd know it was us and would be pulling me out of the car by now."

Lisa cried out, "Shit. Get us out of here!"

After driving several miles, both women breathed a sigh of relief. No one followed them.

Candy's heart pounded so hard it hurt to breathe.

"Who was that?" Lisa whispered as if she were afraid of being overheard.

"I saw a flash of teeth. I think it was another vampire." She cast another look over her shoulder, wondering why he hadn't followed them. *What is a vampire doing at Darlene's? Brett and Dragos just left there. Are they being followed?*

She kept driving, unsure of where they were going. She didn't know what to do.

Lisa ran her hands up her arms as if chilled. "We need to call Brett."

Candy shook her head, long curls falling across her cheeks. Angrily, she brushed the hair behind her ears. "No. No, we need to think about what we're doing."

Lisa gaped at her. "Are you crazy? What would we have done if that thing—that vampire—jumped on the car and attacked us?"

"I would shoot the hell out of it and give us time to get away."

Lisa reached over and gripped her hand. "I know I got us into this, but we've got to stop. We'll get killed or kidnapped. Believe me when I say that kidnapping is not all it's cracked up to be."

A lone tear traced down Candy's cheek. "Don't you see? We can help the guys. We've got to protect them. I am scared shitless, but we can't let this stop us."

Lisa groaned. "I don't—"

"C'mon, Lisa. Just hang in there with me. We can do this."

After several moments of silence, Lisa thrust out her lower lip and nodded. "Fine! But I am not going home to my house after seeing that guy. I'll have nightmares at this point."

Candy forced a smile even as the tears flowed. "Let's go to Brett's. I've got a key. We can surprise them."

Lisa opened the glove compartment and handed Candy a tissue. "Oh, they'll be surprised all right. I just hope they don't kick us out or wonder why we're there."

42

Randall stumbled, grabbing the wall to keep himself from tumbling down the stairs. At the landing, he paused to straighten his shirt and tuck it back into his pants.

His legs trembled from being tied to the bedposts. He rounded the corner and spotted Bobby standing outside Darlene's office. Bobby muttered something to Darlene before looking back at him. Bobby's grin faded on seeing Randall's glare.

Straightening, Randall stalked toward the office. He filled the doorway, watching the slender, cigarette-smoking woman organize papers on her desk.

"What the hell were you thinking?" he barked.

She raised her gaze to him. Her pale blue eyes were wide, as if she were surprised. "What?"

He folded his arms across his chest and fixated his anger on her. "You know what? I'm about to close this place down." He stomped over to her desk and slapped both hands flat on the desk, his face inches from hers. "I almost got killed up there." Drops of spit flew from his mouth.

Darlene gasped and grabbed a tissue. Quickly wiping her face, she rose to her feet. "Don't push me, Detective. I gave you exactly what you wanted. Having pain inflicted on you is not the same as being the one inflicting the pain, is it?"

His eyes bulged. *Who does Darlene think she is? She's just a whore.*

"Be careful what you say, Darlene. You're just lucky that things worked out as well as they did. I could have broken her arm and felt good about it."

He wasn't going to admit it, but Ivana was one talented woman. Once she untied his arms and legs, he was able to fuck the hell out of her. At first he was furious when she tied him up and landed a few punches. He was forced to get her off three times before she freed him. He hated being forced to follow a woman's orders.

Darlene placed her hands on her hips. "Go to hell, Randall. I tried to teach you a lesson, hoping that you would learn restraint. You can't beat or hurt my girls. One more time and you're going to be kicked out and never allowed back in. Got it?"

"You can't threaten me. You forget that I can shut you down."

Darlene threw back her head and laughed. "I don't think you have that type of authority. O'Shea and his friend were here a couple of hours ago. I'm sure that if I spoke to O'Shea, we would stay open."

O'Shea! Damn him. Always a thorn in my side. Randall grunted. "I've got connections too."

Darlene's eye's glittered. She lifted her bony chin and yelled, "Bobby."

Only a few seconds elapsed before Bobby poked his head into the office.

"Escort the detective to the door. He won't be back for a while."

Randall opened and closed his mouth. He decided he wasn't going to waste any more energy on her. Turning on his heel, he stormed to the door with Bobby following close behind.

As the door slammed and locked behind him, he stood

looking up at Ivana's room. She threw open the window and leaned out. Her robe gaped apart. The girls hung out for all to see.

"You come back tomorrow, yes?"

He had to smile. The forty-four Ds drew his attention.

"Not tomorrow, but soon. Keep those girls safe for me, okay?"

She waved and closed the window. With a sigh, Randall turned toward his car. As he reached out to open the door, a hand gripped his shoulder.

Now what? Damn, Bobby is going to get a surprise.

Randall swung around and shoved his hand into a solid chest. "Get your hands—"

Wait a minute. Bobby is beefy, not like the body of steel in front of me. Apprehension built. His gaze lifted up. And up.

The tips of long, dark hair hung down past the man's shoulders. Randall slowly raised his eyes and stared into the deep red eyes.

"Don't you work for Victor?"

The man nodded, continuing to stare down at him.

"Where's Victor?"

Suddenly a black Lexus entered the alley. The back door of the car opened. Instinctively, Randall took a step backward. The man reached out and grabbed his shoulder, pinning him where he stood.

"Victor wants to speak to you. Get in the car."

Randall shook his head. "No. Give me Victor's number, and I will call him while I drive home."

He whipped out his cell, ready to punch in the number. The man jerked the phone out of his hand and tossed it against a tree, where it shattered into pieces.

"Hey, you can't do that!"

"Get in the car or I will break your body into pieces just like the phone."

Randall's gaze darted up to Ivana's room, thinking maybe

she was watching and would call the police. Instead her room was dark. In fact, it looked like all the lights in Darlene's place were turned off. He didn't want to go and meet with Victor. He had a bad feeling.

The man's grip tightened, and they walked toward the car. He was shoved headfirst into the backseat. The man climbed in behind him.

"Do not try to escape. I will catch you, and I will not be careful. Understand?"

Randall nodded. What choice did he have? He had calculated jumping out of the other rear door, but the car had started moving.

They pulled up to Victor's house. The man jumped out and motioned at him. He got out of the car and stared at the unlit house.

"Get moving. Victor is waiting." Victor's goon pushed him toward the house.

Randall tripped, barely catching his balance before hitting the stone walkway. The door was opened by another man working for Victor. As he walked into the foyer, past the men, he shivered. The cold looks in their eyes unnerved him.

"Follow me," a man intoned.

Randall treaded slowly down a few stairs to the entertainment room. He was far away from any form of help.

A single light in the far corner of the vast room cast faint shadows of the occupants on the walls. Victor sat on a low white leather sectional. His arm casually rested on the back of the sofa.

Randall swallowed hard, pushing back his fear. With Victor's dark, unfathomable gaze fixated on him, he found it very difficult not to turn and run—not that he would get very far.

"Detective Randall. So nice to see you again. Alto tells me you visited Darlene's tonight."

He shifted his weight and nodded. "Yeah. There's a new girl there—Ivana."

Victor smiled and ran a sharp fingernail down his cheek. "Yes, I've heard of her. Is she why you are limping?"

Randall rubbed his thigh where a bruise lingered. He broke into a grin until he remembered that he had been brought here at Victor's order.

"She packs a punch like a man. I had to show her who was in charge."

With blazing eyes, Victor's smile widened. "Yes, I imagine you did. That aside, I need information from you. As I mentioned before, I am trying to find a close friend of mine. The man I search for looks similar to Alto here."

Randall's gaze turned toward the silent man in the corner who was ever watching. He immediately thought of the man working with O'Shea.

"I seem to remember you saying something about that. Did the guy do something?"

The next second, Victor stood before him. The man's hand tightened around his throat. He couldn't move. Something dark crawled through his mind, seeking. A chill seeped into his body. He felt as if he were dying. Instinctively, he struggled to raise his hand. His body silently screamed. He couldn't breathe.

Suddenly Victor released his death grip. Randall fell to his knees. With head bent, he tried to suck air into his lungs. Odd noises gurgled from his throat.

"Detective, I want results. Try harder to find the man I want. Alto, take the detective back to his car."

Alto reached down and yanked Randall to his feet. Still coughing, he was dragged outside and shoved into a car. As he tumbled into the backseat, he rolled onto his back. *What just happened?* Randall's head throbbed. He struggled to recall why his throat hurt. The last thing he remembered was coming out of Darlene's place. Puzzled, Randall sat up, noticing it was nearly dawn. *Why didn't I go home earlier?*

When Alto pulled up beside Randall's car, Randall yanked open the door and jumped out. The men in the car sped away without a backward glance. With a yawn, he quickly started his car and drove home. The pain in his head eased. Once in his house, he opted for a hot shower, hoping it would help wash away the fog that clouded his brain. Before sleep claimed him, his last thought was that he needed to avoid Victor—if he could.

43

The sun hovered on the horizon as Brett pulled into the driveway. Brett and Dragos dropped their gear in the kitchen. The smell of coffee lingered in the air.

Brett stiffened until he saw the note on the table. Quickly reading, he sighed. "Candy is in your room. She and Lisa decided to surprise us with a sleepover."

Dragos turned and stalked down the hall.

"What? No good-byes?"

Dragos's laughter trailed down the hallway. Once Brett made his way to his room, he stood in the doorway, gazing at Lisa curled up on his bed. He was tempted to turn around and go sleep on the sofa. If he climbed into his bed, he needed to be sure of what he wanted. She wore one of his old T-shirts. Her little snores made him snicker. He had forgotten the noises she made while sleeping.

Without flicking on the light, he quietly shut the bathroom door. Shedding his clothes, he stepped under the steaming water. Hands braced against the shower wall, he let the water beat down on the back of his neck and shoulders.

A faint sound drew his attention. The shower door opened, and Lisa stepped into the shower. Her blonde curls gathered atop her head.

"Want some company?" Her heavy-lidded gaze caressed him.

He glanced at her lithe body. Full breasts. Slim hips. A sheen of mist clung to her. Dragging his gaze upward, he met her smile.

Without uttering a word, he swept his arm out and pulled her against him. His mouth took control.

"What—"

He ground his lips against hers. Her teeth nipped at his mouth. God, how he missed her.

She wound her arms around his neck and wrapped her legs around his waist, heating his blood even more. Without breaking the kiss, he shut off the water and made his way to the bed. Bumping against the mattress, he fell, taking her with him. She giggled as their bodies bounced into each other.

Wrapping a hand into her hair, he tilted back her head and met her sultry gaze.

"I can't make any promises."

She reached up to stroke his face, her fingers slowly trailing down across his lips.

"Am I asking for any?"

His voice deepened. "Let me show you how much I missed you."

He slid down her body and jerked her thighs apart.

Michael silently groaned. He needed to talk to Brett. He walked into the bedroom, planning on waking Brett up. Instead he was greeted with the sight of his bare ass bouncing up and down. Arms and legs were all tangled together. Grunts and groans filled the room.

Holy smoke! That was a sight he wouldn't forget soon. Vaporizing, he drifted down the hall. He paused outside Dragos's room. *Crap! Even the bloodsucker is getting some. Is there a full moon or what?* All kinds of smooching sounds came from Dragos's room. Michael grunted. He felt deprived.

Back in the kitchen, Michael stared into the refrigerator. He needed a beer, but for some reason he was unable to eat or drink. He got to watch everyone else enjoy. Ghostdom was not quite what he'd imagined.

With a nudge of his foot, the refrigerator door closed. Bored, he drifted outside. A strange black car was parked a few houses down the street. The hairs on the back of his neck stood on end.

He stood behind the car. One man sat inside—a tall one. His head nearly touched the car's roof. The man turned his head to look out the side window. Long hair settled about his shoulders. *Uh oh!*

Slowly, he walked toward the front of the car to get a better look. This didn't bode well for Brett. Torn, he glanced back toward Brett's house. He didn't want to go back to the love shack. It brought back too many memories of his deceased wife; He missed her dearly.

Obviously the guy was just watching the house. It didn't appear he was going to go inside. Soon pink rays from the rising sun filled the sky, and the man started the car and drove away.

Michael glanced upward and nodded. *Okay, okay,* he thought. Everyone had been getting testy lately. The fact that vampires were watching Brett's house was a bad omen. A storm was coming. Michael wasn't sure if they were ready to go one-on-one with vampires—not yet anyway.

44

It was nearly noon before Brett rolled over to look at the clock. He reached out to find the bed empty. The sound of running water came from the bathroom. He could get used to having Lisa at his side day and night.

Her announcement a few months ago that she was taking a job out of state still stung. Maybe it was pride preventing him from asking her to move in. It was like a wall had built up around his heart. Yet after the past six hours, he had hope that things were changing.

He reached for his shorts. His stomach rumbled as he walked to the kitchen. He pulled out a package of refrigerated cinnamon rolls and put them into the oven. He made his way back to the bedroom and knocked on the bathroom door.

"Can I come in?" he asked

Lisa peeked out with a towel wrapped around her body. "Sure. I just finished drying my hair."

He grabbed a toothbrush and flipped on the water. Lisa smacked his bottom as she passed by him.

"Hey! Aren't I supposed to be the one to smack your ass?"

Lisa laughed at him and tossed the towel at his head. "Don't be a caveman, O'Shea." She turned and sniffed the air. "Is that cinnamon I smell?"

He chuckled. "I may be a caveman, but this caveman is baking cinnamon rolls for your breakfast."

She placed her hand over her heart. "Aw. You're so special. Let's eat. I'm starved."

He grabbed Lisa and tossed her onto the bed.

"Sorry, I'm not leaving any rolls for you."

With that, he took off running down the hall. Lisa screamed and ran after him. She hooked the waist of his shorts, yanking them down to expose his half of his butt.

"Hey! Not fair," he yelled as he swatted her hand.

Laughing, they skidded to a stop once they noticed Dragos and Candy sitting at the kitchen table. The pan of steamy cinnamon rolls sat between them.

"Good lord, Brett. Cover yourself," Candy snickered as she stuck a fork into a roll. "We were just going to dig in."

Brett nodded as he threw an arm around Lisa's shoulder. "Anyone want something to drink?"

"Coffee, please," Candy called out.

Lisa kissed his cheek.

A cool draft coursed through the room. Brett rolled his eyes. He knew what was coming.

Michael appeared at the table, eyeing the warm rolls. He briefly met Brett's gaze before muttering, "Glad you all finally crawled out of bed. Lot of hanky-panky going on last night."

Grabbing a cup of coffee and setting it before Candy, Brett muttered, "How would you know?"

"Never mind." Michael snapped. "I need to tell you something."

Settling into a chair, Brett reached for a roll, licking the sticky glaze off his finger. "So what do you want to tell me?"

"You've got someone watching your house."

Forks clattered to the table. Candy gasped. Lisa reached out and gripped Brett's arm.

"Who?"

Michael shrugged. He lifted Brett's plate to his nose and inhaled. "I so wish I could eat one of these things."

Brett grabbed the plate from Michael and dropped it on the table. "Damn it! Who was watching the house?"

"Calm down, sonny. You're starting to irritate me. Now, as I was going to say, it was a guy dressed in black from head to toe. Kind of like our vamp here."

Dragos's eyes narrowed, and he started to rise from the chair before Candy grabbed his shoulder and pushed him back down.

"Damn it, Michael. Quit screwing around. Did the guy have short hair or long hair? What kind of car?"

Michael frowned. "I grew up in the early 1900s. How in the hell am I supposed to know what kind of car it was? It was black, okay—all shiny with four doors."

Candy and Lisa looked at one another and bit back smiles. Brett grew impatient with his annoying ghost.

"Oh yeah, before I forget. The guy had long, dark hair. Like I said earlier, he reminded me of our in-house bloodsucker."

Dragos roared and leapt across the table, reaching for Michael's throat. Brett jumped up, ready to intervene. Michael smiled and disappeared. Dragos crashed to the floor as he grabbed thin air.

Candy jumped up and tried to help Dragos. He angrily brushed away her hand and rose to his feet. "I will enjoy killing that ghost," he said.

Brett laughed. "Be my guest. I've wanted to do it several times."

Muttering to himself, Dragos unclenched his fists before sitting down.

"Well, now that we know someone is watching us, let's set a trap," Dragos suggested.

"Just what I was thinking. I'm guessing that it's one of Victor's guys." Brett grimaced. "Do you agree?"

"Unfortunately, I believe you are correct. We must proceed

with caution. Victor is very methodical and leaves nothing to chance."

Candy cleared her throat. "Excuse me; you guys need backup. Just tell us how Lisa and I can help."

He and Dragos stared at her. Before Brett could say no, Dragos huffed.

"No! I will not allow you to endanger your life. You will stay home, where it is safe."

Brett watched Lisa and Candy glance at one another. *Oh shit! Dragos just lost the battle.*

Dragos smugly stated, "I will not—"

"Hold on; there's got to be a way you two can help," Brett interrupted.

Lisa folded her arms across her chest and glared at Brett.

"Hmmph! Yeah, you men will let us know if we can help. Apparently you've forgotten how I helped you last year."

Candy jerked her purse onto the table and pulled out her gun. "I can protect us quite fine without the help of you guys."

Dragos grabbed the gun. "I do not like the idea of my woman carrying a gun. It is too dangerous."

Brett winced. *Dragos needs to keep quiet. He's just adding fuel to the fire.*

"Guys! Calm down," Brett ordered. "Dragos, you need to listen. Candy is well qualified on how to use a gun. She's a better shot than me, and that's saying something."

Grudgingly, Candy nodded before shoving the gun back in her purse.

"Thanks, Brett."

He turned toward Lisa. "Lisa, remember the York Street case? Your strategy worked then. Any ideas on this case?"

Lisa nodded. "I think we need to fight the battle on their turf, not here at your house."

"I agree. I don't want Victor breaking in here."

Dragos snorted. "That is well and good, but how can we take the battle to them when we do not know where they are?"

Brett leaned in, lowering his voice. "That is why we are going to follow them. If we're lucky, they will take us right to Victor."

"Dragos, you need to figure out how you can break Victor."

Dragos shrugged. "I'm working on it."

45

Allen paced the floor of his office. Humiliation burned inside him. How dare O'Shea and Anders make a public spectacle out of him. Payback was going to be hell for those two.

His phone hadn't quit ringing with calls from television producers, gossip magazines, and lots of scared people in Des Moines. If he guessed correctly, less than a quarter of the callers took him seriously.

Maybe it had been a mistake to boldly announce that vampires existed. Perhaps he should have built up to it and provided more evidence. But it was too late now for regrets. He was determined to prove to the doubters that the creatures existed.

His cell buzzed, interrupting his ruminations.

"Terrence. Are you ready? Yes, I'll meet you outside."

Darkness fast approached. With Terrence, his driver, helping him, they would capture one of the vampires. There was no doubt that with his superior knowledge and abilities, they could get the killer. O'Shea and Anders would be fired by the time he was done.

The limo door was open as he ran out of the office. He climbed into the back. Excitement coursed through him. This was his opportunity to prove himself.

"Did you bring the guns and a stake?

Terrence met his gaze in the rearview mirror. "Yes, sir. I have everything you requested. Are you sure we brought the right things? Is it enough?"

He laughed. "I've carefully planned this. I've thought of everything."

Terrence shook his head. "I don't doubt it, but from the things that I've seen in the movies and TV, vampires are hard to kill. Plus they're supposed to be fast."

Allen leaned forward and patted his driver on the shoulder before leaning back in the seat.

"They may be fast, but we're using the latest technology. By tomorrow morning, we will have the proof we need."

After the fiasco with Michael earlier in the day, Brett retreated to his bedroom as soon as the women left. Dragos was already encamped in his room, barely speaking to him. The women grumbled as they left, clearly unhappy about not going on the ride tonight.

Brett plopped onto the bed. Knowing Lisa and Candy as he did, he'd have to come up with something for them to do; otherwise, they would get into trouble.

Dusk turned the sky into shades of pink and red. Even though it was almost time to leave, he was on the verge of falling asleep.

Pounding on the front door jarred him. Reluctantly, he got off the bed and went to the door. Anders stood on the porch, peering at him through the peephole. His normally combed salt-and-pepper hair was mussed, as if he'd run his fingers through it.

Brett opened the door. "Chief. What's going on?"

Anders stepped inside and walked toward the kitchen. "Where's the coffee?"

"On the counter. Pick the flavor you want."

After watching his boss stare at the coffeemaker for several minutes, he chuckled.

"Here, give me that. I'll do it. I know you're not here for coffee, so what's going on?"

Anders pulled out a chair and sat down. His lips pulled taut. His usual smile was absent tonight.

"Things are bad. I met with the city manager today. A committee has been organized to search for a new chief. They're on a fast track."

Brett's jaw dropped in disbelief. "You're shitting me. Does Foster know?"

Anders got up to grab the coffee and returned to his seat. "Yeah, he knows. The city council wants this case resolved now. As if we don't! I know you're doing everything possible to catch the vampire, but I would feel better knowing that I am out on the streets helping. So, starting tonight, I'm working with you."

Several objections were on the tip of Brett's tongue. "I know it's your prerogative to do that, but what about your other job duties? We're working nights."

Anders waved his hand. "The assistant chief is getting some on-the-job experience. Besides, I miss this type of work. Do you have a problem?"

How was he supposed to respond to that question? "What about your wife? She was upset last year when you were injured."

Anders took a sip of his coffee. "I already talked to Caroline about doing this. She's on board. Listen, I know you probably don't want me to tag along, but if we can expedite this situation, then everyone wins."

Dragos sauntered into the room, pausing when he saw the chief.

"Good evening, sir." Dragos cast a questioning look in Brett's direction.

"Sit down and join us." After Dragos took a chair, Brett cleared his throat. He was worried about what Dragos would say in front of the chief.

"The city manager is looking for a new chief."

Dragos's eyes widened. "Why?"

"They don't think we're doing enough to catch the killer. So the chief has decided that he is going to work the case with us."

Dragos glanced at the chief and then at him. "Work with us? You mean go out and search for Victor with us?"

The chief smiled. "That's exactly what it means. Do you have a problem with me going with you guys?"

Dragos shook his head. "No. I will be honored. Brett told me how the two of you caught the last serial killer. Your experience will be helpful."

The chief clapped his hands together. "Great. When do we leave?"

Brett rose. "We were just getting our gear together. Dragos, have you eaten?"

Dragos nodded. "I had a couple of bags a few moments ago."

"Okay, let's load up and see if we get lucky tonight."

"Get down," yelled Candy. "They're pulling out."

Minutes later, the girls sat up in time to see Brett's car turn the corner. Candy quickly turned on her car and followed the guys.

"Hurry up before we lose them," Lisa hollered.

She was careful to stay several hundred feet behind the car. She leaned forward, hunching over the steering wheel.

"Hey, there are three men in the car."

Lisa's eyes narrowed as she strained to see in the darkness. "I wonder who the other person is?"

Candy sped up, easing closer to the other car.

Lisa gasped. "That looks like Anders!"

Candy stared at the car again. "It does, but why is he with them?"

"It doesn't matter. What matters is not getting caught following the guys. If the chief sees us, Brett could lose his job."

"Did Brett give you the third degree the other night?"

Lisa giggled. "I didn't give him a chance. I kind of surprised him while he was showering."

"You're bad, girl. Dragos quizzed me about what we did all night. I think he's suspicious."

"Then we'd better be careful." Lisa frowned and turned to her. "Why are you dropping back so far? We're going to lose them."

"No we're not. I can see them just fine."

Lisa folded her arms across her chest. "Just don't blame me if you lose them."

The night dragged on. They followed the car as it drove through the northeast side of town. The men pulled into a crowded diner. The smell of barbecue filled their car parked across the street.

Lisa's stomach growled. "Damn it! Do you think I could sneak up to the take-out window and grab us something to eat? I love their chicken tenders."

Candy popped open the glove compartment and tossed several protein bars onto Lisa's lap.

"Here's our supper."

Lisa picked up a bar and stared at it. "This is so not fair."

"Tell me about it," Candy sighed. "Those things have been my dinner more times than I can count."

"At least you two can eat them. I just watch all of you eat!"

Both of them screamed and turned toward the backseat. Instinctively, Candy threw her bar at the speaker.

"Ow!" yelled Michael. "What was that for?"

She reached out and swatted his leg. "Damn it! Why did you have to scare us?"

"Yeah," growled Lisa. She tossed her bar at Michael's head.

"Okay, okay. I'm sorry." Michael held up his hands in surrender

Candy narrowed her eyes and glared at Brett's deceased relative. "Why are you here?"

Michael shrugged. "Something bad is going to happen."

Lisa gasped. "Is Brett going to be hurt?"

He shook his head. "You know I don't always know the specifics. The big guy only gives me hints."

"Big guy? Who's that?" asked Candy.

Michael grinned and pointed upward. "My boss."

She shook her head. "Boss? What am I missing?"

"The guy in charge of angels, heavenly things, and good ghosts—like me."

Good lord. "Does this mean that we're going to get hurt?"

"Ladies! Calm down. I'm here to help you. Don't worry."

Candy watched Lisa tear into a protein bar. "'Don't worry,' he says. I remember the last case you and Brett worked. There were plenty of reasons to be worried on that one."

"Tsk, tsk," Michael murmured. "Don't worry about the details. That's why I'm here."

Candy pointed out the window. "Look! There's a guy doing something by Brett's car."

Just as Lisa started to open the car door, Candy pulled her back into the seat.

"Wait. You can't go running up there. The men could come out any second."

Candy reached under her seat and pulled out a pair of night-vision binoculars. She bit her lower lip in concern. "I don't like the looks of this," she whispered.

Lisa stared at the man. "What? What's he doing?"

"I think he's putting a tracking device on the car. I can't tell without getting closer."

"Screw this! I'm telling Brett right now."

She grabbed Lisa's arm. "Are you crazy? They will know we're following them."

Michael leaned forward in the seat. "I'll go check it out. Be right back."

Michael disappeared. Intently watching the man, they saw Michael appear behind the guy. The man dressed in dark clothing crouched low and ran back to his car.

Minutes later, Michael reappeared in the backseat. He stuck his closed fist toward the women and opened the palm of his hand to reveal a small metal item.

Candy grabbed the item. "I was right. A micro GPS tracking device."

"It's so small. I can't believe the magnets will hold it to a car," Lisa muttered, staring at the small rectangular device.

Michael removed his fedora and set it on the seat. "So this little gadget lets someone know where Brett's car is at all times?"

Candy nodded. "The bigger question is, who is tracking Brett?" Candy opened the window and tossed the microchip on the ground.

Lisa's lip quivered. "Listen, Candy. We need to tell Brett about this."

"No, we will wait. No one can track him now, since we've got the device. As long as we keep checking his car, we can keep him safe. Besides, you're the one who wanted to follow them. We're not going to blow it now. They need us to keep them safe."

Lisa's eyes welled up with tears. "What do you think, Michael? You're close to Brett."

He leaned forward and put an arm around each of them.

"I can keep your secret a little while longer, but no guarantees for the future. I'll hang out with you and see what happens."

Ignoring Lisa's sniffles, Candy pierced Michael with a glare. "You said something bad was going to happen. Was the tracking device it? Is everyone safe now?"

Michael tugged the fedora down over his brow and folded his arms across his chest. "Don't know."

"What do you mean you don't know? Your great-grandson's life could be in danger."

Michael's lips tightened. "Listen here, Missy, I know who the hell Brett is. I wouldn't jeopardize his life or yours. But there are things in this universe that you don't know shit about. So just sit back and let things ride."

Lisa burst into tears. Candy's hand curled into a fist. Never had she so wanted to hit a man. *That damn ghost!* She figured he'd disappear if she took a swing.

Candy jerked forward. The men came out of the restaurant, got into their car, and headed west on the interstate. Traffic was heavy tonight. A pair of semitrucks roared up the road and cut in front of her car, blocking the view of Brett's car.

"Damn. I can't see the guys." With that, she stomped on the accelerator and passed the trucks.

The speedometer showed eighty miles per hour. Candy was grateful that no highway patrol cars were visible. Suddenly a sleek silver sports car tore past them. It came from out of nowhere. She glanced toward the driver, hoping to flip him off, but could see nothing. The windows were tinted black. The car cut in front of her, causing her to slam on the brakes. The silver car closed in on Brett.

"Who the hell is that?" Lisa asked.

"Who knows? The idiot almost ran us off the road."

Candy sped up, hoping to get the license number of the car ahead of them. Unbelievably, they were now pushing eighty-five miles an hour. The risk of discovery or an accident was too much, so she eased off the pedal. She was wound as tight as a firecracker. Nothing was going right tonight. Even Lisa was starting to get on her nerves.

She watched the silver car roar closer and closer to the rear of Brett's car. *What are they doing? Is the driver trying to cause a wreck? Oh shit! This is what Michael warned us about.* As one, they gasped when the sports car rammed into Brett's car.

46

Brett's chest slammed into the steering wheel. Dragos groaned as his arm flew out to keep from hitting the windshield. Brett heard Anders grunt from the backseat. What the hell had happened?

Brett looked in the rearview mirror and saw a small car surging forward to hit them again.

"Brace! We're about to get hit again," Brett yelled.

Anders growled. "The hell with this. Call it in, O'Shea." Anders ripped out his Glock and lowered his window. Leaning his upper body out the car, Anders aimed toward the car behind them.

Torn between watching the road ahead and watching the action behind him in the mirror, Brett struggled to maintain control of the car while calling in for backup. The wind blew through Anders's jacket, causing it to whip about his frame. His grayish hair stood on end. Brett couldn't see Anders's face, but he knew the determination within the man behind him. Anders was pissed, and that wasn't a good thing for the asshole ramming them.

Brett jerked as the sound of gunshots reverberated in his ear. Anders fired two shots at the car behind them.

The other car hit the brakes and fishtailed across the two-lane interstate behind them. Sounds of brakes and the smell of burning rubber filled the air. The sports car spun into the grass median lining the road and slammed to a stop. Smoke filtered up from under the hood.

"Did you get the son of a bitch?"

Anders dropped back into the seat. "Don't know; I was aiming for the tires." With Anders back in the car, Brett hit the brakes and whipped the car around so it was going in the opposite direction. He raced toward the sports car. Ignoring the line of cars stopped ahead of them, Brett roared up to the side of the silver car.

As the car screeched to a halt, Brett jumped out with a gun in hand. Ripping open the silver car's door, he froze. *Empty?* No one was in the car. Not one person. *What the hell happened?*

Seconds later, Dragos and Anders ran up behind him. The disbelief was evident on their faces. Brett exhaled, letting his shoulders cave forward as he realized they could have crashed and died. Sirens and flashing lights swiftly approached.

Anders rubbed his shoulder. "Someone was driving that car. How did they get away so quickly?"

Dragos hung his head. "Only a vampire could have moved so swiftly. Since they were watching your house, we have to assume Victor is behind this."

Anders's eyes widened. "What do you mean they were watching your house? Damn it, O'Shea. You're supposed to report shit like that."

"Sir, it *just* happened."

Dragos cleared his throat. "I don't think they're watching Brett. I think it's me they're after. I can't put your lives in danger any longer."

"Listen to me," Anders ordered. "You're part of our team. If Victor is getting this desperate, then chances are he will make a mistake. This is our opportunity to set a trap."

Anders glanced over his shoulder. Law enforcement cars by the dozen were closing in. "Let me deal with this."

Anders pulled out his badge and walked toward the officers running in their direction. Brett turned toward Dragos. He licked his dry lips as he glanced at the edge of the woods on the opposite side of the road.

"You think it was a vampire?" Brett asked.

Dragos's eyes darkened. "Yes.

❧

An hour later, police finally wrapped up the crime scene and opened the road, letting traffic resume on the interstate. It was backed up as far as the eye could see. Brett and Dragos stood off to the side, waiting for Anders to return. A news crew had cornered the chief and was interviewing him.

The night hadn't gone as planned, but then nothing in Brett's life ever went as planned. Ever since the ghost had entered his life, he had been on an emotional roller coaster and nearly died more times than he could count. Yet he wouldn't trade a minute of it.

Dragos blew out a breath, which drew Brett's attention. His friend was as impatient as he was. Protocol and paperwork were unnecessary burdens. After the adrenaline rush, Brett was crashing. Walking forward, he studied Dragos.

"How are you holding up?"

Dragos stared at the line of cars slowly driving by. "You will not appreciate what I am about to tell you, but I'm pretty sure that I saw the women drive by."

Brett turned, gazing at the line of cars. "What? When, just now?"

"No. Several minutes ago. I was watching Anders, and when I turned back, I saw Candy's car."

"You saw her car?"

"Well, no. I mean I'm not sure. It was a few cars past us. There were two women in the car. I'm pretty sure that is what I saw." Dragos whirled toward him. His long coat swirled about his legs.

"Listen, we went through this."

Anders pulled his jacket tighter about his body and headed in their direction. Dampness permeated the air. Low-lying fog from the nearby river rolled toward them. Anders opened the car door and hesitated. "You guys ready? I'm freezing my ass off. Let's go."

Brett glanced at Dragos and rested his hand on his shoulder. "We can continue our conversation later. I don't want to bring up the women in front of the chief."

Dragos nodded and stalked toward the car, his frame stiff and unyielding. Brett ran a hand through his hair, scratching his head. *What if Dragos really did see the women?* He knew that Dragos had better night vision than he did. *What were the women doing? Following us? Both of them know better than to interfere in police business or put themselves in danger.*

Sighing, Brett got behind the wheel and turned the car toward home.

"Hurry up," Allen hissed. "I need more light up here."

Terrence lifted the lantern, casting a wider circle of light around them. "Sir, I think we should bring in some additional men."

Allen dropped his bag of tools and weapons on the dirt floor. "You're not going to chicken out on me, are you?"

Terrence stiffened. "Of course not. I just want to make sure we have enough men to be successful."

Chortling, Allen opened the bag, searching for gloves. "Oh, don't worry about that. When haven't I been successful? Now bring that light closer."

It took both of them to pull open the cave entrance. Allen took a deep breath and studied the abyss before him. Slowly he took a step, only to realize that he was stuck. He glanced down and groaned. Moist red clay covered the bottom half of his boots. *Damn!* Somehow water had found its way inside the cave.

He shone the light around the cave. Several trickles of water graced the limestone walls, tracing the cracks and crevices of the ancient stones and pooling on the floor.

"C'mon; let's get ready."

Terrence tossed the bag on one of the caskets. Dust swirled up around his face. "Damn it."

Allen tore open the bag and pulled out a long knife and a gun, carefully setting them aside.

"Are you expecting trouble, sir?"

He shrugged. "Just precautions. Look around. Someone has been taking items that belong to me. Several things are missing. I'm hoping to surprise the vampires."

"Shouldn't we let the cops deal with vampires?"

Allen glared at Terrence. "Of course not," he snapped. "Now help me position these cameras around the cave. I don't want anyone to see them."

For the next hour, the men worked in silence as they positioned the wireless cameras. Anyone entering the cave would be caught on camera. As they were about to finish up, the sound of snapping wood came from outside the cave.

Terrence slid out his gun. "I'll go check it out."

Allen nodded. "It's probably a raccoon or possum. Be careful. The damn things could have rabies."

Terrence eased through the doorway, barely making a sound as he made his way through the damp clay. Being ex-military, Terrence knew his stuff. He was the best driver Allen had ever hired.

Anxious to finish setting up the cameras and get back to the car, Allen loaded the bag. When the light flickered, he picked up the lantern and smacked the bottom a couple of times. The light brightened.

He stiffened and turned back toward the entrance. A gurgling sound echoed from outside the cave. His heart stuttered.

He crept to the doorway, flattening himself against the wall. Whispering, he called, "Terrence. Terrence, is that you?" A low moan floated through the darkness. "Terrence, answer me." He picked up the extra gun. It wavered back in forth in his hand. He tried to take a calming breath, but he couldn't move. Fear seized him. *Terrence may be in trouble. I have to go help him.*

With his back against the wall, Allen slid out through the door and into the dark tunnel. He couldn't see Terrence's lantern. Had he gone down farther in the tunnel? Inch by inch, he moved forward. He was afraid to turn on the flashlight or otherwise draw attention to himself.

With his hand outstretched, he used the walls of the tunnel as a guide to keep moving forward. Nothing but blackness met his gaze. Not a sound filled the tunnel. *Maybe Terrence was right about calling in additional men. Too late now.* He had no choice but to keep on moving.

What seemed like hours later, he finally reached the end of the tunnel. Moonlight and shadows filled the dig site. Fresh air tickled his nose. He forced himself to slowly walk toward the car.

Without warning, he stumbled forward, falling to one knee. The gun fell to the ground. Before he could get up, a hand grabbed him from behind and pulled him upward.

Fear rose up inside. "Urgh! Let go." Panic took over. His

arms flailed wildly. Finally, the grip on him loosened and he fell forward on his stomach. Sour acid rose in his throat.

A voice hissed in his ear.

"Sir, sir. Calm down. It's me—Terrence."

Terrence? Allen turned on his back and looked up. His guard leaned down and held out a hand. Scratches lined Terrence's face. Blood spatter dotted his face. Once on his feet, he pulled out a handkerchief to wipe his face.

"Damn it. You scared me to death. Didn't you hear me call you?"

Terrence nodded. "Sir, look down."

Allen's stomach rolled. He winced. The body of a young man lay at his feet. The man's neck was sliced from ear to ear.

"Did you do that?" Allen asked.

"I did. I heard something, so I hid behind a large boulder. I heard him approach me. All of a sudden, he attacked me. Somehow I got my knife out. Luckily I just got him."

Allen bent over the dead man and pulled back his upper lip. Large canine teeth were prominently displayed.

He gasped and jerked upright. "We did it, Terrence. We did it. We got a vampire." Slapping his knee, he gloated. "Let's see what the cops say now. There should be some rope over by the ladder. Bring it here, and we'll get this guy loaded in the car. The coroner will prove that vampires do exist."

Allen pulled out his cell phone and took a couple of pictures of the dead vampire. *Anders and O'Shea's days are numbered,* he thought. He mentally began planning the news conference he would set up tomorrow.

He glanced up. Where did Terrence go? He saw the ladder nearby, but his guard wasn't to be seen.

"Terrence! Hurry up and bring that rope," he called. "We need to get out of here."

He bent down and clicked off several more pictures. Terrence's shadow covered the body.

Rising, Allen muttered, "It's about time. What took you so long?"

"A pity I couldn't have been here sooner. I'm afraid that Terrence will not be returning with the rope."

Allen turned and stared into the face of a stranger. The man was well dressed and looked as if he had come from a formal event. Although he wore a smile, it didn't reach his eyes. A shiver ran up Allen's spine. He glanced around the area, searching for Terrence.

"Where's my guard?" Allen asked.

The man shrugged a shoulder. "As I said, he will not be returning."

Allen took a deep breath. *Who the hell is this guy?* The sound of footsteps drew his attention. He slowly turned and saw two other men standing nearby. When Allen turned back to face the man, he had moved closer—much closer. It was then he noticed that the man towered over him. Unease filled him.

He took a step backward, casting a quick glance in the direction of the parked car. The man laughed, as if he could read his mind.

"Who are you, and what do you want?" he managed to squeak out before stepping back once again.

With his head cocked to the side, the intense stranger studied him. "I have wondered about who unearthed these tunnels and why. Perhaps you would have been better off to leave things as they were." With a wave of his thin, bony hand, the man crowed, "But if you had, I would not have met you and Terrence. Terrence was quite a delight, if I may say so."

What was the man saying? Nothing made sense. The other two men were pressing against his back. One leaned down toward his neck and sniffed. *What the hell?*

Rubbing his neck, Allen stammered, "Why are you here?"

A twisted smile flashed on the man's gaunt face as he threw his hands up into the air. Allen took a step back

"Forgive me. My social skills are lacking. This sometimes happens when I'm hungry. I am Baron Victor Sinclair."

Relief welled up inside Allen. *Thank God.* For a few moments, he had been terrified. The man sounded refined and educated.

He held out his hand to Victor. "Let me introduce myself. I'm John Allen. My ancestors were the founding fathers of our fair city."

"Yes, James Allen. I seem to remember that he was a captain in the army or something. He was a very demanding man."

Allen smiled, pleased that someone else appreciated history and knew of his personal commitment to the city. "You're right. He was an army officer. All the men in my family served, except me. As far as his being demanding, I never heard anyone mention that before. All the journals that I've read indicated that he was duty bound."

Victor's lips thinned. "Duty bound? I daresay that is one way to put it. In my opinion, he was an arrogant bastard."

Allen sucked in his breath. Annoyance rippled through him. "Well I don't know why you would say such a thing when you weren't even alive then to have met him."

Victor stiffened, and his eyes turned red. Alarm bells went off in Allen's head. Before he could run, the men grabbed his arms. They held him in place as he struggled and kicked.

Allen opened his mouth to scream when Victor gripped his chin. Sharp fingernails pierced his skin.

Victor's mouth became a grim, thin line. Victor's nose nearly touched his.

"That is where you are mistaken, John Allen. For I knew your ancestor quite well. I traveled with his company of men to this area. It was so desolate back then—rolling hills and timber as far as the eye could see. It quite reminded me of England. I helped the army plan the system of underground tunnels. How else would I know so much about them? He promised me that this land would be deeded over to me. Alas, he failed to deliver. Thus I know quite well that he was a bastard, as well as a liar, a cheat, and a son of a bitch."

Allen screamed. He prayed that someone would hear him and come to help. *Victor is wrong; no human can live that long. He couldn't have known James Allen.*

"You're crazy. Let me go. We can forget this ever happened."

Victor released his grip and drew back. Sharp, piercing fangs ripped from his mouth. Victor's hot breath swept across Allen's face as he pressed forward. A high-pitched cry tore from Allen's throat. Tears coursed down his face. The men's laughter echoed in his ears. *What is going to happen? I don't want to die. I'm too important to die!*

Suddenly one of the vampires ripped off his left sleeve. Without warning, the man bent and sank his teeth into his shoulder. Allen's legs crumpled to the ground. The monsters yanked him to his feet, holding him upright.

"Mr. Allen, you must cooperate. It's going to be a long night. You may thank your long-lost ancestor for this. It brings me pleasure to know that I am going to kill his relative. I plan on sucking every ounce of blood from your body. We will make it last as long as we can. Trust me; I will enjoy every moment."

Blood trickled down his arm. One of the vampires bent and ran his tongue up to its source. Allen recoiled from the touch. The man licked his lips and grabbed Allen's wrist and bit down.

Allen screamed in terror until his throat burned. His screams were useless. Their sick laughter and lewd comments made his stomach recoil. Vomit spewed from his mouth, splattering across Victor's shirt.

Every muscle in his body went limp. His head sagged to his chest as he wondered when the torture would end.

Suddenly his head was jerked upward. He felt his eyes roll back in his head.

Victor growled in his ear. "You are worse than a woman. See what you've done to my clothes?" Victor raised an arm and swung a hand across his face.

"Please, let me go," Allen sobbed. "Stop. I can't take any more."

One of the vampires smiled as blood dripped from his mouth.

My blood! God! I'm dying. It was becoming harder for Allen to keep his eyes open. He couldn't think straight.

A voice rumbled in Allen's ear. *Victor. May he rot in hell.*

"Wakie, wakie. It's time to bid farewell to this world," Victor said, pressing closer.

Victor's teeth sank into his neck. The initial pain was followed by numbness. Within minutes he no longer felt his arms or legs. Coldness seeped through his body. His heart stuttered. He no longer saw objects—only shadows.

The vampires bit into his wrists and feasted on his body. His head lolled to the side. Darkness pushed away the light until all he saw and felt was darkness. A deep sleep claimed him. He drifted away from the horror, from the pain, until it was no more

47

Eyes closed, Dragos felt a warm body cocoon against his. He smiled until he remembered the chase and gunshots from the day before. Candy wrapped an arm about his waist and squeezed.

"Are you awake?" she asked. "It will be dark soon."

He moved toward the edge of the bed before rising. Candy's arm slid from him.

"Yes. I've been lying here thinking."

He heard the rustling of sheets behind him. Candy rose on her knees and wrapped her arms around his shoulders, pressing kisses on his neck.

"I didn't hear you come in last night. What time did you guys finish up?"

He gently removed her arm and rose. His gaze skimmed her naked figure. He pushed away the temptation to crawl back into bed. "Late. I need to take a shower. We're going out again tonight."

He escaped into the bathroom and shut the door. As he waited for the shower to get hot, he braced his arms against the sink and stared into the mirror. *What the hell am I doing?* He knew he couldn't have a lasting relationship with a woman. He'd had Brett look up known facts about vampires. Much was conjecture or myth—whatever one chose to believe. Supposedly he wouldn't age. She would. How would he find blood once his dwindling supply was gone? No way would he take Candy's blood.

Yet what really bothered him was Candy. Brett didn't believe that he had seen the women trailing them the day before. He knew the truth. His newly improved vision had enabled him to clearly see the women. He wanted to forbid Candy to do such a thing ever again, but it was clear that today's women were much more independent than what he was used to.

"Argh!" He raked fingers through his hair. He hated that Victor had robbed him of a chance for a normal life with his parents and friends. The fact that his parents died never knowing what happened to him filled him with rage. It was a struggle to adjust to this new life being a vampire. He detested this existence of relying on human blood. He found it repulsive—disgusting. How could Candy love him?

His mood had soured by the time he returned to the bedroom. Candy had dressed and gone. He assumed she was mad at him. He would make amends later, but she wouldn't be following them again—not if he had anything to say about it. The house was silent. He pulled out a cell phone that Brett had given him and quickly punched in Brett's number. One of these days, he'd need to learn how to drive one of the four-wheeled death traps that clogged the streets. Until then, everyone would be safer if he wasn't behind the wheel.

Brett pulled up in Candy's driveway and honked. Dragos hurried outside. A damp breeze permeated the car. He rolled up the window and pressed the horn again.

Dragos ran out and jumped into the front seat next to him.

"Hi," said Brett. "Where's Candy? I don't see her car."

Dragos shrugged. "I think she's mad. She left while I was showering."

"Don't worry about it. She'll get over it."

"I'm not so optimistic," Dragos sighed.

Brett pulled onto the street. "Anders called and wants to meet us at Allen's dig site."

"Now what," groaned Dragos.

Brett shrugged.

Within minutes they arrived to see that the parking lot at the dig site was full of official city vehicles, including the coroner's car.

"Hell. There's at least one body here," Brett swore.

"How do you know?"

"The coroner's car. Once a body is discovered, we can't move it until the coroner gives us the green light. C'mon; let's find Anders."

He cautiously made his way through the yellow tape and the detectives working the case.

"Hey, O'Shea! Why aren't you working on this mess?"

He turned and chuckled. "Donnellson. About time you worked a real case."

"Oh, this one is real all right—real bloody. Who's your friend?"

He nodded toward Dragos. "Dragos Eldridge. He's from England and is helping work the prostitute murders."

Donnellson studied Brett's partner. "Really. I hadn't heard that. I guess I'm not sure how someone from another country can help us solve a local case."

Dragos's eyes narrowed as he stepped closer to Donnellson. "I assure you that my expertise is quite unique."

Brett spotted Anders coming toward them. "Hey, there's Anders. Catch you later, Donnellson."

Brett lowered his voice as they walked toward the chief.

"I was afraid you were going to mention the word 'vampire' to Donnellson."

In a droll tone, Dragos muttered, "Just because I was not born in the twentieth-first century does not mean that I'm an idiot."

Casting a sideward glance to Dragos, Brett winced. "Sorry. I wasn't implying that you were. I guess I'm jumpy tonight. Let's ask Anders why we're here."

Anders shook their hands and pointed down to the site. "We've got a hell of a mess again. We have two bodies, and you'll never guess who. Damn, here comes the press." Anders pivoted and walked away. "Follow me. I don't want to be overheard."

The men walked to the edge of the parking lot and stood beneath a streetlight.

"I'll be quick. Once this hits the news, we won't have much time. John Allen and his driver were both murdered. Their throats were ripped apart. Allen had numerous bites and cuts all over his body. It was a brutal way to die."

Brett lowered his head, kicking the dirt at his feet. "Shit! You're joking, right?" Ignoring the chief's glare, Brett muttered, "Ironic isn't it? The guy who was intent on proving that vampires existed ended up getting killed by vampires."

"The coroner agreed to delay his report, so we'll have a few extra hours before the mayor knows about Allen's death—not that the coroner thinks a vampire killed the guy. Yet with Allen spilling his guts to the press about vampires, his death is bound to create questions. I want these bodies out of here ASAP. We don't need the press getting any surprise shots."

Dragos had remained silent as Anders updated them. Brett watched Dragos clench and unclench his hands several times, as though he wanted to punch someone.

"I will kill him! I swear to God I will kill the man before he takes one more human life."

Brett laid his hand on Dragos's shoulder. "Don't worry. Victor's days are numbered."

"I wish I were as confident," Dragos mumbled.

Anders grabbed Brett's sleeve and pulled him away from the scene. "Let's go. We're going to hit the streets every night until we find this guy."

Brett couldn't believe it. *Allen—dead.* He hadn't cared for Allen, but he hadn't wanted the guy dead either. As Brett passed the other detectives working the scene, Donnellson raised a questioning brow. Brett shrugged back in response. The less other cops knew about the case, the less chance for a leak to the press.

"O'Shea, you drive," Anders ordered. "First head somewhere so I can get a coffee." Tearing his fingers through short hair, Anders cursed. "God, I hate this shit. Damn vampires. I'm really getting sick and tired of all this paranormal crap in Des Moines."

Feeling Anders's intent gaze on him, Brett snapped, "Don't look at me like this is my fault."

"Fucking shit magnet," muttered Anders.

Brett bit his tongue. It was clear the chief was worried. The man had a lot of weight on his shoulders, and his job was on the line.

After retrieving coffee for Anders, he climbed back into the car. "Where to?"

Brett saw Dragos staring.out the back window. *Now what?*

"Hey, guys, which way do you want to go?"

"Where's Michael? I haven't seen him lately. He always seems to know what to do in these situations," Anders asked.

"Damn ghost," Dragos hissed.

Anders glanced over his shoulder and chuckled. "Gets on your nerves, does he? Don't worry; Michael can be an ass, but he was a big help with solving the last big case."

"Now that you mention it, I haven't seen him much. We definitely could use his help." Brett pulled out of the convenience store parking lot and drove west down Grand Avenue and past Terrace Hill, the Victorian mansion where the governor lived.

"O'Shea, a car is following us," Dragos growled.

Brett's gaze darted to the side mirror. "Anyone you recognize?" He hoped Dragos didn't see Candy's car again. That was getting old.

"I do not believe so. It appears to be a larger car."

Anders turned in his seat and stared at the car behind them. "Might be nothing. Turn south on Terrace Drive. With the winding roads there, we can lose them."

Brett stomped the accelerator and made a sharp left turn. The road was a succession of turns. Anyone not familiar with these streets could easily get confused. After making a quick turn, he shut off the car lights and pulled up a driveway. The large, affluent homes south of Grand Avenue were graced with manicured yards and mature trees and bushes that provided natural privacy barriers—an advantage for them tonight. Brett drove up a circle drive and parked next to a garden shed.

Minutes ticked by. Only the sound of their harsh breathing filled his ears. Brett took out his gun and set it on the console between him and Anders. The windows of the car grew tainted with the warm moisture trapped in the car, obscuring their vision. He leaned over the steering wheeling and wiped the windows with the palm of his hand.

He glanced at the chief. "It's been quite a while since we've seen a car. Do you think we're clear?"

"Yeah, I think we're good. With Allen's body fresh on our minds, we're all jumpy," Anders rationalized.

Brett eased the car down the driveway, glancing down the street. It appeared to be empty. Anders leaned forward in the seat. His leg nervously tapped up and down.

"You okay, Chief?" Brett asked.

With scrunched-up brows, Anders turned to stare at him. "Of course. Why?"

"Nothing. Just wondered."

He turned the corner and drove toward the main intersection. He felt his body relax a second before Dragos yelled out a warning.

"Brace yourselves!"

48

"Where did they go?" Lisa asked "You said you knew this area of town."

Candy stared at the empty streets. "Damn it! I do. They're hiding somewhere close by."

Lisa felt tears gathering in her eyes. She angrily swiped her face with the back of her hand. "How do you know that?"

"Because that's what I would do if someone were tailing me. Besides, Brett knows what he's doing."

"Candy, we've got to find them. Do something."

Her friend sighed before yanking the wheel to the right, taking them down a narrow winding road.

Lisa could barely make out the outlines of the houses on the street. The trees blocked the views of the homes. The streetlights were few, creating a splattering of small orbs of amber light down the road.

Candy gasped as a car pulled out of a driveway ahead of them and turned in the opposite direction.

"It's them. It's them." Lisa gripped Candy's arm. "I was afraid that something had happened to them." Her good mood faded as Candy scowled at the car ahead of them. "What's wrong?"

"That's not their car. It's bigger. Maybe an SUV. Could they be following Brett and the guys?"

Lisa trembled. "What if it's the vampires?"

She stared at the vehicle ahead of them. *No, it has to be Brett's car. It just has to be.*

Candy laid a comforting hand on Lisa's. "Don't worry. We've got to stay focused."

They continued to follow the car through the darkened streets. As they took a curve, there was a split second where Lisa saw farther down the road. Another car pulled out in front of the car ahead of them. Lisa squinted, trying to make out the details of the car.

The dark car ahead of them decreased its speed. *What is going on?* Candy tapped the brakes.

"What are you doing? Pass them?"

"Damn it, Lisa, I can't pass them on this road." Candy bit her lower lip. "Besides, what if that other car is Brett's? Do you really want to get between the police and the vampires? We're not equipped for that. If we survived, Brett would kill me for dragging you into this."

Lisa smacked her fists on her thighs. "I feel so helpless. We've got to do something."

"I know that," Candy snapped. "I'm doing the best I can under the circumstances. It's not like I deal with vampires every day."

Lisa let out a breath and tried to calm her pounding heart. "I know. I'm sorry to be a bitch. I'm just worried."

Candy stared at the road ahead. "So am I. We need to stay alert and be patient."

They continued to trail behind the car through the twists and turns south of Grand.

Lisa gazed out the car window, absently staring at the dark houses they passed. Would the night never end? All she wanted was Brett back safe in her arms, lying in bed by her side, pressing kisses to her.

Suddenly her body flew forward as Candy hit the brakes.

"Ow! What is going on?

Candy pulled the car to a complete stop and pointed ahead. "Look."

Lisa gasped. The car in front of them had rammed into another car. From this distance, she couldn't tell who they had hit. *Did they do it on purpose? Is it Brett's car?* She grasped the door handle, ready to run toward the cars. She had to know whether Brett was in the car. As the car door opened, Candy grabbed her arm and pulled her back inside.

"What are you doing?" Candy hissed. "Get in here and be quiet."

She shook loose from Candy's grip. "Let go! We've got to go see what's happening." Tears blurred her vision.

Candy pressed the automatic locks. "For God's sake, Lisa, calm down. Do you want them to hear you?"

She swung her gaze to Candy. Her lips tightened into a line as she pressed the unlock button and tumbled to the ground before Candy could stop her. Crawling on all fours, she scrambled to a row of bushes. She saw men exiting the large black SUV and walking toward the car. Cursing under her breath, she scurried forward and flattened against a large oak tree.

With nerves ready to fray, she struggled to draw in a breath. As she peered around the tree, someone slammed into her body. When she opened her mouth to scream, a hand suddenly covered her mouth.

"Shh. Be quiet," warned Candy. "Follow me, and don't get yourself killed."

Lisa trailed after Candy, trying to imitate her movements. Candy had a gun and knew how to use it, so she was sticking close to her friend.

The rear end of the car was crumpled. Four men stood around the damaged car. It was Brett's car.

"Brett," Lisa cried. She couldn't take her eyes off the men. Their threatening size and demeanor would make anyone run.

Candy reached over and pinched her arm. "Be quiet," she hissed.

Lisa's eyes widened when the four men each grabbed a car door and pulled it from the frame. They then tossed all four of them into the street. *Shit! Who does stuff like that? Vampires?* Vampires were supposed to have superhuman strength. *Crap!*

The vampires standing near the right side reached into the car and yanked a man to the ground. The vampire on the driver's side dragged a limp body and dumped it near the other still body.

Lisa rose to her feet, but Candy jerked her back to the ground. Her throat burned from holding in her cries. She had to help Brett. Fear threatened to overwhelm her. Her stomach clenched. She struggled to break free, but Candy held her in a tight embrace.

"Brett. Brett's lying in the street. He's hurt." Unshed tears broke free. "We've got to help him."

Candy whispered, "Dragos and Anders are out there too. They could all be seriously injured. My phone's in the car. Do you have yours?"

Her voice cracked. "No, it's in … in my purse."

"Shit! We don't have time to go back." Candy's gaze was pinned to the wrecked vehicle. "Have you seen Dragos?"

Aghast, Lisa pointed toward the wreckage as two of the vampires dragged Dragos out the other side of the car. Dragos's head slammed onto the cement. He looked stunned and seemed to be unable to move. One of the vampires walked over and stared down at Dragos. A smile broke out on his face—an evil smile. He drew back his leg and kicked Dragos's stomach. A low groan escaped from the semiconscious man in the street.

The vampire took a vial out of his pocket. Using his teeth, he pulled out the cork and spit it to the ground. He pried open Dragos's mouth and poured the liquid down his throat. Dragos choked and rolled to his side.

Lisa heard Candy swear under her breath as her friend jumped to her feet. She jerked Candy down to the ground next to her.

They heard one of the vampires ordering the rest of them to load Dragos in the car.

Lisa sucked in her breath. "Hell. Brett's getting to his feet. What's he doing?"

Candy swore. "Stay down, stay down."

Helpless, Lisa had no choice but to watch Brett stagger to his feet. Wavering from side to side, he drew a gun, aiming it at the vampires.

"Stop right there!" Brett ordered. "Let him go and move away."

"Damn it, Brett," Lisa swore.

All four vampires straightened and turned to stare at Brett. The tension in the air crackled. A crooked smile broke on the leader's face. The vampire seemed to be annoyed. He nodded at the other vampires who had just stuffed Dragos into their car.

"I'm going to go back up Brett. Stay here," Candy whispered.

As Candy rose to her feet, the vampire shimmered and his body disappeared. Lisa's hands flew to her throat. *Vampires can do that?*

The vampire reappeared behind Brett and wrapped an arm around his neck. It also looked as if he bit Brett's neck. The next second, Brett collapsed in the vampire's arms. His gun clattered to the concrete.

Lisa's breath froze in her chest. *Is he alive?* Her hand trembled.

Candy dropped back to the ground. "Damn it."

The vampires tied Brett's hands together before dumping him into the back of the vehicle.

Lisa shook Candy's arm. "Do something! They're taking Brett."

Candy turned and gaped at her. "Are you kidding me? You want me to take on four vampires? Damn it. Now they're loading Anders."

Unable to stop shaking, Lisa shoved her hands into her pockets. "No. What are we going to do?"

"We've got to get our phones. We need to call for backup."

A light breeze sent a chill·through her. Air particles shimmered nearby. Without warning, Michael suddenly stood before them. Adjusting his fedora, he winked at them.

"Did I hear someone call for backup?"

Candy grabbed his arm and yanked him to the ground.

"What are you doing," he yelped.

"Shh! The vampires are over there," Lisa pointed to the wrecked car.

Michael studied the scene. "Why didn't you call me earlier?"

She took her finger and jabbed his chest. "Stop. Brett's tied up in the car. Anders is unconscious. They've taken Dragos too."

Michael laid a hand on her shoulder. "Take a breath. Why didn't you call for help earlier?"

"God, Michael. We couldn't. The phones are in the car." Lisa paused, holding up her finger. "Don't say it! At least we're here trying to help. You're Brett's guardian, so can't you do something?"

Michael snorted and shrugged. "Bloodsuckers make me nervous, and there are four of them."

Candy shot him an angry glare. "In case you two care, they're driving off with our guys." Candy turned to Lisa. "C'mon." She jumped up and ran to the car.

Rolling her eyes at Michael, Lisa hurried after Candy. She jumped into the front seat when Michael appeared in the backseat.

Candy sped down the road, trying to find the black SUV. The roads were eerily quiet. "There it is," she yelled. The vehicle was several hundred feet ahead of them.

"Michael, how about some of that divine intervention of yours."

He closed his eyes. Seconds later they popped open. "Nope. I'm getting nothing. You'd better follow them."

Candy growled. "Lisa, is this how it was last time working with a ghost?"

She sighed and fell back against the seat. "Yes and no. Damn vampires!"

49

Brett's eyes flew open as the trunk door popped open. A man in a dark suit leaned in and dragged him to the ground, where he collapsed. His fingers were numb. The rope wrapped around his hands was cutting off the blood. He struggled to get to his feet.

Anders's body lay sprawled on the ground nearby. Tears blocked his vision. The chief groaned and rolled over to his back. A large contusion covered the side of his face.

"Anders, Anders! Can you hear me?"

The chief's eyes slowly opened. Anders's hand clutched his head. "What happened?"

Brett bent and helped Anders get to his feet before himself falling against the SUV. His legs shook from the exertion of standing. He shook his head, trying to clear his mind. *Where are the guys that attacked us?*

He had no idea where they were. Lights of the city twinkled in the distance. Behind them was nothing but empty cornfields and woods. There were no houses nearby. *Damn, where are we?*

A hand slammed into his shoulder, throwing him off balance. "Hey! Watch it."

A man wrapped a hand around his neck, drawing him closer. "Don't press your luck."

Brett's heart pounded in his chest. The man's eyes glowed as he leaned forward and sniffed Brett's neck. *What the hell. A vampire?*

"Get walking or we will carry you inside," his captor ordered.

He turned and saw two vampires dragging Dragos out of the car. Dragos's hands and feet were tied with what appeared to be some type of metal wire. Dragos appeared to be unconscious, his head lolling forward.

They were herded into a sprawling house; a ranch house with empty lots nearby. With his heart pounding, his gaze darted from left to right. Was Victor here? He tripped down a dark stairway and spotted a dim light down a narrow corridor. At the end of the hallway, a large vampire filled a doorway. Long, dark hair swept his broad shoulders. Brett saw the gold eyes follow their movements. The vampire had a lithe yet muscular body, and his harsh, angular face showed little emotion.

With four vampires herding them down the hallway, Brett searched for a means of escape. There were no windows— nothing. Fear welled up inside of him. A quick glance back at the vampires revealed four pairs of gleaming red eyes. A shiver nearly brought him to his knees.

As they neared the lone figure in the doorway, the vampire clapped his hands. The harsh sound echoed in the tight, confined area.

"Well, well. At last, my dear friend, Dragos, returned to the fold. Whatever took you so long?"

Dragos shook his head, trying to break free from the vampire's grip. Eyes wide, the vampire's mouth opened to reveal deadly looking teeth.

"It was not long enough as far as I am concerned. Let the other men go."

Victor inched forward. Brett braced when Victor's arm

swept upward and a sharpened nail raked across Dragos's cheek.

"Silence! You are not in a position to make demands. Perhaps your friends will ensure your cooperation."

"Dragos, don't worry about us. We'll be fine," Brett murmured. He didn't want Dragos to do something drastic and end up getting killed.

Victor's gaze turned in his direction. His thin lips curled in disgust. "Ah, Detective O'Shea. We meet at last. Are you the one that hid my dear friend Dragos?"

Brett forced a smile. He'd give anything to stab a dagger into Victor's black heart.

"Hiding? No, I just helped out a friend."

Victor's brows rose. "Friend? Humans aren't our friends. They're our dinner."

The other vampires in the room chuckled. Yet their eyes consumed him as if he were a rare ribeye on a platter. Brett cringed while maintaining a nonchalant look.

"Throw the two of them in the basement. Bring Dragos to the pit." Victor curled his lip, revealing deadly teeth.

Helpless, Brett watched two vampires drag his friend down the hall. Dragos's legs were bent, as if he lacked the strength to stand on his own. As he and Anders were shoved down the hallway, he again noted the lack of windows or doors. There would be no quick and easy escape.

A door locked behind them. A lone lightbulb hung from the middle of the ceiling. A twin bed lined one wall. A ratty gray blanket covered a well-used, lumpy mattress. This was not the Marriott by any means. Anders dropped onto the bed and groaned, his eyes barely open. He wiped the side of his head, staring at the bloodstains.

"Hmm. No wonder I have a headache. Do you know where we are?"

Brett shrugged as he searched his pockets. "Not sure.

They slammed something into the back of my head. Do you have your cell?"

Anders felt his clothes and shook his head. "No. Sons of bitches probably took it."

"Some cops we are. Not a clue where we are, no phone, and no way out of here that I can see. Any ideas?"

Anders snorted. "Do I look like I know anything right now? I don't suppose there is any water in here?"

Brett opened an adjoining doorway and saw a half bath. A supply of plastic cups sat near the sink. He filled a glass and brought it to the chief.

After quickly draining the cup, Anders sighed. "Thanks. Sorry to do this to you, but I'm really dizzy."

"Relax. If you fall asleep, I'll wake you up every once in a while in case you have a concussion."

Anders's eyes drifted closed. Mumbling, he asked, "Where's Michael? Isn't he supposed to know when you're in trouble?"

"If he doesn't, we're toast. I don't think those vampires rent this room by the month."

Brett slid down the wall until he was seated. With his knees drawn up to his chest, he lowered his head. Anders's ashen-colored face worried him. The chief needed medical attention. *Where the hell did they take Dragos?*

"Michael. Michael," he whispered. "How about some help here?"

Silence. *Crap.* Now he was worried.

Dragos winced as he was pulled off his feet and hoisted upward. Thick chains wrapped around his arms. The tendons in his arms rippled as they pulled and stretched. With his head bent, his hair shielded his eyes, preventing Victor from enjoying his moment of pain.

Victor grabbed Dragos's hair, jerking his face upward. Dragos poured every ounce of hatred into his gaze. Victor smiled, his putrid breath seeping its way into Dragos's pores.

"You sent me on quite a wild goose chase. All you had to do was wait until I returned, and I could have saved you and the people of this city so much grief."

Swinging toward his captor, he tried to wrap his legs about Victor's throat.

Victor laughed and stepped back out of reach.

"I never asked to become a monster like you. I want nothing to do with you or your kind," Dragos roared.

Victor smirked, and a second later a fist buried itself into Dragos's stomach.

"Is that the best you can do?" Dragos spit into Victor's face. The glob slid down the bridge of his crooked nose and onto his lips. Victor calmly wiped it away.

"As rebellious as ever. You never did make it home to see your father before he died. Such a shame. The poor man suffered, never knowing what happened to his much beloved younger son."

Dragos yanked on the chains binding his hands. His biggest regret was having never seen his parents before they died.

"Shut your mouth, or you will regret it!"

Victor edged closer, whispering, "Do you remember your dear friend Marcus?"

Dragos stared unflinchingly at Victor.

"Ah, I see that you do. He cried like a baby as we drained his blood. Did you know that he called for you near the end? He was nothing but a spoiled young man, much like you at the time."

"Then why didn't you kill me like Marcus? I didn't ask to become this monster. Why me?"

Victor's eyes gleamed with evil as he loomed closer. "You have a will to live. Even seconds away from death, you cursed me and tried to fight me. At that time in history, vampire hunters were relentless. Our numbers had dropped to almost nothing. I needed someone that I could groom in my image—someone to protect what is mine."

It was Dragos's turn to smile. In a smug tone, he laughed, "How did that work for you?"

Victor casually brushed his hand against Dragos's face. "You should learn to be more appreciative. That aside, you have led me on a merry chase. Now we will get down to business."

He shook his head. "You might as well kill me now. I will never concede."

Victor grabbed Dragos's neck and bit deep. Pain resonated through his body. Seconds later, a languorous feeling overpowered his body. His head dropped to his shoulder. He fought to keep the darkness from invading his thoughts when flashes of blood and death leached into his soul. He was seeing Victor's memories.

He became breathless as the vampire's memories became his. He saw Victor as a shy, sickly youth. Tormented by schoolmates and peers, Victor isolated himself on the family estate. Until one night he took a walk in the woods. The bashful youth became a vicious monster. Those who tormented him as a young man did not live long as Victor embraced the life of a vampire. No, Dragos would never feel sorry for Victor—never.

Dragos groaned and tried to open his eyes. He felt ill. The memories were too real—too vivid. Victor's tongue swept out and closed the wound.

Dragos stared at Victor. Disbelief filled him. How could a man become so cruel—so inhuman?

"And that was just a sample of the power that I have over you."

Victor and his men left the room, leaving him to hang from the hooks above with his feet barely touching the floor.

The room contained a multitude of torture devices. A flat metal table with hoops for handcuffs was positioned in the far corner. A drain on the floor looked crusted with dried blood. How was he going to get out of here? Where were O'Shea and Anders? Were his friends still alive? He tugged on the chains, tearing a muscle in his shoulder. He winced from the pain.

A few more episodes with Victor taking his blood, and he would end up like the rest of the vampires. He would rather die than kill an innocent. Even more worrisome was the fact that he might not have a choice.

50

Candy quickly shut off the car lights as they turned down the cul-de-sac. Michael stared at the lone, dark house nestled eerily among the cornfields. The modern-looking home was lit by a single light inside.

"Well, what do you think?" Lisa asked.

Michael swung around to look at Lisa. "We're not going to march up to the front door and ring the doorbell, if that is what you're asking."

Candy reached out and shoved his shoulder.

"Show some respect, young lady. I'm over a hundred years old."

"Stop it. This is serious." Candy glared at him.

"I'll go check out the house," Michael volunteered. "Since they can't see me, it will be safer. You two wait here. Do not leave the car! Am I clear?"

By thinking of the location he wanted to be at, he easily appeared near the house. Staying in spirit form, he slowly circled the house, looking in each window. On the first floor, several vampires lounged about, talking and drinking.

He pressed his face against the glass, staring at the dark red liquid they poured down their throats.

"Saints above! They're drinking blood. Bloodsuckers," he murmured aloud.

Ever since Dragos had shown up, their city had been overrun by the damn creatures. Why Brett trusted the guy, Michael didn't know. He muttered under his breath as he tramped through the immaculately trimmed landscape. At the rear of the house, several small rectangular windows lay level with the ground. Lying on his stomach, he peered into a darkened room. *Nothing.* It was empty. As he rose to his feet, he sensed movement in a nearby room. He pressed through the wall. Anders lay on a bed, barely moving. A splattering of dark stains covered his shirt.

Anders rolled onto his side and stared up at him. The chief's face twisted in pain.

Filled with urgency, Michael rushed to the chief's side. "I'll get you out of here. Don't worry."

If Anders was hurt as badly as he looked, what kind of condition was Brett in? He had to do something—and fast.

Between two overgrown bushes, he found a half-hidden doorway one level up. He turned the knob, and as expected, it was locked. But when had a locked door ever proved difficult for a ghost?

With a wiggle of his fingers, the lock gave way. He needed an easy getaway when he brought Anders out. He then disappeared into the house, where the smell of blood and death filled the air. He descended back into the lower level, where Anders waited. He slipped into Anders's room. Gliding through the door, he surprised Anders when the man rolled over. Michael reached down and wrapped an arm about Anders's waist.

"About time you got back," Anders bit out.

"Can you stand?"

Anders struggled to sit. "Yeah, but I need to get on my feet."

He winced as the chief stood and leaned against the wall. The sound of the man's harsh breathing filled the room.

"You're a sight for sore eyes, Michael."

"I got here as soon as I could. We need to get you out of here. Have any of those bloodsuckers been in to check on you?"

Anders shook his head. "No. They tossed me and Brett in here. They came in an hour ago and moved Brett somewhere else."

"Don't worry. I'll find him. Let's go. And no talking. Just follow my lead."

Michael opened the door to the hallway, looking right and then left. No one was in sight. A scream on the other side of the house gave him pause. *Had to be Dragos.* It sounded like they were pulling his body apart piece by piece by the depth of the sound and continuous moaning. Even though Dragos was a bloodsucker, Michael pitied the man. No person or creature should be tortured like that.

He had to get Anders out of here. The chief was his first priority. Anders staggered and nearly fell as he fought to make his way down the dark hallway. Beads of sweat dotted the older man's face. Anders was an old war horse—a cop's kind of chief—one who climbed into the trenches with them and didn't mind getting his hands dirty if need be. Michael was resolved to get Anders out of here come hell or high water.

Michael grabbed Anders's shoulder as they reached the doorway. A shadow fell across the doorway window. He quickly shoved Anders against the wall.

Anders grunted. "What the he—"

Michael put a finger across Anders's lips and shook his head. Shifting back to spirit form, he quickly relocked the door seconds before the guard reached the door and turned the knob.

The vampire looked through the glass and stared right at Michael. He smiled back at the vampire and flipped up his middle finger. Unfortunately, the bloodsucker couldn't appreciate his one-finger salute.

The vampire turned and disappeared around the corner

of the house. Michael tapped Anders's shoulder and motioned for him to follow. He quietly pushed the door open and leaned over to Anders.

"Run into the cornfield straight ahead. Turn toward the right once you're in the field. Candy and Lisa are waiting in a car."

Anders gripped his ribs. His body shuddered.

"Can you make it?"

"Hell yes. I'm not dying yet." Anders hunched down and jogged across the open yard, nearly stumbling.

Michael watched from the doorway, ready to assist the chief if necessary. He couldn't leave the house without finding Brett, and maybe Dragos. He didn't want to disappoint Candy. Anders disappeared into the dried stalks of corn. He was safe—for now.

Michael turned and locked the door. *Now to find Brett.*

Candy jerked as Lisa screamed. Someone or something slammed into the passenger side of the car. Candy saw Lisa dive for the floor of the car, quickly covering her head. Blood smeared the window. Candy jerked and grabbed her Glock, aiming at the man leaning against her car.

"Who is it?"

Lisa lifted her head and peeked up at the still figure of a man. "Crap! It's Anders."

Candy laid down the gun and jumped out of the car, wrapping an arm around the chief.

"Chief, let me help you."

She opened the back door and helped Anders lower himself into the car. Lisa held out a bottle of water, which he quickly gulped down. She hurried back around to the driver's seat and jumped behind the wheel. He needed medical help, but she couldn't leave yet. Brett and Dragos were still inside.

Candy's grip tightened around the steering wheel.

"We need backup," Anders muttered as he rubbed the side of his head.

Twisting around to look at Anders, Candy stared at his bloody face. "And you need a hospital."

"We can't sit here. We're sitting ducks."

She let out a sigh. "Listen, Chief, I know we need backup, but you've lost a lot of blood. I mean a *lot*. We need to get you help."

Anders stared down at his clothes as if seeing them for the first time. A smile lit his face.

"You should have seen the other guys," he joked even as he winced from pain.

"Seriously? A joke now?"

"I feel better now that I had something to drink." He attempted a half smile. His face softened as his smile grew.

"You'd better not die. I'm just saying. Where are Brett and Dragos? Did you see them?"

Anders shook his head. "They separated me and Brett."

Candy's heart stilled. "What about Dragos? Is he okay?" she whispered.

"Aw, Candy. I don't know. They're doing something to him—something horrible. I heard him scream."

Tremors coursed through her. She couldn't catch her breath. *Oh God! This can't be happening. Dragos can't die. He can't. Not now!* She had finally found a man she loved—the one man she couldn't, and wouldn't, live without.

She wiped unshed tears from her eyes and grabbed the gun. She had resolved to get Dragos out of the house or die trying. The sons of bitches inside were going to pay for hurting the man she loved.

As she opened the car door, it was shoved closed and

nearly hit her in the face. Michael appeared in the backseat next to Anders.

Michael growled, "What did I say? Stay in the car. I can't be watching over you and trying to help the men."

Anders groaned and clutched his head. "That's it. Take me to the hospital. I'll call my guys and get a plan together."

"But—" Candy choked out.

"No buts. I'm pulling rank. I'm not going to sit here and get you or me killed."

Michael nodded. "Good idea, Chief."

She turned around to glare at Michael. Sobs broke from her chest. "Dragos needs help. I need to go to him."

Lisa reached out to her, and Candy fell into her friend's comforting embrace.

"Candy, you can't go out there. They'll kill you. Michael knows how to handle these situations. We need to trust him."

She choked back a sob. "What does he know? He's been dead for decades. He's probably never even heard of vampires." Defeat welled up in her chest, making her want to scream in frustration.

Anders cleared his throat. "Lisa has it right. We have to work as a team if we're going to save them. But, bottom line, Michael brings something special to the fight," Anders added, running his fingers through his graying hair. He winced as his hand touched the large bump on the side of his head.

Candy studied the ghost before them. He pulled the fedora down over his brow as if hiding his thoughts from the rest of them. Although he was Brett's great-grandfather, she wasn't sure about his methods or understanding of paranormal monsters. Did he even understand what they were up against?

"Fine," she hissed. "I'd sure like to know what's so *special* about what he can do."

Michael flashed a crooked smile and shrugged. She

gritted her teeth. People's lives were on the line, and Michael was acting as if this situation wasn't urgent.

Anders and Lisa shared an odd look. *Great. If they don't want to tell me what they think, then fine.*

Lisa touched Candy's shoulder. "Listen, working with Michael has shown us that there are things in the universe that we can't control or manipulate."

Candy blinked. "I didn't understand one thing you just said."

Michael snorted. "What she's trying to tell you is that the big guy sets the stage. We're all players and have certain roles to act out."

She shook her head as if to clear it. "Big guy? What?"

Michael snapped his fingers in front of her face. "C'mon Candy. Catch up with the conversation. Big guy. Angels, God, those things up there." He pointed upward to the sky.

"God? Angels?" she whispered.

"That's what I just said. I've got the inside track—at least most of the time. Unless the guys up there are playing me, which they do sometimes."

When she opened her mouth, Michael held up his finger to silence her.

"Don't worry about the details. I'll figure something out soon."

"Crap, Michael. I'm getting worried listening to you blather on." Turning toward Candy, Anders laid a hand on her shoulder. "I know it's easier said than done, but don't worry. It's almost dawn, so the men should be safe for the time being. We need to get more manpower and get back here before dusk."

Michael agreed. "I'll keep an eye on the house until we're ready to come back and get our men. If anything urgent comes up, I'll let you know."

Candy numbly nodded. A feeling of hopelessness fell over her. She started the car and turned toward the hospital. They had to win; otherwise, Des Moines would become a vampire hot spot.

51

Dragos's arms burned from being strung up from the ceiling. He could no longer feel his upper body. In an attempt to keep his mind from focusing on the pain, he studied the room, which was reminiscent of a medieval torture chamber. The walls were covered with some sort of padding—most likely to prevent outsiders from hearing what went on inside.

Taut muscles in his stomach quivered as he drew up his legs to his waist in an effort to provide relief to his body. Ugly bruises dotted his midsection—a result of pounding fists. Although he possessed superior healing abilities, pain riddled his body. It took all his energy to remain conscious and focused on his one goal—escaping and killing Victor.

He was encouraged when he heard voices in the room down the hall. He knew Brett and Anders were alive. He hid his surprise when he heard Michael's voice earlier. Although Michael and Anders whispered and could barely be heard, he made a point to scream loudly when Victor punched him. He prayed it was sufficient for Anders to escape. The mortal needed medical care. He could smell Anders's blood from his room. The vampires would have made a quick meal of the older police officer. But where was Brett?

Dragos was weakening by the hour. It was becoming difficult for him to keep his mind focused. Lethargy threatened to take over his body. He should have had that extra bag of blood before they left the house.

Steps sounded on the stairway. Someone was coming. He heard multiple footsteps approach the doorway. He remained still and unmoving, with his eyes closed. He tensed as he heard another door open down the hallway. *A reprieve.* A sigh escaped him.

Footsteps rushed down the stairs into a nearby room. His smile widened when he heard Victor's voice. Victor's rage was a living thing. Even from this distance, he felt the fury and evil clawing from his maker's soulless body.

His smile grew as the door to the room where he hung was thrust open. Victor stalked toward him and jerked his chin upward.

"Where is he?" Victor quietly demanded.

Dragos bit the inside of his mouth to keep from laughing. "Who?"

Victor's razor-sharp fingernails raked down Dragos's stomach. "I will ask one more time. Where is he?"

"I have no idea. Did you lose a human?" A surge of satisfaction burst through him. Victor's face twisted in what appeared to be anger.

His moment of joy was instantly replaced with intense pain as a knife slid between his ribs. Victor smirked as the knife twisted, tearing tendons and puncturing his lung in the process. Beads of sweat dotted his brow. It took every ounce of his strength and determination to remain stoic.

"Perhaps your men are not as capable as you believe."

The corner of Victor's mouth curled upward as he tapped the blade against Dragos's stomach. "Yes, perhaps. That is why I chose you as my apprentice all those years ago." Victor sighed. "I fail to understand what you think you gain from being defiant. The two of us could easily control this area of the country. Just think of the possibilities: women, untold wealth, whatever you want. It's all right here. All you have to do is say yes and submit to me. Is that so hard, Dragos?"

Dragos glared at his tormenter. "You are everything that I despise. I will never submit to you and your way of life. I consider death a reprieve from you. So do what you will."

Victor's red eyes narrowed. He pulled Dragos forward and sank his teeth into his stomach, tearing skin and muscle. "Never fear, Dragos. I will win. I have learned to be very patient. It matters very little that the old man escaped. I would have killed him anyway. My men are becoming hungry for fresh blood. Perhaps Officer O'Shea will satisfy them. What do you think?"

Dragos didn't blink. Any flicker of emotion—a response of any kind—would mean the kiss of death for Brett. Dragos stared at Victor.

Victor's fanatical laughter sent fear deep into his bones. Had Victor seen through his facade? He remained determined not to give Victor an ounce of satisfaction.

"We will see how your resolve is tomorrow. Know this, Dragos: you can change the outcome with one word."

As the door closed behind Victor, the smell of evil lingered in the air. Dragos shuddered. He couldn't let his friend die. Yet he vowed not to become Victor's pawn. That would be worse than death. Choices and time were limited. The minutes clicked by. What could he do to change the outcome tomorrow? There was little doubt that Victor would force him to make a choice: for good or bad—for right or wrong. He only hoped that he was strong enough to make the right choice when the time came.

Brett stood, stretching his muscles. He paced the narrow, dark room. He was worried about Anders. He hadn't heard any sound from across the hall since they were separated. Dragos occasionally yelled out from pain, so at least he knew that Dragos was still alive.

There had to be a way to find out if Anders was okay. Someone should be looking for them.

He winced as he touched a cut on his face. Although bruised and battered, he considered himself lucky. He was still alive. What he wouldn't give for a cell phone.

Thoughts of Lisa constantly flitted through his mind. He wouldn't accept that this was the end. He had to tell her how he felt. He had to believe that he would have that opportunity.

He paced the small room, searching for any means of escape. A small slit of a window let in the pinkish rays of the morning sun. Did that mean the vampires were sleeping? He dropped to the dirty mattress, wondering whether this was the day he would escape or the day they would try to kill him.

52

The sun peeked over the horizon. Anders yawned and struggled to keep his eyes open. Even Candy and Lisa had difficulty staying awake. After spending several hours in the ER, he was discharged. Luckily there was no concussion. Anders instructed Candy to drive back to Brett's house.

What a mess. By his estimation, they had about twenty-four hours before crap hit the fan. With all the bodies being discovered, the vampires weren't going to keep Brett and Dragos alive for long.

He tapped Candy on the shoulder as she drove. "Listen; I think we need to head back to the station and grab more ammo. Besides, I want to talk to Foster. We're going to need to bring in men who can keep secrets. I don't know about you, but I will need a couple of hours of sleep if we're going to get those guys."

Candy shook her head. "I can't leave Dragos there."

Lisa's lower lip trembled. "What about Brett?"

With arms resting on the back of the front seats, he leaned forward between the two women. "I don't want to leave them here either, but we need reinforcements."

In the next breath, Michael suddenly appeared next to Anders. He and the women all let out a gasp.

"I agree. Reinforcements are definitely needed." Michael nodded.

"Damn it. Can't you give us warning?" Anders glared at Michael.

The look on Michael's face was one of trepidation.

Anders cursed under his breath. "So what did you find out?"

"It's not good. I did see Dragos. They have him strung up, and they've done a good job torturing him. I haven't seen Brett, but I sensed him moving around in another room. Death lingers in that house."

Oh great. Now the ghost is scaring the women. Jeez! Anders nudged Michael's thigh as the women's eyes filled with tears. Anders growled, "Listen, people. We need ammo and reinforcements before we can go back there."

"What's the plan?" Michael snorted. "I don't think they're going to just let us waltz in there."

"Of course not," Lisa muttered. "Since I have some experience in researching topics, I can put together a plan, like I did last time."

Michael muffled a laugh. "I think you'll be wasting your time. It didn't work that well last time, if I remember correctly."

Lisa swung around, her eyes blazing. "Do you have anything better?"

"Guys, take it down a notch," Anders ordered. "I think Lisa's idea has some merit. If anyone wants to come up with a plan, then do it. We can sit down and combine the best ideas into one plan."

He had to bite back a smile when Lisa grinned at Michael. Candy still looked unconvinced.

"I didn't see any other activity in the house. Do bloodsuckers sleep all day?" Michael asked.

Candy shrugged. "Somewhat. Dragos seemed to cope

pretty well as long as it was a cloudy day and he wore sunglasses and appropriate clothing."

Anders glanced up at the clear sky. "Maybe our luck will hold. It's a sunny day. Whatever we're going to do, we have to do it before it gets dark again. Let's roll."

"You guys go ahead. I'll see what help I can get." Michael popped up outside of the car. "I'll meet you back at Brett's."

Michael watched the car pull away and smiled, thinking about Lisa. They were in a hell of a pickle, and he had to keep her spirits up. He could handle her anger; it was her tears he didn't want to deal with. She should know that he'd do anything he could to save Brett. At this point he'd rile them all up just to motivate them.

Back at the vampire house, he faded into the woods surrounding the house. He shuddered. Evil was real—something that most humans could not see or feel. It encompassed the house like a heavy blanket, barely letting any light into the dark cavities of the structure. The smell of death drifted from the ground, filling his nose. He twitched. The hairs on the back of his neck rose. He slowly turned and faced the house. Someone watched him. It must be one of the vampires.

The blinds in the one of the rooms facing him moved ever so slightly, revealing the dark figure of a man—or rather not a man, but a vampire. The creature stared in his direction even though he was in spirit form. *Impossible! No one should be able to see me.*

The vampire's eyes glittered. The son of a bitch looked as though he thought this was a game—a challenge.

Michael let his body solidify, enabling the vampire to get

a good look at the man who was going to kick his sorry ass back to hell.

The vampire's lip curled before nodding at Michael as if accepting the challenge. He smiled back at the vampire, flashing him a one-finger salute. He hoped the bloodsucker understood that little gesture. It sure gave him a feeling of satisfaction.

Before dropping the blinds back in place, the vampire had the audacity to flash his fangs at him. Michael bristled in outrage. "Bring it on," he hissed between his teeth. "You want a war? You've got it."

53

Lisa's fingers pounded the keyboard as she tried to finish her analysis of vampires—or, as she now called it, "How to Kill a Vampire without Getting Yourself Killed." It was midafternoon. Anders and Candy would be up any minute.

She rubbed her eyes, refusing to quit until she was done. Minutes later, she pressed the print button.

A quick knock on the bedroom door sounded before Anders peeked inside.

"Hey, I'm back with the ammo and few other surprises. You about ready?"

She nodded as she stapled the information together. "Yep. Be right there."

She hurried to the bathroom to wash her face and brush her teeth. Refreshed, she ran a brush through her long curls and pulled her hair into a tight ponytail. She quickly threw off her dirty clothes and tossed them into the corner. She wiggled into a pair of black jeans and yanked a black turtleneck shirt over her head.

When she entered the kitchen, Anders and Candy were staring quietly into their cups of steamy coffee. Anders attempted a smile. Candy refused to meet her gaze.

Her eyes widened as she looked around the kitchen. It looked like an ammo store. She dropped the papers on the table. "Let me grab some coffee, and we can start. Anyone want any lunch?"

Candy cast a surly look her way.

"How can you think of eating?" Anders grunted.

Embarrassed, she set the food on the table. "Sorry, but I need to eat. Eat or don't eat."

No one touched the food. They silently sat, barely looking at one another.

Unable to delay the inevitable any longer, she asked, "Well, I was able to put together some information on how to kill vampires. I think we should be as knowledgeable as possible."

Anders nodded and picked up the paper. Candy shoved the paper before her on the floor. "We should be doing something instead of reviewing information," Candy snapped.

Taking a deep breath, Lisa clutched the papers in her hands. "We are doing something—trying to keep them from getting killed."

Anders folded his hands together on the table and leaned forward. "Knock it off. We're all stressed."

Lisa bit the inside of her cheek to keep from crying. She had to keep it together.

Anders cleared his throat before speaking. "I spoke to Foster and asked him to bring in a couple of sharpshooters. We will need to surprise them before dusk and take them out one by one."

Lisa was surprised when Candy shook her head.

"I don't think that will work. Vampires move very quickly. I'm afraid that they will kill Dragos and Brett before the sharpshooters can kill them."

Anders's eyes narrowed. "What's your plan?"

With eyes downcast, Candy shook her head. "I don't have one."

A whiff of a breeze stirred the air in the room. Suddenly Michael joined them at the table.

"Am I in time?" he asked.

Lisa's hand flew to her chest. "Crap, Michael."

"What?"

She noticed him looking at the papers on the table.

He suddenly burst out laughing. "You didn't?"

Lisa glared at him. "I happen to find information useful."

Michael's eyes glittered with what appeared to be amusement.

"Oh, I'm sure you do. Is the report titled '101 Ways to Kill Vampires' or something goofy like that?"

"Okay! That's enough," Anders barked as he slammed his fist on the table.

Michael's smile faded as he tossed his fedora onto the nearby counter.

Lisa cleared her throat before beginning. The steely gaze in Anders's eyes could unnerve a statue.

"As you know, there is a lot of stuff on the Internet about vampires. Most of it is pure fiction."

"Like what?" Candy asked.

"Wearing garlic around your neck. It's an old wives' tale. I've listed things that aren't true based on what we know about Dragos—things like wearing or flashing crucifixes. According to Dragos, he is able to stay awake longer during the daytime with each passing month. Although he needs blood to exist, he doesn't need to kill to get it—not like Victor and his goons."

"So now that we know what doesn't work, what does kill them?" Anders demanded.

"A wooden stake through the heart seems to be the best solution. Holy water is supposed to slow them down."

Michael grinned, causing her anger to spiral once again.

"Focus, Michael," Lisa ordered.

"Is he always so distracting?" Candy asked.

Michael glared at all of them. "Quit talking about me as if I'm not here."

Lisa resisted the urge to roll her eyes. "Now, as I was saying ..."

"Hey!" Michael shouted. "I have something else to say."

Anders's gruff voice filled the room. "And we're all dying to know what it is."

Michael puffed out his chest and grabbed his hat. "I can move as fast as a vampire. After all, a ghost does have some special abilities."

"What about using some of the heavenly powers that ghosts are supposed to have?" Anders's gaze looked hopeful.

Michael looked downward. He seemed unsure of himself. There was a first time for everything, it seemed.

"We haven't heard you talk about the 'big guy' much lately. Is there a problem?" Anders asked.

"No, it's just that things are different since the case on York Street. I'm kind of on my own."

Anders shook his head. "Well that sucks. This presents a whole new ball game, doesn't it?"

Michael stood. "I'll go get the stakes. How about I dip them in holy water?"

"Can't hurt. Be back within the hour. We have to be at Victor's before sundown." Anders rose to his feet.

"With their acute vision, we're dead if we get there late," Candy added.

Lisa glanced at her friends. She fought back the despair that clawed its way from her soul. She rushed to the kitchen sink and leaned over, her stomach heaving.

Candy wrapped an arm about her shoulder. "Are you okay?"

Finally, Lisa nodded. In a quiet voice, she uttered, "I just hope we're not too late."

Anders patted her shoulder before pulling out his cell. "We're leaving just as soon as my men are here. Right now I'm going to try to get a little shut-eye."

Candy stared at the ammo supply scattered about the

kitchen. "I'll start loading up. With all this, we can slow them up until we can stake them."

Once the kitchen was emptied, Lisa sat alone with her thoughts. It was three hours until the biggest challenge of her life. She prayed that they got there in time. She refused to think about what Brett and Dragos might be going through. It was paralyzing, and she wasn't going there.

She had decided that once Brett was safe, she was going to win him back. She had hope now—something that hadn't existed a few weeks ago. She had so many regrets. Why had she left Des Moines? More importantly, why had she left Brett? She had almost ruined her chance for happiness. Well, it was time to put her life in order once and for all.

54

Victor stared at the papers on his desk. Everything was ready. He was opening a house in Chicago. He even had a new driver's license. He would start over and build a stronger army. With Allen telling the world that vampires existed here, there would too many questions and suspicions if they stayed in Des Moines.

A knock sounded at the door. Without raising his glance, he called, "Enter."

Alto stood before his desk, his eyes downcast.

"Master, we have done as you have asked. The men are ready."

Tossing the pen aside, he clasped his hands together. "Very good. You all have your orders. Do not fail me as you did yesterday."

With a slight bow, Alto backed out of the room. Alone again, Victor rubbed his temple. He was furious that the old policeman had escaped from beneath their noses. How had it happened? Nothing like this had ever occurred before.

He had been intrigued to see the shadow of a man watching the house yesterday. The man didn't appear to be human, but what was he? Was he helping the humans? Had this shadow man helped the old man escape? Whatever he was, the figure was not another master vampire.

Perplexed, yet filled with anticipation, he laughed out loud. How he looked forward to killing those that dared to breach his sanctuary. There would be no mercy—none!

He didn't want to deal with vampire hunters again. In the nineteenth century, he was lucky to escape with only his life. The constant moving was a way to keep his identity a secret.

He poured a drink from a crystal decanter. Victor tipped the glass, thick red liquid coated his narrow lips. His tongue darted out, licking the savory substance. Not a drop was wasted. His thoughts turned to Dragos. He welcomed the battle with his onetime friend. Dragos would soon agree with his way of thinking. He had to. No one ever denied him. It wasn't possible to resist the call of a master vampire—a vampire of his stature and experience.

However, he had been surprised when Dragos's power filtered in and read his mind. That had shaken Victor to the core. No other vampire had the power to do that. How could Dragos break down his mental blocks? Victor found this intriguing. He was determined to soon discover Dragos's secret.

Victor entered the hallway. The guard near the lower level doorway nodded as he passed. It was time to visit the young detective and find out what was so special about the man that Dragos would give up his life for.

Brett rose from the bed as the door opened. He looked at the figure filling the doorway. Instinctively, his hand reached for his gun before dropping to his side.

Harsh laughter filled the room.

"Reaching for a weapon, Detective?"

He clenched his teeth. The desire to wipe that smug look

off the vampire's face grew. "Yeah. You wouldn't be smiling if I did have my weapon."

"Tsk, tsk. Detective, that is not a proper way to greet your host. I believe introductions are in order." With a slight bow, the vampire edged closer to him. "I am Baron Sinclair. Perhaps Dragos mentioned that he and I are acquainted."

Brett shrugged. The man was several inches taller than him. Whoever he was, it was obvious by the fitted Italian suit that he enjoyed modern fashion trends. "Afraid not. He's never mentioned anyone with that name."

The vampire's hair was pulled back and tied neatly in the back. His amber eyes commanded Brett's attention. Brett felt as if the creature were looking into his soul.

The vampire's gaze changed from pleasant to pissed off in a second.

The vampire surged forward, inches from Brett's face. Brett stiffened, his muscles tightening and his gut quivered in anticipation of what was coming.

"Perhaps Dragos mentioned the name of Victor?"

His breath caught in his chest. *Victor—the vampire responsible for all the deaths!* He wanted to kill the man—this monster before him.

Victor stepped back. He snarled to reveal pointed teeth. Wagging a finger in front of Brett's face, Victor taunted, "Ah, I see that you have heard of me. Maybe you even want to try to hurt me or kill me. Let me give you a warning, Detective. You are still alive because I allow it. You will remain alive only if you decide to assist me."

Rage filled him. He forced himself to take a deep breath and try to think clearly.

"Assist you?" he growled.

Victor walked behind him. His finger trailed down Brett's back. Involuntary tremors rippled through Brett's body.

"Yes, I need you to talk to Dragos. He must submit to me."

Is Victor crazy? Why would I help ruin Dragos's life? Or,

worse yet, why would I want to encourage Dragos to be like Victor? Not that Dragos could ever be like Victor.

A voice in his head told him to go ahead and agree. Doing so would buy him time and might even save his ass. Yet there were certain things that he couldn't compromise on.

"I'm afraid I can't do that."

Victor whipped toward him and wrapped a hand around his neck. Victor pressed forward, forcing him back against the wall. Instinctively, he clawed at the hand that squeezed his throat. Even using both of his hands, he was unable to tear Victor's hand away from his body. He grew lightheaded and swayed sideways. He couldn't breathe.

Only when his body started to slide to the floor did Victor's grasp loosen.

"Argh," he coughed as his knee hit the floor. Head bowed and eyes closed, he rubbed his neck. *Damn!* He knew Victor was staring down at him. He could feel the vampire's piercing gaze.

He used the wall as support as he struggled to stand. He glared back at the vampire. "That is not the way to get people to help you," he croaked.

Victor's eyebrow rose. "Really? Would you have helped anyway?"

He shook his head. "Afraid not."

Victor threw back his head and laughed. "Now I understand why Dragos likes you. You're bold but reckless."

Brett stepped forward with fists clenched at his sides. How he wanted to wipe that smile off Victor's face.

Victor held up a hand, his good humor fading. "I suggest you stop there. One more step and I will kill you now."

Indecision tore through Brett. Did it make any difference if he died now or later? Maybe not, but he didn't want to prove Victor right. Where the hell was Michael? He shook his head in an effort to clear his thoughts. Patience and strategy had to prevail.

He grinned at the smirking vampire. "You don't know anything about my friendship with Dragos. And you sure as hell don't know anything about me. Just remember: there are people looking for us. It's only a matter of time before they get here."

"Please, Detective," Victor sighed. "You believe in fairy tales. No one is coming to save you. No one at all. I will leave you to contemplate your sad, short life."

Victor took a step forward. His mouth twisted in a grimace. Instinct told Brett to run, but he held his ground, glaring back at the vampire. Suddenly Victor swung around and exited the room. The door lock clicked in place. Releasing a deep breath, Brett collapsed on the bed, resting his forearm over his eyes. His heart continued to pound in his chest. *I'm going to have a fucking heart attack before this is over.* His frustration grew. He'd never been in a situation where he needed saving. It sucked. He was used to *doing* the saving.

"Michael! Where the hell are you?"

55

Michael frowned as he glanced at the clock. *Four o'clock and not a soul in the kitchen. Where is everyone?*

He walked down the hall toward Brett's bedroom. The sound of sobbing echoed behind the closed door. Edging open the door, he peered inside. Lisa sat on the bed, her face buried in one of Brett's T-shirts.

"Hey there. What's the trouble?" Unease rippled through him. It had been so long since he'd consoled his wife that he wasn't sure what to do.

Eyes wide, Lisa stared up at him. "What if something happens to Brett?"

"Here now! Don't think that way." He reached down and pulled her to her feet. "C'mon; dry those tears. We need you to focus on tonight. Are you able to fire a gun?"

She nodded, wiping her face with the back of her hand. "Brett and I used to go to the target range. It's been a while, but I can do it."

He patted her on the back and smiled. "Good. Where's everyone else?"

"Candy is loading her guns—a bunch of guns. I think she is preparing for Armageddon. I don't know where the chief is."

The doorbell rang.

"You'd better go see who it is. If I open the door and it's Anders's men, they will be weirded out." Seeing the perplexed look on Lisa's face, he waved his arms in the air. "You know— door opens by itself. Most people can't see a ghost. Scary shit."

Lisa flashed a smile. "Got it. I'll get the door."

He stood off to the side in spirit form, just in case vampires were at the door. Something was going to happen soon, and he was edgy. Lisa opened the door. Captain Foster and two other men all dressed in military gear nodded as Lisa let them in.

"Hi, I'm Lisa Winslow. Please have a seat while we wait for Chief Anders. He'll be up shortly. Would anyone like something to drink?"

The men shook their heads. Foster nodded to his men. "This is Ted Nichols and Sean Johnson. They work with me."

Lisa smiled and shook their hands. "We're glad you're all here."

Their bearing and determined looks bolstered Michael's optimism. The men looked to be in their early forties. He'd heard Anders say earlier that both men had served overseas in Afghanistan. They were familiar with tactical operations and knew how to follow orders. *Yep, these men are a good addition to the team. But although they look as tough as nails, will they be able to handle vampires?* He sure hoped so. Otherwise, people were going to die. He skirted the men as they remained standing talking among themselves. *Eavesdropping is so worthwhile. You never know what you might learn.*

A few minutes later, Anders hollered as he entered the kitchen. He plopped another large duffel bag on the kitchen table. As Foster and his men joined the chief in the kitchen, Anders glanced over at him. Michael shook his head, hoping the chief would pick up on the silent message. The men could not see him.

When Anders unzipped the bag, canisters of tear gas, rounds of ammo, and grenades spilled out onto the table.

He reached toward a grenade, but Anders moved it out of his reach. *Crap.* He had forgotten that the other guys were in the room and couldn't see or hear him.

"Oops! My bad," he muttered, earning him an annoyed glance from Anders.

Lisa leaned forward and whispered in his ear. "Hell no. Get your hands off those. Remember last time."

When were people going to let that one go? So he had a little trouble using some weapons. He started to explain, but Anders shook his head.

Candy reached in and grabbed a vest, which she quickly strapped on. She tossed one to Lisa.

"Here. Put this on. We might need it."

Lisa fastened the Velcro straps. "I'd feel better if I had a neck vest," she murmured to Candy.

Foster and his two men flashed puzzled looks at one another. Their hooded eyes studied the rest of them in the room. Tension was thick. It was as if they sensed Michael's presence.

"Hey, Anders," Michael murmured, "the guys are getting suspicious. You need to tell them something so they're prepared."

The chief sighed and nodded. "Foster, bring your men into the other room. I need to share something with you."

Foster's fiery gaze swept the room, assessing Anders and the women. The captain was astute. It was clear Foster suspected something.

After the men left the kitchen, he sat down at the table. His shoulders drooped. After all, how many times had he battled bloodsuckers? None. Nada. When he was a detective back in the 1930s, he dealt with normal cases: robberies, petty crimes, and a few murders. He'd thought killers were the worst until he had to face these paranormal creatures. Even more confusing was why he and Brett had to continually fight these paranormal monsters. Was it his penance? He didn't remember ever having done something so horrible that he deserved this kind of punishment. Innocent people were dying, and that went against every instinct he had. In fact, it pissed him off. *Sons of bitches.*

He leaned back, casting his glance upward, and silently prayed. "Hey. Anyone up there listening? It's O'Shea again. We're kind of in a predicament. We could use some help down here."

After a couple of minutes, he slowly opened his eyes. *Nothing? Really?* Closing his eyes again, he tried to connect with the powers above. "Hello. I'm still here. I have no idea how we're supposed to beat the bloodsuckers, which is why I am asking for help. I know you're up there, so how about giving a guy a break?"

Without warning, a strong gust of wind blew open the front door. His beloved fedora flew off his head and swirled about the room before landing on the floor. Everyone jerked and gaped at the open doorway. Foster and his men whipped out their guns, aiming toward the source of the disturbance.

With eyes wide, Lisa whispered out the corner of her mouth, "Michael, what's going on?"

"Nothing. I think I stepped on some toes."

He stomped over and grabbed the hat before shoving it back on his head. "Hmmph. I guess you were listening, but you didn't have to take it out on my hat." He glanced upward as his gaze hardened. "I'm assuming you've got our backs."

Why was it so difficult to get answers? After all, they all knew he was still on earth to help Brett. If they weren't going to help, then why allow him to keep visiting? He ran his hand over his face and growled. *No use pondering the workings of the universe. There's nothing I can do to change it.*

He turned and froze. *What if there is something I can do?* He walked toward the kitchen table.

With heads together, Candy and Lisa talked in soft tones near the kitchen sink. Anders and the cops hadn't returned to the kitchen yet, so Michael sat down and eyed the duffel bag and its contents—especially the grenades. He slid out his arm and quickly scooped a couple grenades into his pocket. He felt giddy. Grenades had been around for centuries. He knew they had been used in the First World War. *I'll bet that these grenades are even more powerful. Probably powerful enough to blow up a vampire if I had to guess.*

He couldn't wait to try them out tonight. He'd stuff them down the throats of the bloodsuckers. That would give them a shock they weren't expecting.

❧

Anders ran a hand through his hair. Foster, Nichols, and Johnson all stared expectantly at him. Nichols and Johnson were experienced cops and expert shooters. The fact that Foster trusted them enough to bring them was enough for him.

Anders cleared his throat, shuffling his feet. The men waited expectantly.

"Well, I … I'm not sure how to say this."

Foster's brows drew together. "Don't worry about it. We'll be fine. The guys and I know what to do."

"I know you do. I wouldn't have called you if I didn't trust you." He gritted his teeth. "I need to warn you that this won't be a normal case."

Nichols chuckled. "There's nothing normal about the idiots we go after, sir."

"Yeah, but the guys we're going after tonight are anything but idiots. To complicate matters, they have O'Shea."

"Damn it!" Foster swore. "Why didn't you call us sooner? Shit! We need to bring in more men."

As Foster reached for his phone, Anders grabbed it out of the captain's hand. "Listen to me very carefully. We are going after men—I mean things—that are not human. Our guns and weapons will not kill these things."

A nervous laugh escaped Nichols. "Damn, Chief. Are you trying to scare us or what?"

"I'm not joking. I'm very serious. If you want to walk away, then do it. No one will think any different of you."

Foster swore under his breath and stomped toward the window. "Cut the bullshit, Anders. Exactly what are we up against?"

"If you repeat what I'm going to tell you, I'll make sure you write parking tickets the rest of your career." Anders pointed his finger at each of the men. "Got it?"

Anders caught sight of Michael standing in the corner, watching. His men nodded, waiting for Anders to continue. There was no good way to tell them. "We're hunting vampires."

Silence filled the room. The men gaped at him. Michael's grin grew.

"What did he say?" Johnson gasped, looking at Foster.

"Vampires? Like the ones that fly around and change into bats?" Nichols asked.

Foster stared at him, a look of disbelief on his face.

"No, they don't fly around and turn into bats, but they're fast. Listen, guys. I know I sound crazy. There are things in this world that we can't see."

Foster growled, "Like what?"

Anders winced. Michael suddenly disappeared with a glimmer of amusement on his face. *Damn. What is the ghost up to?*

"Ghosts. I may sound crazy, but I've had to face ghosts and demons, and it was scary as hell."

The three men stared back at Anders. Nichols eyed the door, looking as if he were ready to bolt.

"Guys, I didn't use to believe in the hocus-pocus bullshit either. Only crazy people or spiritual people see paranormal things—not an old street cop like me." Anders ran a hand through his hair. What else could he say to convince them?

Michael stepped from the shadows to the center of the room; his body visible to everyone. With his hands on his hips and his head cocked at a jaunty angle, he snorted, "Guys. You need to listen to Anders. We don't have much time."

Nichols and Johnson stepped back, placing their hands on their guns.

Foster growled, "Who the hell are you?"

Michael grinned and glanced toward Anders "You want to tell them, or should I?"

"Since you're here, go ahead."

Puffing out his chest, Michael pushed back his hat to reveal his face. "I'm Detective Michael O'Shea."

Foster frowned and stepped closer to Michael. "O'Shea? You're related to Brett, aren't you?"

Beaming, Michael nodded. "Yep. I'm his great-great-grandfather."

Anders choked back a curse. He could see Foster trying to do the math in his head. He knew what was coming next.

"That would make you over a hundred years old. From where I'm standing, you look like you're in your early thirties." Foster glared at Michael.

"Close."

"If you expect us to believe that your Brett's grandfather, then you're batshit crazy."

Michael's smile faded. "No, not crazy … a ghost."

Foster gaped at him before bursting into laughter. Nichols and Johnson joined in the laughter.

Anders slowly shook his head. Michael glowered at the men still chuckling at his expense.

Suddenly Michael's figure shimmered and vanished. Foster's and his men's faces froze. Their mouths gaped open as they turned about the room, looking for Michael. Foster stopped and looked at Anders. The man's face was as white as a sheet.

Anders almost smiled, remembering the first time he realized that Michael was indeed a ghost.

Foster stuttered, "What ... where is he?"

"Oh, just wait. I'm sure he'll be back to gloat."

Sure enough, a light breeze sifted through the room. Particles of who knew what flew through the air and collected in the center of the room until Michael reappeared. With his arms folded across his chest, his chin jutting forward, he looked every inch a determined detective.

Nichols and Johnson stepped closer to Foster. His men looked nervous. Anders had to give Foster credit; the man didn't cower or back down. But neither did Michael.

"So, believe me now?" taunted Michael.

Foster squinted, reaching out to poke Michael's arm. "Maybe. You seem real enough. How did you do that disappearing thing?"

"That is my secret, Captain. I take it you're a believer now."

Foster glanced at his men, who stood behind him. "I wouldn't go that far, but I know something happened that I don't understand." Foster bit his lip. Frown lines marred his face. "What's really troubling is that if ghosts are real, then vampires might be real. I don't have a clue how to fight either of you."

"And that's why we're all here talking about this now." Relief coursed through Anders. Now they were getting somewhere. "Vampires are extremely fast—Superman fast. Bullets will slow them down, but to finish them off, you need holy water and wooden stakes jammed in their hearts."

"Stakes in their fucking hearts! Man, you're talking crazy shit." Nichols boomed.

Anders held up his hands. "Listen; take a breath. I know this is overwhelming, but these vampires are murdering people in our city. Either we take them out or we might as well give up now."

Foster turned to face his men. "I agree with the chief. If people learn that vampires are real, we will have panic. More innocent people will die. We can't let that happen. With the chief and Michael leading the way, I say count me in. They have experience in fighting paranormal monsters. What about you two? Are you in or out?"

The men glanced at one another before they both stepped forward. They all stood in a circle, arms outstretched, as they fist-bumped one another.

Anders motioned for them to follow him back to the kitchen, where Candy and Lisa waited. He pointed to the counters and table. "There are plenty of knives, grenades, and ammo in here for each of you. Our priority is to get O'Shea and Dragos out of there. Whatever you do, don't let your guard down even for a second. Remember: we take no prisoners. They have to be eliminated."

Everyone looked grim as they silently loaded the rest of the weapons.

Anders glanced at the clock and shoved the last round of ammo into his pocket. "Okay guys. It's showtime. These guys won't play nice, and neither should you. Let's go kick some ass."

56

Brett stiffened. Footsteps echoed from the hallway. They stopped outside his door. Perched on the edge of the mattress, he stared at the door. His heart rose in his throat. The door slowly opened. His nemesis was back. He suspected that the smile on Victor's face was not a good sign.

Two vampires followed Victor into the room. The men marched over to the bed and loomed over him. They licked their lips. Their heated gazes dared him to try to run—anything to give them cause to kill him. He squirmed like a deer caught in the crosshairs of a gun.

Involuntarily, he scooted back against the wall. *How am I going to get out of this mess?*

Victor motioned toward Brett. "Take him to the chamber below."

In a fluid motion, he was jerked to his feet and pushed into the dark hallway. Unable to see, he stumbled, earning the displeasure of his escorts.

A vampire hissed in his ear, "Please run. Try to escape so I can snap your puny neck."

Brett opened his mouth to tell the guy to fuck off but quickly decided this was not the time or place. He grunted, swallowing his anger at being shoved. It would be a cold day in hell before he gave them any sign that he was in pain.

The hallway wound past several closed doors. *How big is this house?* He would never have guessed the house hid such vast chambers. Upon reaching the end, an ancient-looking oak door embellished with wrought-iron gargoyles opened. It looked like something out of a horror movie. Concrete stairs wound down to another level. Eyes wide, he took in the ornate, oppressive features of the cavern. It was impossible to believe that this world existed below a house in this wealthy suburb.

The damp, cloying air from the lower level rose up, wrapping its tentacles about his throat. He swallowed the lump. Tremors shook his body. His skin crawled as if he had walked into a curtain of cobwebs. He resisted the urge to brush the sensation from his skin. Suddenly there was pressure on his chest. He paused at the top of the stairs. He didn't want to go down there. It was as if he knew how the story would end if he did. He knew he wouldn't be coming back up.

"Get moving."

When he glanced down, he saw that a sheen of moisture coated the stairs. One slip and he'd fall onto the stone floor below. There would be no mercy from Victor and his goons.

Before he moved, the vampire behind him gave a shove. His hand clawed at the wall, trying to stop the downward motion. *There has to be something to grab!* His knee buckled, slamming his head into the wall next to the stairs. The movement slowed his momentum and allowed him to collapse in a heap. With the wall now solidly bracing his back, he closed his eyes. Raising a shaky hand, he touched his throbbing forehead. Blood smeared his palm. Glaring at the vampire that grinned down at him, it was obvious that his bloody head had caught the attention of the vampires. They formed a semicircle around him. He shrunk back against the wall. *What I wouldn't give to have a weapon at this moment.*

Victor stood at the top of the stairway. The vampires

glanced up at their master and then backed away from Brett. Yet he didn't relax. He was like a circus animal, an amusement, for these sick bastards. With a groan, he pushed himself to his feet and tentatively descended the remainder of the steps.

Soft footsteps glided down the stairs as Victor followed. Goosebumps trailed down his back. Victor could reach out at any second and kill him. He wouldn't even see it coming.

"Go to the right," Victor ordered.

He followed the vampire into a dark room. The stench of urine and blood made him gag.

"Come now, Detective. It's the sweet smell of blood."

Brett glared at Victor, ignoring his comment. As he glanced around the large room, he noticed a dark shadow dangling from the ceiling. *A man? A dead man?*

Victor motioned to another vampire, who turned on several lights. His gaze traveled up the man's body, pausing at the face.

A moan escaped from Dragos's cracked lips. Brett watched Dragos slowly raise his head and glance around the room. His gaze hardened when he spotted Victor. Dragos's face turned red as he jerked the chains encasing his arms.

Victor stepped forward and grabbed his neck, dragging him forward.

"I have brought you company, Dragos—your detective friend, O'Shea. Like you, he was a little reluctant to cooperate, but that is all in the past."

Brett recoiled as Dragos glared down at him. *What the hell?*

"If you think the human is important to me, you are sadly mistaken."

Brett struggled to keep his mouth shut. The hatred streaming from Dragos's gaze had him rethinking every minute they had spent together. *Son of a bitch. I opened up my house to the bastard because I felt sorry for the guy.*

Victor's gaze grew calculating. The vampire whipped toward him and slashed his bare arm with a fingernail. Blood formed in a dotted line. Victor grabbed his arm and licked it.

Brett fought to pull away from Victor's grasp, but it was ironclad. Fear coursed through him. The dull look in Dragos's eyes scared him. Had Dragos surrendered—given up?

"Really, Victor. Are you showing off for the human?"

Victor flung Brett's arm aside and stormed over to look up at Dragos.

"Are you ready to join us? Ready to release your power and live up to your potential? Dragos, I chose you because you are intelligent. You can have anything that you desire."

Dragos closed his eyes. His muscles relaxed. *What is Dragos thinking? Don't give up!* Brett silently pleaded. Dragos tossed his head, causing the dark hair to fly off his face and revealing a harsh stare.

"No!"

Victor's eyes widened in what appeared to be disbelief, but that was quickly replaced with a look of determination. He turned and nodded at the other vampires. They grabbed Brett and tossed him on a nearby table.

"Argh! Stop!" Every bone in his body burned. He flung his legs off the table, only to receive a punch in the stomach. Instinctively he tried to curl into a ball. Hands grabbed his arms and legs and quickly strapped his limbs to the table. He thrust his body upward, tugging at the immovable straps.

Alto stood near the table, watching Victor. At Victor's slight nod, Alto leaned down. The vampire's teeth lengthened. Brett's eyes flew wide open. *Shit!* He was going to die.

He screamed as teeth sank into his neck. "You bastard. Get away from me! So help me, when I get loose, I'm going to kill your sorry ass."

Breaking through layers of skin and muscle, the intrusion of the bite was a violation of his soul. Little by little, weariness filled him.

"Enough," Victor growled.

Raising his head, Alto slowly wiped his mouth.

Dragos twisted his body, which rippled with strength as he pulled on the chains. "Victor. Enough!"

"Are you joining me then?"

A scream of anger ripped from Dragos's throat.

"I cannot," he groaned.

Victor shook his head. "Alas, you leave me with little choice. Alto, finish the detective. Then toss the body in the fire."

Comprehension hit him. *Finish the detective! Oh crap.* Brett pulled against the restraints, but they remained secure. He looked at Dragos. Dragos's face looked as if it were carved in granite: no emotion, no recognition, and no regret. *So much for friendship.* Had Dragos really been a friend?

Alto stood over him once again. A macabre grin split his face. His eyes glittered with excitement.

A chill swept through Brett. He cast a pleading glance at Dragos. Unshed tears filled Dragos's eyes. *What is going on?*

Dragos squeezed his eyes shut and turned his head away.

Silent tears coursed down Brett's cheeks. His head rolled back and forth. He'd never get a chance to see Lisa again to tell her he loved her. His death would devastate his mother. She'd be alone. There were so many things he wanted to do—wanted to say. He'd never get to be a father. Hell, he couldn't let his thoughts go down this road. It was the road of surrender.

Brett clenched his jaw. His body stiffened. He'd not let them see him give up. He was a fighter. It was never too late to fight.

As Alto leaned closer, Brett landed a ball of spit between the vampire's eyes.

"I hope you choke on my blood, asshole."

Victor's laughter boomed throughout the room.

"Detective, it is such a shame to kill you. You are rather amusing."

Alto hissed in his ear. "Prepare to die, Detective."

He glared up at Alto. He almost laughed as his fear fell away.

He felt the hot breath of the vampire on his skin when Dragos's voice rang out.

"Enough. Leave him alone. I will do what you want."

Alto straightened and turned to Victor. At Victor's nod, Alto moved away from the table.

"Loosen the chains and bring him down," Victor ordered.

Once Dragos was on his feet, he staggered over to the table and ripped off Brett's restraints. Dragos wrapped an arm around Brett and helped him to his feet.

Brett pulled away and glared at Dragos. *You've got to be kidding*, he thought. *A few minutes ago, Dragos had washed his hands of me. Why the change of heart?* Was he supposed to forget that Dragos had thrown him to the wolves—or, more accurately, the vampires?

Victor smoothed some nonexistent wrinkles from his jacket and casually walked over to the bottom of the stairway. The sound of Victor's boot heels clicking on the weathered stone floor sent chills up Brett's spine. Victor paused, turning ever so slightly to face him and Dragos. He stiffened.

"Kill him," ordered Victor, pointing to Brett. "Then join us upstairs. We will be leaving soon."

Dragos's eyes blazed.

"I've agreed to your terms, Victor. Let the detective go. There is no need to take his life."

Victor swung around and stalked toward Dragos. "Kill him. I want you to prove that you are loyal to me."

Dragos remained still. The pulse in Brett's neck pounded. Was it from fear or anger? He stepped back, away from Dragos. He didn't know who to trust at this point.

Dragos's harsh whisper reached his ears. "You'd do better to stay near me, O'Shea."

Not taking his eyes off of Victor, Brett growled. "I'll be the judge of that. You're still a vampire, you know."

Low laughter rumbled in Dragos's chest. "As if I could forget."

"Quit stalling," Victor yelled.

Brett cocked his head and smiled. "Dragos, are we stalling?"

Dragos shook his head and stepped near Brett. "No."

Saliva bubbled from Victor's mouth, as his teeth lengthened. He waved his guards forward. "Kill them both!"

A flurry of motion ensued as two vampires attacked Dragos. With his heart pounding in his chest, Brett backed against the wall, quickly scanning the room for something to use as a weapon—anything! The figures moved too fast; he feared he'd strike Dragos by mistake.

Dragos and one vampire were locked together. Suddenly a cracking sound caused all motion to cease. Dragos straightened. A vampire collapsed at his feet, his head lying at an odd angle. Before his friend caught his breath, the second vampire flew into his body and slammed Dragos to the floor. Punches were thrown faster than Brett could see.

Brett inched toward a workbench and slipped a hammer into his hand, hiding it at his side. He took a few steps toward Victor, thinking maybe he'd be able to surprise the creature. He couldn't just stand here and watch; he had to help. Tension strummed through him as he clasped the hammer.

When Dragos grunted, he swung toward his friend. Strong hands grabbed him from behind, wrestling the hammer from his grip. Victor's lethal-looking teeth were just inches from his face.

"What are you doing, Detective? Your weapon is useless against us." Victor twisted Brett's arm behind his back. He roared from the pain. The vampire's warm breath coated his face. "I've had enough from you. You are mine now."

Victor forced him upon the table and held Brett's upper body in place with only one arm. Brett thrashed and kicked, trying to break free.

"Go to hell!" Brett pushed against Victor, trying to keep the vampire from biting him. His arms shook from the exertion. He couldn't hold him back much longer.

Victor's glittering eyes drew nearer. Instinctively Brett pressed backward. Panic threatened to overwhelm him. A quick glance at Dragos showed that his friend was also fighting for his life. Nothing would save them now.

57

Michael's knee bounced up and down in the backseat. He rode with the two women. Anders and the other policemen drove in a separate car. It didn't take long to reach the vampire house.

With seven people carrying an entire arsenal, the group parked at the edge of the harvested cornfield. Victor's house sat on the far edge of the field. Once out of the cars, they quickly loaded every pocket and bag with ammo and an assortment of knives, holy water, and stakes.

Michael patted the inside of his tweed suit jacket. Yes, the grenades were still there. He chuckled aloud, drawing curious looks from the rest of the group. He adjusted the brim of his hat, ignoring Lisa, who continued to study him.

As the group continued to load and prepare for the battle, Lisa walked up to him.

"What are you up to?"

He barely met her gaze. "Nothing. Why?"

Lisa folded her arms across her chest. "Don't forget that I've worked with you before."

The left side of his mouth quirked upward. "Yes, you did. I take it you remember what a bang-up job I did?"

"Well, I remember it a little bit differently."

His low rumble of laughter drew Anders's attention.

"Are you two about done? We're ready." Anders slammed the trunk lid closed.

"Yes, sir. We're coming." Lisa started to walk away but paused and turned back toward Michael. "No funny business. Got it?"

He smiled. "Got it. We'd better catch up with the rest of them."

Lordy! Lisa was really stressed. Why was she worried about him? It seemed they had bigger worries to deal with.

Michael trailed behind Lisa. Candy and the police officers were clustered together, rehashing the planned strategy. Anders stood off to the side and motioned for him. He would never tell anyone, but he worried about Anders. The chief was in his midfifties and was not in peak physical condition, as were Foster and the other officers. With the head wound and loss of blood, Anders looked pale. He'd have to keep an eye on the chief tonight.

Michael pulled a pipe out of his jacket as Anders sidled up next to him. Anders cocked his head and glanced at him. The chief wiped his brow with the back of his hand. Even though a chilly November wind rustled the leaves at their feet, Anders was sweating.

"Are you okay, Anders? You're not looking yourself. Maybe you should sit this one out."

The chief waved his hand and looked annoyed.

"Don't worry about me. I wanted to have a word with you." Anders's gaze darted to the men walking ahead of them.

"I'm listening."

"Well, I would appreciate it if you would look after Foster and the men tonight. They'll be in the middle of the action and you know ..."

He nodded. It was obvious that the chief was concerned about his men—an admirable trait in any leader. "I'll do my best. You know that getting Brett out of there alive is my first priority."

Anders cleared his throat. "Of course. I'm worried. Maybe I should have brought in more men. Shit! I might get everyone killed tonight."

Michael reached out, clasping Anders on the shoulder. "You've done everything humanly possible. Your men are very qualified. Just remember: stake the bloodsuckers quickly."

"Got it," Anders muttered.

Anders slapped his shoulder and walked ahead to join Foster. He paused to glance up to the star-filled heavens.

"I hope someone up there is watching. These are good people, and I don't want to see any of them end up dead."

His gaze was drawn to a nearby oak tree. The distinct sound of fluttering wings was enough to set his heart pounding. Peering upward, he turned until he spotted a great horned owl glaring down at him. The tufts of feathers on its head made it appear to have horns. The bird's head was cocked to the side. Round yellow eyes followed his every movement.

He stood with his hands on his hips, a pipe hanging out of the corner of his mouth.

"Another owl? Really? Is that the help you're sending?"

The owl hopped down the branch, making hooting noises.

"Chirp away. I'm not happy with this. A damned bird." He shook his head and turned to follow the group.

Suddenly sharp talons dug into his shoulders. Quickly dropping to the ground, Michael waved his arms, hoping to knock the bird off his back. He rolled over to his back and looked to see if the coast was clear. *Nope!* The damn owl landed on his chest, its lethal claws prancing about on top of his body.

Maybe he'd been a little hasty in judging the owl. Its fierceness quickly made him a believer.

"Okay, okay. Just don't attack the good guys."

The owl continued to make high-pitched noises, as if it were agitated. *Not a good sign.* He attempted a half smile.

"Nice birdy. Yes, you are," he muttered in a low tone. "Just fly back to the tree. That's right, fly away. Shoo."

Lisa stood over him. He scrambled to his feet.

"What are you doing on the ground?"

"Didn't you see that owl attack me?"

Her brows rose. "No. All I saw was you rolling around acting crazy. It's getting dark. Hurry up."

He picked up his hat and dusted it off before plopping it back on his head. "I'm coming."

He glanced upward, spotting the owl flying from tree to tree. He knew it was going to be an interesting evening.

58

Lisa's stomach clenched. She stood with the group, who huddled together in the cornfield across from the Victor's house. The last of the pinkish rays from the setting sun dipped lower on the horizon. Her body trembled from fear; fear of the unknown.

The men were trying to decide how to best breach the house. They debated whether they should come in from different locations or blow up the front door and all go charging in? Since Michael had helped Anders escape and had scoped out the house earlier, they asked him for advice.

"Surprise will help us the most. There are cameras, so we need to go in fast."

"Well, I say go big or go home," Nichols grunted.

Anders and Foster glared at the officer, who sheepishly shrugged.

Candy tossed her face camo stick back in her bag. "So who's going in first, and where do Lisa and I fit in?" Her chin jutted out with determination.

Anders cleared his throat and quickly glanced at Foster. "Let us go in fast and heavy. There is going to be lots of gunfire and smoke. I would like you women to hold back, but be ready with the stakes and holy water."

Candy shook her head. "No! I'm going in to get Dragos. I can shoot as well as any man here."

"Well, I'm not staying outside by myself," said Lisa.

"Ladies, think for a minute," urged Michael. "Let the men do the dirty work. We want to keep you safe."

Candy calmly reached for her ammo bag. She lifted out a twelve-gauge, sawed-off shotgun.

Lisa gasped. *What's Candy doing?*

"Put that thing away," Foster ordered. "What the hell are you doing with a riot gun?"

Candy pulled out several shells and calmly loaded the semiautomatic shotgun.

"Shit, woman!" hissed Nichols. "Do you know you're loading military-grade breaching rounds?"

Candy hefted her bag over her shoulder. "Technically, they're M1030 breaching rounds. Lisa, are you coming?"

Anders and Michael glared after Candy. "Shit." Lisa grabbed her bag and hurried after Candy.

"Get back here," Anders hissed. "We're not ready."

She didn't stop or turn around. This way she could pretend she didn't hear his order. By the time she caught up with Candy, her legs felt like noodles. They were ready to collapse at any point. She yanked Candy's arm. "Hey, slow down. What are you doing?"

"I'm going in to get Dragos and Brett. Get your gun, and be ready to start shooting."

Lisa took a deep breath and cast a quick glance to the dark house. *Maybe we should let the police go in first.* "Let's wait for Anders."

Michael appeared by their side. A large grin lit up his face.

"I hope you ladies know what you're doing." He looked over his shoulder. "Oops. Here come the cops. You'd better get going."

Candy crouched down and ran toward the front door. She

brought the barrel of the gun up level with the doorknob and fired.

A loud blast emanated from the gun. Lisa screamed, covering her ears. Shards of wood and metal peppered the ground. Candy kicked the shattered door open.

Lisa gaped after her friend. She had no idea that Candy was so kick ass! Her friend had a low tolerance for pain, but she knew how to get the job done. Lisa jumped aside as Foster and his men ran past her. By the time Lisa set foot in the entrance, Candy and the men had disappeared into the darkness of the house.

She was supposed to help Candy. Fear spiked inside her. As she opened her supply bag, her hand shook. She pulled out a stake and shoved a spray bottle of holy water into her pocket.

She stood in the doorway. Screams and moans echoed throughout the house. Several bursts of light flashed, drawing her attention. *What was that? Gunfire? Shit, shit.* It was so dark she couldn't even see her hand in front of her face. No way was she going to wander off alone. She'd end up getting shot.

Michael suddenly appeared at her side. "Get out of the doorway," he roared. "You're a sitting duck."

He disappeared before she could ask for help. "Michael, get back here. Michael!" She shifted from side to side, needing his reassuring presence.

Several seconds passed before she was able to move, and she cursed Michael with every step. With the wall at her back, all she had to worry about was what was coming toward her. She gripped the stake, holding the sharp point outward. She scooted along the wall, gaining confidence with each step. A silent mantra rang in her head: *You can do this. You can do this.*

Suddenly she stumbled backward. A doorway was open behind her. She whipped around, the stake jerking up and down as her hand trembled. She stared into the dark room. As she stood poised near the doorway, her eyes widened. There was a shadow in the far corner of the room. *Is it Foster or Michael? Probably Michael,* she rationalized. *He enjoys scaring the bejesus out of people.*

"Michael, get over here," she hissed. Why did it have to be so dark in here? She couldn't see anything.

A pair of red eyes suddenly loomed in front of her. Instinctively she stepped back, the stake wavering in her hand.

"Hello, gorgeous. How nice of you to bring me dinner."

Dinner? I don't have any foo … Oh shit! A vampire!

She screamed and whipped around. *Run,* she told herself. Before she took two steps, the vampire grabbed a handful of her hair and jerked her backward. As she slammed back against the vampire, his arm clamped around her waist. No matter how hard she squirmed, he pinned her tight against him. His tongue stroked her neck.

"Hmm. Tasty," he murmured. "You're not going to try to stab me with that little twig of yours, are you?"

His words nearly sent her heart plummeting. She thrashed back and forth, kicking her feet and doing everything else she could to make him loosen his grip. When she pushed back against his body, his erection pushed against her bottom. She froze, glancing back over her shoulder. It was a mistake. His long, dark hair draped over her shoulder. A GQ model's face stared back at her, chiseled cheekbones and all. *Great!* She peeked at him again. He did have those ugly, sharp teeth and scary red eyes. She shook her head, trying to focus on what was important. She was here to kill vampires, not be seduced by one. She had to get it together. After all, he had referred to her as his dinner.

His hypnotic gaze lured her closer. His cold lips nuzzled her neck. The monster inhaled her scent. *This is just creepy!*

Somehow she had to break the spell that wove its way around her.

She rammed her elbow into his stomach. His grip tightened. It was like hitting a rock wall. He didn't budge.

He ran a hand down her curves, lingering on the side of her breast. "You like it, don't you?"

She shook her head. The sound of a zipper made her stiffen with fear. His hand reached around her body and tugged on her jeans.

A woman's scream at the opposite end of the house drew their attention. It was followed by several bursts of gunfire.

Lisa renewed her struggles. It sounded as if Candy was in trouble. "Leave me the hell alone!" Her hand tightened around the stake.

His efforts ceased for a few seconds. "Do not fight me. I can make your body soar."

Her brows drew together. *Soar? Yeah, as he drains the blood from my body.*

She wiggled her bottom up against his dick. A low hiss sounded in her ear.

"Oh, baby. That feels so good," she moaned as she rolled her eyes.

He continued to press and rub against her. His arm about her waist relaxed. Taking a deep breath, she whirled to face him and shoved the stake into his chest. The sound of wood pressing through muscle and tissue sent stomach contents up into her throat.

She slowly raised her gaze to meet his. Red, heated eyes stared down at her. *Damn!* He wasn't dead. Elongated teeth inches from her face dripped saliva on her skin.

"You think a puny thing like you can kill a vampire like me. You are sadly mistaken. I'm going to enjoy sucking you dry, bitch. Prepare to … to …"

His eyes rolled back in his head as he collapsed on the floor.

She shivered, gaping down at the twitching vampire. The stake had embedded deeper in his chest when he hit the floor. Luckily they had soaked the stakes in holy water. She lunged forward and whipped out her spray bottle of holy water and spritzed his face. Red boils quickly covered his once handsome face.

"Take that, butthead." She stared down at the vampire. He appeared to be dead, but she had to make sure.

"Good job, Lisa."

She screamed and swung around, her fist grazing Anders's chin.

"Oh, so sorry. I kill … he's dead."

He smiled back at her. "That's okay. I haven't seen Brett or Dragos yet. Foster and his men are wrapping up their search of this floor. They've already killed one of the vampires. Now you killed one."

Lisa nodded and stepped out into the hallway. She couldn't look at the dead vampire. Anders staked him again for good measure. As she leaned against the wall with closed eyes, a cool breeze brushed her face.

"Hey, kiddo. Great job. You got one." Michael clapped her on the shoulder.

Her eyes remained closed. The evening had just begun, and she was exhausted already.

The sound of rapid gunfire rattled the floors. Lisa straightened and glanced at Michael.

"What the hell was that?"

Michael's eyes closed, the corner of his mouth twisting into a wry grin. He grabbed her hand and turned toward her.

"Foster's guys just found the doorway to the basement."

She threw her arms around Michael, pressing a kiss to his cheek.

"I hope we're in time," Lisa whispered.

59

Michael stormed after Foster and his crew as they descended the basement stairs. He was worried. Where were Brett and Dragos? Were they still alive? Where were the rest of the vampires? Only two had been on the upper level. Now they were both dead.

Nichols and Johnson led the way with guns drawn. With his Glock at the ready, Foster had several stakes poking out of his ammo bag. His large frame filled the hallway. Nothing was going to get by him.

Michael studied Lisa, who was stuck at his side. Killing the vampire had unnerved her more than he thought. If they survived, they'd all have nightmares after this night was over.

The three officers went from room to room, kicking in the doors. When they reached the room at the end of the hallway, Michael started. This was the room he'd heard Brett in when he rescued Anders. He brushed past the officers and entered the room. He breathed a sigh of relief. The room was free of blood. In some of the other rooms, blood permeated the mattresses. Death lurked in this house. It gave even him the chills.

Without warning, a loud crash drew Michael out to the hallway. Three vampires advanced toward them. Lisa froze and stared at the vampires as they ran toward them. *Crazy woman! She's going to get herself killed!* He shoved her into a room and closed the door.

Foster and his men took defensive positions, crouching in empty doorways. The vampires darted from side to side in the hallway. Michael blinked in amazement. They moved so quickly that their figures blurred.

"Shoot even if you don't have a good shot!" ordered Foster. Three Glocks fired rounds down the hall. The vampires flinched as bullets riddled their bodies. Blood spurted, spraying the wall and floor with blood.

"They're still coming," Nichols shouted.

Foster hoisted a grenade in the air. "Take cover!"

Michael rubbed his hands together. He loved this. *Real action!* The hallway filled with smoke. Chunks of drywall rained down to the floor. Nearby doors and windows were blasted into pieces. Pieces of shrapnel stuck out of the wall. Groans and the vibration of shots being fired became overwhelming. He turned back to spirit form in an attempt to slow up the vampires.

As a vampire raced by, Michael swung out his arm and slammed a fist into its throat. His arm throbbed. It was like hitting a brick wall.

Staggering to a stop, the vampire bent over, looking pained. He rubbed his throat, hissing in anger. Foster took advantage of the situation and peppered him with buckshot from a riot gun. The shorter barrel made it easy to use in tight spaces. The vampire staggered, clutching at his body before falling to his knees.

Michael smiled. Edging over to the vampire, he bent down and whispered, "Not so much fun when you're the one getting hurt, now is it?"

The vampire growled, looking around for whoever was talking to him. Spittle flew from his mouth.

"Hey, bloodsucker. Hope you're prepared to die."

The vampire surged to his feet and angrily swiped the air.

Michael's hat flew to the floor. *What the hell just happened? The vampire can't see me, so how did my hat move?* He scrunched his brows together, looking around the room. *Not another complication.*

A man's scream curdled his blood. He turned to see Foster and Nichols both in hand-to-hand combat with a vampire. Foster pulled a large knife from a sheath strapped to his leg. The nine-inch clip-point blade was a lethal weapon.

Foster sustained several minor wounds but held his own. Nichols was severely injured. He kept firing his weapon into the vampire with little effect.

The door behind him opened, and Lisa peeked out. "Get back!"

Ignoring his warning, she ran to Foster's side. She took out a bottle of holy water and sprayed the vampire's face. Roaring with rage, the vampire raised a hand to wipe the water away. At the same moment, Foster lunged toward, burying the blade deep inside the chest of the vampire. The eyes of the vampire widened, as if he couldn't believe what had just happened.

When Foster yanked out the blade, Lisa grabbed a stake and sank it into the knife wound. A spray of blood rose up, splattering her face.

She wiped her face with the sleeve of her shirt. "Oh shit. Nichols is down!"

Foster leapt over the vampire's still body and ran toward the officer. He landed on the other vampire's back, locking him in a neck hold. Roaring to his feet, the vampire slammed into the wall. Foster flew through the drywall before sliding to the floor.

Michael grabbed Lisa's arm, glancing down at the staked vampire. "You will have to finish him. He's still moving. Hurry! It's dangerous standing here."

Her lower lip trembled. "Uh, I'm not sure I can do it."

He gripped both of her shoulders and gave her a gentle

shake. "No argument. I've got to help Foster and Johnson. Do it!"

The sound of thudding footsteps drew his attention. A vampire ran toward Lisa. *Shit!* He jumped in front of the vampire and swung his fist. And it went right through the vampire. What the heck! The vampire skidded to a stop and turned. The vampire stared right at him yet couldn't see him.

With a shrug, the vampire spun back around toward Lisa, who gripped a wooden stake. The vampire roared and stormed toward Lisa. She froze, gaping up at the towering creature.

Foster and Johnson were fighting for their lives. There was no one to help Lisa. Michael's arms fell to his sides, bumping against a lump in his pocket. *Wait! A grenade.* He smiled as he held one in the palm of his hand. Time to play ball!

The vampire stood over Lisa. Michael crept up behind the vampire and held up the weapon for her to see.

"Lisa, you need to dive into that room behind you. I'm going to blow this guy up. Ready?"

At her nod, several things happened at once. He dropped the live grenade down the back of the vampire's shirt. The vampire stiffened and turned toward him. Lisa ran into the nearby room and slammed the door. He stood, grinning at the vampire, who unfortunately couldn't see him.

He decided at the last second that maybe it wasn't the smartest idea to stand so close to an explosion. The vampire reached down his shirt and pulled out the grenade as it exploded.

The blast slammed Michael into a wall. Pieces of two-by-fours littered the floor. Drywall dust drifted through the air, creating a cloud. His ears rang from the explosion.

"Ow!" He limped away from the wall and turned to where the vampire once stood. His eyes widened as he took in the carnage before him. Blood and body parts were stuck to the wall and ceiling. The torso of the vampire lay at his feet.

Lisa jerked the off-center door open and peered out. "Is he gone?"

He nodded. "At least we don't have to worry about staking him."

Lisa gasped and pointed down the hall. "Look, Foster and his men are down."

She ran toward the officers, attempting to stay upright as her feet slipped on the blood- and goo-covered floors. Michael stared after Lisa, shaking his head in admiration. How many other people could accept the fact that vampires and demons existed and then act as if nothing out of the ordinary had happened? She was a good match for Brett.

He jerked to attention when something hit him from behind. A hand rested on his shoulder. Had someone sneaked up on him? He tensed and reached up, intending to flip whoever was behind him. He grabbed the hand and pulled, but it flew out of his grip. It was a hand, but there was no body attached to the limb. He shivered from the heebie-jeebies. *Ew! That was just gross.*

Stepping over the withering limb, he hurried after Lisa. The third vampire had disappeared. The three officers lay on the floor. Foster's body was the first one they reached.

Michael blinked the moisture from his eyes, shaking his head. *No, this can't have happened. The good guys weren't supposed to die.* His shoulders sagged. *This wasn't the plan.*

Lisa collapsed to the floor and began to brush the dust from their bodies. A moan filled the air. A leg moved.

"Quick! Help me roll Foster over to his back," she cried.

They gently rolled Foster over. His chest heaved in sporadic movements. She leaned in to help him sit.

Thundering footsteps drew louder. Michael turned to see Anders rushing down the hall.

"What the hell happened? I heard the blast." Anders turned pale as he saw his men on the floor.

"Chi … chief," Foster said, his voice cracking. "Are you okay?"

Anders nodded as he turned his head and quickly wiped his eyes. "Yeah, I'm fine, but you look like hell."

Foster groaned as he raised his arm. Blood flowed from several gashes. "Where are my men?"

Michael gently dragged Foster off to the side. He motioned to Lisa. "Tear off his shirt and put a tourniquet on the arm. Don't worry, Captain; your men are right here beside you. I'll check on them right now."

He pulled chunks of drywall and wood off of the other two men.

Johnson coughed, spewing dust off his face and holding an arm over his stomach. "Shit. What happened? I feel like I've been hit by a truck."

Michael helped Johnson sit up and then turned to help Nichols. The officer hadn't moved or spoken. *Damn it!* His lips were blue. The man's neck was ripped to pieces.

Michael's eyes filled with tears. *No, no. This can't happen. Nichols was joking around just a couple of hours ago. Damn it! The man has a family—a baby!*

Bending down, Michael touched Nichols's neck, praying and hoping for a pulse. There was nothing—not one breath or movement. His head dipped to his chest. Lisa touched his shoulder.

"Is he okay?" Her voice shook with emotion. It was as if she knew.

His throat tightened. He tried to breathe but couldn't. Panic ripped through him as he scrambled to his feet. He brushed Lisa aside and ran several feet before collapsing against a wall. *Why? Why Nichols?*

He heard a cry and turned toward the fallen officer. Foster dragged Nichols into his arms and cradled him. His tears dropped across the dead officer's face. Foster's body rocked back and forth. The captain's face contorted with grief.

Anders and Johnson crouched down next to Foster, their heads bowed and their shoulders gently shaking. Lisa stared down at Nichols. Her fist covered her mouth.

A round of gunfire snapped them back to action. In that dim hallway, they glanced at one another, silently assessing the scenario. Sadness and loss quickly faded from their faces, replaced with anger and the need for retribution.

Michael wiped his face and rose to his feet. Foster carefully laid Nichols on the floor, using his jacket to cover the upper part of the body. Lisa held out a hand and helped Johnson to his feet. The five of them stood in a circle and silently reloaded their weapons. Michael grabbed another grenade.

A muscle twitched in Foster's jaw as he yanked out some stakes and put them in his knife sheath.

"I saw a vampire disappear through a door at the end of the hallway." Foster's hoarse voice cracked. "It looked like it was hidden by that bookshelf. It could be booby-trapped, so be careful. I'll go first. If anyone wants out, now is the time to leave."

The four men looked at Lisa.

"Don't look at me. I'm not leaving without Brett and Candy."

Anders turned to Foster and Johnson. "Are you two able to continue?"

Foster hoarsely muttered, "Nothing is keeping me from finishing these assholes now."

"I'm in," chimed Johnson.

Michael grinned. That was the kind of attitude he liked to see.

"Chief, if you don't mind, I'll take the lead," Michael announced. "They can't kill me. I don't want to see any of you hurt or—"

Anders cut him off. "Appreciate it."

With a grenade in hand, Michael was ready to blow another vampire to kingdom come. They quietly made their way to the end of the hallway, checking each room they passed. They didn't want any more surprises. A heavy bookcase lined the wall. Someway, somehow, there had to be an opening behind that wall.

"Step back, guys. I say it's time to wake up these bastards," Michael warned. He pulled out two grenades. "Take cover. It's going to be loud."

He lobbed the live grenades against the bookcase. The entire foundation of the house rattled. Waves of smoke and dust rolled toward them. Heads covered, they waited for the air to clear so they could see. Foster stepped forward and looked into the gaping hole in the wall.

Foster shook his head. "You're not going to believe this, but there are stairs leading down to another level."

Michael peered down into the darkness. He had never liked killing. Even if it was part of the job, it took a toll on a man's soul. It drove some cops crazy. But in this case, it would feel damn good to kill the bloodsuckers. They were going to pay for what they'd done.

He leaned in and hollered down the hole, "Attention bloodsuckers! We're coming for you!" It was time to go find his grandson. Dead or alive, he wasn't leaving without Brett.

60

Brett fell back on the floor as a loud blast rattled the house. He lay there, his head covered, as debris from the ceiling rained down. He crawled to his knees, coughing from the dust in the air.

"O'Shea, are you okay?" Dragos croaked.

Clouds of dust filled the cavern. Brett couldn't see a thing. "Where are you?"

"Right next to you."

He brushed the grime from his face and rose to his feet. Dragos stiffened and grabbed Brett's arm.

Someone pushed at the door at the top of the stairs. A man wearing a hat squeezed through the broken opening.

"Michael!"

"Brett! Thank God you're okay." Michael materialized next to Brett and enveloped him in a hug, lifting his feet off the ground.

Brett's eyes widened as he saw everyone crawl through the hole in the wall. Lisa shrieked before throwing herself into his arms. Anders approached him with a wide grin and a pat on the back. He set Lisa on the ground, pressing a kiss on her mouth. He smiled as Foster and Dragos clasped each other on the back. He was alive. Help had come, and he was going home.

Lisa's smile faded as she turned about the room. "Where's Candy?"

Dragos growled and walked over to Lisa and grabbed her arm. "Candy? Is she here?"

Brett couldn't hear himself think with everyone talking. His head was spinning. He gave a shrill whistle. "Quiet!" He turned to Anders. "Did Candy come with you tonight?"

Anders's mouth stretched into a thin line. He nodded. "She blew open the front door to be the first person in the house. Foster, did you guys see her when you were searching the basement?"

Foster and Johnson glanced at one another, each shaking his head.

Brett glanced at Michael, who looked as grim as he felt. "How in the hell can you lose one of your team members?"

Michael cleared his throat. "Hold on a second, sonny. No accusations."

Dragos's eyes closed as he let loose with a string of curses. His eyes blazed with fury.

Lisa wrapped her hand in his. Her voice trembled. "Where's Candy?"

"We've got a problem. Victor is still alive. There's at least one other vampire with him," Dragos softly muttered.

Lisa gasped and clasped her hand over her mouth. "Could Victor have Candy?"

Michael nodded. "Maybe. We need to thoroughly search the house. She could be injured somewhere."

A wild look filled Dragos's eyes. "If Victor harms one hair on—"

Brett rested a hand on Dragos's shoulder. "Don't let your mind go there. If he did take her, where would he go?"

Dragos shook his head. "The tunnels by the river. That has to be it."

Anders turned toward his men. "Foster, you and Johnson

go get the cars and bring them here. The rest of us will search the house to make sure she's not inside."

After the two officers ran up the stairs, Brett turned to Lisa and placed a hand on either side of her face.

"I need you to be safe. I want you to go home."

Tears welled up in her eyes. "I can't. It's my fault that Candy is now in danger."

He sighed and wrapped his arms around her lithe frame, drawing her to him. "It's not your fault. She knew the risks, just like you. We'll find her. Please, I couldn't stand it if something happened to you."

She sniffled while nodding her head. "Drop me off at the station, and I'll get a ride home."

He squeezed Lisa tighter, wishing this were over.

Michael walked over to him. "What are we going to do about the mess here? We've got several bodies lying around."

"Get the bodies and put them in a pile. We'll have to torch the place. At least there are no neighbors to worry about. I'll call the fire department once we get out of here."

They all moved up to the first floor of the house and started dragging the bodies to the family room.

Brett paused as he neared the front door. A body lay nearby. A quick glance at Anders was all he needed to see. It was as though someone had punched Brett's gut. He bent down and slowly pulled the cover off the man's face. He gasped. *Nichols.* He'd known Nichols since the academy. He bit down on his lower lip. He wanted to punch something; scream at the unfairness of Nichols's death. His fists clenched. He stared down at the body, unable to see through the salty tears clouding his view. Nichols had died trying to save him. He was resolved to make Victor pay for this even if it was the last thing he did.

Anders stepped to his side. "He was killed in the line of duty. I'll make sure his family is taken care of."

Brett's throat tightened. His words were barely audible. "We can't burn his body."

"Of course not. We're going to leave it outside. When we call it in, they'll find him and call the coroner." Anders wiped the dampness from his cheeks. "I'll come up with some reason why he was here. It's not your problem. C'mon, O'Shea. Let's go. We need to find Candy."

61

Brett's hands clenched the steering wheel as he glanced over his shoulder. The yellow glow of the house fire bellowed out the front door. Anders silently climbed into the front seat of the car next to Michael.

Nichols's body lay near the street. Brett didn't feel right leaving his friend alone in the cold. Somehow the reality of seeing the body made the horror of this night more real.

"O'Shea! Let's go," Anders roared. "The fire department will be here any minute."

He grunted and looked up, catching Lisa's stare in the rearview mirror. She was on Dragos's lap, scrunched between Foster and Johnson. No one spoke. She reached forward and squeezed Brett's shoulder. No words were necessary. It had been a costly night.

Brett drove toward the police station, wanting to get Lisa out of harm's way. Johnson was severely injured and needed medical attention, but after Nichols's death, there was no way any of them were opting out at this point.

As they pulled into the parking lot along the Des Moines River, Foster hopped out of the car to let Lisa out. Brett got out and walked around the side of the car.

Lisa stepped toward him, wrapping her arms about his waist. Her cheek pressed against his chest.

"I'm so sorry about Nichols. Are you going to be okay?"

He nodded, his hand absently massaging the back of her neck. He lowered his head, pressing a kiss to the top of hers.

"Yeah. The important thing right now is to get Candy back safe and unharmed."

Brett stepped back; wet splotches stained the front of his shirt. He gripped Lisa's chin, tipping her gaze upward.

He leaned in, inhaling the sweet scent that was uniquely hers even with the hint of smoke and gunpowder. "I need you to be safe. Go home, and when I get done with this, we're going to talk. I need you, Lisa."

Without waiting for a response, he captured her trembling lips with his. The urgency of the situation and the depth of his emotions welled up in that one kiss. He willed her to understand. He couldn't say or do anything more—not with four hardened cops and a vampire waiting for him.

He broke away. His hand trailed down her damp cheek.

She pressed a hand to his face. "Go. We'll talk when you get back. Stay safe."

He drew in a deep breath and returned to the car, where he waited until she entered the station before driving away.

"So, Dragos, is there a back way into the tunnels?" Brett asked.

Dragos shook his head. "I don't think so. After I awoke, I briefly explored the tunnels, but I didn't see any other openings.

Anders muttered, "Perhaps we can trap them underground."

"Yeah, then burn them out," Michael added.

"What is the matter with you people?" said Dragos. "Candy may be in there."

Anders nudged Michael. "Dragos is right. Besides, what's the fascination with fire about?"

Michael shrugged. "You noticed, huh?"

Brett rolled his eyes. He wasn't in the mood for jokes. "Knock it off, Michael. How's everyone sitting on ammo?"

Everyone agreed they had enough ammo. After a short drive to the ball field, the group quietly got out of the car.

Foster pulled out his gun, and Johnson quickly turned to Foster. "Got any grenades left?"

"No talking," Anders snapped. "And no flashlights."

Single file, they wound their way down the dark path toward the dig site. As they got closer, Anders motioned for everyone to hit the ground. Crawling on their stomachs, they made their way to the edge of the site.

Brett glanced down into the site. Nothing moved, and there were no lights. Dragos, lying next to him, growled.

"What's wrong?" Brett whispered.

"Victor is down there."

He peered down, unable to see anything. "Are you sure?"

Dragos punched his arm.

Damn that hurt.

Dragos slithered forward, crawling down into the pit. One by one, they followed. They paused outside the tunnel doorway. The muffled scream of a woman drifted toward them.

Candy!

Dragos stiffened and rushed toward the tunnel entrance. Brett grabbed his friend's arm. "Wait. It's what they want us to do," he warned.

Dragos pulled away, shaking off Brett's hand. Anders stepped toward the vampire.

"Brett's right. You'll be an easy target if you go running in."

Suddenly a large barn owl swooped down, nearly missing their heads. Michael's hat fluttered to the ground. The owl chirped and circled them several times. It swept low, causing Foster and Anders to fall flat on the ground.

Foster drew his gun and aimed it at the owl. Michael sprang forward and grabbed Foster's arm.

"No! Don't shoot," Michael whispered.

"Shh!" Anders growled.

Michael grabbed his hat and stared at the owl as it flew toward the river.

The men gathered by the tunnel entrance, ready to enter. Brett saw Foster draw his knife. *Damn!* He'd never see Foster in action until now. *Impressive.* Foster motioned for him to follow. They crawled five feet before hitting a large boulder that nearly filled the opening. Brett tapped Foster on the shoulder, and they returned to the tunnel entrance.

Brett shook his head. "Not good, guys. There's a large rock blocking the tunnel. We'll never get through this way."

Anders stomped his foot, whispering, "Son of a bitch."

Dragos stood at the entrance and held out his hand, silently assessing the situation. Looking disheartened, he shook his head.

"We cannot go in that way. It is a trap. If we try to move it, many more rocks will fall down on us."

"Now what?" asked Anders, turning toward Brett.

When Brett turned to see if Michael had any ideas, the ghost was gone.

"Michael. Michael, where are you?"

Foster snarled, "Your ghost doesn't seem to be helping much."

"No offense, Captain, but Michael is a little unorthodox in the way he does things."

"Sir, I think we need to call in the heavy equipment and open up that tunnel," Foster stated.

Anders's mouth twisted in a grimace. "Take it down a notch, Foster. O'Shea will lead us."

Everyone swung his gaze in Brett's direction. He wished he were as confident as Anders appeared to be. He was getting pissed off about Michael, wondering how he could just up and leave them.

Dragos walked over to his side. "Where's Michael?"

"I wish I knew."

The sound of footsteps running toward them drew their attention. It was Michael, crashing through the small brush. His hands waved in the air. Michael skidded to a halt in front of Brett and Dragos.

"I found a way in."

62

The owl swooped down and landed on Michael's shoulder. He smiled and turned toward the bird, giving it a one-finger scratch.

"Watch the claws. Not too hard." Michael cringed. He turned toward Brett, whose mouth hung open. "Sonny, close your mouth. Bugs will fly in there."

Dragos flapped his hand, causing the owl to chirp angrily. Michael gave Dragos a shove.

"Don't push me," warned Dragos. "Get that bird out of here."

"Hey, be nice. The owl found us a way into the tunnel."

Anders drew closer. "What did he say, O'Shea? A way in?"

The owl chirped into Michael's ear. For some reason, the bird wanted them to leave this area now.

"Guys, we've got to leave now. Follow me." Michael turned and walked toward the timber.

Glancing over his shoulder, he saw that most of the group followed. Foster and Johnson hadn't moved, but they stared after them. He stopped and motioned for them to follow. Foster shrugged and shook his head.

Anders turned and waved at Foster. Michael sighed. The captain stood there with indecision written on this face.

A rumbling sound from deep within the tunnel bellowed

toward them. A large boulder came shooting out of the tunnel, directly toward Foster and Johnson. Michael jerked into motion and disappeared. He reappeared behind the two police officers and gave them a shove. They took off running as if the devil himself were after them.

Once the boulder rolled past them, a large mass of bats flew toward them. Michael screamed. Although they were just little brown bats and relatively harmless, the idea of thousands of the furry creatures caught in his hair or creeping over his body sent him running for his life. And he didn't even have a life to lose.

Dragos swore aloud as he ran by. The swarm of bats flew directly on their heels.

He heard the rest of the group running behind him.

Brett yelled, "Do something, Michael!"

At that moment, the owl swept down in front of him. *Right!* The owl had shown him another way to get into the tunnels.

With a loud whistle, he pointed toward the river.

Anders jumped in front of Michael. "Are we following the owl?"

"No." Michael shook his head and gasped as a bat flew past his head. "The owl is leading us."

"Son of a bitch!" Anders flashed a glare as he ran to keep up.

Changing course, the group turned toward the river. The men yelped and swore as their feet slipped on the mud. As one, they slid down the deep embankment to the water's edge. Michael's chest shook with contained laughter. Covered in mud and slime, the men struggled to get to their feet.

Anders took a finger and scooped mud from his brows. Brett tilted his head and tried to pick the mud from his ears.

Foster and Johnson leaned against one another, looking as though they wanted to kill him. *Jeez! It wasn't my fault,* he thought

Anders bent down and cupped his hand. He took the river water and splashed it on his face. He then leaned over and spit mud from his lips. "Michael, where's this new tunnel? It's getting late."

Dragos pressed against Michael, forcing him to back up against the riverbank. "I must get to Candy now."

Michael pointed to a small opening in the riverbank. They would have to crawl in, but once inside the tunnel, they would be able to stand. During normal river levels, the opening would be hidden from view. Thanks to the owl, they had a way in to the tunnel system—a way to surprise the vampires.

With one hand on his hip, Michael pointed. "There's our way in. Who's first?"

Dragos growled and knelt down quickly, disappearing through the hole. One by one, they crawled through the opening. Once inside, they gathered in a circle, looking ahead.

"Dragos and I can lead the way, since we can see." Michael said, pushing back the brim of his hat with the back of his hand. "We want to surprise them, so no talking or flashlights. Got it?"

"No more talking; let's go," demanded Dragos.

The tunnel lacked the twists and turns of the other tunnel. Occasionally Dragos would stop and move a rock or some other obstacle out of way.

Nearly thirty minutes later, Dragos suddenly stopped. Brett and Anders piled into his back.

"Shh!" warned Dragos. He pointed ahead. A golden glow from a faint light flickered in the distance. It appeared the light was moving in their direction. "Move back. Someone's coming." He swung toward them. "If it's Victor, he's mine."

They all pressed against the walls of the tunnel, stakes and guns drawn.

"Be careful," Brett warned. "They may use Candy as a shield."

This brought another growl from Dragos.

"Okay, guys. Here they come," Michael whispered. He only hoped they were prepared enough to take out two more vampires.

A noise behind brought them to a halt. No one breathed. Footsteps grew louder. Had Victor set another trap? If vampires were coming up from behind them, then they were trapped. With vampires in front of them and behind them, there was no way out.

63

Brett motioned to Anders. He would circle back and try to surprise whoever was coming.

"Be careful," Anders warned.

Brett slowly made his way back the way they came. Whoever or whatever was coming was not very stealthy. Every few seconds, a curse or moan reverberated through the tunnel. He doubted that it was a vampire trying to sneak up on them. With their superior eyesight, vampires wouldn't be banging into things.

With the footsteps becoming louder, Brett heard a man mumble.

"Damn. How many frickin' rocks are in this tunnel?" the approaching man swore.

Oh no. It can't be. Randall! What the hell is he doing here?

In a low voice, Brett whispered, "Randall, Randall. Put the gun down."

Randall jerked and pointed a gun at Brett's chest. Brett instinctively dropped to the ground and covered his head as Randall fired. The bullet ricocheted off the stone walls. The gun clattered to the ground.

Randall dropped the flashlight and screamed. "Argh! Son of a bitch. Is that you O'Shea?"

Brett rose to his feet and leaned against the stone wall,

trying to slow his pounding heart. Randall was holding his own hand. "The bullet bounced off the wall and hit my hand."

Brett wiped his brow with the back of his hand. "You're lucky you didn't kill yourself or me." He lunged forward and grabbed the front of Randall's shirt. "What the hell are you doing here?"

Eyes wide, Randall trembled. "I've been keeping an eye on Victor. I saw you and Anders running, so I followed you."

"How the hell do you know Victor?"

"We met at Darlene's and went to a few parties together."

He was furious. He wanted to shake Randall. In a low voice, he leaned closer to Randall. "Do you know what Victor is?"

Randall shook his head. "Is? What does that mean?"

"Nothing." He dropped his hand, pushing away from his coworker.

The sound of footsteps hurried toward them. Randall made a strange sound and then ducked behind Brett, who bent and picked up Randall's gun. As he handed it back, he warned, "Lower your light. I'm with a task force including Anders and Foster. For God's sake, don't shoot them."

Michael suddenly stood in front of Brett. Concern filled his face. "Are you okay? We heard a gunshot."

"Yeah, I'm fine. Detective Randall was tracking Victor and spotted us, so he decided to find out what's going on."

Randall gulped. "Where did he come from?"

"Didn't you see him running down the tunnel?"

"No." Randall's voice shook.

"This is Michael. He's working the murder case with us. Hurry up. We need to get back to the group."

Michael turned and frowned at Randall. "Should we take his gun so he won't shoot us?"

Randall drew the gun closer to his chest.

Brett chuckled. "No, but you have my permission to kick

his ass if he shoots any of us. Now turn out the light and stay close."

They quickly made their way back to the group.

Dragos snarled. "Randall."

"Guys, Detective Randall has joined us."

Anders snorted. "Randall. What the hell are you doing here?"

Randall nervously shifted. "I was—"

"Chief," Brett interrupted, "it's too late to send him back."

He turned toward Randall. "Victor has kidnapped Dragos's girlfriend. He may have other men with him."

Randall cast a look at Dragos. "Sorry," he muttered.

Brett grabbed Randall's arm. "Listen up. We don't have much time. The guys with Victor are very fast and lethal. If they get close to you, just shoot like hell."

Dragos raised his head, listening to something down the tunnel. Without a word, he took off running.

"Let's go," Brett said.

By the time they caught up with Dragos, the vampire had come to a complete stop. Brett felt the fury pouring from Dragos's body. Brett's gaze took in the scene before them.

They stood at the edge of a large cavern. Trickles of water dripped to the floor, running through the cracks in the rocks to the outside river. Sconces were strategically placed to provide lighting. Tens of large shipping trunks were set on the floor. Large crates were stacked in the corner. Furniture from the past three centuries was wrapped in plastic, ready to be moved. It looked as though someone planned on leaving town.

Several vampires were in the process of loading boxes. Victor and Candy were noticeably absent.

Brett turned toward Dragos. The vampire's dark, piercing gaze assessed the situation before them. Dragos twisted his head, cracking the bones in his neck. Straightening his shoulders, Brett watched Dragos walk toward the vampires.

"Gentlemen, are you going somewhere?"

Everyone froze. The vampires' dangerous gazes fixated on Dragos before giving the rest of the group a cursory glance.

As one, the vampires smiled, the tips of their teeth showing. Dragos smiled as well.

Brett wished he knew what Dragos had planned. Randall came up to his side.

"Pssst. O'Shea, what the hell are those guys?" Randall's body trembled.

"Vampires."

Randall gasped. "You're shitting me."

Michael walked up on the other side of Randall and smacked the back of the detective's head. "If I were you, I'd quit talking and get that gun of yours ready."

Brett turned toward Anders and the other officers. "Spread out and find cover."

Before Anders got into position, the vampires surged forward. He dived behind a rock as the bullets flew. Brett peered around the stone and saw Randall standing frozen in place. His face was twisted in fear. His gun hung at his side—not a good thing when vampires were attacking.

A vampire smiled and stalked toward his coworker. Brett cursed under his breath. Randall seemed to be completely oblivious to the danger he was in. Pulling out a stake, Brett lunged for the vampire approaching Randall's side. The vampire was so intent on his victim that he wasn't prepared for Brett's attack. Brett plunged the stake deep into the vampire's chest.

Randall screamed as Brett and the vampire rolled on the ground in front of him. Out of the corner of his eye, Brett saw Randall waving the gun at them.

"Don't you dare shoot that gun, Randall," he bellowed. He drew back a fist and punched the vampire's jaw, and the vampire retaliated by trying to bite him. "Grab a stake!"

A few seconds later, Randall returned with a stake in his

hand. The vampire suddenly lunged forward, overpowering him. Brett braced for the pain. Instead the weight of the vampire collapsed on top of him.

Opening his eyes, he saw Randall kick the vampire to the side and jam the stake deep into his heart. The vampire's body twitched, and blood gurgled from his mouth.

After sucking in a deep breath, Brett rolled over and rose to his feet. He jumped as the other detective leaned down and shot the vampire in the temple.

Randall glanced at him. "Just wanted to make sure he was dead."

Brett shook his head and looked for Anders or Foster. They were ripping off shots at two vampires. The bodies jerked in a ghoulish manner as they tried to reach the two officers. Johnson crept up behind them and planted stakes deep in their chests. He hit them so hard the tips of the stakes poked out the other sides of the bodies. Anders hurried over to the bodies and splashed them with holy water. Screams of dying vampires filled the cavern.

Where is Dragos? More importantly, where are Candy and Victor? Brett picked up a couple of stakes. Gun in hand, he walked toward a connecting tunnel. When a woman's scream ripped through the air, he started running.

He entered a smaller cavern. Dragos and Victor were locked together as they fought. Candy was tied to an old bed. Dried blood was caked to her arms and neck. He ran to her side, cutting the ropes to free her. She jumped into his arms, sobbing.

"Do something. Dragos needs help." Tears coursed down her flushed cheeks.

Brett glanced at Dragos, who was holding his own against Victor. "Are you okay? Did they hurt you?"

Her eyes filled with tears. "It was horrible. He forced me to go with him. He snapped my gun as if it were nothing. He let the vampires bite me; over and over." She angrily swiped the tears from her cheeks. "They're planning to leave tonight. They were going to kill me. Take my blood and kill me." Candy choked back a sob.

He wrapped her in a tight hug, pressing a kiss on the top of her head. "You're safe now. Stay here. I need to see if your boyfriend needs any help."

Dragos saw red. He entered the cavern and saw Candy. Alive and tied to a bed. She was bruised and bloodied. He'd barely taken a step toward her when Victor's laughter stopped him.

He turned as Victor slammed into him, knocking him across the floor. He jumped up with arms outstretched and attacked Victor. He wrapped his hands around the vampire's neck. Victor's grin faded as bones cracked under the pressure Dragos applied. Victor hit him in the face and tossed him to the side.

He scrambled to his feet. Pleased that Victor didn't look so cocky any longer.

He spit the blood from his mouth and glared at Victor. His lip curled in derision. "Are you worried?"

Victor threw back his head. His laughter echoing through the cavern. "Do not get ahead of yourself, Dragos. I've been a vampire much longer than you. My powers are much stronger than yours."

Dragos took one step, and then another, until he stood in front of Victor. His chin jutted outward, his gaze focused on his target. "That may be. However, I happen to believe in the power of justice—the power of good over evil. And you, sir, fall into the evil category."

Victor rolled his eyes, and his fingertips lengthened. His head tilted slightly to the side; he studied Dragos as if seeing him for the first time. "Evil? Vampires were set upon this earth to take control over those weaker than us. We were made to rule."

Dragos stared unblinkingly at Victor. The bloodied vampire didn't have the capability to show empathy or compassion. "You made me this ... this creature, thinking that I would be like you. You couldn't be more wrong. I will never be like you."

Victor hissed and turned away from him. "I don't know what I ever saw in you. You could have had so much more. Now you are nothing but a weak vampire who needs to be killed. I will make sure my next creation is superior to you."

Dragos briefly glanced over Victor's shoulder before facing his nemesis again. A large smile lit his face as he stepped back. A look of puzzlement filled Victor's gaze.

"Unfortunately you will not have the opportunity to create anything ever again."

Victor swung toward him, anger blossoming across his face. "You're a poor excuse for a vampire, I will end your ... your li ..."

Victor clasped his chest before collapsing to the floor. A wooden stake protruded several inches from his chest. As Victor lay on the ground, he looked up at Dragos with a quizzical gaze. Blood seeped from his body and pooled nearby. Victor clutched the stake and writhed in pain. The holy water was eating away at Victor's insides.

Dragos leaned down, "What's wrong, Victor?"

Brett joined Dragos at his side. Dragos turned and hugged the detective.

"Hey! Let's not get mushy."

Victor gasped for air. A trickle of blood ran out the corner of his mouth. Victor's dark eyes glared at them.

"Detective O'Shea. It was yo ... you?"

"Yeah, it was me. Your rants were growing tedious. And more importantly, you hurt my friends."

As Victor moaned and hissed on the floor, Michael walked over and stood over the vampire with another stake in hand. Holy water dripped from the stake. Terror flashed in Victor's eyes.

"Say good bye, Victor." Michael plunged the stake into the vampire's chest. Almost immediately, the body began to decompose.

Candy's voice drifted toward Dragos. He turned and saw her running to him with arms outstretched. He drew her close. His heart clenched as her soft sobs filled the air. He brushed the curls from her face and pressed his lips over every inch of her face. When his lips met hers, he sighed. He had found home once again.

Epilogue

Brett loaded the last suitcase. He forced a smile as Dragos and Candy piled into the car. Lisa waited in the front seat.

Lisa yelled out the car window. "Hurry up, Brett. They're going to miss their plane."

The past four weeks had been nothing but a blur. As far as the public was concerned, the murders had ended as quickly as they had begun. Anders held a press conference and announced that the primary suspects had been killed in a shootout near the river. They burned all the vampires' remains and sealed up the tunnels and caverns in the hope that they would stay hidden forever.

Nichols was given a hero's burial. Unfortunately, Officer Johnson decided to take early retirement. Johnson didn't want to face any other paranormal entities. Not that Brett blamed him; he didn't want to see any more creatures either.

Detective Randall made a complete turnaround. He believed he was now Brett's new partner. The guy experienced a major attitude adjustment. It would take some time before Brett trusted Randall. But at least Randall's opinion of women appeared to have changed for the better. Brett and Randall were pleasant to one another, and that was a start.

They pulled up to the curb of the airport. Candy and Lisa

jumped out and hugged one more time. Tears freely flowed down their faces.

Dragos walked up to Brett and embraced him in a hug. "I can never thank you enough for everything you did. You gave me a home, believed in me, and introduced me to the most beautiful woman in the world. Thank you. We want you to come visit us in England as soon as you can."

"Are you sure that you want to go back to England?"

Dragos nodded. "I can never bring back what was lost. Now that I am the only heir left to inherit my family estate, I welcome the chance to return there and run the family property and business. If Candy hadn't done an investigation of my family, we wouldn't have a home to go back to."

Brett turned aside, already missing Dragos and Candy. If he wasn't careful, he'd end up crying like a baby.

"From what Candy has told me, you've inherited a very large estate. This should provide you with the needed privacy."

Dragos nodded. "Yes, being a vampire does require a certain amount of privacy. Hopefully we can learn more about vampires and figure out a way for the two of us to grow old together. I won't live without her."

Brett paused. Dragos's words brought home how he felt about Lisa.

Candy called to Dragos and pointed to her watch. It was nearly time. He was losing his childhood friend. As well as losing Dragos, a close friend and brother.

"Well, buddy. I think it's time." Brett's throat tightened until his words were no longer audible. He embraced Dragos and squeezed hard, not wanting to let go. He finally released Dragos and took a step back. "I mean it. If you two need anything, call me and I'll be there."

Dragos's serious gaze bore through him before he nodded. It was as if Dragos were memorizing what he looked like. Dragos draped his arm around Candy. Newly married, they giggled and kissed, barely able to take their eyes off of each other. The pair entered the airport, ready to embark on their new life and adventure.

As if sensing Brett's sadness, Lisa looped her arm around his.

"Are you okay?"

He nodded. "Let's go."

In a melancholy mood, he decided to drive south out of town. He didn't want to go home. It would be so different with Dragos and Candy both gone. Lisa reached over and held his hand. He brought her hand to his lips and pressed a soft kiss to it.

"Since we're going this way, I take it we're not going back to your house."

"Nope. I'd like to drive for a while. Do you have anywhere you have to be?"

She flashed a brilliant smile, her soft golden curls cascading over her shoulders.

"No. I think we deserve some quiet time."

He nodded. Words weren't always necessary when you were with someone you loved. He and Lisa needed to talk about their future. After the past few weeks, he knew he wanted to be with Lisa. He was beginning to trust her again. A broken heart was something he didn't want to experience a second time.

He continued to drive south on I35. After the past two years, he had been under an extreme amount of stress. It had probably skewed his thinking about a relationship with Lisa. Because there were so many times that he had almost died, he held back. Did he want to leave a wife and child if he died? He didn't know the answer to that question.

After a couple of hours of being on the road, Lisa yawned and stretched her arms. "How about a coffee break?"

Shortly after spotting the sign indicating that the Missouri line was only a few miles away, he pulled into a convenience store to refuel.

"Do you want anything?" she asked.

"Yeah, just a bottle of water. Thanks."

He leaned against the car. With a deep breath, he inhaled the fresh country smell. The crisp north breeze ruffled his hair. He zipped his jacket. Snow was in the air. He could feel it.

A bald eagle flew over the store. He raised his gaze, watching the graceful bird float effortlessly across the sky. A feeling of peace permeated his soul. This was what he needed: a change of pace—a vacation. But where would he go? England? No, he'd wait until Dragos and Candy were settled. His eyes drifted shut. He let his mind drift in order to imagine. He'd always wanted to go to North Africa. Maybe see the pyramids. *What a sight that would be.*

Someone nudged his shoulder. He didn't have to open his eyes to know who it was. He peeked open one eye and burst out laughing. Michael was lounging against the car with his hat tilted down, obscuring most of his face.

"What are you doing out here in the middle of nowhere?" the ghost asked.

Brett laughed, feeling lighter than he had in days. "Pondering."

Michael pushed back his hat with the palm of his hand. His brow wrinkled. "Pondering what?"

He shrugged. "You know. Everything. I've decided I need a vacation. Can you go?"

"Afraid not. I'm being called back for a while. It seems I stepped on some toes. But you definitely deserve one. Where you thinking of going?"

"Maybe Europe or the Middle East—I'm not sure."

"Well, you need to go. Since I'll be gone for a while, be careful. I can't come save your ass, you know."

He patted Michael's shoulder. "Here comes Lisa. Do you want to ride back home with us?"

"No, I'll pass," Michael mumbled. "I need to report in today. Better get it over with."

"Okay, see you soon. I'll leave a note at the house when I take off so you'll know where I am and when I'm due home."

Michael tipped his hat and bowed before fading away.

Brett greeted Lisa with a kiss and turned the car back toward home.

"How about moving in together," he blurted.

Lisa's head swung toward him. "Really?" Her grin grew wider.

He nodded. "Yep. I think it's time that we went all in. I love you, Lisa."

Her eyes misted over. "I love you too." She reached out, running her fingers over his lower lip.

He took her hand, kissing it lightly. "I know you want more. So do I."

Lisa leaned over to press a kiss on his cheek. "This is a great first step. I'll never be bored with you around, O'Shea."

His eyes grew heavy. "Honey, I'm going to make sure you're never bored."

Lisa licked her full lips and pursed her mouth into a pout. "Too bad we're two hours from our bedroom."

"Damn, woman! Tighten that seat belt. I'll have us home in an hour."

Brett smiled to himself. All the fears and worries he'd had for the past several months fell away and disappeared. He felt lighter than he had in years. He couldn't wait to let his mom know about Lisa. She would be as excited as Lisa. He was beginning a new chapter of his life.

They drove in silence, enjoying each other's company. He'd come up with a surprise for Lisa. He hoped she was game for an adventure, because he would be calling the travel agent in the morning. It was time for a fun adventure with no hocus-pocus stuff. He figured that after two crazy cases, there couldn't be any more of this unusual paranormal activity in Des Moines. He had seen it all and survived. Now it was time for him to have a normal life.

Printed in the United States
By Bookmasters